SF Boo

LOST STARSHIP SERIES:
The Lost Starship
The Lost Command
The Lost Destroyer
The Lost Colony
The Lost Patrol
The Lost Planet
The Lost Earth

DOOM STAR SERIES:
Star Soldier
Bio Weapon
Battle Pod
Cyborg Assault
Planet Wrecker
Star Fortress
Task Force 7 (Novella)

EXTINCTION WARS SERIES:
Assault Troopers
Planet Strike
Star Viking
Fortress Earth

Visit VaughnHeppner.com for more
information

The Lost Earth

(Lost Starship Series 7)

By Vaughn Heppner

Copyright © 2017 by the author.

ISBN-13: 978-1973956693
ISBN-10: 1973956691
BISAC: Fiction / Science Fiction / Military

PROLOGUE

"Focus," the commandant demanded. "I need greater focus." She was a tall woman wearing a Star Watch uniform, and she was concentrating on a large wall screen.

At the console, the tech's features were shiny with sweat. His narrow hands shook as he adjusted the sensor images.

The picture sharpened abruptly. What they thought they'd seen became horrifyingly clear. Thousands of warships boiled like maddened ants out of a hole in the middle of empty space.

"Could those be ghost images?" the commandant whispered.

With a sleeve, the tech wiped sweat from his forehead. "I've run a diagnostic, sir. There's nothing wrong with the scanner."

The commandant gave him a fearful glance. The tech was supposed to be the best, had received instructions from Professor Ludendorff himself. The tech operated the Builder Scanner brought back from Sind II in the Beyond.

The scanner had gone operational four and a half weeks ago. It had taken months to install and even longer to figure out. The master control room was here, deep inside Pluto, in one of Star Watch's most heavily fortified bases.

The commandant resumed her study of the wall screen. The opening in space must be the terminus of a hyper-spatial tube. How far back did this one stretch?

She feared it stretched all the way to the dreaded Swarm Imperium. The number of warships pouring through staggered

1

the imagination. Hundreds of spaceships per second came through, and moved aside to make room for more…more…more. The invaders already had a 100 to 1 advantage against Star Watch's combined fleet. If they kept coming through like that, it would soon be 200 or even 300 to 1.

The commandant massaged her throat. The saucer-shaped vessels to the left of the mass must have come from the Builder Dyson Sphere one thousand light-years away. Those vessels surely belonged to—

"Commander Thrax Ti Ix," she whispered under her breath.

There was a pause at the terminus. Was that it then? No. Invader warships hurriedly moved aside from the hyper-spatial tube terminus. That seemed ominous. The commandant groaned as a massive round ship seemed to squeeze out of the opening. It moved aside, and another vast ship squeezed through. Then another and another… How big were those things? They dwarfed the largest merchant haulers.

The commandant grew faint, finally realizing she'd forgotten to breathe. "How far away…?" she whispered, unable to finish the sentence as she inhaled.

The tech tapped his console and adjusted a rangefinder. He looked up in alarm.

"They're twelve light-years from Earth," he said in a choked voice.

She was going to be sick. "Twelve?" she whispered.

The tech didn't hear her. He was adjusting the picture frantically, searching for something.

The Builder Scanner used a fantastic technology. It could search one hundred by one hundred light-year blocks. This was the fifth sensor sweep so far, the first to use a special anomaly-finding device.

"I wonder…" the tech said. "They must have appeared in empty space on purpose. Do they want to get set up first and scout around before they attack?"

The commandant reexamined the Swarm warships— *probable* Swarm warships—a mere twelve light-years from the Solar System.

"Where are the nearest Laumer Points?" she demanded. Those were regular wormhole openings and exits that linked Human Space in a web of faster than light paths.

The tech tapped his console. A yellow symbol appeared at the edge of the wall screen.

"How far away is the Laumer Point from the mass of ships?" the commandant asked.

He studied a small screen embedded in the console. "Three-quarters of a light-year, sir. The Laumer Point is at the edge of the Tau Ceti System, in its Oort cloud."

"Can you calculate the fleet's present velocity?"

"It's almost zero."

"We have time, then," she said.

The tech looked up at her. "That depends on their ships, sir, depends on what kind of drives they have."

The commandant bit her lower lip as she stared at the invaders once more.

The Swarm had made it to Human Space, and so dreadfully close to the Earth. Thank God, Captain Maddox had found the Builder Scanner and brought it home in time to see this. Yet…given the Swarm numbers, did it matter that they could see the horrible event? Might it have been a mercy to be unable to see it?

"Even if it takes them a year to get here, or two or three years," she whispered, "what can we do to stop them?"

"It's worse than that," the tech said. "They obviously control a nexus. That's how they made the hyper-spatial tube."

"Yes?" she said.

"What's to stop them from making a second hyper-spatial tube, this one directly into the Solar System as they dump a second fleet on us?"

The commandant spun around. It was time to send a priority message to the Office of the Lord High Admiral. This could be the beginning of the end for the human race. Even if the New Men lent Star Watch their armada of star cruisers—

"No," the commandant whispered. She wasn't going to despair. Star Watch had advance warning of the greatest invasion in human history. Now, they had to do something about it.

PART I
NULL SPACE

-1-

Sergeant Treggason Riker had been drinking heavily. He was sitting around a raised fire pit at the Sheraton Hotel on the island of Kauai, the Garden Island of the Hawaiian Chain.

Ocean waves crashed nearby on the nighttime beach, lending a weighty undercurrent to Riker's melancholy spirit.

He was an older man with leathery skin. He possessed a bionic eye and a fully bionic arm. Years ago, he'd lost both originals on a desperate mission on Altair III. He was an old dog, a veteran in Star Watch's Intelligence Service. For the last few years, he'd gone on the space missions with Captain Maddox aboard Starship *Victory*.

Using his real hand, Riker raised a shot glass of good Scotch whiskey. With a silent oath, he tossed the contents into his mouth, swallowing and wincing as it burned its way down.

He was seriously drunk. He had a right to be. He was making the biggest decision of his life. Now that Captain Maddox had married Meta, maybe it was time for him to retire. He'd watched over the young buck long enough. He'd helped keep Maddox alive through thick and thin. He wasn't sure he'd performed his main duty well—that of acting as a brake on the impulsive captain.

Riker shook his head. Maddox demanded obedience from his underlings yet the man had a hard time taking orders from those above him. The young terror always thought he knew best.

"I've had my fill of it," Riker said in a soft growl. "It's time to relax."

Riker stared at the fire in the raised stonework. The flames danced so hypnotically. He could watch them for hours. He snorted. He *had* been watching them for hours.

What time was it anyway?

Riker checked his wrist, but he'd set aside the watch in his room before heading out here. Mumbling, he put his hands on the chair's rests and shoved upward. Then he shoved the chair back from the fire pit. Leaning forward, eyeing the space around the fire, he realized everyone else had left. They had each said good night, the other vacationers, when they had departed. Could he do any less?

"Good night," Riker said in his gravelly voice.

No one answered, of course, as he was alone.

"I *am* alone," he announced. He'd never married. Maybe that had been a mistake.

A sly smile stole onto his leathery face. He could still marry, lying abed in bliss for the rest of his life. If Maddox could get married, *he* could certainly do the same.

"Bah!" Riker said a moment later, shaking his head, staggering sideways as he did so. He was too old a dog to change his ways.

With a sigh—

Riker froze. A second later, he turned as fast as he could to the left, thinking to have spotted someone in the shadows under a nearby archway.

"Hello?" he called.

No one answered. The fire flickered to his side and the waves crashed nearby against the beach.

Riker took a moment to focus. He had drunk far too much tonight. He—

He made a dismissive gesture and began walking. There was no one else out this late. It was just his lonesome. He moved along the sidewalks, past the hotel swimming pool toward a high-rise complex.

Riker wasn't staying at the Sheraton, but at a condo in the Plantation next door. The condo belonged to Star Watch. Brigadier O'Hara had told him to think things over before he made his final decision. The Iron Lady was a good commanding officer, the best in the service.

After passing the complex, Riker chose an indirect route, heading onto a twisting garden path to the Plantation. The gardens in Kauai were flower, bush and tree marvels, ones Riker could well appreciate. It was almost like a mini-jungle, although an exceedingly well-kept one.

He stopped suddenly. Small things moved on the ground—on the grass to the side of the crushed gravel path.

Old Riker smiled at what he saw. The "small things" were big old frogs hopping around. He wondered how old they were. He—

Riker felt a tingle in the center of his back. He raised his good hand onto the hidden blaster under his other armpit and spun around. He'd just felt a fierce scrutiny.

His glassy eyes roved about over the bushes and trees.

The ocean wind blew gently, causing palm leaves to rustle. He could hear the waves from here. Normally, he liked the sound. Right now, in the dark, in the garden, in his current state of mind, the crashing waves had an ominous quality.

"Hello?" Riker called.

Like before, no one answered. He was alone in the dark well after the witching hour. He was a jumpy old man letting shadows startle him. And yet...he'd learned to trust his senses. Something was out there, something bad, something...

"What's wrong with you, Old Man?" Riker asked himself.

"I'm drunk," he answered.

"That doesn't mean you have to act like a fool."

"No," he answered himself, "but at least it explains it."

Riker might have grinned to himself at his dialogue. He was not an eccentric like Captain Maddox. Riker knew himself as a hardnosed old salt who knew his trade. He did not take crazy risks. He did not jump at shadows—

He made a rough noise in the back of his throat and waved both hands at the darkness. He turned for his condo and staggered along the path.

He would have liked to feel as calm and easy-spirited as he pretended to be. He most certainly wasn't, though. Riker kept his gun hand near the hidden blaster. There was something following him. He did not think it was an android or a New Man spy. This felt different. This felt primordial and slimy, like something escaped from an ancient abyss.

"Get a grip, you old fool," he muttered under his breath, less to poke fun at himself and more to bolster his courage by hearing his own voice.

Riker cast a worried glance over his shoulder. He used the power of his bionic eye. There was nothing he could see tracking him. Yet, he still felt a presence.

He spoke crudely under his breath and actually broke into a run. It was smoother than his unsteady gait a second ago would have foretold.

Riker had been in all kinds of dangerous places, including the prison planet Loki Prime. He had kept his head in all of them. Tonight, it felt different. Tonight, it seemed as if he were the last person on the island. He had to restrain himself from shouting as loud as he could for someone to help him.

He ran flat out, panting from the effort. He kept looking back, saw nothing, ran even faster, looked back again—

Riker shouted as his feet tangled with each other. He slammed against the sidewalk, hitting his chin. That stunned him, making him blink as tears welled in his eyes.

Instead of the jolt bringing sanity to his drunken midnight madness, Riker scrambled as fast as he could back onto his feet. He ran harder, white-faced and terrified, with his chin throbbing and blood running onto his shirt. He could not explain the dreadful feeling racing through his brain. It shamed him on a fundamental level, and yet he knew better than to ignore the feeling. He trusted himself. Even drunk, he trusted what he felt.

Riker slammed against his condo door, Number 142, and worked madly to find his card key and thrust it through the slot. It seemed to take ages for the light to blink green. He felt the presence closing in on him, yet he could not look back to stare it down. He twisted the handle, opened the door, slipped inside and began to close the door when an irresistible force flung the door open and tried to grab his good shoulder.

-2-

With a terrified shout, Riker slipped out from under the grasp and bolted up the long flight of stairs.

Two bedrooms and two bathrooms made up the bottom floor of the condo. A long staircase starting near the door led up to the living room and kitchen. The upstairs had two balconies.

Here in Kauai, few people had air-conditioners. There was no need. The sliding glass doors were open. A comfortably cool ocean breeze blew through the screens. The ceiling was fifteen feet above the second floor, with a single ceiling fan twirling lazily.

Still finding it hard to think, Riker ran to the bigger living room couch. It was made of rattan and cushions. He spun around and found that he was trembling.

He heard footsteps coming up the stairs.

Riker's trembling turned into outright shaking. He'd never felt like this in his life, not even while fleeing from the kill-squad on Loki Prime. It made him sick. He was deeply ashamed of the fear.

"No," he said. "I will face this."

It didn't help the shaking any. He wiped a sleeve across his eyes and under his nose, catching a little of the clotting blood from his chin. He tried to think. He had to defend himself—

A head and shoulders appeared on the stairs.

Riker groaned in terror.

The head turned toward him. It seemed common enough. The man—it was a man or had the body of a man, anyway— had sparse dark hair and dark eyes. He was wearing a shiny suit like a stage performer. He continued climbing until he reached the second floor. He had shiny baggy pants and dark shoes. There was something familiar about the man. He was Asian, small-boned with pallid features, with even whiter markings around his eyes—

"You're a Spacer," Riker said in a stage whisper.

The Spacer stared at him, neither admitting nor denying the charge.

Spacers belonged to a set of people who lived aboard starships. They followed the tenets of a robotic Builder. The "Nation" of Spacers had vanished some time ago. The Visionary, a Spacer leader, had named Captain Maddox as *di- far*. It meant Maddox was a focus for change. The captain could lift the human race from one track onto another. The Spacers were techies but believed all kinds of mumbo jumbo. Several voyages ago, Shu 15—

"Who are you?" Riker said in a rasp.

The man in the shiny suit did not smile, did not nod. He was wearing silvery gloves, which seemed odd.

"Why aren't you wearing goggles?" Riker asked, his voice firming.

The small Spacer inhaled lightly through his nostrils, but instead of speaking, he glanced both ways. He settled on one of the screens. He gave a tiny nod, heading for the first glass door. Once there, the Spacer shut the sliding glass door, thumping it a little harder than seemed necessary. Then, he locked it.

"What are you doing?" Riker demanded.

The Spacer in the shiny suit held up an admonitory finger before walking across the rug to the kitchen area. He closed the sliding glass door there, locking it as well.

At that point, Riker's knees lost strength. He sat down hard on the couch, staring at his traitorous knees. This was his chance to escape. If he fled down the stairs—

The small Spacer in the shiny suit had walked back. He stood across from Riker before the low rattan table in the middle of the living room.

10

"What are you?" Riker asked.

The sergeant no longer felt drunk. He was tired, though. The fear had changed, too. He no longer had the flight fear, he had the waiting kind that freezes a man. He knew fate was about to deal him an exceedingly unfair card. He knew it, and yet, he couldn't do anything about it. That was possibly the most maddening feeling in the world for him.

"Sergeant Treggason Riker?" the Spacer asked in a dry voice.

Something in the voice dragged Riker's gaze up to meet the Spacer's. He locked onto the other's face. There was something desperate in the narrow features. The eyes no longer had a normal tint, either. There indeed seemed to be a hellish swirl in them. The Satanic swirl had just begun, though, hadn't been there earlier. It wasn't yet radiating at full intensity. Even so, the swirling eyes caught Riker's attention with tractor-beam-like force.

Yet, Riker was a stubborn old coot if he was nothing else. He'd had to be stubborn to deal with Captain Maddox all these years. If one couldn't deal via the direct route with the captain, one used a more perverse way to challenge the boy.

Riker began to fight the hypnotic power of the eyes. He'd sat before a fire for hours tonight drinking his Scotch whiskey. He hadn't heard much of the conversations going on around him. He'd been too busy trying to figure out whether he should retire or not.

"Why...?" Riker said. After that, he could no longer form words.

The power of the brightening eyes was starting to batter down the last vestiges of the sergeant's resistance.

"You do not know me," the Spacer said. "I am, in fact, nobody as far as you are concerned."

"What?"

The Spacer frowned in a troubled way. "I am unsure I shall survive our meeting, Sergeant. I am almost used up, almost finished with my dreadful task."

"Huh?"

The eyes lost a bit of their power. The narrow face, now shining with sweat, seemed put out. "I don't like this interference. I am referring to your…monosyllabic utterances. They are annoying. I demand that you cease them, at once."

Riker latched onto that with the remaining vestiges of his will. He struggled to speak.

"Stop it," the Spacer said.

Riker's head swayed back. He felt a force against his mind. It was like a heavy wet blanket attempting to subdue his thoughts. No…that wasn't exactly right. It attempted to subdue his will.

The sergeant struggled with mulish perseverance. He had to win this fight. He could not let the thing inside the Spacer—

Riker's eyes widened in horror and grim understanding. The Spacer was a vessel for something.

"Wh…?" Riker said. It was all he could manage.

The Spacer shook his head. "Your resistance is useless and annoying. You are also straining my final resources. Thus, I forbid you to speak. Do you hear that? Speech is forbidden you."

Riker struggled to pronounce a single syllable. He could not. He found his lips frozen, his teeth almost welded together. Some intuition deep in his soul told him he had to struggle to speak nonetheless. It didn't matter if he couldn't speak. He had to make the thing expend energy to keep his lips shut. That would allow him a chance later…maybe…if the sergeant still had a little luck on his side.

"Why do you fight so hard?" the Spacer whispered. "I didn't. I accepted the inevitable. Don't you realize this is your fate? It has chosen you."

Riker's staring eyes grew larger yet so the whites showed. He wanted to ask who had chosen him and why?

The Spacer in the shiny suit moved to another couch. He pulled up on the edges of his pants over his knees, lifting the shiny fabric as he sat down. The small Spacer clasped his silvery-gloved hands together between his knees.

"I am a messenger," the Spacer said. "Soon, you will take my place. You will carry the message to its terminus."

The Spacer must mean that he, Riker, would carry the entity inside him. What was happening? Where did this thing come from?

The Spacer took a small item from a suit pocket. As he clicked it, a shiny sharp blade popped up.

"It is almost time," the Spacer said. He reversed the blade so the point aimed at his suit. With a sharp, swift motion, the man stabbed himself in the chest. The blade went in deep as the man kept pushing. He grunted painfully nonetheless. The Spacer let go of the handle as blood welled in his mouth.

"I'm almost finished," the Spacer wheezed. "You have no idea how long I've wanted to pass on the charge. I'm weary of life, Sergeant. I suppose in a few moments you're going to understand what I mean."

The Spacer smiled, showing bloodstained teeth. "Any second now," he whispered. "Then, you will know…"

-3-

Riker sat on the couch, numb with horror and frozen by a strange paralysis. The self-induced knife-thrust sickened him. He yearned to shout in dismay. He struggled to demand an answer from the demented Spacer.

Yet...Riker knew something else was at work. If he believed in demons, he would say the man had one. Yet, Riker had been in Star Watch Intelligence and in the Patrol too long to subscribe to such an old-fashioned answer. He had seen some crazy aliens in his time. Surely, the Spacer carried an alien thing in him.

The sergeant half-expected to see a slimy wormy thing ooze out of the knife-made opening in the chest. Did a parasitical creature control the Spacer? If that was true, what gave the parasite the mind power it radiated?

"I reject the idea that you're mentally stronger than me," the Spacer wheezed. "I have trained my entire life to understand the unusual. I have two modifications. I can see electromagnetic phenomena. I know that you cannot. I can also analyze data faster than ordinary with my computer enhancement. That it chose me makes perfect sense. I have no idea why it desires a beat-up old relic like you."

Riker saw blood stain the shiny suit where the knife was sticking out. The Spacer sat back now, wearing the knife like an ornament. He made gurgling noises in the back of his throat.

The two of them waited in silence.

The blood from the knife wound kept soaking into the suit. It seemed to flow more easily now. The Spacer's life weakened as the redness in his suit grew larger.

"Last voyage…" the Spacer suddenly wheezed. "Your captain found something last voyage. I believe it happened quite by accident. He entered a null realm. Did he tell you about it?"

Riker was frozen. He couldn't even shift an eyebrow.

"Oh," the Spacer wheezed. "Your captain said nothing, eh? That is interesting. I wonder why the captain kept the knowledge to himself. Do you know he spotted two…I believe you call them Destroyers? You did not even know the species name that made the war vessels. Someone has called them the Nameless Ones. They were not nameless. Oh no, Sergeant Riker, they have a profound name. It has been my horror to learn that name much more intimately than I would have ever desired."

Riker swayed back the slightest bit. This had something to do with a neutroium-hulled Destroyer?

"Where did you acquire such stubborn strength of will?" the Spacer whispered. "It is maddening. If I cannot complete the transfer, my last year of existence and this hideous burden will have all been in vain. Do not do that to me, Sergeant."

Riker's lips parted the slightest bit, emitting a slight croak.

The dying Spacer's eyes swirled with horrible force. The power slammed against Riker's mind. He almost passed out, his eyelids drooping—

Riker croaked another sound.

"Maddox is going to need the Destroyers, you old fool," the Spacer whispered. "That is a small price to pay for freeing me."

"What…?" Riker whispered.

"Do you think I could come with my full being? No, no. The Builders fashioned their trap too cunningly for that. They were wily foes, the cleverest we ever faced. They caught me, caught three of my vessels. Now, the Swarm has come to Human Space, Sergeant. They will obliterate your puny race from existence. That is certain. Your paltry fleets cannot destroy them. You need more. The Juggernauts might help, but

15

there are too few of them to turn the tide. What, then, can save your witless race? Clearly, two Destroyers would tip the balance in your race's favor. I can give you the two powerhouses. Their price is my freedom."

"Who…?"

"Yes, who am I and how did I snap up this wisp of a Spacer into my service? How did I force him to carry a fragment of my ego in himself all these lonely months? I am much greater than you realize. You are a mite before me. Know that your captain woke me from an endless slumber. I used the opening he created with Starship *Victory* when he escaped the null realm. It appears he wisely kept silent about me, about my Destroyers. But now the need is hard upon humanity. Now is the moment I knew must eventually arrive. You, Sergeant Riker, shall carry my ego-fragment to your captain. Then…"

The dying Spacer laughed maniacally, blood dribbling onto his chin. He coughed afterward with long drawn out wheezes.

"Finally," the Spacer whispered. "I am almost dead, Sergeant. That's the only way to pass the thing on to you. I am sick of life. I still can't believe—"

The Spacer abruptly stopped talking. He put his bloodied gloved hands onto his knees and grunted horribly, spraying spittle and blood as he rose to his feet.

The Spacer had glazed eyes. With a slow, deliberate movement, he used his left hand to tug at the fingertips of the right-hand glove. Finally, he gripped the loosened fingers of the glove and pulled the bloody, shiny cloth from his hand.

Riker blanched in renewed terror.

The hand had turned a mottled green color. It stank, too. Worse, it pulsated with a weird radiating light.

"I have been dying for some time," the Spacer whispered. "It is possible I began dying the moment the ego-fragment entered my being. Now, you shall begin to die, Sergeant Riker."

On unsteady legs, the Spacer bumped against the rattan table, shoving it out of the way.

Riker strained to move. He could not. He strained so hard his heart pounded with fierce beats. His vision swam before him.

"Now," the Spacer said. He reached down with his rotted shining hand and grasped Riker's bionic hand.

Nothing seemed to happen.

The dying Spacer frowned. He gazed at Riker.

"Oh," the Spacer wheezed. "Hm.... I believe *this* should help."

He squeezed the bionic hand. His own rotted hand glowed more fiercely.

Riker's head jerked minutely. He stared in horror at his metal hand. Glowing force grew on the Spacer's hand, transferring to his metal appendage.

Riker's heart beat manically. He roared with raw force. That unleashed him. Sergeant Riker stood. He used the bionic arm, hurling the bleeding Spacer from him.

The Spacer landed on the rug in a crumpled heap.

"Too late," the Spacer wheezed. "It's too late now. I have made the transfer. The ego-fragment is on you, Sergeant Riker. It will seep into your—"

"No!" Riker howled in desperation. He tore the blaster from its rig under his shoulder. He used his flesh and bone hand to do it. Aiming at the glowing bionic hand, Riker pulled the trigger.

A torrent of energy burned from the blaster. It made the metal glow hotter, hotter, and began to devour the bionic appendage. He burned his bionic hand continuously, until it dropped heavily onto the rug, making that area burst into fire.

"No," the Spacer wheezed. He struggled to rise.

Riker backed away from his fallen bionic hand. He stared at the Spacer in horror, turned the blaster on him.

The fumes of molten metal and burned flesh and bone made Riker retch until he coughed hoarsely. He couldn't stay here. He had to run away, get away from the thing.

No, something said in his mind. *You are mine by right of conquest.*

Riker dropped the blaster and fled for the stairs. He tripped, tumbling down them head over heels. He crumpled at the bottom landing dazed and hurt, with blood dripping from his nose.

It didn't matter. He had to escape this place. He had to leave so he could get far away from the ego-fragment. This thing was evil beyond anything he'd ever faced.

With a cry of despair, Sergeant Riker climbed to his feet and fled into the balmy Kauai night.

-4-

SEVEN DAYS LATER

Aboard Starship *Victory*, Captain Maddox was wearing shorts and gym shoes as he stalked around a heavy bag. His fists were heavily wrapped and raised for combat.

He was tall, with handsome features, dark hair and whip-corded muscles.

One moment, he stalked around the bag. The next, he moved in, throwing a flurry of blows. They were faster than an ordinary man could strike, each one thudding hard, making the heavy bag swing a little more.

Captain Maddox was half New Man and half regular *Homo sapien*. He had a faster than normal metabolism and intense intelligence.

Maddox had recently returned to duty from his honeymoon. Meta was still on Earth, looking for a new place to rent as their home. She'd become dissatisfied with his old apartment.

Maddox stepped back from the heavy bag, beginning to stalk around it again. Although sweat had begun to shine on his lean physique, his efforts had not even caused him to breathe hard.

It was different being married. He liked it. He loved Meta. They had spent a glorious two weeks together. They'd had two quarrels in that time, each resolved in an hour.

Maddox stepped at the bag, hammering it before sidestepping away.

He often did his best thinking while hitting the bag.

The Lord High Admiral and the Brigadier of Star Watch Intelligence had holed up in Star Watch HQ in Geneva, Switzerland. Something was troubling them. Maddox was certain that something dire had occurred that neither of them wanted anyone else to know.

Maddox was not unduly concerned about that. What did trouble him was that Sergeant Riker had gone missing. No one seemed to know where he was. As far as Maddox could learn, there had been an incident in a Kauai condo at the Plantation. There was a burn mark on the carpet of Room 142 with specks of blood hidden in the rug, both facts that the police investigators had not reported.

Two days ago, Maddox had requested Star Watch Intelligence to check into the matter. Major Stokes had assured him he would look into it personally. So far, nothing had happened. Maddox had contacted Stokes earlier this morning. The major had told him not to worry about it; the investigation was proceeding well. Intelligence would soon find Riker.

In the gym aboard Starship *Victory*, Maddox moved toward the heavy bag once more. He landed body blows one after another. They were shockingly powerful strikes. They—

Maddox stepped back abruptly, letting his long arms swing at his sides.

"Galyan," he said.

A second later, an Adok holoimage appeared. The image possessed deep-set eyes in a strangely lined alien face. He was a deified alien AI, the last member of a lost race.

"I've decided to accelerate the Riker investigation," Maddox told Galyan.

"I believe that is a euphemism," Galyan said in a slightly robotic voice. "What you really mean is that you are about to take matters into your own hands."

No hint of a smile appeared on the captain's lips. This one smelled funny. Maddox simply said, "Major Stokes is lying."

The holoimage floated back a few centimeters. "I am curious as to how you deduced this, sir."

"There are too many anomalies present. First, Stokes would have moved mountains to find Riker if he thought someone had murdered or kidnapped the sergeant. Second, the specks of blood in the rug in Room 142 should have goaded the Kauai police to greater action. It did nothing of the kind. Instead, the police stonewalled me."

"Are you going to the scene of the crime for a second look?"

Instead of answering, Maddox said, "I'm surprised you haven't already analyzed the situation."

The holographic AI only hesitated for a fraction of a second before saying, "I assume you realize I have analyzed it and are chiding me for doing so. Did I presume upon a liberty I did not actually possess?"

"What was your conclusion?" the captain asked.

"To the situation or to your probable response?"

"To…my response," Maddox said.

"I have concluded that you are not going to waste time investigating on the ground. Instead, you are going to request that I infiltrate classified Star Watch computers to find out what they know about Riker."

"That's not bad, but wrong," Maddox said.

Galyan's eyelids fluttered. It meant his AI unit was processing. "Let me rephrase. You will not request I do this, but order it."

"There won't be anything about Riker on classified Star Watch computers that we don't already know," Maddox said.

"I do not understand how you have arrived at this conclusion."

"The information we seek will be in the Brigadier's personal files."

"How do you know this?" Galyan asked, sounding genuinely interested.

"Through intuition," Maddox said.

"That is not logical. Intuition is merely a person's subconscious arriving at a conclusion before the conscious mind does so. The subconscious uses logical references to achieve this. Thus, I should easily be able to duplicate your subconscious' process."

"What does that tell you that you didn't?"

Once more, Galyan's eyelids fluttered. "You have received information that I do not yet possess."

"Wrong. The correct answer is that my intuition is still superior to your logic processors."

Galyan studied the captain before nodding in a noncommittal manner.

"What?" Maddox said, almost sounding nettled.

"Nothing," Galyan said.

"Have I hurt your feelings?"

Galyan did not reply.

"I...*request* that you tell me what's bothering you," Maddox said.

"You will not like my findings, sir," Galyan warned.

Maddox raised an eyebrow.

"But I will honor your request as a command," the AI said. "The statement regarding your superiority is an indicator of your New Man parentage. You have continued to slip into their arrogant patterns of—"

"That's enough," Maddox said, interrupting with the hint of a frown.

Galyan fell silent, waiting.

"My statement struck home," Maddox said. "Thus, you attempt to strike back at..." He shook his head, and began to unwrap the binding from around his fists, revealing a gold wedding band on his left ring finger. It was his only piece of adornment.

"I want a glance at the Brigadier's personal files," Maddox said.

"May I offer a conjecture regarding such action?"

Maddox hesitated a second. "Go ahead," he said reluctantly.

"Breaking into her personal files will anger the Iron Lady," Galyan said. "I have no doubt we can achieve the feat—"

"Yes!" Maddox said, deciding. "Thank you, Galyan. We are going to do this the old-fashioned way."

"We are going down to study the scene of the crime in detail?" Galyan asked hopefully.

"No," Maddox said, as he strode for the exit. "We're going to use *Victory's* sensors and computers to locate the needle in the haystack."

-5-

It took far longer for the bridge crew to find Riker than Maddox had expected. During the last hour, he had begun to believe that Star Watch Intelligence had whisked the sergeant somewhere off planet.

As Maddox silently played with that conclusion, Galyan announced, "I have discovered Sergeant Riker's whereabouts."

Lieutenant Valerie Noonan turned in her seat. "Don't keep us guessing, Galyan. Where is he?"

"Do I have your permission to speak?" Galyan asked Maddox.

"Of course," the captain said.

"The sergeant is in a special ward of a heavily fortified asylum for the criminally insane," Galyan said.

"What?" Valerie cried.

"The facility has a pristine name," Galyan said. "I am simply speaking factually. Riker is in a facility outside the city of Athens, Greece. There is a Space Marine barracks nearby. No doubt, they could deploy to the facility in minutes, if needed."

"Why is Riker there?" Maddox asked.

"I have not yet entered the facility's computers," Galyan said. "My sensors located his body, while I assessed the facility's purpose. Would you like me to hack into their computer system?"

"At once," Maddox said.

24

"Please give me a moment," Galyan said. His eyelids fluttered for a long moment before abruptly opening with a look of shock.

"What happened?" Valerie asked.

"This is incredible," Galyan said. "The system is heavily encrypted. I made it halfway through the core when fail-safes crashed into place. I believe I can still invade the system, but it will be days, maybe even a week before I can give you the results."

"How is that possible?" Valerie asked. "You once invaded a Builder—"

"I gave a detailed report on the Builder system invasion," Galyan said, interrupting. "It appears Star Watch personnel have invented a secure site against my unique abilities."

"The asylum must be a maximum-security site," Maddox said softly. "Clearly, Major Stokes knows about it and knows about Riker's incarceration."

"As you surmised, sir," Galyan said, "the major knowingly lied to you."

Maddox stroked his chin, thinking. What had happened in Kauai that had put Riker in such an institution under heavy guard and total secrecy? What's more, the Brigadier and the Lord High Admiral were in Geneva, out of contact with anyone. Were the two events related?

"I doubt Riker is insane," Valerie said.

"What?" Maddox asked, looking up. "Don't be absurd. Riker is as level-headed as they come." Maddox shook his head. He opened his mouth to say something more, and slowly closed his mouth instead.

"Are we going to leave him there?" Valerie asked.

"I am surprised at you, Lieutenant," Galyan chided.

"What do you mean?" Valerie asked.

"You are a rules stickler," the AI said. "You love to follow the chain of command and procedure. It is unlike you to suggest we break the sergeant out of a probably lawful—"

"Galyan," Maddox said, interrupting.

"Sir?" the AI asked.

"Enough," Maddox said.

Galyan turned to Valerie. Perhaps he noticed her crimson features. "Have I embarrassed you, Lieutenant?"

"No," Valerie said, as she turned back to her station.

"Was that an accurate statement on your part?" Galyan asked her.

Valerie spun back around. "We can't just leave Riker in the lurch. Somebody must have framed him. I know I follow the rules. They're for our protection. But I can learn, too, you know. The captain stands by his crew. One way or another, we have to get Riker out of there."

"Against the orders of Star Watch?" Galyan asked.

"Who ordered us to leave Riker in there?" Valerie asked.

"No one directly told us that," the AI said. "The implication, however—"

Maddox pointed at Galyan. "Right," he said. "The implication is that someone has nabbed Sergeant Riker under Star Watch's nose. Major Stokes doesn't even know about it."

"But we have determined that Stokes is lying," Galyan said.

"That's right," Maddox said. "Officially, we're going to believe his lie."

Galyan's eyelids fluttered. Soon, a smile crept upon his Adok features. "That is quite underhanded, sir. I like it."

"Count me in," Valerie said.

"Yes…" Maddox said, as he stroked his chin once more. "Galyan, get me a schematic of the asylum and the exact location of Sergeant Riker."

"I have a schematic on file," Galyan said.

A holoimage of the asylum appeared before the captain. As Maddox studied it, a light began to blink on Valerie's comm board.

The lieutenant listened to it and then turned around swiftly. "Sir," she told Maddox. "You've just been summoned to an emergency briefing in Geneva at Star Watch Headquarters."

"Regarding…?" he asked.

"The Iron Lady did not elaborate. But she does want you down at Geneva in an hour. The meeting will start in two."

"What should we do about Sergeant Riker in the meantime?" Galyan asked.

Maddox nodded slowly, as if to himself. "We'll shelve the rescue attempt for now," he said. "But I want both of you ready for an immediate strike."

"Will you ask the Brigadier about Riker?" Galyan asked.

"I'm going to play this by ear," Maddox said. He faced Valerie. "Call Keith. Tell him to get a flitter ready. I'm going down."

-6-

Maddox sat in a stark conference chamber in a deep underground chamber beneath Star Watch Headquarters.

Brigadier Mary O'Hara sat beside him at a round table that could have comfortably held fifteen or sixteen individuals. The room had steel walls and two heavy doors. Marine guards in battlesuits stood outside the one Maddox had come in.

Mary O'Hara was an older lady with gray hair and matronly features. She'd run Star Watch Intelligence for as long as Maddox had been around.

In many ways, the Iron Lady treated him as the son she'd never had. She was a good woman, and had cried at his wedding. He felt embarrassed thinking about it.

Fortunately, he didn't have to. What the Iron Lady had just shown him was deeply sobering.

The holoimage recording of the invading Swarm Fleet heading for the Tau Ceti System at sub-light speed still hovered over the table. According to the specs, the fleet was building up velocity at a steady rate.

Maddox had recognized the saucer-shaped ships. He'd seen them at the Builder Dyson Sphere. He recognized others that he'd seen at the Golden Nexus System where the Swarm fought the Chitins. Since the Swarm had reached Human Space, they must have defeated the smaller bugs there.

"How much time do we have left?" Maddox asked.

O'Hara shook her head. "Admiral Fletcher is racing home with the Grand Fleet. Luckily, they started home a month ago.

Thanks to Professor Ludendorff, we've already come to a tentative agreement with the New Men. Ludendorff did the right thing giving them Strand. I wouldn't have agreed to that at the time…"

O'Hara shrugged.

"Will the Grand Fleet arrive in time to face the Swarm in the Tau Ceti System?" Maddox asked.

"Oh, no," O'Hara said. "Fletcher will make it home, but he won't go there. Tau Ceti is doomed. We can't possibly gather enough ships in time to face the Swarm there. We're going to have to pick the perfect engagement to give us the best odds we can get. We'll have to gather every ship we can. We'll have to begin a crash building program…"

She shook her head.

"Even then…" she added, "I'll doubt that will be enough to defeat such a vast fleet."

Maddox drummed his fingers on the table. "You're going to need the New Men's help."

"Bringing them here is a grave risk in and of itself."

"It's also preferable to extinction."

The Brigadier stared at Maddox. "In truth, we're not sure how to broach the topic with them. Why would the New Men help save us?"

"For the best of reasons," Maddox said. "After us, the Swarm will go after them. It's in the New Men's self-interest to combine our forces while we're able."

"Our best strategists and tacticians have made the calculations," she said. "Even with the New Men's help, we're doomed."

"The Spacers…" Maddox said.

O'Hara laughed bleakly. "Tell me where the Spacers are hiding."

"I have no idea."

"No one does."

"We have to find them," Maddox said.

"Could you find them?"

Maddox blinked at her. "Yes," he said finally.

"How would you start?"

"By talking to Shu 15," he said.

29

The Brigadier's features hardened. "You've just gotten married, Captain. I do not believe you trying to persuade Shu would be a good idea. Meta wouldn't like it."

"Maybe not," Maddox admitted, "but that's also beside the point given possible human extinction."

"Even if Shu gave you a lead," O'Hara said, "I doubt you could find the Spacers in time. Don't you realize that it's possible the Spacers would side with the Swarm?"

"For what possible reason would they do such an insane thing?" Maddox demanded.

"The Spacers have strange beliefs. They might believe the Swarm are the superior species. They may even have already fled far away to start over."

"Maybe," Maddox said. "Whatever the case, we can't stop trying just because the enemy has a few more ships than we do."

"No…" O'Hara said softly, staring at a wall.

Maddox could read the signs easily enough. Mary O'Hara had a different idea. Neither she nor the Lord High Admiral had any plans on giving up. If the Spacers couldn't shift the odds in humanity's favor, what could?

The Iron Lady inhaled sharply through her nostrils. She brought her focus back to him. Against all past protocol, she reached out, touching his face. Her features softened, and she smiled at him very sadly.

Maddox could not say what he felt. He'd never known his mother. She'd died soon after his birth, after she'd escaped from a New Man breeding facility. The Iron Lady had treated him like the…

"Ma'am?" he asked.

O'Hara let her hand linger against his cheek just a little longer. Finally, she removed it.

"I'm glad you married Meta," the Brigadier said. "That was a wonderful idea. Meta is a fine woman."

Maddox nodded. The spot on his cheek still felt warm. He…missed the Brigadier's touch. A second later, he squared his shoulders and lifted his chin. He refused to allow himself any weakness.

The Brigadier's smile became even sadder. "It's been so very difficult for you. I'm sorry."

"No," he said.

O'Hara looked away. Her shoulders actually shook. Was she crying?

Maddox wanted to put a hand on her shoulder, to console her. He could not. It wasn't his way. He was an island. Yes, he had Meta. He had his crew. Even so—

The Brigadier faced him as she wiped her eyes. "I'm sorry for that little display," she whispered.

"I don't understand."

"There may be a way to save Earth."

"Yes?"

"It will mean using *Victory* again. This will possibly be your hardest mission yet, the most dangerous. I don't want to ask you to do it…"

"If it will give us a chance against the Swarm, I'm for it," Maddox said. He glanced at the holoimage stellar map. The number of Swarm warships out there…

O'Hara stood. She seemed listless. What was wrong with her?

Maddox stood as well. "Do you have something to show me?"

O'Hara nodded.

"Is it Sergeant Riker?" he guessed.

Her eyes widened before narrowing in suspicion. "What do you know?" she asked.

"That the sergeant is being held near Athens in an insane asylum."

"You used your starship against us?" she accused.

"How can you say that? I used *Victory* to locate Riker. Stokes told me Star Watch had no idea concerning his whereabouts."

"Don't lie to me," she said.

Maddox stopped talking.

"You used your starship against Star Watch."

Maddox said nothing. He would not lie about it. That didn't mean he had to agree with her.

"What do you know about Riker?" she asked.

31

"Not much," Maddox admitted. "I don't believe he's insane, though."

"No..." O'Hara said softly. "It's much worse than that."

Maddox frowned.

"Come," O'Hara said. "It's best if you see and hear it if for yourself."

-7-

Maddox exited the underground railcar, following the Iron Lady into a corridor. They'd used the small vehicle, moving underground on a special rail to a new location sixty kilometers from headquarters.

"We can't be in Athens," Maddox said.

"We transferred Riker while you came down," she said.

Maddox said nothing to that.

They passed underground checkpoints and moved through heavy hatches. More battlesuited marines lined the way. Finally, they entered an area with nurses and doctors. Muffled screams sounded behind some of the doors.

They entered a long sterile hall, passed another checkpoint and finally arrived at a two-way mirror. On the other side, Sergeant Riker sat in a padded room wearing a straightjacket. Poor Riker's face was twisted with fear. He did not look about or mumble to himself. Instead, he sat like a man awaiting a terror that would consume him.

"What happened?" Maddox demanded. He yearned to kill whoever had done this to Riker.

O'Hara glanced at the captain. "We have deactivated his bionic arm. Otherwise, he could tear off the straightjacket."

"Take it off him," Maddox demanded.

"He feels more comfortable with it on."

"I don't believe that."

"It is hard to understand, I agree," O'Hara murmured.

"Are you saying he's tried to kill himself?" Maddox asked.

33

"No…but he's certainly thinking about it."

"Let me talk to him."

O'Hara sighed. "That's what he fears most."

Maddox stared at her. "Why?"

"It has to do with a null region in space."

"What does that even mean?" Maddox asked.

"The region holds two Destroyers of the Nameless Ones," O'Hara said, as she watched Maddox closely.

The captain's face drained of color. In a quick jerk, he stared at Riker again.

"So, it's true…" O'Hara whispered. "You can actually reach two Destroyers? He wasn't lying about that?"

The realization of her words penetrated Maddox's thoughts. "I see," he said. "You want me to retrieve the Destroyers."

"We're considering it."

"Who is we?"

"The Lord High Admiral and I, among a few others in charge of the Commonwealth's defenses."

"Why wouldn't we attempt this?" Maddox asked.

O'Hara studied his face. She seemed unsure. She seemed to doubt him. "Do you know what happened to your sergeant?"

"I haven't a clue."

"He won't tell us how it happened. He won't say anything knowingly. But we have monitors in his room. He talks in his sleep. That's how we've come to learn as much as we have."

"Let me talk to him."

"He dreads that," O'Hara said. "He's pleaded with us to keep you away from him."

"Why?"

"Did you find specks of blood in the rug of Room 142?" O'Hara asked.

"You know I did."

"And a burn mark?"

Maddox nodded.

"We found the sergeant's bionic hand on the rug. The other one couldn't have done it, at least, not according to the fingerprints."

"What are you talking about?" Maddox asked.

"Riker used a blaster to burn off his bionic hand," O'Hara said.

Maddox began shaking his head. "That's it. I demand you let me speak to him. I have to know what's going on."

"What if speaking to him means your damnation?"

Maddox frowned. What kind of question was that?

"I don't know," she said. "I want to know if we can save humanity. I don't want to sacrifice you, Riker and possibly Meta to do it."

"I'm tired of these hints. Are you going to let me speak to him or not?"

"Don't you have any sense of self-survival?" O'Hara asked. "Can't you realize there are wicked dangers in the universe best left alone? Sometimes, those evils can consume you."

"I believe in fighting as hard as I can, Ma'am."

"The boastfulness of —"

His eyes grew haunted.

"—youth," O'Hara finished.

The haunted look vanished almost as quickly as it had appeared.

The Iron Lady nodded. "I suppose I knew it would come to this. Why else did I bring you here? I expected nothing less from you, of course."

"You're going to let me in to see him?"

O'Hara nodded, walking toward a hatch a moment later.

-8-

Maddox entered the padded cell. Riker looked up from where he sat. His face twisted with dismay.

"Sir..." Riker whispered. "No..."

Maddox moved closer, reaching out, touching one of the sergeant's straightjacketed shoulders. The captain let his arm drop to his side after that. He sat down, moving his legs into a cross-legged position.

Riker turned away, shaking his head.

"I hear you burned off your bionic hand, Sergeant," Maddox said in a chiding tone. "That's pretty awful aim, you know."

Slowly, Riker faced him. The fear no longer shined in his eyes. The twisted muscles of his face no longer strained.

"The thing only whispers in my mind now," Riker said in his gruff voice. "I no longer think it's alive in me. I did at first. That was maddening, sir. I thought about...a terrible deed."

"A voice drove you to that?"

"Oh, no, sir," Riker said. "I wanted to kill its voice, its offer. I wanted to silence it before it could tempt you to a deed better left undone."

"You're referring to the Destroyers in the null region?"

The fear reappeared for a moment before vanishing again. Riker let his head droop before raising it once again.

"I should have known the Iron Lady wouldn't let it go," Riker said. "I should have realized the desperation of the hour."

"You're referring to the Swarm?"

36

"I am, sir."

"How did you learn about their invasion?"

"The Spacer told me."

"The man you slew?"

Riker laughed bleakly. "I didn't kill him. I burned him, that's true. First, he stabbed himself with a knife, killing himself."

"Why?"

"I suppose starting from the beginning is the best way to tell it. So that's what I'll do, sir, if you have the time."

Maddox nodded.

Riker proceeded to tell his tale starting with his leaving the fire pit at the Sheraton Hotel in Kauai. He told of his fear, his panic, the flight up the stairs and the strange conversation in the condo's living room.

"Did you really go into a null region last voyage?" Riker asked.

"We all did," Maddox said matter-of-factly. "There's a weird energy drain there. Everyone slept through it except for Galyan and me."

"Galyan knows about the Destroyers?"

"No," Maddox said. "Only I do."

"And you kept it to yourself, sir. That was wise of you."

"I had no idea this entity lived there. It told you the Builders fashioned a trap for it. There's clearly more going on than we know."

"I'll agree to that," Riker said. "The problem as I see it is that the Builders are gone. No one can contend with this thing in the null region."

"You contended with it, Sergeant. You did rather well, all things considered."

Riker shook his head. "It miscalculated, that's all. It grabbed my bionic hand. If the dying Spacer had grabbed my real hand, the ego-fragment would have invaded my soul with full force instead of only scratching it."

"Your soul, Sergeant?"

"My mind then, if that makes you feel better."

Maddox let that pass. "You said you heard it speak in your mind?"

37

Riker nodded.

"The voice has fallen silent since then?"

"I could feel it trying to remain in place," Riker said. "I should have hidden somewhere. I may not have been thinking straight for a time."

Maddox tapped his chin.

"Sir, I'm asking you for a favor. I've saved your hide a time or two. This is the moment I'm cashing in my chips. Don't try for the Destroyers. They're a lure to bring you back to the null region. Somehow, we slipped into it. We got away, too. That was pure luck, I'm thinking. I doubt we'll have the same luck with this thing awake."

"What choice do we have?" Maddox asked. "The Swarm is here, and humanity is at stake."

"I realize that. But there has to be another way of defeating the Swarm."

"I'm open to suggestions."

"If we can't think of a way, the New Men can surely think of something."

"We've beaten the New Men," Maddox said testily. "We're better than they are."

"Begging your pardon, sir, but I don't believe that. Not man to man we aren't."

Maddox frowned.

"The professor might have an idea of what to do."

"And if he doesn't?" Maddox asked.

"Then we're going to have to release Strand and let him figure it out."

"That will never happen," Maddox said.

"Use the Juggernauts, then," Riker said in a pleading tone.

"The Spacer, or the thing in the Spacer, already said the Juggernauts won't do it."

"Maybe it was lying. I mean, why would it tell us the truth if it wanted freedom?"

"Maybe you're right," Maddox said. "And maybe the Destroyers really are the only way to save humanity from the Swarm."

"What about the waiting entity?" Riker shouted. "Don't you realize it's a horror? It could destroy us just as easily as the Swarm could."

"That's a supposition on your part."

Riker began shaking his head frantically.

"Stop that," Maddox said. "I know when you're pretending. You're scared. I can appreciate that. The Spacer and this ego-fragment have badly frightened you. Yet, we've faced long odds before. We're like the legendary sailor."

"Who?"

"Odysseus," Maddox said. "He had to sail between Scylla and Charybdis, the two a mere arrow shot away from each other. Each thing was on the opposite side of the Strait of Messina between Sicily and Italy. Scylla was a six-headed sea monster and Charybdis a terrible whirlpool. They stand for no good choices in a situation. I don't doubt this entity is evil. Maybe it was the driving force behind the Nameless Ones. Maybe that's why they destroyed everything they found."

Maddox stopped talking as he regarded Riker more closely. "Did you happen to learn the Nameless Ones' real name?"

Riker shook his head.

"I'm certain Ludendorff will want to join the expedition," Maddox said.

Riker groaned. "You haven't really listened to what I'm saying. You think this is like all the other aliens we've faced before. It isn't. The entity can enter us. It has terrible powers, and it's purified evil. How do you fight something like that?"

"I don't know," Maddox said, "yet. But I plan on figuring out a way. I'm *di-far*, remember?"

The two men stared at each other.

Maddox stood. Riker kept sitting. Maddox pulled out his monofilament knife. "I'm going to cut that hideous straightjacket off you."

"I might grab your knife and turn it on you," Riker said.

"Sergeant, I want your help."

Fear reentered the sergeant's eyes. "I'm retiring, sir."

"The others need you, too."

"Please, sir, don't use that card on me. I'm too old. I'm too beat up. This thing has mastered me."

"No, Sergeant, that it did not. You've told us everything. Now we know the real danger. Now, we have time to prepare for the entity. I want you along, Sergeant."

Riker licked his lips, seeming to consider the idea, and finally shaking his head.

Maddox sighed and looked away. Then, he moved closer, lowering his head so his lips almost touched one of Riker's ears. The captain pitched his voice low.

"I need your help, Sergeant," Maddox whispered.

Riker stared up at Maddox. The fear was still there, but there was something else, too.

"Very well," the sergeant said gruffly. "In that case...I'll do it, sir. Count me in for this mission."

-9-

"You're making a dreadful mistake, Captain," the Iron Lady said. "Normally, I am inclined to give you your head on these missions. In this instance…I believe you are letting emotions cloud your judgment."

Maddox glanced out the window, seeing the Congo jungles below. They were heading for a particularly deep old gold mine in South Africa.

Maddox and O'Hara were the only two occupants in the passenger area of a supersonic shuttle. Two hours had passed since his talk with Riker.

The sergeant hadn't yet reached *Victory* in orbit. The doctors were still checking him. According to Valerie, to whom Maddox had just spoken to, Keith would take the sergeant up to the starship in another half hour.

Maddox turned to O'Hara, who sat beside him. "Begging your pardon, Ma'am, I'm not the one being emotional about this."

"What's wrong with trusting your emotions?" O'Hara said, changing course as she stared into the captain's eyes. "I've long trusted mine. Shu 15 is dangerous, too dangerous to trust."

"People say the same thing about you and me."

O'Hara brushed that aside. "You barely defeated her once in order to regain control of your starship. I doubt Shu has forgotten the incident. She's been in solitary confinement for quite some time. She must have learned to hate you by now."

41

Maddox shrugged. "I've studied her situation. If the confinement was so terrible, she could have given up her modifications at any time. That would undoubtedly have nullified her Spacer programming and removed the inner compulsions. I believe those were your conditions for her freedom. I realize Shu is loath to give them up. She earned her modifications through hard toil and they're held in high esteem among the Spacers. Still, I doubt she holds any ill will toward me."

"She might consider her long confinement cruel."

"Do you think *she* believes that? Or is that what you've come to believe?"

O'Hara tried a new avenue. "She tried to kill you before."

"So did Major Stokes. You don't seem to have any problem keeping him on your staff."

"That's different."

Maddox raised an eyebrow.

"The Spacers are unhinged with their modifications, programming and compulsions," O'Hara said. "We didn't realize their mania before. We do now, though. There's something fundamentally wrong with the entire race."

Maddox would agree that the Spacers had made some bad choices in the past. Even so, Shu had helped *Victory's* crew in the end. The Spacer Nation was in hiding at present. No doubt, they were waiting somewhere in the near Beyond, watching events and making their strange judgments about what to do next.

"Ma'am, whatever lies in the null region..." he trailed off.

"What were you going to say?" O'Hara asked after a moment.

"It just occurred to me. Does Star Watch have anything on file concerning null regions?"

"I've already checked," O'Hara said. "The answer is no."

"What about strange entities in relation to the Nameless Ones?"

"Everything about the Nameless Ones and their Destroyers is a blank to us, Captain. Likely, because you've been in one of their vessels, you know more about the Nameless Ones than anyone else."

"Maybe Ludendorff knows something about them…"

A predatory look appeared on the Iron Lady's face. "Where is Ludendorff, by the way?"

"You mean you don't know?"

"Why would I ask you if I did?"

"I can think of several reasons," Maddox said.

"In answer to your question, no," she said, "I don't know his present whereabouts, although we believe he is hidden somewhere in the Alpha Centurial System. Some of the Commonwealth's best mental specialists are there. The last I could discover, the professor was still attempting to restore Doctor Rich's full mental faculties."

"I wish him luck in that," Maddox said.

O'Hara made a face. "I feel sorry for Doctor Rich. What does she see in the egotistical Methuselah Man?"

"I suspect Ludendorff loves her."

"Him?" O'Hara scoffed. "Do you truly believe that's possible?"

Maddox nodded.

"Ludendorff is a charlatan of the first order," O'Hara declared. "He imprinted himself on Dana when she was an impressionable young university student. Dana has never gotten over that. Now, she may have lost her brilliance because of following that old goat all over the galaxy."

"Dana loves the Methuselah Man. And I don't believe it has anything to do with youthful imprinting."

"This time, you're wrong, Captain."

Maddox rested his hands against his lean stomach. He wished Ludendorff luck with Dana. They would need the doctor before this was through. The mission sounded ominous indeed. What exactly had attacked Riker's mind? What was an ego-fragment? Was the entity in the null region physical or gaseous, or were there such things as spirit beings? If the thing was a spirit, how had the Builders been able to trap it?

The problem was they didn't know enough about the entity. That the Builders had trapped it gave Maddox hope they could find a weapon against it.

The pilot made an announcement over a loudspeaker. They would soon be landing.

"Shu is going to want to come on your voyage," O'Hara said.

Maddox glanced sidelong at the Brigadier. "I may need her."

O'Hara shook her head.

"What if the mission hinges on what Shu can do for us?" Maddox asked.

"I'm not going to release Shu with her modifications intact," O'Hara said in a firm voice. "I suppose you think you can whisk her out of confinement. Well, this time, I dare you to try. This time, I challenge you to use all of *Victory's* alien technologies. But I should warn you first. If it appears you will succeed, I will have Shu shot."

"I have no plans on breaking her out," Maddox said quietly.

"I'm not always sure when to believe you."

Maddox smiled. "Ma'am, while it might not be polite, I have the same reservations about you."

It took a moment before O'Hara smiled back at him. "You're not going to change my mind about Shu."

"Can you give me any inducement I can offer her?"

"None," O'Hara said.

"Not even with humanity's survival in the balance?"

"Captain, it is because of the high stakes that I refuse to let her set foot on *Victory*. Fool me once, shame on you. Fool me twice, shame on me."

Maddox absorbed that, wondering if he would have to break Shu out of her maximum-security prison after all. He—

"What's that?" Maddox asked, pointing out the window.

In the distance, a large mushroom cloud bloomed into existence.

"Emergency!" the pilot simultaneously shouted over the loudspeaker. "Buckle up."

Maddox instantly clicked his buckles into place. The Iron Lady had never taken hers off. That probably saved her from serious injury.

The supersonic shuttle swerved violently. The G forces tugged at them harder and harder. The Iron Lady's head slumped forward as she went unconscious. Her body lifted, but the straps held her into place.

"This is going to get rough," the pilot shouted over the speaker.

Maddox gripped his armrests as the blast from the nuclear detonation struck the shuttle. As the shaking continued to worsen, Maddox wondered if they would flip...

Finally, the shaking lessened. Maybe the shuttle had been far enough away from the blast to escape destruction.

Several minutes later, the worst of it was over.

"Pilot," Maddox called.

"Captain," the pilot said over the loudspeaker.

"Where did the bomb originate?"

"My navigator is checking—it was the underground detention center, sir."

"Where Shu 15 was kept?"

"Do you mean the secret Spacer prisoner, sir?"

"Yes," Maddox said.

"That's what I'm hearing, sir. The nuclear explosion appears to have originated underground. No one knows more than that at this point."

The timing of the explosion wasn't a coincidence. Somebody hadn't wanted him talking to Shu 15. He didn't believe the Iron Lady had a hand in that. Could it have been the Lord High Admiral? No, he doubted that, too.

The most likely person not wanting him to talk to Shu...was the entity stuck in the null region. But it was impossible for the entity to have engineered such a blast in a maximum-security prison. It was impossible for the entity to know he'd planned to talk to Shu.

Even so, Maddox was convinced the entity had attacked the prison, destroying the entire complex...in order to hide something critical.

Maddox's eyes shone with interest. This was a puzzle, the kind of thing he lived to solve.

Beside him, the Iron Lady groaned.

That snapped Maddox back to the moment. "Find a medical center," he told the pilot. "We need to get the Brigadier to one as quickly as possible."

-10-

The answer to the deep prison destruction eluded Maddox.

Three days of intense detective work brought the captain nothing concrete. Major Stokes led Star Watch's Intelligence investigation, which was also coming up empty handed. The evidence might have been in the prison's security systems. Those systems had all been destroyed, along with any backups.

"It's too thorough," Maddox told his wife five days after the blast.

They lay in bed together in his quarters aboard *Victory*. The starship neared the Laumer Point that led to the Alpha Centauri System. Maddox wanted to pick up Professor Ludendorff. Then, he would head into the Beyond where he had fought the first Juggernaut during their last voyage.

It was strange, but Maddox had shown little interest in Star Watch's efforts to build a vast coalition fleet to face the Swarm invaders. Few people knew about the Swarm yet. Maddox knew the Builder Scanner kept a constant eye on the enemy fleet's doings. He knew the Lord High Admiral had already spoken to the Emperor of the New Men via long-range communicators. Maddox didn't know the state of the negotiations, though.

The captain was concentrating on his mission, his goal. He would let the Lord High Admiral deal with matters of grand strategy. He had to bring two alien Destroyers to the table. Those two super-ships could well turn the odds in humanity's favor. Several years ago, just one Destroyer had devastated the fleets attempting to engage it. Maddox also knew the Destroyers had annihilated Swarm fleets in the past. Would the bugs remember the Destroyers?

First, I have to get them, Maddox told himself. That was far from a done deal.

Soft hands ran across his shoulders. Maddox turned, smiling at his wife. Meta had long blonde hair and beautiful features, with a voluptuous figure—

Maddox turned around more fully, putting his arms around her, pressing the naked Meta against him. He kissed her for a time.

"Say it," she whispered. "Tell me again."

"I love you," he said.

Meta closed her eyes, snuggling up against him. "I love you, too," she whispered.

For a time, they simply enjoyed one another.

Afterward, Meta said, "Are you still thinking about Shu?"

"I want to know who killed her," Maddox said.

"You believe it was the entity in the null region."

"I suspect the entity. Yet, I don't see how it could have done it. Whoever set off the nuclear device made sure we couldn't piece together the clues because the clues would no longer exist after the detonation."

"The backup systems—"

"Yes," Maddox said. "They've been wiped clean."

"Someone with electronic skills must have done it."

"You must be thinking the same thing as I am," Maddox said. "This seems like something an adept Spacer could do."

"Have you talked to Riker about this?" Meta asked.

Maddox shook his head. "I don't see the connection."

"Riker's mind touched the entity. If the entity had a hand in Shu's death…"

"Yes," Maddox said. "That's brilliant." He kissed Meta on the forehead and rolled to his side of the bed.

Meta grabbed his shoulder and pulled hard, causing him to fall back. She pounced upon him, kissing him on the mouth.

"We're married," she said. "A peck on the forehead is no longer going to suffice. Do I make myself clear?"

47

Maddox grinned, pressing her against him one more time. He kissed her forcefully on the mouth. Then, he wriggled free and sat up on the edge of the bed. He hadn't talked to Riker much since his sergeant's departure from Earth.

Maddox frowned. In fact, he hadn't talked to Riker at all since the sergeant had come aboard the starship. Was there a reason for that, one he didn't fully understand?

Maddox stood, reaching for a shirt. He'd hated Shu's mental interference during the voyage into the Deep Beyond. If that kind of thing was happening again…it was time to put an immediate end to it.

-11-

"Galyan," Maddox said, as he walked down a ship corridor. The holoimage appeared, floating beside him.

"Anything to report on Sergeant Riker?" the captain asked.

"He has not left his quarters since we left Earth orbit."

"I already knew that. What's he been doing in his room?"

"When he arrived, the sergeant began searching for bugs. It took him thirteen hours until he had found and deactivated the last one."

"How many were in his quarters?"

"Seven," Galyan said.

"You can no longer see into his quarters?"

"I have to become invisible and enter his quarters to do so."

"Did the sergeant rest in any manner until he'd found and deactivated the last bug?"

"No, sir," Galyan said.

"Did you invade his quarters after the seventh bug was destroyed?"

"Yes, sir."

"What did you observe?"

"The sergeant no longer seemed as agitated, but I would not call him tranquil. He was at greater ease than before. He sat cross-legged and stared at a bulkhead for a long time."

"Did you run experiments?"

"It is interesting that you should ask, sir. I did. I left and reappeared at oddly timed intervals. Each time, I found him

49

studying a bulkhead. He seemed…troubled, but not as troubled as when the spy devices had been concentrated upon him."

"What was your conclusion?"

"I have several," Galyan said. "First, Sergeant Riker is acting differently than is his wont. There are facets of his old personality in play, but there is something else as well. Second, he does not like to be observed. Third, I am unsure if he can detect me when I am invisible. I have a suspicion that he senses me, although he is uncertain about my presence."

"Can you scan anything foreign in him?"

"I have tried on several occasions. I did not detect anything."

"What about testing his brainwave patterns?"

"I admit, sir, I did not think of that. Would you like me to conduct that type of test?"

"Yes."

Galyan vanished.

Maddox continued his quick stride. He made it halfway to Riker's quarters before Galyan reappeared.

"Sir," the holoimage said. "I am detecting a slight variation in his brainwave patterns."

"Have you detected these differences before in Riker?"

"Never," Galyan said.

"Can you extrapolate from the odd brain patterns that a foreign entity is using Riker?"

"I cannot."

"How do you account for the different brainwaves?"

"I cannot, sir."

"Is Riker acting differently than usual?"

"Without a doubt, sir," Galyan replied.

Maddox pursed his lips. Did the altered brainwaves indicate a change done to Riker, or did it indicate a foreign entity in Riker at the moment? It was a troubling question on several fronts.

"I want you present in the room when I talk to Riker."

"Should I remain visible?"

Maddox shook his head.

"Should I speak up for any reason?"

"None," Maddox said.

50

For a time, they moved down the corridor in silence.

"What are we really attempting to determine about Sergeant Riker, sir?"

A soft smile appeared on Maddox's face, although he said no more as they moved toward the sergeant's hatch.

-12-

Riker stood as Maddox entered his chamber. The sergeant seemed more subdued than usual, his leathery features somewhat withdrawn. He didn't hold his shoulders back as he normally would have, but let them slump forward.

The sergeant had been sitting on a spot on the floor. He was wearing his regulation uniform. That did not include a weapon of any sort. The hatch had been locked on the outside. Riker was free of the insane asylum, but Maddox didn't yet trust him enough to allow him free use of the ship.

"Mind if I come in, Sergeant?"

Riker made a bland gesture.

Maddox moved to a desk, turned a chair around and sat down, facing the sergeant.

After a moment's hesitation, Riker stepped to a bulkhead, sliding down against it, using it as a backrest as he sat on the floor.

"Is Galyan in here?" Riker asked.

"Do you sense him?"

The sergeant did not reply.

"Was that an unworthy question?" Maddox asked.

Riker leaned the back of his head against the bulkhead. A shy grin slipped onto his face.

"I understand, sir, believe me, I do. You don't trust me."

"Would you if you were in my position?"

"I'm the one who warned you to leave me behind."

"True," Maddox said.

"So, why didn't you?"

"Surely you understand—"

"Excuse me for interrupting," Riker said. "You said you needed me. You pitched your voice in such a way as to make me believe the indomitable Captain Maddox needed his faithful sergeant on the expedition."

"Was I convincing?"

"At the time, sir. It was perfectly done."

"Perhaps because I meant it," Maddox said.

Riker shrugged.

"Have you lost heart?" the captain asked.

The sergeant sighed. "I've begun feeling it again. It's a weight I don't want. The idea of some entity using me—"

Riker shivered.

"You hate it?" Maddox asked.

For a moment, Riker's eyes hardened. "Damn straight, I hate it." The look vanished a moment later. "How do you fight something like that?"

"I aim to find out."

Riker moved the back of his head off the bulkhead. "Sir...this one is bigger than you. This one is tougher than you."

"A lot of them have been tougher."

"You're not going to find an easy solution this time. It fights dirty."

"I plan to do the same, only better."

"You're too confident, sir. You should be quaking in your boots, terrified."

"Who says I'm not?"

"You don't look terrified."

"Didn't you just say I'm a good actor?" Maddox asked.

The old Riker grin appeared. "That I did, lad." He sobered almost immediately. "Can I ask why you're here?"

"I've hit a wall," Maddox said. "I've tried every avenue I know to pierce the wall and see what's on the other side. Everything has failed. You're the last connection I know to what happened."

"I have no idea what you're talking about."

"Shu 15 is dead."

Riker stared at Maddox. Finally, the sergeant rubbed his chin. "Nuclear detonation?" he asked.

"Care to explain how you knew that?"

"I'm right about that?"

"Why act surprised?"

"It..." Riker licked his lips. "It was a guess. No. That's not right. It was a feeling I had when you said her name. Now..." The sergeant frowned, rubbing his eyes. "I'm getting sleepy, sir."

Maddox did not sit forward or give any outward sign of it, but he felt exhilarated. He had been right. There was a connection, and it had to do with the entity in the null region.

Maddox stood abruptly.

Riker's head swayed. His eyelids were red with fatigue.

Maddox strode to the sergeant, leaned down and slapped him across the face.

"Hey!" Riker said, opening his eyes. "What's that for?"

Maddox slapped him again. Each slap left a red mark on the sergeant's cheek.

Riker scrambled to his feet. He swung at Maddox. The captain grabbed the wrist and held it in place.

Finally, Riker stopped applying pressure. When Maddox let go, the arm swung down. Riker didn't sit. He nodded, though.

"The thing tried to drive me to sleep, didn't it?" Riker asked.

"That was my guess," Maddox said.

"Why has it stopped?"

"I believe its power is limited. I believe the more you fight it, the more you'll exhaust it."

"How would you know that?" Riker asked.

"By observing you these past days," Maddox said.

"Is this really about Shu 15?"

"Partly," Maddox said.

Riker nodded again. "Go ahead, sir. Let's get started on whatever you're planning."

Maddox moved back to the chair, sitting once more. After a few moments, Riker stepped to his bed, sitting on the edge.

"Are you thinking about Shu 15?" Maddox asked.

"I'm trying not to."

"Think about her."

Riker nodded but soon raised his hands palm upward.

"She was small and fine-boned," Maddox said. "She had a pretty face. I've always suspected that she had pretty eyes."

"She always wore goggles," Riker said.

"Shu 15 had two modifications. She could see electromagnetic impulses. She could…"

Maddox stopped speaking because he saw Riker's glazed condition.

Trying to contain his excitement, Maddox asked in the same voice as before, "Can you see Shu 15 in your mind?"

"Yes," Riker said in a dull voice.

"What is she doing?"

"Sitting in a chair looking at papers," Riker said dully. "Star Watch had confined her in a deep abandoned gold mine. I sensed her, and she sensed me. I…I…found a way to her door. I could not open the door, but I passed the message to her. She was terrified after that. She fought the message. I think…"

Riker frowned. "I think the message strengthened her modifications. The message told her to wait for the right moment to escape."

Riker looked up at the captain.

Maddox had the feeling that Riker was staring right through him.

"She was frightened. She didn't want to comply. She hated the message. I think…I can only suspect that she felt you coming to her place of confinement. I believe she used her powers as never before. I believe she reached out to the fail-safe device embedded in the mine."

"What device?"

Riker cocked his head. "A nuclear warhead," he said softly. The sergeant's forehead furrowed. "How can I know about that? How can I know any of this? I'm not a storyteller. I don't usually make up—"

"Sergeant," Maddox said.

Riker blinked several times. The frown departed. The glassiness left his eyes.

"I believe I understand," Maddox said. "I suspected it might be true. I wanted to test the theory on you."

Riker waited.

"The Spacer messenger you burned in Kauai went to Shu first," Maddox said. "It's possible he put some of the ego-fragment into her. The entity appears to have tried to cover its bets. If Shu sensed us coming—me coming—and she knew that she would put the 'message' into me..."

Maddox turned away. A feeling of sorrow he'd never felt before swept through him.

Riker chuckled softly.

Maddox turned to the sergeant in surprise.

"Ice cold Captain Maddox has feelings after all. I knew you had it in you, lad. I think you're right. Shu 15 killed herself to save you."

"No..." Maddox said.

"She must have loved you, sir."

Maddox shook his head.

"This entity is making mistakes," Riker said. "Maybe you have it right, sir. Maybe we can beat this thing. Yet..."

"Go on," Maddox said.

"We're defeating echoes of its power. When we face the real McCoy, I have a feeling it will be a new ballgame."

"Ludendorff..." Maddox said. "Let's hope the professor has some idea about what we're facing."

-13-

"I have no idea," Ludendorff said 47 hours later. "I've never heard of such a thing."

Starship *Victory* was in the Alpha Centauri System, near Proxima Centauri.

Alpha Centauri was a multi-star system. Alpha Centauri A had a mass 1.1 and a luminosity 1.519 times that of the Sun. Alpha Centauri B was a smaller and cooler star. The double stars orbited a common point between them. A and B varied between a Pluto-Sun to Saturn-Sun orbit. Alpha Centauri C or Proxima Centauri was a red dwarf. It was gravitationally bound to the other two, but orbited 15,000 AUs from the others. That was approximately 500x Neptune's orbit.

Professor Ludendorff was an older man with thick white hair, tanned skin and a thin gold chain around his neck. He and Maddox met in the starship's main cafeteria. Doctor Dana Rich was in their quarters. She'd been subdued, hardly acknowledging the many salutations.

Keith had brought the two from the space habitat where they had been staying. Now, the starship headed for the next Laumer Point. They would travel as fast as they could for the Beyond where they had passed through last time on their voyage to Sind II.

At the cafeteria table, Maddox stirred his coffee, having just added cream.

Ludendorff slurped his coffee, grinning as he did so. After finishing the cup, he lifted the pot from the table and poured himself more.

"Coffee is outlawed in the Alpha Centauri System," the professor said. "Can you believe that?"

"That's an outrage," Maddox agreed.

"It's not because they can't grow any or import it. It's a religious tenet for the entire star system. I had to keep a low profile while there. Otherwise, I would have contacted smugglers for some good Colombian beans."

"Perhaps you don't understand the seriousness of our voyage," Maddox said.

"My boy, I've listened to every word you've spoken. I fully understand the significance of your story. Likely, I understand the situation better than you do. I'm sure I've already picked up several nuances that you missed."

"I doubt that," Maddox said.

"That's your problem, Captain. You're too arrogant, too cocksure. You're going to have to temper that if you hope to succeed this voyage."

Maddox sipped his coffee. "You've never heard of such an entity belonging to the Nameless Ones?"

"What did I say a moment ago?"

"What about a null region?"

"*That* I've heard about. But it's only a legend."

"Clearly, that is not the case. We were in one last voyage."

"Describe the event. I'm curious if this is a real place or if you were merely dreaming."

"The entity is real enough," Maddox said. "We've seen its effects."

"The reality of the entity might be reason enough for you to have imagined the null region," Ludendorff said.

"We fought a Juggernaut after exiting the long Einstein-Rosen Bridge. Do you remember? The Juggernaut caught us with its tractor beam."

"I remember the incident quite well," Ludendorff said.

"The Juggernaut had not yet gripped us fully. We used the star drive to try to escape. The partial tractor beam kept us from leaving. I suspect we built up power all the while."

58

"Yes, yes, that makes sense."

"When we finally tore away, the starship must have moved like a stone from a slingshot."

"Possibly," Ludendorff said.

"Whatever it did, that propelled us into this null region. Everyone fell unconscious there but for Galyan and me."

"I would imagine I should have stayed awake as well," Ludendorff said.

"But you didn't," Maddox said. "I think I remained awake because… Not to put too fine a point on it, I have superior reflexes and metabolism. You have a few superior properties, but you're old these days."

Ludendorff's eyes narrowed.

"Galyan remained awake," Maddox said, as if failing to notice the professor's reaction. "He spoke of a vast power drain. The AI powered certain ship functions. At that point, Galyan went offline. I saw two Destroyers afterward. I clearly remember that. I also saw a light in the distance. I steered us to the light."

"And?" asked Ludendorff.

"And I recall wishing we were at the Junkyard Planet, what we called Sind II then."

"Go on."

"We passed through the light. I fell unconscious. When I woke up, we'd traveled over thirty light-years in an instant. I believe the light read my thoughts and moved me to the place I desired."

"It read your thoughts?" Ludendorff asked in disbelief.

Maddox nodded.

"That's a preposterous tale," the Methuselah Man said.

"Yes," Maddox said. "I quite agree."

Ludendorff gave him a searching sideways glance. "Why didn't you say anything about the null region before this?"

"I thought it best the Destroyers remain a secret."

"Hmm…" Ludendorff said. He picked up the cup and drained the coffee. Afterward, he poured himself more.

"What do the legends say about a null region?" Maddox asked.

"It's quite complicated, scientifically speaking," Ludendorff said. "But I'll keep it simple so you can comprehend." The professor fell silent as he swirled his cup. "I suppose the easiest way to describe it would be as an antimatter pocket or reality. Only, it isn't antimatter, exactly. Otherwise, our starship would have blown up in a titanic explosion while we were there. Instead, we had the massive power drain. That drain happened because many properties are reversed in a null region."

"Could that trap a Destroyer?"

"It's possible," Ludendorff said.

"Does that sound like a Builder operation?"

"Oh, yes. That part I can easily see."

"Would the null region keep the Destroyers intact all this time?"

"*Victory* remained intact in regular space. Why couldn't the Destroyers remain intact in the null region?"

"But you don't believe in the actual existence of the null region?" Maddox asked.

Ludendorff's right hand seemed to tremble. Maybe he'd had too much caffeine already.

"I suppose I shouldn't be hasty about this," the professor said. "We had a freak occurrence that day. Who's to say Strand didn't have something up his sleeve as a backup plan against us in case the Juggernaut failed."

"You think Strand knows about the null region and this Nameless entity?"

Ludendorff made "tsking" sounds. "I hate to admit such a thing, my boy. But Strand knew far too many oddities for his own good. I suppose if anyone would know about such things, it would be him. But Strand can't help us now. The New Men have him."

"Maybe we should get him from the Throne World."

Ludendorff looked up in alarm. He chuckled a moment later. "You're pulling my leg, of course."

"Why would I do that at a time like this?"

Ludendorff scowled. "Strand must remain where he is."

"Professor—"

60

"No!" Ludendorff said, making a decisive motion with a hand. "Strand cannot help us."

"But if he knows—"

"Don't you understand? Strand will concoct any lie in order to escape the New Men. You cannot trust anything he might tell you. No, no, my boy, you must forget such a notion. We went to exhausting effort to capture the scoundrel. He will have to live out his days—"

Ludendorff raised a shaky hand as he spoke, with another cup of coffee headed for his lips. Maddox struck quicker than a cobra, smacking the cup out of the professor's hand. Hot coffee spilled on the floor as the cup flew across the cafeteria to shatter against a wall.

The professor yanked his hand back far too late. He shook his fingers, finally looking up at Maddox.

"What's gotten into you?"

Maddox began to lean forward as hot intensity shone in his eyes. He gripped the edge of the table—abruptly, the captain leaned back in his chair. The intensity vanished from his features. Something hooded the fire in his eyes as an easy urbanity took its place.

"I…shouldn't have…" Maddox didn't finish the thought.

"You shouldn't have done that," Ludendorff snapped. The professor gave the captain a second glance before shaking his head. "You're overwrought. I understand. The threat of the Swarm invaders has gotten the better of your already questionable manners. As I said a few moments earlier, you're too cocksure. Yes, yes, I understand this is an extinction-level threat. But humanity has faced those before, believe you me."

"I suspect humanity has never faced a full-scale Swarm attack before," Maddox said.

"There may be something to your idea," the professor conceded. "Still, slapping my hand…"

"Questionable manners, I think you said. Why don't we leave it at that?"

Ludendorff shrugged as he flexed the struck fingers.

"You've caused me plenty of inconveniences in the past," Maddox said. "Perhaps I owed you that."

61

"If we're leaving the subject, why are you still addressing it?"

For just a moment, the fire in the captain's eyes slipped past his guarded look. He tightened that back into place a second later.

"Being married must have added to your stress," the professor muttered. "Dana talks about marriage because of your impulsive act. She wishes to emulate you. I have to distract—"

The professor shook his head abruptly. "Women," he said. "Troublesome creatures, don't you agree?"

"They have their pluses."

"Oh, certainly," Ludendorff said. "I obviously agree to that. In fact, I know more about women than any man alive. I know how to please them better than any man alive. If you'd like a few pointers…"

Maddox raised his eyebrows in a sardonic manner.

"It's Meta's loss," Ludendorff said. "You could have her crying out in ecstasy for hours if you listened to me."

"You will leave Meta out of your lecherous comments."

"Oh, ho, I do believe I've found a chink in your icy armor, Captain. That was a mistake letting me see it."

"Just so you remember what I said."

"Threats, Captain?" Ludendorff asked.

Maddox sighed.

A few moments later, Ludendorff turned away. He nodded. "I need Dana for this. I need her brilliance. But it's not there, and I don't know how to revive it."

"Could Galyan aid you?"

The professor regarded him. "Yes. That's a good idea. The two of us…" Ludendorff frowned with growing severity. "If the null region exists, Galyan and I shall figure out how to duplicate your former feat of entering it. Let us for the moment, anyway, consider that problem solved."

Maddox waited.

"We have several other problems to address. Who knows what awaits us on the Destroyers? The last time you boarded one…"

"Yes," Maddox said. "That could be a problem."

"Let's also set that aside for a moment. The elephant in the room is the entity. I suspect it poses the greatest threat to us. We shall accomplish nothing if we cannot deal with it."

Maddox could see the wheels turning in Ludendorff's mind.

The professor let his right thumb slide under the small gold chain around his neck. He moved the thumb back and forth across the underside of the chain.

"What is the entity?" the professor asked.

Maddox shrugged, saying, "Might it be gaseous or spirit-based?"

Ludendorff's head jerked up. "Spirit-based?" he asked in surprise.

"We can't discount the possibility," Maddox said.

"What does spirit-based even mean?"

"A spirit, like a demon or an angel," Maddox said.

"I am familiar with the *concept* of spirits," Ludendorff said testily. "However, there is no factual, observable data that leads me to believe in them."

"Can we see the wind?"

"Oh, yes, yes," Ludendorff said in a tedious voice. "I am familiar with those tropes in trying to explain—"

"Why are you so resistant to the idea of spirits?"

Ludendorff opened his mouth to reply, but then slowly closed it. He shrugged a moment later.

"Let's refine your definition," the professor said. "What do you mean by a spirit?"

"I just said—"

"No! *Refine* the concept. Help me understand *exactly* what you're trying to say."

Maddox tilted his head. "A material object has three known states: solid, liquid and gaseous."

"So you are suggesting that spirits are non-material?" the professor asked.

"It would seem so."

"Can you refine that definition?"

Maddox tapped his chin. "I suppose…natural versus supernatural objects."

"Natural is something made or formed by natural causes," the professor said. "Spirit entities are made or formed through supernatural causes."

"That sounds about right."

"Nature gives us nature-based weapons. Supernatural..." Ludendorff spread his hands. "How do you propose to find a supernatural weapon to deal with the entity?"

Maddox chewed that over. "If the entity is supernatural... I don't know where to find a supernatural-based weapon."

"Neither do I."

"Maybe we haven't exhausted the possibilities of natural entities," Maddox said. "Perhaps an entity could be electrical in nature."

"That's an interesting hypothesis. In fact, your sergeant's story tends to lend itself to that belief. His bionic hand glowed. That would imply an energy source." Ludendorff's voice had risen with excitement as he spoke. "Yes, yes," he said, grinning. "That would also make sense of why this...ego-fragment used a passing Spacer. In some manner, the entity could reach from its null-region trap when a Spacer with greater modifications came within its radius."

Ludendorff positively glowed. "That is remarkable, my boy. I think we have stumbled onto the right direction to search."

"You seem relieved it's not supernatural."

Ludendorff laughed. "Of course, I'm relieved. I'd rather face a thing I can understand, a creature that I can defeat. We simply need the right kind of weapon."

"Would a blaster work against an electrical creature?"

Ludendorff drummed his fingers on the table. He stared at the pot of coffee for what seemed an eternity. Then, he picked up the pot, opened the lid and sipped some of the coffee inside. He grinned at Maddox afterward.

"I have it," the professor said.

Maddox waited.

Ludendorff slid off his chair and began to pace. "The starship is about here in Human Space..." he said to himself. And then he seemed to freeze. The professor remained like that for several heartbeats as if he'd turned into a statue. Then, just as suddenly, he began pacing again. "If we moved there…" He snapped his fingers and turned to Maddox. "I believe we need to make a slight detour, my boy."

Maddox studied Ludendorff, wondering what had happened during that frozen moment.

"Is something wrong?" Ludendorff asked.

Maddox opened his mouth, but decided to let the incident pass. "No," he said.

"Why are you staring at me then?"

Maddox hesitated just a moment longer before asking, "Where would this detour take us?"

"To a hidden planet Strand and I used to explore," the professor said. "I haven't been there…in two hundred years. It shouldn't take us long. I just have to remember the route. It's quite tricky."

Once more, Maddox became suspicious. This was Professor Ludendorff. The man usually had something up his sleeve. Yet, the frozen seconds had seemed different. It was almost as if someone had changed…settings, like old-fashioned radio stations, in the professor's mind. Inwardly, Maddox chuckled to himself. That had to be wrong. It had simply been the Methuselah Man thinking harder and more deeply than normal. With all those memories packed in his mind, it must take some effort to dredge up old thoughts.

"Why do you need to go to this place?" Maddox asked.

Ludendorff's eyes shone with a strange light. "I don't know how I'd forgotten. It's been so long, I suppose, but it was an interesting voyage that we had there." The Methuselah Man shrugged. "I just remembered an excavation with some strange symbols that never made sense before. They're making more sense now that we're talking about null regions. I need to see those symbols again to be sure."

"Will going to this place be dangerous?"

Ludendorff laughed. "Quite dangerous, my boy. I think you're going to love the place."

-14-

The circuitous route took *Victory* near a blazing star, through a vast gaseous cloud that stretched more than a light-year and through the thickest asteroid belt that Maddox had ever witnessed. It also took them away from the place in the Beyond where they needed to go.

"Maybe we should head to Sind II," Maddox told Ludendorff a week after their conversation.

"Patience, my boy, we're almost there."

Six days later, the starship entered yet another Laumer Point, one that took them five light-years in a hop into a nearly empty system with a cool red giant star. The system was closer to the edge of the galaxy than Maddox had ever gone before.

"I'd think the more exotic wisdom would be nearer the galactic core, not at the galactic edge," Maddox told Meta.

Ludendorff happened to be on the bridge today. He overheard the remark.

"You're quite wrong, my boy," the professor said. "The Destroyers came from outside our galaxy, remember? Surely, I've told you that before."

"It must have slipped my mind," Maddox said from the captain's chair.

"That's one of my greatest problems," the professor admitted. "When you hold as much knowledge as I do in my brain, you're bound to forget more than most people will ever learn in a lifetime."

"I hate to think we're on a wild goose chase," Maddox said.

"No, no, that's the wrong way to look at this," the professor said. "Gaining the understanding of a thing is worth the detours. Most people aren't willing to risk the loss of time in order to gamble for knowledge. It's one of the foibles that keep the masses ignorant. The other is a low IQ, but they really can't help that, can they?"

"I suppose not," Maddox said, as he gave Meta a knowing look.

She smiled back at him.

That made Maddox grin.

The professor "tsked" his tongue several times. "Newlyweds," he said. "I never thought I'd see you in such a condition, Captain. It doesn't become you, let me be the first to tell you."

"Why is he so angry?" Meta asked Maddox.

"Dana wants them to get married."

Meta clapped her hands. "That would be a wonderful idea, Professor."

Ludendorff gave Maddox a thunderous glare. "I told you that in the strictest confidence."

"Don't you love Dana?" Meta asked.

"Now, now, it's not a matter of love," the professor told her. "These things must take time to fully mature."

"Maddox is a captain," Meta said. "He could marry you two."

"I'd be delighted to help," Maddox said.

Ludendorff smiled at Meta and frowned at Maddox. Finally, the Methuselah Man waved a hand in the air. "I'll give that my highest priority. I give you my word. Unfortunately, we're almost at the planet."

"Captain," Valerie said sharply. She was at her console. "I hate to interrupt the good times—"

Maddox swiveled forward, glancing at the main screen. He saw four bright dots speeding toward *Victory*.

"Are those missiles?" the captain asked.

"Yes, sir," Valerie said. "We're under attack."

"Why didn't you warn us about this possibility?" Maddox asked Ludendorff.

The professor grumbled something under his breath about it having slipped his mind. "If you'd let me concentrate instead of belaboring me about matrimony—"

Maddox barked orders at Galyan, who had materialized on the bridge.

The starship's antimatter engine began to build up power. Soon, a purple neutron beam flashed into the void. One of the speeding missiles vaporized.

"Nothing to it," Ludendorff said. "They're quite old."

"How old?" asked Maddox.

"Ten thousand years, at least," the Methuselah Man said.

Maddox glanced in astonishment at the professor. At the same time, the neutron beam flashed again, and a second missile blew apart.

"Captain," Valerie said. "I have the sensor analysis. These are thermonuclear-tipped missiles."

"Oh," he said.

"Of ten thousand megatons each," the lieutenant added.

"That's can't be right."

"If one of those goes off…" Valerie said.

The neutron beam flashed again, and the third missile and its warhead exploded harmlessly, destroyed before it could ignite.

"The fourth one is getting ready to blow," Valerie shouted.

"I can hear you, Lieutenant," Maddox said. "Shouting isn't going to solve anything. Galyan," he said.

"Give me another few seconds, sir," the holoimage said.

"Full power to the shields," Maddox said.

Galyan's eyelids fluttered.

The neutron beam flashed. As it did, the enemy warhead ignited in a fantastic explosion of nuclear power.

Fortunately, the missile and its warhead were still quite a distance away. Perhaps it had a computer in the warhead, and the device had concluded that it would never get closer to the targeted offender.

"Here comes the wave," Valerie said.

The blast, heat and radiation struck *Victory's* shields. The blow slammed the entire shield, which may have saved the starship. If the blast had struck at a single concentrated point…

The entire shield turned red. The glowing red color deepened to purple and headed toward a darker hue.

"Do you see any more of those missiles?" Maddox asked Valerie.

"I'm looking," the lieutenant said in a strained voice.

Maddox studied the shield outside the ship. He believed he could detect a slight brightening to the nearly black hue.

"I see hundreds more missiles," Valerie whispered.

"Are they heading toward us?" Maddox asked.

"Back up," Ludendorff said. "Back up fast. I forgot about the ancient defenses. Strand was with me last time. We did something to stave them off." The professor bowed his head. "If I could just remember…"

"We're going too fast to just back up," Valerie said in a scathing tone.

"I'm altering our trajectory," Keith said from the piloting console.

"Galyan," Maddox said. "Have you pinpointed the missiles?"

"I have, sir," the AI said. "Look at the screen."

On the main screen appeared hundreds of symbols for the—

"Are those floating missiles, as it were?" Maddox asked.

"Affirmative," Galyan said.

Maddox swiveled his chair to face the Methuselah Man. "Are they mines?"

Ludendorff looked up in astonishment. "Yes, that's right. They are a type of mine."

"From an ancient war?" asked Maddox.

"I believe so," Ludendorff said. "I can't quite remember all the details. I do know the mines were activated ten thousand years ago."

"Is ten thousand years a euphemism?" Galyan asked.

"I suppose…" Ludendorff said as he rubbed his forehead.

"I see more missiles," Valerie said. "I count five turning toward us."

"Emergency jump," Maddox said.

The shield remained purple as they tried to shed the terrible energies caught in its electromagnetic force.

Keith manipulated his piloting board faster and then seemed to be tapping the board in frustration.

Lieutenant Keith Maker was a Scotsman, a sandy-haired individual with, normally, a mischievous grin. Valerie and he were still seeing each other, but they weren't as open about it as Maddox and Meta or even Ludendorff and Dana.

"Is something the matter?" Maddox asked Keith.

"Yes, sir," the pilot admitted. "The star drive isn't responding."

"Galyan?" Maddox asked.

"Checking," Galyan said. "Keith is correct," the holoimage said a moment later. "Something is dampening the star drive. We are unable to jump."

"We'd better do something fast," Valerie said. "Those five missiles are accelerating. I don't think the shields can take another explosion of that magnitude."

"Evasive maneuvers, Lieutenant," Maddox told Keith. "Get us the hell out of here."

"If anyone can do it, sir," Keith said. "It's me."

-15-

The next fifteen minutes proved harrowing. The neutron beam flashed into the void, destroying one of the new missiles.

"Hold off firing," Maddox told Galyan. "Their computers will likely reach the same conclusion as before. Get the disrupter cannon ready. We're going to take them all down at once if we can."

As he spoke, Keith slowed *Victory's* forward velocity. The starship applied massive thrust as the gravity dampeners strained, protecting the crew from excessive G forces.

"Do you remember what Strand did before to contain those missiles?" Maddox asked the professor.

"I'm afraid not."

Maddox kept himself from saying more. The seconds ticked away. He wanted to know what kept the star drive from working, but he didn't want to overload Galyan just now in order to find out.

On the main screen, the four new missiles zeroed in on *Victory*. This place was a giant trap. How could Ludendorff have forgotten about the floating missile-mines?

"Ready, Captain," Galyan said.

"Fire," Maddox whispered.

The disrupter cannon and neutron cannon worked in tandem. In less than thirty seconds, the four new missiles were smashed atoms.

"Lieutenant…?" Maddox asked.

"It takes time to stop our mass, sir," Keith said.

71

"The greater, thus hotter, thrust will surely activate other mines," Ludendorff said, "as *Victory* will appear on their possibly sluggish sensors."

"Do you have a suggestion?" Maddox asked.

Ludendorff shook his head. "It's merely an observation."

Maddox had lurched forward in his chair. He didn't like the idea of a ten thousand-year-old minefield doing-in Starship *Victory*. What could this planet possibly tell them about the entity in the null region? Ludendorff and his archaeology—the man loved the past. There was no denying that. Yet, why did he remember in fits and starts about this place? That seemed odd.

"Sir," Valerie said.

Maddox nodded, expecting the worst.

She pointed at the main screen.

Seven ancient missiles had begun a hard burn for the starship. Behind those, thirteen others rotated so the nosecones faced *Victory*.

"Professor," Maddox said. "You'd better start remembering better."

Ludendorff stood stiffly with his head bowed and his arms crossed. He shook one of his hands as if using it to pry out an old memory. Suddenly, he looked up.

Yes," Ludendorff said. "That's it. Lieutenant," he told Valerie. "You must—" The Methuselah Man hurried to her station. "Would you vacate your chair?" he asked.

Valerie hopped out.

Ludendorff sat down in it. He stretched his fingers like a master pianist readying for a concert. He flexed them several times. Then he addressed the comm board, tapping, adjusting and moving markers.

"What are you doing?" Valerie asked him.

"Remembering an old sequence, a code," Ludendorff said. "The Fishers were an aquatic species. You could think of them as Earth dolphins but with appendages, I suppose, like squids. They spoke in whistles and other high-pitches sounds like dolphins. I'm trying to key into the missiles, to tell them to abort."

"To blow themselves up?" asked Valerie.

"Do not distract me," Ludendorff warned her.

Valerie stopped talking and stood tensely, watching the old master at work.

Finally, Ludendorff sat back in the comm chair. He straightened a second later and swiveled around. "Stop firing at them at once. This won't work otherwise."

"Stop firing," Maddox told Galyan.

The AI obeyed. The disruptor and neutron cannons ceased firing. The antimatter engine still labored, powering the shield to renewed strength.

"Well?" Maddox asked.

"It seems to be working," Keith said from the piloting board. "The missiles are no longer accelerating at us. If we can keep it this way for another ten minutes, I can get *Victory* turned around."

Maddox glanced at Ludendorff.

"I know, I know," the professor said. "I did it again. I saved the ship and our lives. You are all quite welcome."

"Ah…" Maddox said.

"Yes," Ludendorff said, as if answering a question. "I believe we should be able to proceed to the planet as planned."

Maddox considered speaking his mind. He did not like all those missile-mines waiting out there. It was more than possible that there were even more mines out there than they presently detected. Valerie hadn't detected them until the last minute. That implied cloaking devices. Yet, if they backed away from the planet now, would they ever come back?

"What exactly are you looking for?" the captain asked Ludendorff.

"The Fisher oceans dried up long ago," Ludendorff said. "The red giant scoured the other planets—"

"What are you *looking* for?" Maddox repeated.

Ludendorff blinked several times before nodding crisply. "I finally recalled an argument Strand and I had over the Fisher ruins. Strand suggested an electrical entity had plagued the Fishers near the end of their existence. He suggested those stories weren't mere myths, but truths. I, on the other hand—"

"Thank you," Maddox said. "I understand."

73

Ludendorff scowled, although he held his peace. The professor did not like anyone interrupting him, nor ending his stories abruptly.

"We're heading for the planet," Maddox told Keith. "If the professor can keep those missiles at bay, we might as well see what we came for."

The others merely stared at him.

"Steady as she goes," Maddox said in a level voice.

Reluctantly, Keith turned back to the piloting board. "Aye, aye, Captain. We're heading for an insertion orbit."

-16-

Four hours later, the starship moved in low orbit around a desert world. According to sensor scans, harsh winds blew across a barren planet. There were several low mountain ranges, but nothing grand or majestic like Mount Olympus on Mars or even the Himalayan Range on Earth.

"According to our original findings," Ludendorff said, "the Fishers used to live in a vast ocean world with tens of thousands of low reefs. A few of the areas were dry land, and those were veritable garden spots."

Maddox thought of Kauai, wondering if it had been anything like that.

"The star turned into a red giant," Ludendorff said. "In its enlarged state, it devoured the other planets and boiled away the once mighty oceans. The vast majority of the Fisher ruins were also burned away."

"What about the civilization, the people?" Maddox asked.

"Oh," Ludendorff said, shaking his head. "The Fishers passed away like the Adoks."

"The Swarm hit here?"

"No, no," Ludendorff said. "Haven't I made myself clear? The Destroyers struck here, the Nameless Ones."

"I thought Destroyers ravaged a planet?"

"They did."

"Why is the planet still here then?" Maddox asked.

"That's a good question. I don't know."

"What?" the captain asked. "I thought you were the great archeologist."

"I am," Ludendorff said.

"Maybe the Fishers drove away the Destroyers?"

"What part of 'I don't know' don't you understand?" the professor asked.

Maddox grew thoughtful. "I'm curious. Why do you think the Fishers knew anything about the entity in the null region?"

Ludendorff blinked several times as a blank look entered his eyes. "Yes!" he said decisively, as if the lights had suddenly turned on again in his mind. "Strand had a theory about that. I'd quite forgotten it. Strand believed the Fishers spoke to the Nameless Ones. He believed the two sides came to an accord."

"Are you feeling well, Professor?" Maddox asked.

"Quite well," Ludendorff said. "Why do you ask?"

"You don't seem yourself."

"Nonsense, my boy," Ludendorff said, slapping his chest.

"You keep…blanking out."

"Dredging up old memories," Ludendorff said. "Don't let the process scare you."

"It's as if someone is feeding you these memories."

"What?" Ludendorff asked. "That's preposterous. Firstly, who could do such a thing?"

That's what Maddox was asking himself. He'd never seen Ludendorff act like this. It was strange and unsettling.

"I'm utterly fine," Ludendorff said. "You try being as old as me and remembering everything. Then, you won't think it odd that a man has to conjure up old thoughts before he can relate them."

Could that be the answer? Maddox wondered. It was possible. His instincts said otherwise, though.

"Are you interested in the Fishers or not?" asked the professor.

"How could the Fishers have made a deal with the Nameless Ones?" Maddox asked. "I thought they annihilated everyone they met."

"I'd always believed that myself," Ludendorff said. "Strand had a different idea. In areas of archeology, I seldom listened to his heresies, though. However, suppose the Nameless Ones worshiped electrical creatures like the entity now stuck in the null region? If we could think of them as supernatural creatures, surely simpler aliens like the Nameless Ones could be more easily fooled."

"I'm not following your logic," Maddox said.

"That doesn't surprise me. My advanced thoughts—"

"Please, Professor," Valerie said, cutting in. "Spare us your grandiose self-praise. There are too many missile-mines waiting out there to kill us for you to engage in long monologs."

Ludendorff crossed his arms. "Strand suggested the Fishers adopted the Nameless One's gods. In this case, that might be the entities in question. Strand suggested this had never happened before. In doing this, the Fishers escaped extinction."

"These Fishers are all dead now," Valerie said.

"True," Ludendorff said. "All things die. Some of us sooner than others. Some, like me, seem to last forever."

Maddox, Valerie and Meta studied the planet on the main screen. It was a dry yellow color, a desolate desert world.

"I propose we head down at once," Ludendorff told Maddox. "As Valerie has suggested, I'm not sure how long my sequencing will keep the missiles at bay. Last time, we miscalculated and nearly got ourselves killed."

"How long do you think we have?" Maddox asked.

"Several hours at the most," the professor said.

"At the least?"

"An hour, maybe a little more."

Maddox inhaled deeply, standing afterward. "Lieutenant," he told Keith. "You'll be taking us down to the planet."

"Aye, aye, sir," Keith said, straightening from his piloting board.

-17-

Maddox wore a skin-suit with a rebreather helmet. Despite the oceans having boiled away into space, the planet had retained an atmosphere. He didn't see how that could be, if Ludendorff had told them the truth about what had happened in the past. Did that mean Ludendorff had told a false story? Or did it mean the planet had regained an atmosphere? Maddox was inclined toward the simpler answer that Ludendorff was wrong at least in certain areas of his story.

The shuttle had landed on a sandy beachhead that stretched out into a red-tinted horizon. Lieutenant Maker had remained inside the craft. Maddox and Ludendorff presently crunched across sand, heading deeper into a vast rocky cavern.

The pitted volcanic rock was black, burned no doubt by the expanding red giant. Ludendorff was right about the oceans having disappeared. Boiling away was the likeliest explanation. What would it have been like as the oceans boiled away? The red giant must have burned hotter back then as it wasn't that hot now. The professor and he would have roasted if that had been the case.

Being on the dead Fisher world had transformed Ludendorff yet again. The Methuselah Man walked quickly as if excited. The old man pulled out a flashlight, beaming the ray in the lengthening cavern.

"Look, look," Ludendorff said excitedly over a comm. "I remembered correctly."

The skin-suited Methuselah Man ran across the sand, pulling away from Maddox, with his beam first playing before him and then washing across the black rock of the monstrous cavern.

Maddox had never seen Ludendorff so giddy. How could someone get so excited over rock drawings and pottery shards, as it were? Maybe being old like Ludendorff meant watching people age and die time after time. Old relics might hold greater worth for a man in that instance.

Maddox rounded a corner Ludendorff had already passed. He raised his flashlight—the captain stopped in shock and then awe. He swept his light over a wall of ancient structures. They had been chiseled, it seemed, from the very rock. There were tall columns, great stone porches, round stairs and many fluted entrances into places.

"Professor," he called over the suit comm.

"Hurry, my boy," the professor panted over the comm.

Maddox looked around but couldn't spot the man. Where had Ludendorff gone?

"What is this place?" Maddox asked.

"The ruins I told you about. It's here just where Strand and I found them over two hundred years ago. We searched then— come, my boy. Do try to keep up."

Maddox broke into a run. What had the professor said earlier? The Fishers may have worshiped the same entity the Nameless Ones did. How could Ludendorff know any of that? Wouldn't that imply he knew more about the Destroyers and the Nameless Ones than he'd said? Or did this have something to do with the sudden memories? What would cause Ludendorff to compartmentalize subjects like this?

Maddox nodded to himself. The man always had a scheme. It would not be any different this voyage.

"Captain," Ludendorff called.

Maddox unsnapped the cover of his outer holster. With a gloved hand, he drew a blaster. Would Ludendorff try something weird down here in the ruins of an ancient planet? It seemed like the perfect place for the professor's kind of trickery.

"Captain," Ludendorff called over the comm.

Maddox no longer accepted the professor's vast enthusiasm. He almost called up to the ship. He slowed as he neared the strange monuments chiseled out of the black volcanic rock. These were symmetrical in a wave-like fashion. As the captain studied them, he could almost envision aquatic creatures hammering wet stonework.

As Maddox resumed his advance, he noticed that the stonework glittered in the light. The Fishers must have placed different kinds of rocks into the work. Had the red giant burned down here too? Had it changed the substances of the…gems, perhaps?

"Where are you?" Maddox called over the comm in irritation.

The captain swept his beam back and forth. Suddenly, he felt small as he realized the extent of the cavern. The ruined artwork towered two hundred meters, as high as his beam could travel.

"Where are you?" Maddox called again.

Ludendorff had fallen silent.

Maddox's grip tightened on the blaster. He passed the wave-like monuments. Before him in the wall were small round openings. They were not lined up in rows, but there was a pattern. The openings went higher and higher. What had the professor said before? The Fishers had been a cross between dolphins and squids. Squid-like creatures might have been able to squeeze into the narrow openings.

What was inside the holes?

Maddox was curious, but felt a strange reluctance to peek inside.

Maddox halted. On impulse, he clicked off the flashlight. Darkness settled over the vast wall. Light shined from the now hidden cavern entrance in a diffuse and subdued manner.

Something deeper in the cavern shined eerily. Maddox hadn't noticed it before. Could Ludendorff have gone down there? Why hadn't the professor answered his last call?

Following his instinct, Maddox began trudging toward the faintly glowing something down there. It might be five hundred meters away. As he walked, a feeling of unease grew in

80

Maddox. A strange pressure tightened on the back of his neck. Should they have brought Riker along?

"Professor," Maddox called over the comm. He waited for an answer. Could Ludendorff be in trouble? That had happened before.

"Captain," a scratchy noise sounded in his ears. Was that Ludendorff? "Help," the scratchy voice said.

"Damnit," Maddox breathed. "Where are you?"

"Down," the voice said.

Maddox's stomach tightened. He switched on his flashlight, beaming it at the glowing thing. For just an instant, he thought he saw something distinct. It had several legs, tentacles maybe, and it scuttled away from the light, zipping into an opening and disappearing.

Maddox stood frozen in shock. He couldn't believe what he'd seen. The Fishers were long dead, an ancient race. Yet, that had been a squid-like creature. He had seen it.

Ludendorff could be in trouble.

Captain Maddox broke into a run, chasing after the glittery creature that should not exist.

-18-

Maddox hesitated before a rock opening. He detected a faint glowing substance on the edge of the black rock hole. Could the Fisher he'd seen—if that's what it was—have brushed against the rock as it went into here?

"That's preposterous," Maddox told himself. This was a dead world. The red giant had obliterated the ancient civilization and boiled away the oceans.

"What did I see, then?" Maddox whispered to himself.

He shivered in superstitious dread.

The captain shook his head. Yet, he trusted his five senses. He was not like some men who could doubt what they had seen. He had seen a squid-like thing. It had not borne a suit. How did it breathe? How had it subsisted all this time? Why hadn't Strand and Ludendorff run across the creatures the last time they had been here two hundred years ago? Or was that something else the professor had conveniently forgotten?

With determination, Maddox ducked his helmeted head and poked inside. Using his flashlight, he saw that the way was tubular, narrow and smooth. He did not like the idea of entering such a place. If Fishers had squeezed through eons ago—with a silent oath, Maddox moved in. This was rash. He knew it. Sergeant Riker would have bitterly disapproved of him heading in. That thought did not bring a smile to Maddox's face. The disquiet in his gut was growing. Despite that, he moved on his hands and knees through the narrow path.

He had seen what he had seen. Humanity was in peril from the Swarm. The Destroyers were possibly the only way to defeat the massed might of the bug fleet. Thrax was no doubt along, hoping for revenge. If finding a way to defeat the entity in the null region meant crawling in a claustrophobically narrow tunnel, then that was what he would do.

Maddox's unease grew with the length of his passage. "Ludendorff," he called over the comm.

There was no answer.

Using his chin, Maddox reset the comm. "Galyan, come in."

There was nothing but static in his ears.

Changing the setting once more, Maddox said, "Keith." He waited—

"Captain?" Keith asked in a scratchy voice.

"Are you still in the shuttle?"

"Sir?" Keith asked. "I can't hear you, mate. Can you move to a different location?"

Maddox stopped crawling. That caused his gut to tighten worse than before. A horrible feeling of claustrophobia struck. He had no choice but to keep crawling.

"Captain…" Keith said in a tiny voice, the volume fading away to nothing.

The churning in Maddox's stomach wasn't as bad as long as he kept moving. He decided the feeling was a trap or a goad of some kind. How the glowing Fisher existed, he had no idea.

His eyes narrowed. He had a blaster. He had light, and he had his wits. "I am Captain Maddox," he told himself. *That will have to be enough.* "No," he said. It would be more than enough.

Maddox increased his crawling pace. He thought he could see something farther down. The desire to confront the glittery Fisher had begun to intensify.

After another hundred meters, Maddox eased through another opening. This place let him stand. He used the flashlight. The beam went higher and higher. He turned it onto a wall—

Maddox mouthed a silent exclamation. The beam played upon a monstrous mural. It showed Fishers as upright squid-like creatures wearing glittery garments. They advanced upon a dark cloud, beaming it with rays of light. The cloud emitted rays of its own that burned oceans and destroyed flying craft and fortress citadels.

Maddox played the flashlight across the scene. For a moment, he seemed disoriented. The mural blurred—but that passed in seconds. His mind hurt some, but not enough to worry about it.

The captain reexamined the mural. It showed the dark cloud entering the star, causing it to expand. The implications seemed staggering. Could the cloud represent the entity of the Nameless Ones? Did the cloud possess a weapon that could make a star expand? What force could resist a red giant burning the inner planets? No force Maddox knew. Had the Nameless Ones possessed greater weapons than mere neutroium-hulled Destroyers?

We know so little, Maddox realized. This star system seemed to hold ancient secrets. What kind of titanic battles had raged here in the past?

An impulse caused Maddox to turn to his left. He froze. There was no doubting what he saw this time. Twenty meters away, the glittery Fisher was watching him. The thing stood on squid-like tentacles. It regarded him with a row of eyes along the upper bulbous body. It seemed to be studying him.

At that point, Maddox heard whistles and strange squeaking-like breathy sounds. He believed the Fisher was attempting to talk to him.

"Is this a sacred fane?" Maddox asked.

The Fisher did not stop talking. Maybe it hadn't heard him.

Maddox repeated the question.

The Fisher made louder, urgent-sounding noises. It raised a tentacle, and it waved as if it were trying to get Maddox to follow it.

The captain realized his tongue had gone dry. He had begun trembling. He did not like that. He was beginning to believe the thing over there was a ghost. That nearly unnerved him.

Maddox raised the blaster. Maybe he should fire and be done with it.

The Fisher stopped waving. It seemed to be waiting.

The urge to fire beat in Maddox's brain. This could not be happening. This was impossible. "Stop it," Maddox told himself. If it was a delusion…

With a decisive move, the captain holstered the blaster. He couldn't tell if the thing was hostile or not. The waving seemed to indicate he should follow. If he failed this mission, the human race was likely dead or left to a few scrabbling worlds. If ever there was a time to take crazy risks, this was it. He took a step toward the creature.

The glittery Fisher turned and headed down a ramp. Captain Maddox followed.

-19-

Aboard Starship *Victory*, Sergeant Riker lay on his cot in his quarters. He was stretched out with his hands on his chest and his eyes shut in apparent slumber. Before the start of the voyage, Star Watch techs had given him a new bionic arm and hand and energized them.

Abruptly, Riker's eyes flew open and he stared at the ceiling. He sat up. A vast feeling of wrongness filled him. Swinging off the bed, he stood, went to the hatch and tried it.

Locked.

Riker tilted his head, wondering why he felt this way and what caused it. Something about the planet down there... Something—

"Captain Maddox," Riker whispered.

He tried the hatch again. It was just as locked as before.

How did he know—? A chill swept over the sergeant. This had something to do with the ego-fragment. While it hadn't seeped into his soul and possessed him, it could whisper to him occasionally and try to convince him of things. Did that mean it had survived, or had the touch of the ego-fragment done something to his mind and senses?

Riker did not know. He decided to incline toward the latter view. Otherwise, it was too much. But that wasn't the point right now.

So what was the point?

Riker made a fist with his bionic hand. He was the captain's right-hand man. In the end, he was supposed to keep the captain out of trouble or save the man from his rashest decisions. That's what this was about. The captain was in danger and quite possibly needed help.

For reasons Riker could not explain, he was the only one who could help Maddox now.

"Right," Riker growled.

He raised his fisted bionic hand and began to hammer on the hatch. It made a terrible din as he hammered the metal. If he had to, he would batter his way out of confinement.

It did not come to that, however. Riker had not thought it would. While he had found and dismantled all the listening devices in his cabin, there would be some just outside his quarters.

"Sergeant Riker," a robotic voice said behind him.

The sergeant quit hammering the hatch and turned around. Galyan regarded him quizzically.

"You have to listen to me," Riker said.

"First, you must stop denting your hatch."

"I have stopped."

"Yes," Galyan said. "That is true. I am listening, Riker."

"The captain's in danger."

"Indeed," Galyan said. "How do you know this?"

"I don't know."

"You are spouting a partial falsehood. Remember, I can monitor your bodily functions. They have shown me the signs of a liar."

"Partial liar, I think you said. I spoke the truth. I don't know, but I have my suspicions. Yet, does that matter if I'm right?"

"No, I suppose it would not."

"I have to help Maddox."

Galyan shook his head. "I doubt that is the correct procedure. It is more probable that you wish to stop him."

"Galyan, it's me, Sergeant Riker. I've always helped the captain. I want to do that now."

"I must ask Valerie. She is in charge while the captain is away."

"Then ask," Riker said. "The longer you wait, the more likely it is that Maddox will die."

"What is endangering him?"

Riker only hesitated a second. "I don't know."

"Now you are indeed lying. You do know."

"I won't say."

"I give it a high probability that Valerie will not agree to this supposed rescue attempt unless you tell us what is threating the captain."

"A Fisher ghost," Riker said.

"A supernatural ghost or a holoimage?" asked Galyan.

"I'm done talking," Riker said. "You get me Valerie's answer. If it's the wrong one, I'm busting out of here and taking a shuttle down to the planet anyway."

Galyan disappeared.

-20-

On the planet, Maddox continued to follow the glittery Fisher. He'd tried reaching Ludendorff, Keith and the ship in that order with his helmet comm. He had failed each time.

During the process, he'd moved farther into the hollowed-out wall and deeper into the sandy planet. Maddox hadn't seen any more murals in that time. Instead, he saw incredibly high ceilings. Finally, he realized these weren't ceilings, but simply other paths. When the Fishers had chiseled the structure, it had been filled with water. Ocean water would have filled this place, allowing one to swim in any direction.

Maddox glanced over his shoulder. How was he supposed to find his way back once this was over? The captain halted. He clicked his flashlight on and off several times. The Fisher ahead of him stopped and turned around.

"This is as far as I go," Maddox said.

The Fisher used a tentacle to wave the captain onward.

Maddox shook his helmeted head. "Sorry, no. Either explain what you want or I'm going back. It's time for me to report in."

The Fisher waved more urgently.

Maddox continued to shake his head. "If you're a ghost, you must understand me. If you're not a ghost, I have no idea what you could be."

The Fisher seemed frantic now. It waved the tentacle. It whistled and made the squeaking breathy noises.

Maddox concentrated on the thing. Thus, he did not detect the spaceman until the last minute. He began to whirl around when a gun of sorts jabbed against his back. Maddox almost grabbed the gun. He noticed two other spacemen behind the first. All three wore crinkly spacesuits with helmets and dark visors. All three had weapons aimed at him.

Using his chin, Maddox clicked an outer speaker. "Who are you?"

The last spaceman pointed in the direction the Fisher had wanted Maddox to go.

"Who are you?" Maddox repeated.

"If you don't go," the last spaceman said, using a distorter to garble his voice, "we will burn you down and leave your body."

Maddox glanced at the Fisher. It was gone. Finally, the captain shrugged, heading in the direction the spaceman pointed. He wondered who these men were. One thing seemed clear. They were real people, not ghosts. He also wondered if the Fisher had been trying to warn him, or if the ghostly thing had been trying to distract him so the three could sneak up on him.

In the end, it probably didn't matter.

***

The three spacemen with their guns forced Maddox down a string of narrow corridors. At last, they came to a big circular area. In the middle of the area was a large dome-like stone building. It must have taken the Fishers quite some time to chisel that out of the volcanic rock.

There was a small circular opening into the dome. Maddox approached it. The spacemen had flashlights, and those beams played upon the stone. Gruesome images adorned it. With chisel-like knives, Fishers put creatures to death on what appeared to be altars. Was this some sort of sacrificial chamber, then?

Maddox wondered why the spacemen hadn't taken his blaster. That would prove to be a mistake on their part. He hadn't tried to draw it yet. Maybe they had a scrambler aimed at the blaster. He didn't want to try for it and be burned down in the process.

"In there," the same spaceman as before told him.

"Why?" Maddox asked.

"Go! No more questions."

Maddox faced fully around, regarding the three. He attempted to determine who they represented. The spacesuits were unlike any that he'd seen before. Could the spacemen control the missile-mines out there?

"Are you human?" Maddox asked.

"Inside."

"Why won't you tell me who you are?"

"Go," the spaceman said. "Your questions will be answered in there."

"Are you sure?"

"Let us burn him and be done with it," a different spaceman said.

"If he won't go inside, we will burn him," the first one said.

Maddox calculated his chances, found them wanting and thus turned around and faced the dome.

"Wait," one of them said.

Maddox faced them again.

"Put your blaster on the deck."

Deck? Maddox wondered to himself. Oh. He thought he understood then. It left him feeling chagrined. He should have realized this from the first. It likely answered the question of the Fisher.

Slowly, Maddox removed the blaster and set it on the stone floor. Then, he faced the small opening, pushing through to see who was waiting for him inside the dome.

-21-

Maddox had to shove against resistance, a membrane of some kind, before pushing through into the dome. Immediately, bright light surrounded him. He staggered into an area with several goggle-wearing guards with guns pointed at him. Two other Spacers worked a large boxlike instrument on a tripod. It hummed with power and possessed several blinking lights. The last Spacer sat on a large folding chair. She had white hair and wrinkled skin, and wore a polar bear garment. Like the others, she wore goggles. Like the others, she did not use any breathing equipment or wear any kind of spacesuit.

Maddox removed his rebreather helmet, giving the old woman a slight head bow. "We meet again, Visionary," he told her.

"Captain Maddox," she said in a hoarse voice. "I am unsurprised the Methuselah Man led you to this barren planet. Where is Professor Ludendorff, by the way?"

Maddox shrugged.

"We know he is down here. My guards almost captured him once. Don't you find it interesting that he did nothing to help you? Instead, he saved his own skin. That is the nature of the selfish creatures. He and Strand are the last. Once they're gone, the Spacer Nation shall rejoice."

"Is this a conference of *di-fars*?" Maddox asked.

The Visionary frowned. "That is no joking matter, Captain. You should show greater reverence."

"For myself?" he asked.

"No, for the concept of *di-far* that you imbibed from us. Few understand reality like the highest Spacers. We have learned the deep secrets of the universe. You would do well to heed me, Captain."

"I'm listening."

She seemed to study him. "Tell me why you are here."

"You're not going to say anything about the last time we met?"

"Events have moved on," she said. "That is often the case with those like us. I have no use for revenge, if that is what is troubling you."

"Do you realize the Swarm has invaded Human Space?"

"Of course," she said.

"Will you join the Grand Alliance?"

"There will be no Grand Alliance."

"The New Men have refused the Lord High Admiral's offer?"

"You did not let me finish," she said. "There will be no Grand Alliance that will be able to halt the Swarm invasion. Humanity's final hour has arrived."

"The Spacers will also die?"

"We are leaving this region of the galaxy, Captain. You must realize that."

"Why interfere, then, with those of us trying to save our miserable hides?"

"Because I fear you are going to attempt an abomination. We suspected Ludendorff would lead you here. That is why we watched and waited."

"Why would the professor bring me here?" Maddox asked.

The Visionary chuckled. "You seek to learn while you can. You are a monomaniac, Captain. Instead of worrying about a future you won't have, you should make your peace with the Creator while you can."

"Why are you here?"

"I have already hinted at the purpose," the Visionary said. "I am here to stop you."

Maddox debated with himself. Sometimes, a man had to gamble. That meant putting chips on the table when one couldn't afford to lose them. One did that in order to entice his opponent to lay down chips. Winning meant gaining those chips.

"We need the Destroyers in order to defeat the Swarm," Maddox said.

The Visionary leaned forward on her chair. "So, it's true," she breathed. "I can hardly believe it. You are *di-far* indeed to have stumbled upon...Destroyers you said. That would indicate more than one."

"Two at least," Maddox said.

"At least," she breathed. "It's possible there are more?"

Maddox shrugged.

"More Destroyers," she said. "I can see why the greed has eaten at your good sense. Do you see yourself as a galactic conqueror, perhaps? The Great Captain Maddox, bringing humanity under his heel."

"What happened to you?" Maddox asked. "How did you get so off-course? How did the Spacers learn to hate themselves the way they do? Do you wish to see humanity ground under by alien races?"

"You have no idea what you're talking about."

"You must indulge in self-hatred to say the things you do. It is the nature of a healthy organism to wish to reproduce its own kind. The human race faces extinction at the hands of the Swarm. We can avert that if we try hard enough."

"You fool," she said. "Do you realize that the cure is worse than the disease?"

"No."

"Exactly," she said. "That is why I'm here. That is why I strained to see into the future. I can only see dimly, that is true. But I saw you tramping about this dead planet. You seek a thing in order to attempt to slay the Ska."

"What, pray tell, is a Ska?"

The Visionary made a sign in the air as the guards shifted uneasily.

"The Ska are terrible creatures," she said in a dreadful whisper. "They are ancient beyond time. That is a saying, of course. Some of us have conjectured that they come from a reality beyond ours. They do not conform to our laws. I do not mean man's paltry laws and customs, but the laws of physics.

They are not made of flesh and blood like everything else living. They are not pure energy, as some would say. That would be senseless. They are not gaseous. They are something else."

"Spirits?" asked Maddox.

The Visionary shook her head. "That would merely mean that you have no idea what a Ska is. It is not a demon or an angel."

"Don't demons and angels come from a different reality?"

"I do not know," the Visionary admitted. "I have never met a demon or an angel. They are myths."

"Is the Creator a myth?"

She scowled. "Do not try to confuse the issue. The Ska must remain in the null region. Do not seek to know how I learned of this. I am the Visionary. It is my place to know."

"Sure," Maddox said.

"Do not mock me, half-New Man."

Maddox became quiet. Without being consciously aware of it, he began to judge distances between the various guards. If they were going to kill him, he might as well attack.

"It seems I cannot persuade you," the Visionary said. "That is unfortunate."

"Wait," Maddox said. "Let me see if I understand your position. You're willing to let the rest of humanity perish, but you don't want us setting this Ska free? Therefore, you're going to deny those of us willing to fight the Swarm—"

"Enough!" the Visionary said loudly. "Don't you understand? You can't save humanity with purified evil. You must use reason. In this case, the Swarm are too powerful for us. Thus, do as we are doing."

"Running like wet hens?" Maddox asked.

"Surviving," she said. "That supplants your vain heroism. What good is this fighting belief if you die in the end?"

"All things die."

"Why die before your time? Humanity has much potential. Don't throw it away."

"How is using the Destroyers throwing it away?"

"The Fishers perished because they made a bargain with evil. They accepted several Ska among them. Because of that, the Nameless Ones moved on."

"That sounds like a good bargain."

"Does it indeed?" the Visionary asked. "Do you know what caused the star to become a red giant?"

"The Nameless Ones caused it."

"You have seen the mural. It is false. The Ska among the Fishers caused the destruction. But the Ska multiplied, growing and expanding. This part of the galaxy became barren until finally the Ska rejoined the Nameless Ones as they burned through planets and civilizations."

"We're going to destroy the Ska in the null region."

"You fool. No one can destroy them."

"They're immortal?"

The Visionary looked away.

"Do they age?" Maddox asked.

"The way stars age," she answered.

"Stars burn out. Maybe there's a way to cause a Ska to burn out."

"It is a vain hope."

"How can you know that?"

She faced him again. "Because I am the Visionary," she said.

"I am Captain Maddox."

She shook her head as if in disbelief.

At that point, Maddox struck. He leaped sideways, punching the nearest guard. Maddox's fist went through the guard—the holographic image. He fell onto the floor, surprised.

With an oath, Maddox leaped up. The Visionary glared at him.

"It doesn't matter," she told him. "The guards outside are real enough. Goodbye, Captain Maddox. It is too bad you are so stubborn."

Maddox rushed the machine on the tripod. He half expected his hand to pass through it. Instead, he whacked his hand against it, nearly spraining his wrist.

The Spacers attending the machine, the guards and the Visionary all flickered and winked out. At the same instant, the interior dome went dark. The machine shut down, and the membrane over the opening disappeared. That allowed the planet's atmosphere to come rushing in.

It did so while Maddox stood alone in the dark, his rebreather helmet somewhere behind him on the floor.

-22-

Maddox held his breath, turned and dropped to his hands and knees. He fumbled around until he reached the rebreather. Working with haste, he slipped it onto his head and inhaled deeply. The good air revived him.

Maddox wondered why the outside guards hadn't charged in already. Maybe the Visionary had been lying about them. Maybe the guards waited out there to gun him down.

The captain gathered himself, and charged through the opening. He halted in surprise.

Wearing skin-suits and rebreather helmets, Sergeant Riker, Keith and Meta stood over obviously dead Spacers. Each of the spacesuits had burn or bullet holes in it.

"Maddox!" Meta cried over the rebreather comm. She rushed him, giving him a powerful hug.

Maddox grinned inside his rebreather. "I'm okay," he said.

Meta didn't respond.

Maddox used his chin to turn on the comm. "I'm fine, I'm fine," he said. "How did you find me?"

"I showed them the way," Ludendorff said.

Maddox turned around. The professor in his skin-suit and rebreather stood near a large stone block with strange designs on it.

"We have to get out of here," Maddox said. "The Spacers are here. I just spoke to the Visionary."

"In there?" Ludendorff asked, pointing at the dome.

"She used a projector," Maddox said. "I think they're in orbit around the planet. Maybe they can summon the missile-mines. Maybe they used a dampening field to keep us from using the star drive earlier. Whatever the case, we have to contact *Victory* and let them know the danger."

"Our communication with the ship is jammed down here," Keith announced. "Is this a trap?"

"Right," Maddox said. "Professor, can you lead us out of here?"

"Yes," Ludendorff said decisively. "Follow me."

***

Lieutenant Noonan was on *Victory's* bridge with Galyan beside her.

She did not like this star system or planet. She had not liked the strange places they'd passed to get here. She deeply distrusted the professor. She dearly hated Keith being down there on the planet.

"I have detected a ship," Galyan told her.

"Where?" she asked.

"It is on the edge of the planet's horizon in relation to us. It is almost as if the ship is daring us to chase it."

Valerie moved to the command chair, sitting down. "Can you contact the landing party?"

"Negative, Valerie," Galyan said. "Oh, no."

"What now?" she asked.

"Some of the missile-mines out there are turning toward us."

"Great," Valerie said. "That's Murphy's Law in action."

"Whatever can go wrong will at the worst possible moment?" Galyan asked.

"That's right."

"Who's out there at the edge of the horizon challenging us?"

"Would you like me to guess?" Galyan asked.

"Of course," Valerie said. "We need all the edges we can get."

"I doubt they are New Men. It is not their style. I doubt—"

"Just tell me who you think it is. Don't belabor the issue."

"Spacers," Galyan said. "This is their style."

"Great," Valerie said. "Spacers have tricky toys. You're right. This does stink like them. Galyan, how low can we take *Victory*?"

"I presume you mean without destroying the ship."

Valerie rolled her eyes. "Yes, yes. That's what I mean."

"I would calculate—I see a shuttle attempting to gain escape velocity."

"Just one?"

"Yes, Valerie. It is the original shuttle. Wait. I detect the second one. It was delayed. Now, it is also building up velocity."

"I want to talk to them."

Galyan's eyelids fluttered. "I have established communication with Captain Maddox."

"Put him on," Valerie said.

The main screen split into two parts, one showing space and the planet, the other showing Captain Maddox staring at her.

"There are Spacers here," Maddox said.

"Galyan already deciphered that," Valerie said.

"They're going to try to stop us."

"Missile-mines are pointing at us. Galyan has caught glimpses of someone at the edge of the planetary horizon."

"That's them," Maddox said. "Your first priority is to save the ship. The second—"

"I'm saving you," Valerie said.

"Oh, oh," Galyan said. "Look on the screen, Valerie. Two Spacer ships have left the safety of the planetary horizon and are heading for the shuttle."

"Oh no you don't," Valerie said. "Galyan, ready the disruptor cannon."

"The Spacers are hailing us," Galyan said.

Valerie hesitated a moment. "Put them on," she said.

The Visionary appeared on a half-screen. "Lieutenant Noonan, I presume," the old woman said.

"Harm the shuttles and I'll blow your ships away," Valerie said.

"My," the Visionary responded. "You say that so elegantly. I have a counterproposal. I am going to destroy Starship *Victory*."

"Fire, Galyan," Valerie said. "Destroy the nearest Spacer craft."

The antimatter engine purred with power. The great disruptor beam struck. A second later, the neutron beam followed. The seconds lengthened.

The first Spacer craft's shield glowed red, brown—the intensity of the disruptor beam hammered the shield with ferocious power. The shield turned black and collapsed altogether. The hull proved as weak as paper. The twin beams smashed through—the Spacer craft exploded, showering hull and bulkheads everywhere. Some of the debris peppered the second Spacer's shield. The second starship had stopped heading toward *Victory*. The vessel appeared to possess the uncanny Spacer ability of changing its direction of travel as if the laws of physics didn't apply to it. The ship accelerated all-out for the protection of the planetary horizon.

Valerie had hunched forward on the command chair, scowling thunderously. "Why did they charge out at us like that? The Visionary has to know that her ships can't resist the disruptor beam for long. If they had more vessels—six or more—they could have possibly engaged us without some of them dying." She shook her head. "The attack doesn't make sense." Valerie sat up. "I don't like this. The Visionary is no fool."

"Valerie," Galyan said. "Four surface-to-space missiles are climbing fast from the planet. They appear to be Spacer missiles, and they are targeting the shuttles."

"Destroy them!" Valerie shouted.

"Targeting," Galyan said.

"Did the Spacer ships make a suicidal attack in order to try to cover the missile launch?" Valerie muttered.

At that point, the twin beams stabbed down toward the climbing missiles. The missile hit by the disruptor beam exploded. A second later, the neutron beam destroyed its missile. At that point, one of remaining missiles detonated. The nuclear explosion powered aiming rods on the nosecone. Those rods beamed gamma and X-rays at the lower shuttle.

It blew up in a blast of red light.

Valerie internalized her groan of dismay as a sick feeling swept through her.

"That was Captain Maddox's original shuttle," Galyan said. The Adok holoimage stared at the fleeing Spacer ship. The vessel had almost crossed the planetary horizon to make it onto the other side.

"We must destroy that ship," Galyan said in a strange voice.

"Belay that," Valerie said. "Prepare to go lower into orbit, Galyan. We're not going to lose anyone else. We're going to retrieve the surviving shuttle."

Before the last surface-to-space missile could detonate, the disrupter cannon rayed again, destroying it. The Spacers must have placed launchers down there some time ago.

"Spacers," Galyan said in his altered voice. "Why would they do this?"

"I have no idea," Valerie said, heartbroken at the thought that Lieutenant Maker might have bought the farm. She should have told Keith that she loved him. Why did she always wait when it came to such things? Now, she was going to pay a bitter price for the rest of her life.

"Valerie," Galyan said. "The last shuttle is hailing us. Should I put the speaker on the screen?"

Valerie hesitated. She didn't want to know the worst.

At that point, Galyan gave her a renewed warning. One of the missile-mines out in space had begun a hard burn planetward. But instead of heading for Starship *Victory*, the missile-mine headed for the last shuttle.

102

-23-

As Keith Maker piloted the last shuttle for orbital space, he turned to Maddox in astonishment. "It's a good thing you relayed your message through the other shuttle and had everyone travel in here. But how did you know the Spacers would use surface missiles against us?"

Maddox shrugged from his seat. He hadn't known. But he'd believed the rest of them would have a better chance of reaching *Victory* if one of the shuttles acted as a decoy. The trick had been in making the decoy seem like the real deal, and making their shuttle act as a decoy. In that, he'd guessed correctly.

"Do you see the approaching missile-mine?" Ludendorff asked behind them.

The professor was strapped to the seat in front of the shuttle's weapon board. It was to the side of Maddox and Keith. Ludendorff indicated the missile-mine straining for the planet's atmosphere.

Maddox tapped his board.

"This could get rough," Keith said as his teeth rattled.

The shuttle shook as it roared for space. The pilot ejected chaff and a decoy emitter. That wasn't going to make a difference with the size of the warhead in the approaching missile. Old habits died hard, Maddox supposed.

The captain tapped his board again. The screen in front of him wavered until Lieutenant Noonan regarded him.

"We're coming up, Lieutenant," Maddox said.

"You're alive," Valerie shouted in amazement.

"Not if that missile-mine reaches us," Maddox replied. "I assume you know which one I mean."

"Galyan is working on it," she said with glee. "Is...is Keith with you?"

"Right here, love," Keith shouted. "It's nice to be missed."

Valerie blinked on the tiny screen and rubbed her watery eyes. She was smiling hugely.

Keith glanced at Maddox with a stupidly huge grin on his face as well. "What do you think of that, mate?"

Maddox nodded. "Get ready for evasive action," he told Valerie. "The Spacers—"

"I know they're here," she said, still smiling.

"The Visionary is here, as well," Maddox said.

"I know," Valerie said. "We chased her vessel—"

"I saw what happened," Maddox said, interrupting. "I would guess the Spacer ships you targeted were decoy vessels. If the Visionary is here, that means the Spacers have come in strength."

It took a second, but Valerie's smile faded.

"I suspect the Spacers also beamed a dampening field at us earlier so we couldn't use the star drive to escape the system," Maddox said. "None of that matters, however, unless Galyan destroys the missile-mine—"

Beside him, Keith whooped with delight. A bright flare of light from space showed that Galyan must have just annihilated the offensive missile-mine.

"We're going to do this, mate," Keith shouted.

"I can hear you just fine, Lieutenant."

Keith glanced at Maddox. "Yes, *sir*," he said. "I have to say, sir, you're the slyest starship captain in the fleet."

Maddox gave the barest of acknowledgements. He appreciated the pilot's enthusiasm and cheery outlook. He much preferred that to doom and gloom attitudes. Still, the Visionary was out there, likely hidden on the other side of the planet. How many Spacer ships did she have with her? Would they have the regular Spacer cloaking devices?

Yes, of course they would. But Starship *Victory* had Galyan and ancient Adok sensing devices. Maddox had bested the

Visionary quite some time ago by bluffing her about a self-destruct switch aboard the starship. He doubted that would work a second time. Besides, it looked as if the Spacer outlook had shifted. The Visionary had tried to reason with him to abandon his quest. Now, it appeared, she wished to obliterate him and the starship in order to stop them from possibly freeing the Ska from the null region.

"How can we convince the Spacers to join our side against the Swarm?" Maddox asked Ludendorff.

"Forget it," the professor said. "They're fanatics. They lost their collective minds some time ago."

"We could use their starships against the Swarm."

"The Spacers?" asked Ludendorff. "They hate direct confrontation. They like playing from the shadows. The hidden dagger, the silent ray in the back is more their style. They'll never risk their ships in a battle if they can find another way. No. Forget about the Spacers. They lack the essential balls for manly battle."

"You love battle?" Meta asked from the back area.

Ludendorff grinned at her. "In terms of balls, my dear, mine are the biggest of all. That is why I have such zest for life. That is how I've survived the ages as the other Methuselah Men dropped by the wayside. Do not—"

"You've made your point," Maddox said. "I would still like to find a way to enlist the Spacers. The Swarm invasion should erase old hatreds."

"That's one of the advantages of running away," Ludendorff said. "You get to keep your prejudices. The Spacers loath Methuselah Men, don't you know. They hate having anyone around who knows more than they do. In this instance, I believe that means you as well."

"How did they know to make an image of a Fisher?" Maddox asked.

Before Ludendorff could answer, Keith began high-G maneuvers. The shuttle's gravity dampeners strained. The small craft shook harder, and the visible atmosphere of the dusty planet slowly moved behind them.

"Soon," Keith said between clenched teeth.

Maddox's vision became blurry. Even so, he saw his sensor screen. He noted an enemy ship on the edge of the distant planetary horizon. If it tried to beam them...

Likely, this was going to be close.

-24-

Through the main shuttle window, Maddox spied *Victory* in space above them. The ancient Adok starship was composed of two large oval sections. The disruptor cannon quit firing just then.

Maddox checked his sensor screen. For the moment, no Spacer ships were in direct line-of-sight of *Victory*, unless, of course, the Spacers had cloaked ships watching them.

With the yellow planet below them, Keith began braking as the starship—as home—grew larger and larger. A big hangar-bay door should be opening about now.

"It looks like we're going to get aboard, sir," the pilot said.

Galyan the holoimage appeared in the cockpit. "Welcome back, Captain."

"It's good to be back," Maddox replied.

"I launched probes earlier, sir," the AI said. "Seconds ago, enemy fire destroyed them on the other side of the planetary horizon. Before the probes disintegrated, I saw the Spacers. There are six of the saucer-shaped vessels, sir. Each is approximately three-quarters the size of one of *Victory's* ovals."

"Excellent work, Galyan," the captain said.

The little holoimage puffed up his chest. "Thank you, sir. I appreciate that. Do you have any orders?"

"Are you trying to suggest I launch antimatter missiles at the Spacer concentration?"

"That seems like a tactically sound idea," Galyan said.

"I have a possible solution," Ludendorff said.

"Why didn't you speak up sooner?" Maddox asked.

Ludendorff lightly kicked a large backpack strapped near his feet. "I recovered something critical Strand left behind on the planet two hundred years ago. We were never able to go back down and get it."

Maddox glanced at the backpack. That sounded suspicious. "What did you find?" he asked.

"Several items, actually," the Methuselah Man said. "One of them...I prefer to test it before I make grandiose promises. May I use my old laboratory?"

Maddox thought briefly before nodding.

Ludendorff rubbed his hands in obvious anticipation.

"What should I tell Valerie?" Galyan asked Maddox.

"Are we in immediate danger?" Maddox asked.

"The missile-mines could begin targeting us at any moment," Galyan said. "I also believe the six Spacer ships are grouping together in order to attack *Victory* as one."

Maddox turned to Keith. "Can you get us aboard any faster?"

Keith glanced at him before he punched it, the shuttle picking up speed as it zoomed for the now apparent open hangar-bay door.

***

Maddox refrained from moving his head for just a moment. He breathed heavily, his body pounding from the half-crash-landing Keith had just achieved.

"We're here," the pilot announced.

Around them, the dented shuttle groaned metallically. A vent hissed before falling silent.

"That was the worst landing I've ever survived," Ludendorff declared.

"The captain wanted us inside faster," Keith said. "So that's what I did."

Maddox unbuckled. "I appreciate that," he told Keith. "Speed is of the essence. A few bruised muscles are a small price to pay."

"That's what I say," Keith said.

Maddox had unbuckled. Meta soon followed. The others did so more slowly and gingerly.

"Get to work, Professor," Maddox told the man. "Give me your option."

"My head is still ringing," the Methuselah Man complained. "But I'll do what I can."

"I'm not interested in your trying," Maddox said. "I want success. No one pays us to come in second."

With that, the captain headed for the hatch. His muscles ached and he felt strained. That had been a horrible landing. It was amazing they were all in one piece. But he'd wanted speed, and that's what he'd gotten.

Jumping to the hangar deck, Maddox saw personnel racing to the smoking and dented shuttle. He didn't have time for niceties. The Visionary was concocting a new shift in her overall plan. He wanted to be on the bridge, implementing a plan of his own before she could beat him to the punch.

Maddox forced himself to begin running. His muscles were tight. A man called him. Maddox didn't bother acknowledging the salutation. He forced himself to run faster, letting his muscles loosen by the action of contracting and relaxing over and over again. In moments, Maddox flashed through a hatch, hitting a corridor at speed. His long legs pumped now as he ate up the distance. He breathed hard with his arms swinging in rhythm. At this point, Maddox began to sprint at full speed, his toes barely touching the deck. He was glad to have made it off the planet and definitely glad to be out of those narrow tunnels. He never wanted to crawl in an ancient ruin again.

How could he defeat the Visionary and the missile-mines out there? This was one of the times he would like to simply jump out of danger. He couldn't do that if they had an enemy star-drive dampener aimed at them. If he tried to engage the Spacers in combat, they could simply stay ahead of him around the planet, using the alien missile-mines to eventually destroy *Victory*. Of course, the Spacers might use all six ships to attack the ancient Adok vessel.

The conclusion was obvious. He had to buy Ludendorff time, hoping the Methuselah Man had found something useful on the surface that could change the present equation.

-25-

Maddox sat in the captain's chair as he tried to control his rapid breathing. He used a towel, blotting his forehead, before stuffing the towel beside his right thigh on the chair.

Valerie had hailed the Spacers, offering to surrender.

The Visionary now appeared on the bridge's main screen. The old woman wore her goggles and sat in a throne-like chair. Around her, Spacer techs worked at their stations.

"Have I heard correctly?" the Visionary asked in her hoarse voice. "You wish to surrender *Victory* to me?"

"This is painful for me to say," Maddox admitted.

The Visionary appeared to study him. After a time, she pulled the polar bear fur a little tighter around her throat.

"I do not believe you, Captain. I doubt you would ever knowingly surrender your starship. Last time I demanded such, you threated to detonate your vessel in order to keep it out of our grasp."

Maddox spread his hands. "I see and have finally accepted the situation, Visionary. You have a jump dampener aimed at my ship. I don't know how you can keep it targeted on us, but you..." He turned to Valerie.

The lieutenant muted the connection.

"I should have already thought of it," Maddox said. "There has to be a cloaked ship in our line-of-sight. It must be doing the dampening. You have to find it."

"If it's dampening our star drive," Valerie said, "maybe it can dampen our sensors as well."

110

"Galyan," Maddox said. "Work on that."

"Yes, sir," the holoimage said.

Maddox nodded.

Valerie pressed a switch.

"This is quite nefarious of you, Captain," the Visionary said. "Offering to surrender to me indeed. Obviously, you are attempting to buy yourself time. The questions is, time to do what?"

"How can I convince you that my offer is genuine?" Maddox asked.

"Lower your shields," the Visionary said promptly.

"Gladly," Maddox said, "once you give me your personal assurances that you will accept our surrender."

"I give you that assurance now," she said.

"And you will let us live?" he asked.

"Prisoners have no rights."

"I am...requesting those rights," Maddox said. "They are part of my condition for our surrender."

"I demand unconditional surrender," the Visionary declared.

"Come now," Maddox chided. "When I finally surrender, you shall gain *Victory* and all that entails. The Adok starship will surely give you new technologies useful for your extended journey as the Spacers seek a new home."

"That is an interesting proposal," she admitted.

Galyan gestured Valerie. The lieutenant hesitated, and then muted the main screen again.

"Sir," Galyan said. "I have been running personality profiles and probabilities. The Visionary knows you are stalling."

"She already said that," Maddox said.

"She is letting you stall because she is attempting to...pull the wool over your eyes, sir."

Maddox considered that. "How?" he asked.

"I do not know," Galyan said. "But my conclusion fits with what I know concerning the Visionary's personality. My point is this, sir. You are taking a risk by stalling. Perhaps our better option would be direct conflict before the Visionary can complete whatever she is attempting."

"Put her back on," Maddox said.

"Captain, I do not care for this continued rudeness," the Visionary said as Galyan unmuted her connection. "I am the Spacer Visionary. Mere starship captains do not cut me off in mid-speech."

"You have my abject apology, Ma'am," Maddox said. "I have a zealous crew, each trying to outdo the other. It can make for a tedious—"

"Captain," the Visionary said in a silky voice. "Do you not think I know when someone is attempting to snow me?"

Maddox spread his hands once more.

The old woman cocked her head as if listening to someone unseen. She sat straighter afterward. Even though she wore goggles, it seemed as if she stared at Maddox triumphantly.

"I am detecting an energy spike on the planetary surface," Galyan said. "I shall—Captain Maddox. We must take emergency procedures."

"Surrender, Captain," the Visionary said gleefully on the screen. "I have targeted your starship with a planetary Fisher defense cannon. If you do not immediately lower your shields, I will unleash a torrent of energy against you. By the time the cannon finishes firing, Starship *Victory* will be gone."

"What planetary cannon?" Maddox asked.

"This is your final warning," the Visionary said. "I cannot allow you any more time for maneuvers. Either you accept my offer or you and your crew are dead."

"I have it," Galyan said. "I am using a split-screen. Please, observe the left half."

The main screen split into two sides. On one, the Visionary continued to grin gleefully. On the other, fresh sand and tumbled rocks lay below a vast metallic cannon that continued to rise, presumably, into firing position. The barrel of the cannon seethed with orange-colored energy that bubbled like an ancient broth.

"What is that?" Maddox asked.

"It is the weapon that drove off the ancient Destroyers," the Visionary said. "Imagine what I'm saying. Those cannons defeated a Destroyer's neutroium hull. There used to be more of them. One is enough to destroy your starship. You have ten

112

seconds, Captain. What will it be? Oblivion? Or will you finally enter the Spacer service?"

-26-

"You can't surrender," Valerie told Maddox. "We have to go down fighting. We have to save the human race."

"So..." the Visionary said. "Your original offer of surrender was false, as I suspected. I realized you were a liar, Captain, but it hurts me to see that you are such a bald-faced scoundrel."

Maddox stared at the goggle-clad old woman. It galled him that she'd outwitted him. Could he surrender? Could he truly—

"I surrender," Maddox said.

"Lower your shields and shut down your antimatter engine," the Visionary said.

"It will take us a few moments to do that," Maddox said.

"You are stalling, Captain. The ten seconds have already passed. It has been almost twenty seconds now. Lower your shield and shut down your antimatter engine. That is the only way you can save your lives."

"Lower the shields," Maddox said.

"But, sir," Valerie complained.

"Do it, Lieutenant."

"I...I don't think I can, sir."

"Then you are relieved of duty. Galyan, you will lower the shields."

The Adok holoimage stared at Maddox. Finally, glumly, he nodded. "The shields are lowered, sir," Galyan said.

Maddox faced the Visionary. "There you are. Send over whatever shuttles you wish. *Victory* is yours."

The Visionary laughed scornfully. "Do you think I'm that witless? Do you believe lowering your shields convinces me? You can raise them in an instant. Power-down your antimatter engine, Captain. You must do it now or the planetary cannon fires."

Maddox stared at the Visionary. He turned to Valerie. He—

Even though she had been relieved, the lieutenant noticed a blinking green light on her board. She tapped it.

Maddox stood up with his features twisted with anger. "I told you to obey me," he said in a loud voice. Maddox stalked to Valerie's station.

He reached her, seeing Ludendorff speaking urgently on a tiny comm screen. Maddox continued to glare as he put a hand on Valerie's shoulder.

She looked up at him, blinking twice, signaling him.

"I am the captain of this vessel," Maddox declared. "I have grown infinitely weary of working with you—"

"Sir," Galyan shouted. "The planetary cannon is firing."

"Shields up," Maddox said. His pretense dropped as he moved back to his chair. He sat down, looking at the main screen.

An orange roiling blob of something sped upward at them from the surface.

"Evasive action," Maddox said in an even voice.

Keith manipulated his panel. The great starship began to move.

"Galyan," Maddox said, "what is that?"

"Unknown, sir," the AI said.

"Fire at it," Maddox said.

"I do not have time to align the disruptor cannon," Galyan said. "I am firing the neutron cannon."

A purple gout of power struck the orange blob. It seemed to devour some of it. The rest continued upward in a roiling riot of—

Victory shook as the orange energy blob struck the shields. They glowed instead of turning red, and in a second, the shields went down. The remainder of the orange blob struck the ship.

This time, everyone went flying. The entire bridge shuddered as klaxons rang, lights blinked and electrical smoke trickled from some of the boards.

"We cannot take another hit like that," Galyan said. "Hull integrity will shatter with a second strike."

"Sir," Valerie said. "Look at the planetary horizon. Six Spacer ships are accelerating toward us."

"Get us out of here, Lieutenant Maker," Maddox said. "Get us moving as fast as you can."

"Aye, aye, mate," Keith said.

Victory turned in orbit quicker than seemed possible. A long energy tail burned from the exhaust ports. The starship began leaving its orbital station.

"Do you think that will save you?" the Visionary said on the main screen. "It is charging up, Captain. Once it is ready, the cannon will fire again. Can you survive the next shot?"

Maddox stared at the Spacer witch. A moment later, he let his shoulders slump and hung his head.

"Turn off the antimatter engine," the Visionary said.

Maddox began to tremble. "Please..." he said, without raising his head.

The Visionary laughed with glee. "I have tamed the arrogant Captain Maddox. *Di-far* indeed. You are nothing compared to me. This is your final warning, Captain. Then, you shall die."

Without looking up, Maddox raised a hand.

Valerie broke the connection with the Visionary.

Maddox's demeanor changed abruptly. He looked up as Ludendorff's face took the place where the Visionary had just been on the main screen.

"I've done it," the professor said. "Valerie is implementing the sequencing. I believe she has overridden the planetary cannon. The missile-mines will be harder. Do you wish to bait a trap for the Spacers?"

Maddox nodded silently.

"Continue to flee," Ludendorff said. "Like many cowards, the Spacers love to chase a defeated foe. They will congratulate themselves on outwitting you. By the way, your act was magnificent."

116

Victory headed for space, leaving the desert planet behind as it gained velocity. The starship headed away from the red giant. The starship strained to reach a Laumer Point at the edge of the system.

"Sir," Valerie said. "According to my indicators, the planetary cannon has almost built-up another charge."

"What does it fire?" Maddox asked the professor.

"Trillium plasma," Ludendorff said.

"What is that?" Maddox asked.

"I'll explain later," the professor said. "I still have a few final calculations to make."

At Maddox's orders, Ludendorff disappeared from the main screen. The split screen showed the stars and nearest waiting missile-mines out there, while the other half showed six saucer-shaped Spacer warships chasing them.

"Galyan," Maddox said, "have you found the cloaked ship yet?"

"I have, Captain."

"Feed its coordinates to Valerie," Maddox said. "Lieutenant, retarget that ship with the planetary cannon."

Seconds passed.

"The cloaked Spacer vessel is almost out of the planetary cannon's line-of-sight, sir," Valerie said.

"Fire at it anyway," Maddox said.

Valerie tapped her screen, waited, tapped again, and said, "I'm ready."

"Fire," Maddox said.

Valerie stabbed a button.

On the sandy surface, the giant planetary cannon emitted a huge glob of Trillium plasma. In a roiling riot of orange mass, it boiled upward into space. This time, the mass did not chase *Victory*. Instead, the blob cut across the planet as it zoomed toward the cloaked Spacer vessel.

At the last moment, the cloaking quit as hot exhaust poured out of the vents from the targeted vessel. The orange blob struck the Spacer shield, dissolved it and battered against the vessel.

"Fire the disruptor cannon," Maddox told Galyan. "Finish the stricken ship."

A second later, the antimatter engine roared with power. A hot disruptor beam flashed from *Victory* to the glowing Spacer vessel. The beam cut into the softened hull armor. It crashed through bulkheads, storage bins, living quarters, and smashed into the reactor core. A second later, the Spacer vessel exploded in a fiery death, the glowing hull armor flying in every direction.

"Are we going to turn and face the other Spacers?" Keith asked from the piloting board.

"Negative," Maddox said. "We're heading for the Laumer Point."

"What about those missile-mines?" Keith asked. "Some of them have begun turning toward us."

"Professor," Maddox asked over his chair comm.

"I'm giving the sequences to Valerie," the Methuselah Man said. "We'll know if we can get through them soon enough."

"Will we be able to target the Spacers with those missile-mines?" Maddox asked.

"I'm not as sanguine about that," Ludendorff said. "Is it important that we do?"

"We'll know soon," the captain said. He regarded Valerie. "As soon as the planetary cannon is ready again, fire at the nearest Spacer ship."

"Yes, sir," Valerie said. "Oh. The Visionary is hailing us."

Maddox shook his head. "I'm done talking to her for the moment. Let's see what she does next."

-27-

Victory gained velocity as it left the dusty planet behind. The missile-mines with their amazingly powerful warheads received radio signals from the starship. None of them turned toward the double oval vessel. They remained inert.

On the planet, the giant cannon fired again. An orange glob struck another Spacer ship. The shield and ship disintegrated under the terrible plasma. That left five Spacer warships chasing *Victory* into the void.

"They have more mass, sir," Galyan said. "I am not convinced they have superior weaponry. I believe we can defeat them, sir."

"That isn't the question," Maddox said.

Galyan waited. Finally, he glanced at Valerie as if for help. The lieutenant shook her head. Galyan sulked after that, disappearing from the bridge shortly.

"The Visionary is hailing us again," Valerie said.

The starship had begun to thread through the giant minefield.

Maddox clicked a button on his armrest. "Professor, could it cause the missile-mines to lock onto us if we speak to the Visionary?"

"I don't see why it should," the professor replied. "Still, I would not recommend you speak to her."

"I want to hear what she has to say."

"Bah," Ludendorff said. "She's old and pompous with a bizarre philosophy. You'll learn nothing more from her, at least nothing worthwhile considering the risks."

"You said it was low-risk."

Ludendorff scowled on the screen.

"Thank you, Professor," Maddox said.

"Wait," Ludendorff said.

Maddox paused.

"Bah, never mind," the Methuselah Man said.

Maddox wondered what Ludendorff had wanted to tell him. He knew better than to ask, though. Then, the professor would know that he'd been curious. It was better to feign disinterest. Maddox had learned that many people wanted to share their secrets. One of the best ways to get them to talk about themselves was to seem uninterested and maybe even exasperated at hearing about such things. Why this worked, the captain didn't know. Perhaps it was good enough to know that it often did work.

Ludendorff disappeared from the screen. The Visionary appeared in his place. She did not seem the same as only a short time ago. Some of the arrogance and superiority had departed. She almost seemed crestfallen.

"Captain," she said. "I wish you would listen to reason."

"Why are you still following us?" Maddox asked.

"You fool," she said angrily. "I have to destroy you. I can't allow you to free the Ska."

"Help me destroy it, then."

"Impossible."

"Ska can die. You said so yourself. That means it is possible to kill them with the correct weapon."

"Can you make them grow old?" she asked.

"Perhaps a weapon that ages cells—"

"They're energy creatures, remember?"

"Then I must find a way to age the energy."

"It doesn't work like that," she said.

"How does it work? I would like to know."

She considered him for a time. "Give me your word that you won't try to enter the null region. If you do, I will let you live."

Maddox cocked his head. He debated giving his word. Yet, this was different. He did not believe the Visionary could destroy the starship at this time. Therefore, he did not need to lie to her. Finally, the captain shook his head.

"You're a stubborn man."

"Thank you," he said.

"I did not mean that as a compliment."

"Yet that is how I've taken it."

"You're too clever by half, Captain. This time, though, the odds are too stacked against you. If you release the Ska—"

"Visionary," Maddox said. "Your logic is flawed. Ska have already been through this part of the galaxy. We're all alive. We—"

"You have no idea how long ago the ancient conflict took place. Yes, the Nameless Ones and the Ska have been through this part of the galaxy. Don't you think the Builders have sought a weapon that could kill the Ska? Don't you understand the breadth of effort the Builders expended to fashion a null region? Why do you think they went to such lengths?"

Maddox shrugged.

"You can do better than that," she admonished. "The Builders did so because they could not find a weapon to slay a Ska. Thus, they had to trap it in a place it could not escape. Yet now, you want to free it."

"Just because the Builders couldn't do a thing doesn't mean it can't be done."

"It comes close to saying that," the Visionary told him. "You are a mite compared to the Builders. Do not think to pit your puny skills against their glory."

"Okay," he said.

His answer seemed to exasperate her. "You lack reverence for your betters, Captain."

"While you truckle to an ideal," Maddox said. "Which of us should people pity? You think it's me. I think it's you. Let the results determine which of us is right."

"If I'm right—"

"Kill me if you can, Visionary, or teach me about the Ska."

The old woman grew motionless on her throne. At last, at a hand motion from her, the connection vanished.

Shortly after that, the Spacers vanished.

"Did they cloak?" Maddox asked.

Valerie had been checking her panel. "I can't detect them. It's possible they have a star drive and used it to leave."

Maddox didn't feel like summoning Galyan at the moment. The Adok was sulking. He would leave the poor AI alone for now.

The captain stood. "Lieutenant," he told Valerie, "you have the bridge."

She rose from her station and moved toward the command chair. As she did, Maddox headed for the exit. Maddox wanted to know what things Ludendorff had taken off planet...and why Ludendorff hadn't already explained to him about the Ska.

-28-

Before Maddox went to see the professor, he stopped off at his quarters. He showered, shaved, donned clean clothes and then went to the cafeteria. He ate four eggs and several strips of bacon, drowning it all with several cups of coffee.

He headed to Riker's quarters second. The sergeant admitted him. Maddox questioned Riker about how he had known that he—the captain—had needed help on the planet.

Riker explained it as a gut feeling.

"Is the ego-fragment alive in you?" Maddox asked.

Riker turned away, finally shrugging. "I don't think so, but I don't know for sure."

"Good enough," Maddox said. He slapped Riker on the man's real shoulder and headed for the exit. He noticed the dents on the hatch. On impulse, Maddox turned to regard the glum sergeant. "Thank you for what you did."

Riker nodded.

"That's one of the reasons I brought you along. I did need you in the end."

Riker regarded him. Finally, the leathery face broke into a shy grin.

Once in the corridor, Maddox's stride ate up the distance. It was finally time to talk to Ludendorff.

***

They met in a dim lounge with viewing ports showing the red giant and the already dwindling desert planet. The background stars were few in this direction. Valerie had reported that Galyan had been unable to detect any cloaked vessels following them. The Spacers must have used a jump drive to flee.

Ludendorff sat on a cushioned chair with a goblet of red wine in his hand. He swirled the cup, inhaled the aroma and sipped.

"Wonderful vintage," the Methuselah Man said as he smacked his lips.

Maddox had declined any wine. Only the strongest alcoholic beverages affected him, and any of those for only a short time. His greater metabolism burned away alcohol in his bloodstream much faster than the average individual's could do.

"We did it," the professor declared.

Maddox cocked his head. "What did we do?"

Ludendorff laughed with delight. "We beat the pharisaic Spacers, the moralistic lecturers who preach about what we should and shouldn't do."

"Did you know the Spacers would be down there?"

"What rot and nonsense," the professor said.

"I see."

"Oh, don't get yours feathers in a ruff, Captain. I had no idea the Visionary would poke her nose into this." The professor shrugged. "We beat them soundly, and that feels good. Doesn't it feel good to you?"

Maddox nodded. It did feel good.

"So, we celebrate yet another victory," Ludendorff said, raising the goblet into the air before taking a sip and putting the glass on a side table.

"There are a few things I don't understand," Maddox said.

"You've come to the right person, my boy. I'm feeling expansive. Ask away."

"How could a plasma cannon survive down there for as long as it did?"

"Yes. That is interesting, isn't it? The short answer is that I don't know how."

Maddox studied the Methuselah Man. "You and Strand didn't find any evidence of ancient weaponry two hundred years ago?"

"Indeed not. In case you don't believe me, the proof is in the New Men."

"Oh," Maddox said. "Yes." The star cruisers would have possessed trillium plasma cannons if Strand had known about the ancient weapons. That was a good point.

"It's a delight to speak to a person of true intelligence," Ludendorff said. "I get so bored having to explain every little detail to people. Even with you, though, discussions can become tedious. I hope this one remains on a high plane of thought throughout."

A wry grin slid onto the captain's face. Ludendorff was acting expansively. Was this real or was the professor faking for reasons he did not yet understand?

"The Visionary spoke about the Ska," Maddox said.

"Did she now?"

"How did she learn so much about the null region and the creature in it when the great Professor Ludendorff knows so little?"

"The riddle is easily solved. The Spacers are repositories of deep knowledge. Despite their moralistic nagging, they are erudite. It's what makes them so exasperating. Perhaps you could relate to me your conversation with the Visionary in the stone dome."

Maddox thought about that. He could try to pry critical information out of the professor, trading fact for fact, or he could try a different approach. The captain shrugged. Why not try something new? He told the professor what he remembered of the talk.

"Interesting, interesting," the professor murmured. His eyes were alight as he listened, drinking in the details. Finally, Ludendorff slapped a knee. "Notice her surprise at there being Destroyers in the null region. Perhaps she knows less than you think."

"That may be true," Maddox admitted. "Or perhaps she can collect data in ways we don't understand."

"You think this because of her 'Visionary' title?"

"Maybe…" Maddox said.

"Yes…" Ludendorff said, finally nodding. "The possibility exists, I suppose."

"Which means you think it's true," Maddox said.

Ludendorff picked up the goblet, staring at the gently swirling wine. It seemed he'd fallen into a trance. Finally, he reached to set down the goblet without drinking from it. The glass clicked on the side table.

"Throughout the years I've heard a mention here and there of the Ska," Ludendorff said slowly. "I've never heard the Ska mentioned in the same breath as the Nameless Ones. That is new to me, quite interesting and...troubling."

Maddox waited.

"I should have confided in you sooner, my boy. From what I know, the Ska are the next thing to immortal. They age like the stars. That was a poetic turn of phrase for the Spacer witch. The Ska are old indeed, and I suppose the word evil fits their actions. The idea of an ego-fragment—" The professor shook his head. "That is nearly inconceivable to me. Perhaps it wasn't a fragment at all."

"What then?" Maddox asked.

"A spawn, I would think. From my understanding, a Ska can split like a body's cell. Each half receives the collected knowledge and wisdom of the original and yet gains a youthful vigor. Perhaps the spawn, the half, used this vigor to...detach a part of itself and reach the Spacer messenger."

"How could it do this and not entirely escape its null region prison?"

"That, my boy, is the question. Maybe it doesn't matter precisely how you're asking it. The key is how do you kill a thing like the Ska?"

"Did you see the mural down in the ruins?"

"Of course I did."

"The Fishers shot the dark cloud—a Ska, I imagine—with weapons emitting rays of light."

Ludendorff shuddered before smiling again. "That could mean a variety of things. For instance, the rays of light could have a metaphorical meaning."

Maddox took his time. What had the shudder just now signified? What was going on with Ludendorff? Maddox had a feeling the professor didn't realize how strangely he had been acting. If that was true—

"Did I say something wrong?" Ludendorff asked, breaking into Maddox's reverie.

"You're the archeologist," Maddox said briskly. "You must have a better idea than metaphorical meanings. What did you find on the planet, Professor? What did you take to your laboratory?"

The professor took the goblet and drained the remaining wine. He picked up an open wine bottle beside his chair and poured himself another glass. He drained that cup, too. Finally, he set the bottle and the goblet, unfilled, beside him on the side table.

"Strand and I had to leave the planet in a hurry two hundred years ago," the professor said. "Spacers chased us off, if you can believe that. I have concluded the Spacers view the planet as a shrine."

That didn't seem right. "Why?" Maddox asked.

"Please, my boy, don't interrupt as is your habit. Let me conjure up the past from memory. That isn't as easy as you would think. I am much older than you are, with thousands of more interesting memories that have squeezed into my mind."

"Ah," the captain said.

"I know, I know," Ludendorff said with a sigh. "I have wounded your vanity. Others think you are a creature of ice. I realize that you are inherently vain. All New Men are like this. I'm not sure you know that about yourself."

"I do now," Maddox said. "And I am only half New Man, by the way."

"You are taking offense, and that was not my desire today, tonight, whatever time it really is." The professor sighed again, glanced longingly at the wine bottle and shook his head. "I've had enough. If I loosen my tongue any more, I'll tell you truths that will blast your self-conceit into pieces. I have no desire to harm your vaunted efficiency."

Maddox wondered if the professor had been drinking before he'd agreed to the meeting.

Ludendorff coughed into a fist, grinned at Maddox and leaned his head back against the chair's rest.

"Where was I?" the professor said. He closed his eyes. "Ah, I remember. Strand and I had to leave in a hurry due to pesky Spacer moralizers. I learned through the years that Strand had left behind on the planet an interesting number of relics stuffed into a carrying bag. I'd hoped to retrieve the bag—the reason I urged you to come to this planet."

Maddox remembered the bag Ludendorff had kicked while on the shuttle.

"One of the relics gave me the sequences that have been allowing us to travel through the missile-mine belt," Ludendorff said.

"The Fishers put up those mines?"

With his head laid back, Ludendorff frowned. "I told you not to interrupt. I mean it, my boy. I won't tell you a thing if you keep squawking."

Maddox decided to wait. He could be patient when he needed to be.

Once more, Ludendorff sighed. "In answer to your question, no, the Fishers did not put those missile-mines in place. Another ancient race did so. We must head to their planet next."

Maddox surprised himself. He found it difficult to keep quiet. He forced himself to listen instead of asking about the new planet.

With his head resting back against the back of the cushy chair, Ludendorff seemed to be waiting. He almost seemed to be disappointed.

"You didn't interrupt," the professor said. "How very interesting, Captain. That tells me you dearly want to know what I have to say. In other words, I have your undivided attention."

Maddox still remained silent.

"Oh, I'm impressed now," Ludendorff said. "I can feel the heat of your desires from here. Very well, here is what I know: The Fishers fell under the spell of the Ska left in their system. I don't know why the Nameless Ones did that. The Ska turned the Fisher civilization onto an evil path. For reasons neither Strand nor I have determined, a subset of Builders managed to corral the Ska, keeping it from leaving the Fisher System. In time, they drove it mad. That's how the story puts it, at least. The Ska used the Fisher star, causing it to expand like a red giant far before its time. That killed the Fishers. Perhaps the Ska thought that with them dead, the Builders would let it leave the system."

Ludendorff put his hands on his stomach, beginning to twiddle his thumbs.

That proved to be too much for the captain. "Did the subset of Builders kill the Ska?"

Ludendorff shrugged.

"That's not an answer," Maddox said.

"I don't have an answer. I don't know. That's as far as the legend goes."

Maddox frowned as he considered what Ludendorff had said. "Wait. That doesn't jive. You said we should go to the planet that built the missile-mines."

"I did."

"But you said a subset of Builders corralled the Ska in the Fisher System."

"You're listening, I can see. The subset of Builders used the other planetary system to manufacture the missile-mines. Whether those aliens also built the weapon that halted the Ska, I don't know."

"Have you ever been to that planet?"

With his head on the back of the chair, Ludendorff rolled it from side to side.

"I would think that would be an interesting planet to visit," Maddox said.

"You and I are in full accord there."

Maddox controlled his temper. The professor was likely trying to goad him. At times, it was better to let Ludendorff have his fun. The Methuselah Man usually made more mistakes that way.

The captain reasoned out the correct response as a thought bubbled up from his unconscious. He almost snorted to himself. Instead, he said, "You've just learned most of this."

Ludendorff's head jerked upright as he opened his eyes. "That's a remarkable deduction, Captain. You're right. I have read Strand's notes left in the old carrying bag. The man—" Ludendorff glowered. "I would dearly like to know where Strand acquired that knowledge. As much as I am loath to

129

admit it, in this instance, Strand's knowledge surpasses mine on the subject."

"What else do you know about the Ska?" Maddox asked.

"That about sums up my knowledge," the professor said. "The next star system might or might not hold what we're looking for."

"Does it have a name?"

"The star system is over two hundred light-years from here," the professor said. Fortunately, it's near the system with the null region. I have never gone there, as I've said. Strand called it the Gnome System."

"Gnome? That's an odd name. What does it signify?"

"This is just a guess on my part," Ludendorff said. "But I believe Strand meant to imply an alien race of artificers. Remember, they belong to the same time-period as the Fishers. That is ancient beyond belief, much older than your Adok starship."

"The Gnome System will give us a weapon to face the Ska?"

"I thought you were listening. I don't know if it will. But if any place can, I would wager that is the place to go."

"Do you have the coordinates?"

"Indeed I do, my boy."

"Are you eager to go there?"

Ludendorff reached for the wine bottle, letting red liquid gurgle into his goblet. He set down the bottle, picked up the goblet and stared at it. He glanced at Maddox.

"I am eager, my boy, and I'm…concerned, let us say. The Gnome System will be dangerous, of that I have no doubt."

Maddox nodded.

Ludendorff quaffed his drink, smacking his lips afterward. "Dangerous and exciting—the same two words I'd use to describe us, Captain. Wouldn't you agree?"

"Without a doubt," Maddox said, wondering how much Ludendorff had left out.

-29-

Victory used star drive jumps as well as regular Laumer Point transits to race from the galactic edge up through the Orion Spiral Arm. They reentered Human Space, and from there, learned that more people had heard about the Swarm threat against Tau Ceti.

How this had seeped out so quickly struck Maddox as fantastic. They were far from Earth. Yet, the news seemed to travel faster than a quick frigate could go from the Solar System to way out here via Laumer Points. According to the news, the knowledge had begun to create panic in many star systems. With the terrible news came some strategic information. It seemed the Swarm Fleet headed for Tau Ceti at high velocity. That was still at sub-light speeds, though. If Thrax's saucer-shaped vessels had star drives, they had not revealed the ability. The bugs moved together in a mass just as Earth bees swarmed from their hive.

"Rumors fly on the wind," Ludendorff said in the cafeteria.

"That's all well and good," Maddox said. "But there is no wind in space."

"Solar wind," Keith suggested.

Ludendorff clapped his hands, nodding in delight.

The Adok starship continued to jump as a terrible sense of urgency had begun to take hold of the crew. Time kept ticking. When would Thrax's saucer-shaped warships make their move? What would happen to the Tau Ceti System when the Swarm reached there?

"I can easily envision mass chaos at Tau Ceti," Ludendorff told Maddox.

The captain seldom responded to such thoughts. Maddox had fixated on the Ska in the null region. If they couldn't find a way to destroy it, or to drive it off the alien Destroyers, how could they dare to enter the null region?

That was the other problem. *How* would they enter the null region? Last time, they'd made it into the strange space through an accident. Could they duplicate the feat?

At last, Maddox decided they must have more information about the Ska. He could put Ludendorff under interrogation. That might work, particularly with Galyan's help monitoring the Methuselah Man. Yet, the professor had many tricks, many sleights he no doubt kept in reserve. That was the trouble with using Ludendorff's help—the Methuselah Man's incredibly devious nature. When it came to milking the professor for information that he did not want to give…

Maddox and Meta were lifting weights in the starship's gym. Maddox bench-pressed while Meta did pull ups nearby.

She was wearing tight-fitting garments and had tied her hair into a ponytail. Keith had suggested once that she cut her long hair to make things easier for her. Meta had scoffed at the idea.

"Besides," she'd said, "Maddox likes it long."

"Is that a good enough reason to keep it long?" Keith had asked.

"Of course," she'd said. "I look more feminine with long hair."

"I can't deny that," the pilot had said, ending the debate.

Maddox racked the four-hundred-pound bar against the rests. He sat up, breathing heavily, having done ten reps.

"Fifty-one, fifty-two, fifty-three," Meta said between clenched teeth.

Maddox grinned as he watched Meta. She'd been genetically altered like him. She'd also grown up on a 2-G planet. She was strong all the way around, including mentally. It was one of the reasons he loved her.

"Keep going," he said.

Meta didn't nod, but she continued to pull her chin up over the bar. Finally, after eighty-eight reps, she let herself hang down all the way and let go, dropping to the mat under her.

"My biceps are burning," she said.

"You're getting closer to one hundred pull-ups," he said.

She nodded as she massaged an arm.

Maddox looked back at his bar. He kept staring at it, staring and—He felt Meta's hands on his back. He turned with a smile.

"What's wrong?" she asked.

Maddox made a face as he sat on the end of the bench-press bench. They were the only two in the gym at the moment.

"I'm troubled," he admitted.

"About what?"

"I think you know what."

"The Ska?" she asked.

Maddox nodded.

"We don't know enough about it," he said. "I'm afraid we're not going to learn enough in time. If we fail to drive it off…"

Meta became thoughtful. She stood closer and ran her fingers through his hair. "You always come up with a way in the end," she said.

"Maybe. But maybe I won't this time."

"Too bad you couldn't use Dana."

Maddox looked up at Meta.

"What?" she asked. "Did I say something wrong?"

"How can I use Dana?" he asked quietly.

"She helped me remember once."

Maddox had forgotten this. Once Meta had secrets locked in her head. Dana had helped release the needed memories.

"If she could tease more information out of Sergeant Riker…" Meta suggested.

"Yes!" Maddox said. "That would be—" He shook his head. "Dana has yet to regain her full intellect. Until she does, I don't see how she can help us."

"Figure out a way to restore her intellect."

"Me?" Maddox asked. "Ludendorff has tried and he can't do it."

"You're not Ludendorff. Maybe Galyan has a program—"

Maddox stood abruptly. He kissed and hugged Meta. "You're the greatest," he said.

She smiled with delight.

"Come on," Maddox said, grabbing her hand, pulling her with him.

-30-

Galyan had retreated inside the great Adok computer system. He saw himself as he'd been when he had been Driving Force Galyan, the living commander of his people.

That had been before the terrible Swarm invasion six thousand years ago. Now, the Swarm had returned to destroy his friends, the humans. He had to help them. The thought of remaining in this place alone, with Maddox, Valerie, Riker, Meta, Keith and the others dead and gone—that was too terrible to contemplate.

Yet, how could he escape the obvious conclusion? A Swarm fleet had entered Human Space. The Swarm Imperium controlled a nexus. He had to strive with everything in him to save his friends. They had to return to that dark realm where only the captain and he had been awake.

Yet, how could he help restore Doctor Dana Rich's intellect? It had taken a terrible beating last voyage...

Inside the computer, which acted like a perfect holo-deck, Galyan stood on *Victory's* bridge as it had been in the beginning. Ludendorff had tried to enlist his aid last voyage to help Dana, but he had not begged Galyan to exhaust every possibility.

Galyan did not breathe, but he did sigh. The captain and Meta *had* asked him to exhaust every possibility. Galyan did not want to do that. There were some memories that were too difficult to remember. There were some things that made him infinitely sad and lonely.

135

He did not like to be lonely. He had been alone for six thousand years. He knew something about the subject that few others ever would.

Galyan wondered if the Ska in the null region was alone. He suspected it must be. Could they use that—?

"You are evading your responsibility," Galyan told himself. "Your family has come to you for aid. You are the elder in this situation."

Professor Ludendorff thought of himself as a long-lived person. Had Ludendorff survived for six thousand years? No, the professor had not. He knew very little about loneliness and long age compared to Galyan. As the elder, the protector—

"Must I do this?" Galyan whispered to himself. "Must I torture myself in order to help Dana?"

Galyan already knew the answer. He must exhaust every possibility. He had to restore Dana's intellect. That was a difficult assignment, and yet, he had completed many difficult assignments for his new family. They had come to him as a last resort. They had finally realized that he could do what possibly no one else could.

Yet, they had not understood what they asked of him. They did not understand the pain he would have to endure by doing this. Galyan knew no other way to exhaust the possibilities.

"My dearest love," Galyan whispered. "I beseech you to come to me."

The self-identity of Galyan began to tremble with sorrow. Long ago, perhaps three thousand years ago, he had stored an immense amount of data in the image of his mate. There had been a strange ion storm that had come through the system. The storm had threatened his existence and threatened to erase all Adok knowledge. The only way he had thought to save this knowledge...

"Galyan," a female Adok whispered.

Galyan dreaded this even as his electronic heart soared with delight. He turned around and looked upon the holoimage of his beloved mate.

A human would not have been able to discern any difference in her appearance, but Galyan most certainly did.

She was achingly beautiful. He had not done this for a long, long time, an eon. He had not—

"My love," she said. "Why are you so sad?"

Galyan wanted to howl with agony. He missed his love, his mate, with an intensity that should have been impossible for an AI creature. It nearly drove him to despair. He wanted to hold her, kiss her, love her as he had when he had been flesh and blood. Alas, he could never do that again.

"I. Miss. You," he whispered. "I miss you more than you can imagine. I would gladly have died with you, my love, my life, my dearest one."

"Oh, Galyan," she said. "You should not do this to yourself. You should accept your new family. You should build a life with them—"

"Dearest," he said, holding up a ropy arm, pressing a finger against her lips. "That is why I've summoned you. That is why I'm torturing myself once more. I…must know how to cure the mind of one of my sisters."

"Galyan?" his dearest asked.

"I never thought I'd need the medical knowledge. But I did not want to lose it. I put it in you."

"Yes," she said. "How can I aide you, my mate?"

He told her Dana's problem.

His mate's eyelids flickered faster than Galyan's had ever done. She accessed an immense goldmine of data. She processed, crosschecked—

"Driving Force Galyan," she said. "I may have a solution."

"Tell me," he whispered.

She did.

Galyan closed his eyes afterward. He did not want to say this. He wanted to remain in this moment for the rest of his existence. How could Captain Maddox and Meta have asked him to do this?

"Because they do not understand," Galyan whispered.

"What is that, love?" his mate asked.

"Dematerialize mate program," Galyan whispered in the softest voice he'd ever uttered.

After that, Galyan remained rooted to his spot on the bridge. Time passed. It seemed like an age. He debated deleting himself for good. Why should he suffer like this? Why should he torture himself with the loneliness of existence?

"Because I am Driving Force Galyan," he said. "I am the last of the Adoks. I must show the universe the greatness of my people, the greatness of my love. I will help my family. We will stop the Swarm. I will not allow the bugs to destroy any more species. That I vow as the last acting commander of my people."

He still felt achingly alone. Yet, he had a burning purpose. If Galyan could hate, he hated the Swarm with an undying rage.

He opened his eyes. The bridge still existed. He was the only one on it. With great sorrow, Galyan disappeared from his inner bridge. He went to bring Captain Maddox the answer to the problem.

-31-

Two days later, Doctor Dana Rich slowly woke up, disoriented. She opened her eyes but couldn't see a thing. Slowly, a ceiling above came into focus. She frowned. This was—

"Starship *Victory*," she said softly.

Doctor Rich was dark skinned with intensely brown eyes. She had beautiful dark hair and exquisite features. She had grown up on the Indian world of Brahma. She'd been a university student there when she first met Professor Ludendorff. He had been unlike any man she'd met before or since. He had a great breadth of mind. That was important to her—

Mind. Dana touched her head. Slowly, she sat up, looking around. This was her quarters aboard the starship. She remembered—

Dana's eyes widened. She remembered last voyage. She recalled that she had been injured. She had lost use of some of her intellect—she touched her open mouth. She'd lost some of her razor-sharp abilities. Ludendorff had tried everything to restore her mind. The professor had stayed at her side…

She smiled. Many people thought that Professor Ludendorff was a selfish prick. While that was true on many occasions, he could also be wonderful and protecting. He was a good man, at least some of the time he was.

It was at that point that Dana recalled what had happened to her in the last two days. It had proven painful and exhausting.

She felt exhausted. Yet, Galyan had restored her full mental capabilities to her.

"Thank you, Galyan," she said softly.

The holoimage appeared in her quarters. "You are welcome, Dana," Galyan said.

The doctor pulled up the blanket to cover her breasts. "Is my room bugged?"

"Of course, Dana," Galyan said.

"I don't like that."

"It is for your own protection."

"I don't need protecting. I can take care of myself."

Galyan stood there as if he didn't know what to say.

"No," she said. "I'm sorry. You just helped me. Thank you indeed, Galyan. I appreciate it."

"You are part of my family."

"Yes," she said. "And you're part of mine."

She reached out to touch him. Her hand passed through his holoimage. She jerked her hand back. "I'm sorry," she said.

"I understand why you did that," Galyan said sadly. "I will go so you can dress. The professor will be overjoyed to hear you are better. None of us knew whether the process would work or not."

She nodded as she stared at him.

"What is wrong, Dana?"

"Galyan, I…" She didn't know what to say. She wondered in that moment what it was like being Driving Force Galyan. She supposed none of them would ever know. Had the Builders been cruel to give the Adoks deification technology? It was more than possible.

"Wait a minute," Dana said. "The others need me restored, don't they?"

"Yes," Galyan said.

Dana thought about that. "Couldn't they have tried this before?"

"Dana…" Galyan said hesitantly. "I would not say anything under normal conditions, but finding your cure was costly."

"How so?"

Galyan said nothing.

140

"To whom was it costly?" she asked. "To Maddox?"

Galyan shook his head.

She scowled.

"I would not have said anything," Galyan told her, "except that my probability psych program has detected anger on your part toward them. I wish to dampen that."

"Why?" she asked.

"Because your cure proved costly...to me," he added in a small voice.

"Costly to you, Galyan?" Dana asked. "I don't understand."

"And I cannot explain it. Or maybe I don't want to explain it. Please, Dana, I beg you—"

"No, Galyan," she said. "I don't ever want you to beg me. By your Adok arts, you restored my full mind to me. I am grateful for that. I will help the others in order to repay, in part, whatever this cost you."

"Thank you, Dana."

"What exactly am I supposed to do?"

Galyan explained the problem.

"Destroyers?" she asked. "Why would we possibly want to get those horrors?"

"Did I not tell you?" Galyan asked. "The Swarm has reached Human Space."

Dana stared at him. "I did not realize," she whispered. "Yes, of course. Go tell the professor. I will have to eat, walk around a bit. Then, I will be ready to get started with Riker. The Swarm," she said softly. "It has finally happened."

-32-

Sergeant Riker lay on a couch. He was in a dimly lit room with Doctor Rich. She'd used her specialist techniques to calm his mind and put him in a reflective state.

"This will hardly hurt at all," she said softly.

Riker felt like opening his eyes, but refrained because he didn't quite feel strongly enough about it.

"I—oh," Dana said. "I forgot about your bionic arm."

Riker could hear her fabric rustle as she moved around him. A small stab of pain flared against his real shoulder.

Even so, the sergeant kept his eyes closed. He felt greater contentment than he had in a while. He tried to remember when he'd felt this good. Not since the last time he'd he worked at home in his garden. He loved planting trees in particular.

He'd heard a saying once that had stuck with him for life. An old man who plants a tree whose shade he will never use is the primary component of civilization.

Riker saw himself as imminently civilized. He loved his society, his culture. He manned the borders in order to keep invaders at bay. Those invaders could be aliens like the Swarm. They could be New Men spies or simply those who broke the rules of civilization. Such would have to face men like him. Barbarians broke the accepted rules. Barbarians spat on the culture. The best way to deal with barbarians was to keep them outside civilization's borders. Once the barbarians were inside the gates in large numbers, the civilization was likely doomed.

The Swarm were inside the borders and in fantastic numbers. Because Riker loved his nieces, his blood and heritage—the bounty of his father, grandfather and great grandfather and beyond, and his mother and grandmothers—he would fight with all his might. The Swarm thought to eradicate what Riker had received as a gift with a duty to pass it on to his blood.

On the couch, in the dimly lit room, Riker moved his head from side to side. The good feeling was beginning to evaporate.

"Relax," Dana whispered in his ear. "You must stay calm, Sergeant."

"Duty," he whispered.

"You will do your duty by remaining calm, by relaxing."

"How can this be?" Riker asked gruffly.

"You are the spy for our side," Dana whispered.

Riker frowned while he kept his eyes closed.

"The enemy has thought to use you by infiltrating you," Dana said.

"The barbarian is inside the gate?"

There was silence until—"Yes, Sergeant," a feminine voice whispered in his ear. "But you can turn the spy if you remain calm."

A hard grin slid onto the sergeant's face. He *would* turn the spy and use the barbarian against others of his kind. They would not destroy Riker's civilization. It was uniquely his, built by many generations. His ancestors had passed on duties and privileges to him won through their sweat and toil. He would not be the weak link that broke the great chain. He would rise to the task. He would do so because he was proud of his lineage, of those who had gone on before him. Any who thought to steal his heritage from him—

Riker made a growling noise in the back of his throat. He would grind into dust any who thought to trick or overpower him. He would prove to be a good son of his ancestors. He would not let his birthright go because others thought he had too much privilege.

In his heart, Riker spat on such fools and knaves. He manned the border. He would remain vigilant until he was dead.

"Riker," the soft voice said.

"What?" he asked.

"Why are you so tense?"

"I will fight to the end," Riker said.

"That is good," the voice whispered. "You are a soldier. It is a soldier's duty to fight."

"It is a man's duty to protect his loved ones."

"That is true. But now you must relax."

"Are you asking me to shirk my duty?"

"No, Sergeant," the soft voice said. "I am asking you to do the hardest thing of all."

"What is that?"

"You must face a monster that can crush you with a thought."

"Do I have to go alone?"

"Are you afraid?"

"I...am afraid," Riker admitted. "I am too weak."

"No, Sergeant," the soft voice said. "Being afraid isn't wrong. Listening to your fears is the problem. I want you to listen to your courage."

"I will," he said.

"Then you must relax and go inward. There in the depths is a monster that seeks to withhold knowledge of the weapon we need to destroy it."

"I'm not sure I understand."

"Relax, Sergeant Riker. You are going to use your mind, will and memories to defeat a monster greater than any man."

Riker squirmed on the couch. This sounded frightening. And yet, for the sake of his nieces, he would do this thing.

"I'm ready," Riker said.

"Then let us delve deeply into your subconscious."

-33-

Baffled rage consumed him. A trick, a monstrous trick by the computing people had lured him into this place. He had brought three of the hard material machines with him to investigate and annihilate. Instead, terrible darkness filled this void and battled his every effort to escape.

Worse, he felt tired and sleepy. What caused such a thing? It made no sense. He had never known sleepiness like this except for the long journey through the seemingly infinite void to get to this exciting realm of endless matter.

Stars had surrounded his kind, and planets full of juicy tastes. They had multiplied the hard material machines and built clickers to run them.

He had ranged through the small dark realm so unlike the material world of stars, planets and juicy treats of hot emotions. Letting the hard material machines devour others brought joy because the prey's terror and hopelessness warmed him so beautifully. That had been the source of his power: endless fear and terror radiating into them had caused each of his brothers to puff up with energy.

They were the Ska, the eaters of fear, the feasters upon hopelessness magnified into mindless terror. Oh, he had gobbled so many of these puny flesh and blood races. He had warmed himself on the heat of their psychic emanations.

Oh, how wonderful, oh, how powerful it had become. Now, though, he had slipped into an inconceivable trap of darkness.

The computing people had done this to him.

He Who Could Kill with Speed—the Elder Ska—had known something approaching sorrow. It would take endless ages before he perished in this draining null place. He would linger for time upon time. If he could have used that time to find a means of escape...

No! A great and final sleepiness had settled over him. His awareness shrank. He almost woke up again when the third hard material machine blew up. The clickers in it had attempted a jump.

If he could have, the Elder Ska would have tormented the clickers an eon for destroying their machine. Instead, he lost his awareness and fell back to sleep.

Ages slipped away. Eons and eons later, something sharp and lively entered the dark realm.

The Elder Ska began to awaken. He saw the alien starship and felt the pulsating life within it. Even more amazing, there appeared an opening that could possibility be a way out of the trap.

The life forms in the starship acted faster than he could. They moved to the opening, passing through it, vanishing—

The Elder Ska wailed in misery. The opening vanished with the tasty morsels of flesh and blood, taking their hot emotions with them. That was almost too much to accept. He debated ending his existence.

Instead, he forced a split, and with the renewed energy of youth, he struggled to understand about the opening.

One part of the split tried to wriggle through. Pain, searing agony almost blasted it apart. Before the other ended, a spark of his once vast force latched onto a passing Spacer vessel. He found the most modified among the crew and entered into the creature.

That hurt so much and that confined him. But he had a plan. If he could get the prey to go back into the null realm, he could reunite with his brother and reemerge later whole and powerful again.

It was a good plan. It would have worked. But the creature known as Sergeant Riker—

***

146

In the dimly lit room aboard Starship *Victory*, Riker bolted upright on the couch. The sergeant's eyes flew open and he howled as if he was a demented soul burning in Hell.

Dana fell off her chair in fright.

Riker continued to howl.

Galyan appeared.

That made Riker berserk. He stood, grabbed the couch and grunted as he raised it over his head. He was going to beat the surprised Dana Rich to death.

The hatch opened and Maddox and Meta rushed in. Riker hurled the couch at Meta. She tried to dodge, but the couch caught her, hurling her against a bulkhead.

Maddox shouted as he moved into a flying kick, hitting Riker against the chest so the sergeant tumbled off his feet, rolling across the floor.

Maddox landed on his feet like a cat. Riker shook his head, snarled as if he'd gone mad and jumped up. He charged Maddox.

The captain sidestepped the bionic arm, stretched out a foot and tripped Riker. The sergeant crashed headlong against a bulkhead.

The old sergeant didn't seem to feel it, though. He spun around, popped to his feet and charged again. Like a professional matador, Maddox once more moved aside.

"I'll kill you, morsel!" Riker shouted.

Maybe he would have, but at that moment, Professor Ludendorff poked his head into the room. The Methuselah Man raised a gun and fired a heavy dart against the sergeant's chest.

Riker looked down at the dart. Maddox looked and so did Ludendorff. The sergeant plucked the dart out of his chest, laughed like a predator—his eyes fluttered until, like an axed tree, Riker fell headlong onto the floor, out cold.

147

-34-

Several days later, Maddox held a meeting in the conference chamber.

Meta was there with a cast around her torso. The hurled couch had broken several ribs. It might have done more, but Meta had tough muscles and stronger bones. She used an accelerated bone therapy drug. The ribs should knit together perfectly within another week. She had complained to Maddox about a sore back, but no one else knew about that.

An apologetic Sergeant Riker sat beside Meta.

He'd just come out of a stasis tube. Dana had run a battery of tests on his mental state. There was a small anomaly that she couldn't understand or explain. Otherwise, Riker seemed mentally fit. That one unknown, however, had most of them concerned.

Dana sat beside the sergeant. She seemed like her old self, confident, healthy and wearing her white lab coat.

The professor sat at the opposite end of the table from Maddox. At Ludendorff's left side was Galyan, who stood. The Kai-Kaus Chief Technician Andros Crank sat beside the holoimage. Andros was a stout and rather short man with blunt fingers and unusually long gray hair. The Chief Technician seldom said much, but he had observant gray eyes that seemed to miss nothing.

Finally, Valerie sat between Andros and Captain Maddox at the head of the table.

The captain cleared his throat. "We've had an interesting few days, to say the least. We've also delved into the sergeant's memories to get at the Ska ego-fragment that tried to use him."

Sergeant Riker looked around with a hint of wariness at the corners of his eyes. He seemed a little like a cornered beast watching the net-handlers whispering among themselves.

"Today," Maddox continued, "I'm hoping to pool our thoughts and observations in order to figure out what the Ska fears."

"It obviously fears remaining trapped in the null region," Dana said promptly.

Maddox nodded. "No doubt about that, Doctor. Thank you. Do you have any idea if it fears a particular weapon?"

Dana shook her head.

"Sergeant?" asked Maddox.

"I wish I knew," Riker said with his head hunched. "I hate the Ska. They're barbarians at the gates. They're just like the Swarm. Too bad we couldn't send the Ska at the Swarm."

"That would be risky," Ludendorff said. "The Ska might attempt to king itself and lead the Swarm to even greater devastation."

"Would repeated nuclear blasts hurt the Ska?" Maddox asked the professor.

"I find that doubtful," Ludendorff said. "The reason is simple, really. If all it took were a few nuclear explosions, why didn't the Builders do that in their day?"

Maddox looked around the table, seeing if anyone had anything to add.

"The Destroyers annihilated flesh and blood," Dana said slowly, "yet the Ska seem to thrive off heightened negative emotions."

"Would laughter and joy wound it, then?" Meta asked.

"I wouldn't think so," Ludendorff said. "If it warms itself through extreme fear, joy would simply be a lack of warmth."

"How do you know that joy and laughter wouldn't be like freezing cold?" Maddox asked. "A man caught in a snowstorm can freeze to death."

"How do you aim joy and laughter?" the professor asked.

"How does a non-physical creature warm itself off terror?" the captain countered.

"I think that's a critical question," Dana said. "If we could answer that, we might be that much closer to our solution."

"I don't agree," Ludendorff told her. "The Builders—"

"Aren't gods," Dana said in a huff. "And the Ska aren't demons," she told Maddox. "They're alien entities. The Ska thought of the Builders as the computer people."

"Which is meaningless to our discussion," Ludendorff told her.

Maddox wondered if the professor and Dana had had an argument in the past few hours. It seemed likely from the way they were acting.

"Did the Ska directly kill people?" Maddox asked.

"That seems obvious," Ludendorff said.

"If it's so obvious," the captain said, "why did the Ska employ the hard material machines and the clickers? Why not go as themselves, especially if no one could kill them?"

Ludendorff opened his mouth to rebut the idea—

"Think about what he said before you rattle off an answer," Dana told him.

The professor regarded the doctor.

"It's a reasonable question," Dana added.

Ludendorff rubbed his chin, nodding a moment later. "Yes, I suppose it is. Perhaps...perhaps we've been looking at this the wrong way."

"How do you mean?" Maddox asked.

"Instead of asking what can kill the Ska," Ludendorff said. "We should be asking how the Ska can influence or touch material objects. Those objects would include people, clickers and stars."

"I would say they influenced those things through the Destroyers," Maddox said. "Yet, according to the Fisher mural, the Ska entered the star and caused it to expand prematurely."

"The Fishers shined lights at the cloud," Ludendorff said, "the representation of the Ska."

"Not necessarily," Dana said.

"Must you object to everything I say?" Ludendorff asked testily.

Dana turned away as a secret smile slid into place. Maddox saw that. He wasn't sure the professor did.

"Are you suggesting the Ska built the cloud?" Ludendorff demanded.

"What does the cloud represent?" Dana asked, facing him.

"The Ska," Ludendorff nearly shouted.

"The cloud is material," Dana said. "The Ska is immaterial."

Ludendorff rubbed his forehead. "This is making my brain sore."

"Go on," Maddox told Dana.

The doctor frowned thoughtfully. "I'm not sure what I mean. I am beginning to think the Ska operates on a psionic plane."

"Telepathy?" asked Maddox.

"I know," Dana said. "That is a rubber science, as people say. We haven't found a telepathic race, and certainly humans have shown no ability at reading minds or foretelling the future. Yet, the Ska are not like us. They come from a different reality. But what does that mean?" She shrugged.

"That doesn't help us find a weapon to defeat the Ska," Maddox said.

Ludendorff snapped his fingers. "It just may, Captain. It just may."

Dana stared at the professor. The professor returned her scrutiny.

"What if the Ska use telepathy, psionics, whatever word you wish to use?" Ludendorff said, "in order to communicate with their creatures? I would suggest it even goes farther than that. They use this psionic ability to absorb fear. It's how they sense the warmth, as the creature in Riker put it. The psionic ability is the Ska's hands. Unfortunately for them, this telepathy cannot act in a telekinetic manner. Remember, telekinesis is the ability of mind to move material objects. But the Ska cannot do this. If they could, they would not have needed the Destroyers. The Destroyers acted as their material weapon, their gun. That gun killed in order to create terror. The terror is what the Ska feeds off. I suppose a crude analogy would be a man using a hammer to break an oyster in order to

151

get to the meat inside. The man can't use his hands to pry open the oyster, but he can manipulate a hammer."

"That is an inelegant analogy," Dana said.

Ludendorff scowled.

"But it does make your point," the doctor admitted.

Ludendorff nodded curtly.

"Wait," Valerie said. "If the Ska can't do anything directly to material objects, how did it make the first Destroyer and the clickers who run it?"

Everyone stared in silence at Valerie.

"I don't know," Dana finally said.

"Maybe the Ska stole the first Destroyers," Ludendorff said. "It hijacked the hard material machines from others. After that, the clickers always built more of their kind."

"And Ska can control the clickers?" Valerie asked.

"That seems self-evident," Ludendorff said.

Valerie tugged at her lower lip. "Wouldn't that mean that each Destroyer has some sort of psionic receiver in its command center? This receiver gives the orders. Maybe this receiver knows terror unless it obeys its Ska master."

Ludendorff shook his head. "That is a marvelous insight, Lieutenant. I'm impressed. Yes. I think you're right."

Valerie beamed at the professor's rare compliment.

"Suppose this is so," Maddox said. "Ska cannot directly...touch or manipulate hard matter. They use the Destroyers to terrify, and in the center of each machine is a control unit that it can terrify. How then could the ego-fragment terrify Riker and the Spacer messenger so easily?"

"Interesting," Ludendorff said with growing excitement. "That's because the Ska telepathy can...touch a human mind. With the telepathy, the Ska can turn dials in the human mind, so to speak. The mind controls the body, and the rest is history."

Maddox thought about that.

"I see your point," Dana told the professor. "So instead of looking for a weapon to destroy the Ska—"

"Which no one seems capable of doing," Ludendorff added.

152

"Right, right," Dana said. "Instead of searching for a nonexistent weapon, we should be looking for a defense against the Ska's telepathy."

"Telepathy or psionics are merely words we're using to describe a thing the Ska does," Ludendorff said. "I doubt it is like telepathy as we think of it, but it's the closest concept we have to what the Ska is doing."

"If this is true," Maddox said. "Why didn't the Builders figure it out?"

"I don't know," Ludendorff said.

"Maybe because they're the computing people," Dana said. "Maybe Builders don't have emotions like we do."

"Ah…" Ludendorff said. "So, the Ska couldn't directly touch Builder minds."

"None of this makes sense," Riker croaked.

"Possibly not," Ludendorff told him. "But maybe it gives us enough of an inkling that we can figure out a method that will work long enough for us to achieve our goal."

"What are you suggesting?" Maddox asked.

The professor stared at Dana. "We have to come up with a device that protects the mind from this altered-reality Ska telepathy. That will allow the wearer of this device to power up the ancient Destroyers and pilot them through the white light."

"How do we manufacture the bright-light exit in the null region?" Maddox asked.

"Figuring that out could be a problem," Ludendorff admitted.

"And how do we keep the Ska from coming through with us?" the captain asked.

"The only way I can think of is by moving faster than the Ska does," Ludendorff said.

Maddox blinked several times. "Are you suggesting we're going to be like kids racing through a yard, grabbing a ball and running out before the dog wakes up and mauls us?"

"Right," Ludendorff said. "That's the essence of my plan."

"I'd rather have a weapon to kill the Ska," Maddox said.

"We don't always get what we want," Ludendorff said.

Maddox nodded. It was a good point. "Very well," he said. "Professor, I'm going to put you in charge of figuring out how to make the bright-light exit appear in the null region."

"I already know," Ludendorff said.

Maddox raised his eyebrows.

"I'll wave my magic wand," the professor said.

"What magic wand?" Meta asked.

Ludendorff turned to Meta, pointed at her, and said, "Precisely."

-35-

The days lengthened as the starship sped through Human Space. Ludendorff and Dana spent an inordinate amount of time together in the laboratory. At times, Galyan aided them.

Meanwhile, Maddox prowled the corridors, speaking to his crew, reassuring them and judging their morale. He knew they were going to have to perform miracles if they were going to get into the null region, board the Destroyers, power them up, flee through the white light ahead of the Ska and make sure nothing evil from the Nameless Ones remained aboard the Destroyers.

Riker spent more and more time alone. Maddox decided that was bad for the sergeant. He thus ordered Riker to work out with Meta and him. The sergeant walked on a treadmill at those times. But at least he wasn't in his room, brooding.

One day, Riker confided in Maddox, "Sir, I think I'm the weak link in the plan."

"How's that, Sergeant?" Maddox had just racked his curl bar.

"The Ska in the null region will certainly be able to sense me. I have the feeling I'm going to be like a neon light on an otherwise dark night."

Riker seemed to wrestle with his next words, finally saying, "You should drop me off at one of the Commonwealth Worlds."

Maddox shook his head. "That seems like a foolish waste of an asset."

"I don't understand, sir."

"I think you do."

Riker stared at Maddox for a time. Finally, the sergeant shook his head. "You've already thought of that, haven't you, sir?"

"It's possible."

"In some manner, you plan to use me, or the thing in me, to trick the Ska."

"The idea has occurred to me." Maddox grew silent, finally adding, "Unfortunately, there might be some risk to you."

"I'd say there is going to be a lot of risk to me."

"Yes," Maddox said.

Riker turned away.

"If you'd rather not do this…" Maddox said.

"I'd rather not," Riker said.

"Oh," Maddox said, trying to keep the disappointment out of his voice.

"Except that I'm a member of Star Watch," Riker said. "That means something, doesn't it, sir?"

Maddox watched him, waiting.

"It means I have to put my money where my mouth is," Riker growled. "It means that if I have to sacrifice myself for the good of the Service—"

"It's not going to come to that," Maddox said.

"You hope."

"I'll do more than hope. I'll strive with all my might."

Riker nodded. "I understand. We're going balls out, aren't we, sir?"

"Yes," Maddox said. "You could say that."

***

Over the next three weeks, they received news a few times. The New Men appeared to have agreed to aid the Commonwealth. The rumor mill said an armada of star cruisers was heading directly for Earth.

"I wonder if that's wise," Meta said.

Maddox handed her a dish of ice cream. They were in the cafeteria, sitting with Andros Crank.

"From Earth, the Alliance Fleet will surely head to Tau Ceti or to whatever system the Swarm heads to after Tau Ceti," Maddox said. "There's another thing to consider. If the Swarm opens a second hyper-spatial tube, Earth is the obvious target. It's best to have all the ships in one location waiting for the enemy."

"I do not think the Swarm will use the tube again anytime soon," Andros said.

"What's the basis for your deduction?" Maddox asked.

"If I were the Swarm overlord," Andros said, "I'd already have created a second hyper-spatial tube directly into the Throne World System. It wouldn't matter if I just sent a few Swarm warships. The threat would keep the star cruisers guarding the Throne World instead of coming to help the Commonwealth. In that way, I would defeat my enemies in detail."

"That's sound strategic thinking," Maddox admitted. "However, the lack of a second hyper-spatial tube isn't conclusive evidence it doesn't or can't exist."

"No," Andros said, "but it should give our side more confidence. If the Alliance Fleet can destroy the Swarm Invasion Fleet, that should eliminate the problem."

"That's a big if," Maddox said.

"Can't we talk about something else?" Meta asked, removing the spoon from her mouth.

"Of course…" Maddox said.

***

The ancient Adok starship left Human Space once more, heading into the Beyond. Ludendorff spent more and more time on the bridge, rather than in the laboratory.

"We need more data," the professor told Maddox.

The captain sat at a sensor station, collecting information for the Patrol arm of Star Watch.

At the professor's words, Maddox looked up. "How much longer until we reach this ancient star system of yours?"

"You know as well as I how soon," Ludendorff said. "Seven more jumps should put us there."

"Should?" asked Maddox.

157

"My information regarding the star system is not precise. It was simply as close as I could come. If the system proves barren, there are three other possibilities we should check."

Maddox turned back to the sensor board, but looked back up at Ludendorff a second later. "Time is critical."

"Captain, I am a wunderkind. There is no denying that. Yet, I am human after all, even if altered into an incredible specimen of intellect."

Maddox stood up, motioning to a warrant officer. He let the woman take his place at the sensor station. Moving to the command chair, Maddox told Ludendorff, "Have you ever wondered why you were the chosen one?"

"Plenty of times," Ludendorff said. "Why? Does that bother you regarding yourself?"

Maddox shrugged and grew silent.

"It's a burden," Ludendorff said shortly. "I decided a long time ago that I might as well enjoy my difference from everyone else. Otherwise, I might go mad or become depressed. A person can't change who they are."

"I quite disagree," Maddox said. "One can mold himself into many different forms."

"Yes, I suppose we each have a range of possibilities." Ludendorff held out his arms with about a meter between his hands. "One man can move within this realm of possibilities." He moved his hands closer. "A different man can only go from this point to here. In the end, however, he is still the same man."

"It depends on how you define same."

"What's your point, my boy?" Ludendorff asked.

"I've been thinking about fate and responsibilities. We're on a quest like a knight of old."

"No knight ever went on quests like this," Ludendorff said. "Besides, those were fantasy stories."

"How do you know that?"

"Common sense tells me so," Ludendorff said.

"Yet, man is not always a sensible being. Sometimes he does the irrational. Some men kill themselves, some act cowardly, some are heroes—"

"Are you going to do something irrational, Captain?"

"I am."

Ludendorff stared at Maddox, finally nodding. "Yes, I suppose you have a point. We could be rushing to our doom, and doing it with considerable enthusiasm. We have no choice, though."

"Wrong," Maddox said. "We have the greatest starship ever built. We could flee to the other end of the galaxy if we wanted."

"Could you live with yourself if you did that?"

Maddox shook his head.

"So, you don't have a choice," Ludendorff said.

"There are always choices, Professor. Irrational thoughts batter at a man's mind. So do sacrificial thoughts and those of love. In the end, we have to decide which thoughts to follow."

"Love..." Ludendorff said. He glanced sidelong at the captain. "How does one know if he should marry the..." he trailed off.

"Here's an easy maxim to apply to your situation," Maddox said.

"Which situation? Creating a defense against the Ska's telepathy?"

"Rate how you would feel if another man slept with Dana," Maddox said. "If that would bother you, cherish her. If you would only be mildly annoyed, the two of you only have a short time left together. If you wouldn't care or maybe you'd even be glad of it, get rid of the woman immediately."

"I'd kill such a man," Ludendorff said.

"Now that wasn't so hard to figure out, was it?" Maddox asked.

Ludendorff stared at the captain, then finally turned away, saying, "Bah! That's an emotionalist system."

"Correct."

"I'm a man of intellect."

"Part of you is. Clearly, you are also a man of great emotion. Your endless bragging proves it."

"Is it bragging if it's the truth?"

"I could easily defeat you in hand to hand combat," Maddox said.

159

Ludendorff rubbed his chin until he grinned at Maddox. "Who would believe that a child in terms of experience could teach the master a lesson? It is amazing, and instructive. Good day, Captain. I must return to the laboratory."

Maddox grinned to himself as the professor exited the bridge. Soon thereafter, the captain focused on the present star system. A few more jumps and they would reach the system of yet another ancient race.

They weren't going to refight the ancient war, but they might be able to use the tools or the information gleaned from that time in order to help save the human race from ending its short time in the galaxy.

-36-

Fifty-two hours later, Maddox stood on the bridge, viewing the burnt cinders of what had once been a planet.

Masses of debris circled the largest central piece. The debris was composed of igneous rock—the world's former crust—and iron and magnesium rock—the former mantle—and iron chunks—the once molten core of the planet. Only the solid iron core of the planet remained: the locus of the gravitational force that locked the debris around it.

"This is frightening," Valerie said from her station.

"What kind of weapon did this?" Maddox asked.

"Nothing we own," the lieutenant said. "Nothing we even know of."

Ludendorff stood to the side. The professor kept shaking his head. "We must check the other planets for artifacts," he said.

Maddox looked up. He had his doubts about the utility of checking the other planets, but since they were here, they might as well look.

Thirty-four hours later, it was clear that whoever had destroyed the once Earth-like planet had also burned down any evidence of the ancient alien race's existence elsewhere in the system.

"I must conclude that a fierce emotion motivated the destroyers of this system," Ludendorff said. He regarded the others. "We must extend our search to the other nearby star systems."

161

"I disagree," Maddox said.

"We need answers," Ludendorff declared.

"Perhaps, but we're also running out of time. Not only do we have to retrieve the Destroyers, but we have to get them running and reach Earth before the Swarm Fleet arrives."

"This isn't the time to quit, Captain."

"No one is quitting," Maddox said. "This is the time for a reality check. We're not going to find more data regarding your ancient race. We have what we have."

"But that's not enough," Ludendorff said.

"It has to be enough. We're not going to get more. That means we have to use what we have."

"It's precious little."

"Nevertheless, it is what we have. Figure out how to make a mind shield, Professor. That's up to Dana and you."

Ludendorff shook his head. "You're asking too much of us."

"You're right," Maddox said. "I'm counting on the great Professor Ludendorff to pull another rabbit out of his hat."

"Saying that in a stirring way won't change the grim situation," Ludendorff said moodily.

"I'm not hoping to change it."

"Yes," Ludendorff said with a sigh. "I am well aware of what you want to change: you hope to pump me full of enthusiasm so I'll work harder and harder—"

"Quit telling me about it," Maddox said, interrupting. "You know that actions speak louder than words. Well, start shouting."

Ludendorff stared at Maddox.

The captain turned to the navigator. "Set a course for the Ezwal System. We'll use the Einstein-Rosen Bridge like we did last time. We made it past the black hole and gained nearly four hundred light-years in a swoop. Let's hope there's no Rull Juggernaut waiting for us on the other end this time."

"I have a better solution," Ludendorff said. "Forget about the Ska, the null region and the Destroyers. Let's go to Sind II and collect the Juggernauts. They can take the place of a Destroyer."

Maddox nodded curtly. "You've just outlined Plan B. That should relieve some of the pressure from you to produce Plan A. Yet, I have to admit, Plan A has a much higher chance of giving us victory over the Swarm."

"No pressure?" Ludendorff asked.

"Maybe a little," Maddox admitted. "Is there anything else?"

"What are you talking about?"

"Why aren't you in the lab manufacturing our miracle?"

"I have to have the brainwave first," Ludendorff said.

"Start experimenting. If that doesn't work, ask Andros Crank to assist you. The Kai-Kaus have a different way of looking at these things. That may be just the impetus you need."

Ludendorff pursed his lips, nodding after a moment. "You may have a point." The professor made a half salute, turned and headed for the exit.

-37-

As *Victory* raced through the Laumer Points and used its star drive to jump to strategically placed wormholes, Ludendorff, Dana, Galyan and Andros Crank strove tirelessly to resolve several pressing dilemmas. Yet, it was Valerie who came up with the idea of how to reenter the null region.

The professor explained on the bridge to Maddox how difficult it would be to find a place no one had ever spotted before.

"Think about it," Ludendorff said. "We don't know how the Builders created a null region. We don't even know what a null region is. Where does it belong? Supposedly, the Ska came from a different dimension. But what does that mean? What was the mechanism of travel? What—"

"You were talking about the Builders creating the null region," Maddox said.

"I hate to admit it," Ludendorff said. "But I'm mentally exhausted. I've been striving for weeks on end, my boy. In the final analysis, that drains even the Methuselah Man."

"I would think it would be *more* draining on you than on others," Maddox said.

Ludendorff waved that aside. "I'm going to let the insult pass. I simply don't care anymore."

"There was no insult intended."

"I certainly took it that way," the professor said. "You're implying I have less energy than the others do."

"Of course," Maddox said. "Isn't that obvious?"

"Now I am angered, sir. My energy outdoes others by many magnitudes. It is one of the reasons I survive year in and year out."

"You're claiming normal aging doesn't affect you?"

"Explain your meaning."

Maddox shrugged. "A child is always moving because he has boundless energy, while an old man just wants to sit still. A child can do a thing over and over again because of his great zeal. The older we get, the more easily we're bored. That is due to a lack of energy. Thus, logically, as a Methuselah Man, you must have less energy than the rest of us."

"What about your supposed Creator, then?" Ludendorff asked. "He must be the oldest of all. Is God motionless?"

"Maybe God has the zest and energy of a newborn child. Maybe that's what it means to be the Creator, and why He created in such magnificent abundance. Even on Earth we don't have one or two species of birds, we have tens of thousands, showing the creative exuberance of the Creator and thus His boundless energy."

Ludendorff scratched his cheek. "I'll say this, Captain. It is an interesting hypothesis. I wonder if I could incorporate it in our scheme to thwart the Ska." The professor shrugged a moment later.

"It doesn't help us solve the problem of finding the null region," Maddox said. "Nothing gets done if we can't find it."

"I think I can find the null region," Valerie said, piping in from her station.

Ludendorff whirled around. "You?" he asked. "You must be joking. How are you going to find a place no one had ever seen before Maddox fell into it?"

"Easily," Valerie said. "I thought of it some time ago, but I thought that must be too easy. Yet, I haven't heard any of you suggesting the method."

"Please," Ludendorff said. "Don't hold me in suspense. What is your glorious technological breakthrough?"

"None at all," Valerie said. "I used to substitute-teach math classes before I entered the Space Academy. It was how I made extra money."

"How utterly fascinating," Ludendorff declared while rolling his eyes at Maddox.

"If you don't want me to explain it…" Valerie said.

"No, no, please continue," the professor said. "You substitute-taught math…"

"I substitute-taught many classes," Valerie said. "This just happens to explain how I figured out our present problem. Kids were always asking for help on their algebra and geometry assignments. Sometimes, I remembered how to use the correct formulas they were working on. Sometimes, I'd already forgotten. Those times, I used simple logic to figure out the right mathematical answer. That seldom helped the student, though. They just wanted to know the method the teacher had taught them."

"What does any of that have to do with the null region?" Ludendorff asked.

"We don't have to *find* the region," Valerie said. "We just have to get into it."

Ludendorff stared at her. He didn't seem mocking anymore. Instead—his eyes widened abruptly.

"I guess you see it now, too," Valerie said.

Ludendorff turned to Maddox. "I can't believe this. It's so easy a child could figure it out."

"But a child didn't," Valerie said. "I did. When the great and mighty—"

"Forget about that," Ludendorff said in a rush of excitement. "That was inspired thinking on your part, Lieutenant."

Valerie allowed herself a small smile.

"Yes," Ludendorff said. "Now, I can go back to figuring out how to negate the Ska's telepathic powers."

"Before you do any of that," Maddox said, "I want to know how we're going to enter the null region."

"Should I tell him?" Ludendorff asked Valerie.

The lieutenant nodded.

"We duplicate the former situation," Ludendorff told Maddox.

"We don't have a Juggernaut to hold us back with a tractor beam," Maddox said.

166

Ludendorff turned to Valerie, "Am I correct in assuming that you have the starship's exact coordinates last voyage before it jumped into the null region?"

"Yes," Valerie said.

Ludendorff spread his hands in Maddox's direction. "Do you finally see?"

"Oh…" Maddox said. "Yes."

"Good," Ludendorff said. He hurried off the bridge, no doubt back to the laboratory.

Valerie turned back to her comm board. A few moments later, she became aware of someone standing nearby. She looked up to see Maddox frowning down at her.

"Sir?" she asked.

Maddox cleared his throat. "What is the method?" he asked quietly.

"What method is that, sir?" she asked.

"Of entering the null region."

She realized in that moment that the captain had not yet figured it out. With as straight a face as possible, she explained. "We go to the exact location *Victory* was before when the Juggernaut attempted to lock onto us with its tractor beam. Then, we apply the same amount of power using a star drive as we did last time."

"We'll simply jump normally as we tried to do last time?" Maddox asked, perplexed.

"No," Valerie said, "as a tractor beam will lock us in place."

"Where do you and Ludendorff hope to find another Juggernaut?"

"We won't need one," she said.

"Lieutenant," Maddox warned.

Valerie relented. "We'll use *our* tractor beam, sir. We'll latch onto something and anchor ourselves. Once we've reached the same stress level as last time, we'll cut the tractor beam and hopefully launch ourselves into the null region."

"Ah…" Maddox said. "That *is* simple and elegant. You think Ludendorff understands the plan?"

"I do, sir."

Maddox rubbed his chin as he moved back to his captain's chair. He glanced at her—

Valerie hurriedly looked down at her board. She glanced sidelong at him a moment later. The captain was still rubbing his chin.

Valerie smiled. She might not be a genetic superwoman. She might not be able to live forever like a Methuselah Man, but this time, she'd figured out the problem before anyone else could. That made her feel more than good. It made her feel important.

-38-

Halfway to the Ezwal System, Ludendorff, Dana and Andros Crank were arguing in the laboratory. They could not find a method to stop something when they didn't know how it worked.

"If I could probe more deeply into Riker, I might be able to learn more," Dana said.

"Why don't you do just that?" Ludendorff asked.

"The captain won't approve it," Dana said.

"Then we have to convince him of the urgency—"

"I've tried," Dana said. "He won't budge. He's worried the sergeant won't recover from the process next time."

"We must risk it anyway," Ludendorff said. "By what method or property does a Ska communicate with a person?"

"If we cannot determine the method," Andros said, "maybe we should do what you figured out in the first place?"

Ludendorff nodded encouragingly.

"You realized we couldn't kill the Ska," Andros said, "but maybe we could block its mind power."

"If that's the right way to say it," Ludendorff said.

"No," Andros said. "Instead of stopping its mind power, we block it in a different manner altogether."

"How?" Ludendorff and Dana asked together.

"Put earphones on a man and play loud music," Andros said. "Instead of listening to the Ska, the person will be too busy listening to his music."

Ludendorff laughed. "Yes. That might work under certain circumstances. It's an interesting idea. Yet the music will work better on a less disciplined person. The disciplined person would be better able to ignore the music and thereby hear and obey the Ska."

"Maybe the disciplined person could ignore the Ska's power altogether," Andros said.

"I'm the likeliest candidate then," Ludendorff said.

"The second likeliest candidate," Dana amended.

"Don't tell me you think Maddox is better dis—"

"Yes!" Dana said. "I suspect he is the most disciplined. That might also explain why the Ska failed to thwart him the first time *Victory* went into the null region."

"That's good for another reason," Andros said. "We still don't know why the null region drains energy, and thus we have failed to develop a counter. The captain remained awake last time when the rest of us fell asleep. Thus, it is good that the captain can best resist the Ska."

"We need to give our side better odds than that," Ludendorff said. "I like your idea, Chief Technician, because at least it's a method. But we must find something more certain. We know the Ska was sleepy last time, last to the party, so to speak. What do we do if the Ska is early this time?"

Andros opened his mouth before closing it without saying a word.

Dana did the same a few minutes later.

Finally, Ludendorff snapped his fingers. "I have an idea. It's imperfect. But it extrapolates from your music-listening idea. The key to the idea is having something so the bearer or wearer ignores the Ska. Maybe we should drug the selected people. Given the right drugs, a person often isn't scared when they should be."

"A drugged person would also make stupid decisions," Dana said.

"That is one of the drawbacks, of course," Ludendorff said.

"Still..." Dana said.

"It is a good extrapolation," Andros said.

"Are Kai-Kaus always this agreeable?" Ludendorff asked.

170

"No. We learned to tell the truth, because only the continued and stark truth kept us alive as we battled the Swarm."

Andros Crank referred to the Builder Dyson Sphere, where a Builder had experimented with Swarm and humans in an enclosed environment.

Ludendorff acknowledged the answer with a grunt. "So far, our answers are substitutes for solid tech edges."

"We may not find one of those," Dana said. "That's why we're trying to steal Nameless Ones' technology in the first place."

"True," Ludendorff said.

At that point, klaxons began to blare.

Looking up, Dana asked, "Now what has gone wrong?"

-39-

On the bridge, Captain Maddox sat forward on the command chair. They had just completed what had become a routine star-drive jump.

By this time, they had refined the process so no one felt any Jump Lag. That included the equipment. It meant that Valerie, Galyan and other sensor operators could begin scanning the moment the starship arrived at its new destination.

This time, Galyan had been operating the ship's scanners.

The system had a G-class star with two terrestrial planets in the inner system and one super-Jupiter in what would have been the trans-Neptunian region in the Solar System. The system had two valuable Laumer Points, one near the star and the other near the super-Jupiter gas giant. *Victory* had appeared at a Mercury orbital-like distance from the system star. That was extremely near. This was an unusual Laumer Point because it shifted its position in an orbital manner like a planet. Today, the Laumer Point was on the other side of the star from *Victory*.

"I have double-checked my findings, sir," Galyan said.

On the main screen, Maddox examined a faint image of a saucer-shaped starship. The vessel was halfway between the star and *Victory*.

"There are more starships present," Galyan said.

"Put them on the screen," Maddox said.

172

Two more faint images appeared on the main screen. The three were equally spaced, almost covering the breadth of this side of the star.

"Have you determined their exact type?" Maddox asked.

"Affirmative," Galyan said. "They are regular Spacer vessels."

"Cloaked, I presume," Maddox said.

"I am using my advanced Adok methods to pierce their cloaking."

"Have they spotted us yet?"

"I believe so, sir."

"Here's the big one," Maddox said. "Are they waiting for us?"

"I am straining to scan near and around the star," Galyan said. "By the pitch of your voice, you seem to already suspect what I do."

"The Visionary is here?" asked Maddox.

"Affirmative, sir," Galyan said.

"Should we hail them?" Valerie asked.

Maddox glanced at the lieutenant with the hint of a frown. He did not like his crew second-guessing him. The lieutenant should know that by now.

"I'm sorry, sir," Valerie said.

After a moment's hesitation, Maddox waved that aside as if it didn't matter. He did it for her morale. He didn't like doing it, but the crew had become increasingly tense the longer they traveled.

"Do not hail them yet," Maddox said. "Let's see what they do."

"I have detected signals, sir," Galyan said. "The last ship to our right has sent a signal. I suggest it is to another starship we cannot see that is also positioned near the star."

"May I ask a question?" Valerie asked.

Maddox suspected he already knew what she wanted to know. He said, "I want to see who shows up before we hail anyone."

"Oh," she said. "Thank you, sir."

Maddox nodded.

"It is my turn to query you," Galyan said.

173

"I don't know," Maddox told the AI.

"You don't know if I can ask you?" Galyan asked.

"No," Maddox said. "I don't know how the Visionary knew we would come to this system."

"How did you guess my question, sir?"

"Pure genius on my part," Maddox said.

"That is a Ludendorff-style response, sir. It is not your typical Maddox response."

"Sometimes it pays to try another person's style," Maddox said. "Maybe it's effective."

"Are you suggesting I attempt Ludendorff-style answers?"

"No," Maddox said.

"That is a relief, sir," Galyan said. "According to my studies, humans react more positively to humble speech. They resist arrogant or boastful talk."

"Are you continuing to scan, Galyan?"

"Affirmative, sir."

As Maddox watched the screen, more faint images of starships came around the star.

"Galyan, I want high-intensity scans to our sides and rear," Maddox said. "For this to work, the Spacers need someone trying to dampen our star drive so we can't escape."

"I am scanning—sir," Galyan said. "There are three odd vessels moving in behind us."

"Switch main screen view," Maddox said.

The star and the faint images vanished. In their place were faint flatter saucer-shaped vessels. They seemed to glide toward them.

"Are they emitting any rays at us?" Maddox asked.

"Affirmative, sir," Galyan said. "As you foresaw, they are beaming dampening rays. I do not think we can use the star drive until they desist."

"Target the nearest inhibiting ship," Maddox said. "Power up the disrupter and neutron cannons."

"Sir," Valerie said. "The Spacers are hailing us. Sir," she said, with surprise. "The Visionary wishes to speak to you."

"Put her on," Maddox said. "But before you do—Galyan, the minute the disruptor cannon is ready, begin destroying the inhibiting vessels coming in cloaked behind us."

"Affirmative," Galyan said.

Maddox nodded to Valerie.

A second later, the Visionary appeared on one side of a split-screen in her usual polar bear robe, goggles and other paraphernalia.

"Greetings, Captain," she said in her hoarse voice. "I suppose you are surprised to meet us here."

"Yes and no," Maddox said.

"Let me get to the point," the Visionary said. "Since we last met, I have gathered reinforcements. I now want to aid the Alliance Fleet and stop the Swarm invasion."

"Really?"

"I have taken the liberty—"

The Visionary stopped talking as the disrupter cannon fired. The beam reached across the void, striking the flat saucer-shaped cloaked vessel behind *Victory*. The beam burned against the shield, causing a quick collapse. Seconds later, the disrupter beam began to chew through the alloy hull.

"What are you doing?" the Visionary shouted. "We come in peace."

Maddox waited until the disruptor beam caused the inhibitor vessel to explode spectacularly.

"Target the next one, Galyan," Maddox said.

"At once, sir," the holoimage said.

"Are you attempting to sabotage us?" the Visionary asked in a demanding tone. "We have come in peace."

"Do peaceful vessels beam dampener rays on another ship's jump drive?" Maddox asked.

The Visionary only hesitated a second. "I wanted to speak to you," she said. "They're only to make sure you heard my message."

The disruptor and neutron cannons fired at the second inhibitor vessel. This one blew up faster than the last one.

"This is an outrage," the Visionary shouted. "You are deliberately sabotaging a Spacer-Commonwealth union."

"You seem to think I'm an idiot," Maddox said. "You think I'll fall for the easiest lies. I don't think so, Visionary. Remember, you yourself named me *di-far*."

175

"I am sorry to interrupt, sir," Galyan said. "But what do you want me to do with the last inhibitor vessel?"

"Destroy it at once," Maddox said.

"You are killing Spacers, Captain," the Visionary said.

"That is true," Maddox said.

"You're a butcher, a murderer."

"A patriot of the human race," Maddox said.

"The last vessel is no longer aiming dampening rays at you," the Visionary said.

"Thank you," Maddox said.

"You must let it survive."

"Sir?" asked Galyan.

Maddox stared at the Visionary's goggles as he said, "Destroy it at once, Galyan."

"No!" the Visionary shouted. "My son is on that ship."

Maddox's face became even calmer than before. "I take no delight in his death, Visionary. But you have pitted yourself against me. You believe I'm a dupe. Next time, maybe you won't put Spacers in harm's way."

"Next time, you die," she hissed. "I will hound you until the end of time. You can flee to the other end of the galaxy, but I will kill you, Captain Maddox."

The twin cannons burned hot against the last inhibitor vessel. Like the others, it exploded in a savage blast.

By this point, twenty-eight Spacer vessels had swung around the star. More kept coming. Each of them strained as they accelerated at *Victory*.

Maddox stared at the Spacer witch on the screen. He stood. He gave a faint head bow and turned to Keith. "Take us out of here, Mr. Maker."

"Aye, aye, sir," Keith said.

Seconds later, *Victory* jumped again, heading out of the trap the Visionary had set for it.

-40-

The next few jumps were tense. Each time the starship arrived at the next destination, Galyan, Valerie or the warrant officer scanned intently.

There were arguments regarding the source of the Visionary's ability. Ludendorff believed the old woman had access to something like the Builder Scanner Star Watch now possessed.

"Maybe it's simpler than that," Maddox replied. "Maybe Star Watch routinely checks on our progress with the new scanner. They see where we're headed, and a Spacer spy using a Builder communicator informs the Visionary. What could be easier?"

"Brigadier O'Hara has surely flushed out all the spies by now," Meta said.

The three of them sat in the dim lounge.

"I doubt it," Maddox said. "Certainly O'Hara has rid Earth of many enemy spies, but not all."

"What other kind are there except enemy spies?" Ludendorff asked.

Maddox fell silent.

Soon, Ludendorff got up and took his leave.

Meta put a hand on Maddox's hand. "You shouldn't let him get you angry."

"I know," Maddox said. "But I dislike people interrupting me."

"He didn't," Meta said. "But you interrupt others all the time."

"Only when necessary."

"That's not always the case."

Maddox shrugged. "This voyage is different from the others. There's more at stake. We're also bouncing around more, and staying out longer. Stress is building."

"Because we have a nearly impossible assignment," Meta said.

Maddox stared out of a viewing port at the passing stars. "I don't want to return to the null region. It was so strange last time. Being in the dark, being alone except for Galyan, making that fantastic jump to the Sind System—"

Meta's grip tightened on his hand.

"There's more going on than I understand," Maddox said. "There seems to be a hidden player. Is a Builder behind this?"

"Why doesn't he come out and say so?"

Maddox shook his head. "I have no idea. This Ska...it's terrifying. I'm not used to that kind of...problem."

"We've faced plenty of terrifying problems in the past."

"Desperate problems," Maddox said. "Not ones that could sear a man's soul."

"You're a strange man, Maddox. You seem so practical and often so rational. Yet, you worry about cosmic issues."

"Issues of the soul," Maddox said.

"Who would have ever taken Captain Maddox as a metaphysical person?"

"It's far from that," Maddox said. "I'm religious in nature, as I know there is more than I can see and feel. I want to know more, and why, and how, and—"

Meta got up, moving closer to him. "You know what I wonder?"

Maddox shook his head.

Meta climbed up into his chair, straddling his lap. "I want to know what you taste like." Meta grabbed his face and kissed him passionately.

Maddox laughed. He grasped Meta around her bottom and lurched up to his feet.

"What are you doing?" she giggled.

178

Maddox shifted her so he carried her in his arms. "I'm taking you to my quarters. Do you have any objections?"

"I do," she said.

"That's too bad," he said. "For you." Maddox continued striding to his quarters, still carrying Meta in his arms. She snuggled against him, loving it.

***

Finally, the starship reached the Ezwal System with its white dwarf star. The star was a little bigger than the Earth but had the mass of Earth's Sun. The star was extremely dense, composed of electron-degenerate matter. It no longer generated heat through fusion, but radiated away its stored thermal energy.

The system lacked planets, but possessed a black hole. Near the black hole was a Laumer Point. This one led through an Einstein-Rosen bridge three hundred and eighty-four light-years long.

As per the last few jumps, Galyan scanned relentlessly for signs of cloaked Spacer ships.

"The system seems clear," Galyan said.

"Let us proceed, Mr. Maker," Maddox said.

Victory headed for the black hole. Soon enough, the heavy gravitational force tried to pull them into the event horizon. The ancient Adok starship used its antimatter engines to aim for the ER bridge entrance. It was a struggle, but finally, *Victory* entered the bridge—and came out on the other side, three hundred and eighty light-years away. The new system had a cool blue star and five terrestrial planets. There were no gas giants. There were no Juggernauts waiting, either.

"Start scanning, Galyan," Maddox said.

The AI made its most thorough scan yet. "Nothing to report, sir."

"Look for any anomaly you can find. Report the slightest deviation."

"You want me to find the null region, sir?"

"If you can, Galyan, if you can."

After two hours of relentless scanning, Maddox let Galyan stop. There was no evidence of a null region or a way to enter a null region.

Maddox called a briefing.

Ludendorff, Dana and Andros Crank had come up with a possibility for functioning while in the null region. It was a photon energy suit.

"It took some doing," the professor said, growing expansive. "I doubt I could have accomplished the feat without Andros's exceedingly practical turn of mind. He is the master artificer, par excellence."

Andros blushed and stared down at his hands, folded together on the conference table.

"In any case," Ludendorff continued. "The suits might allow the wearer a greater length of time against the null region's power drain. Unfortunately, constructing the suits has proven difficult. There are four of them so far." The professor turned to Maddox. "You will have to decide who should wear the photon suits."

Maddox nodded.

"The Ska is another matter," the professor said. "Doctor, if you would care to explain?"

Dana smiled wryly. "We didn't have as great a breakthrough against the Ska. Instead, we have a way, we hope, that works around the problem. Maybe that's why the professor is letting me explain it."

"Nonsense," Ludendorff said under his breath.

"Our problem was clear," Dana said. "How can we keep the Ska from terrifying said people and/or controlling them? We thought at first that wearing headphones, listening to music, could help. The person would listen to the music instead of the Ska. In time, we refined the process. Why bother with music? The wearer could turn it off if the Ska got to him. The direction of the idea was correct, though."

Dana scanned the others. "We have produced a drug, a happy pill, if you will. The drug will induce euphoria, which should counteract whatever the Ska does to terrify. Here is where we're making a guess. We think the Ska uses the terrifying process to control the person. But, if the person cannot be terrified, theoretically, the Ska cannot control him."

"Will the happy pill negatively influence a person's judgment?" Maddox asked.

"Yes," Dana said.

"It's a tradeoff," Ludendorff said.

Dana gestured toward the professor. "Under the circumstances, that's the best we can do."

Maddox turned to Ludendorff. "Do you think four people can power up the Destroyer and pilot it out of the null region?"

Ludendorff shook his head. "You'll have to drag it out with *Victory's* tractor beam."

"Drag a fifty-kilometer-long vessel with our comparatively tiny ship?" Maddox asked.

"Once we're out of the null region, we can scour the Destroyer and clean it out if we have to," Ludendorff said.

"None of this is acting swiftly," the captain said. "Remember? That's how we're supposed to counteract the Ska, right?"

"We realize that," the professor said, "but this is the best we've been able to achieve."

Maddox drummed his fingers on the table. "It might take two trips to drag out two Destroyers."

"That is a distinct possibility," Ludendorff said.

"We will, of course, have pulled out the Ska by that time," Maddox said.

"We have a theory regarding the null region and the Ska," Ludendorff said. "The theory isn't by any means certain, but the possibility exists." Ludendorff took a deep breath. "Maybe the bright light you saw before wasn't an exit for the Ska. Maybe the Builders created the exit so only they—or any material being—could come into and leave the null region."

"That's illogical," Maddox said. "The ego-fragment made it out of the null region."

"The ego-fragment is what gave us the first clue," Ludendorff said. "According to Riker's memories of the Ska, the entity burned away most of its essence trying to leave."

"It didn't have a bright exit at that time," Maddox said.

"I have come to believe there was a residue exit, so to speak, a 'shadow' of the bright exit."

Maddox appeared perplexed.

"It is a complex theory, to be sure," Ludendorff said. "Yet, there is reason for believing this."

"I'm dubious," Maddox said.

"And I as well," Galyan added.

"Nevertheless," Ludendorff said, "that is my belief."

Silence filled the room.

Maddox stirred. "You still haven't told us how we can induce or create the bright exit."

"I have no idea how to do that," Ludendorff said. "But again, I believe the bright light was a Builder-constructed... I suppose 'reflex' is the best word I can use to describe what I'm thinking. I believe the bright exit appears immediately after, or shortly after, one enters the null region."

"Why?" asked Maddox.

"A built-in fail-safe for a Builder researcher," Ludendorff said.

Maddox studied the professor. "Why do I get the feeling you're hiding some of what you know?"

Ludendorff shrugged—it seemed a trifle uneasily.

"Am I wrong?" Maddox asked.

"Yes," Ludendorff said a little too quickly.

Maddox drummed his fingers on the table. He looked around. "Are there any more questions?"

No one spoke.

"Lieutenant Noonan," Maddox said. "What object do we aim our tractor beam at in order to build up...power for a null-space jump?"

"The moon of the second planet will do," Valerie said. "Unfortunately, we'll have to wait eight days until it's near enough to the correct location."

"That long?" asked Maddox.

"No, no," Ludendorff said. "In this, we have gotten lucky. Eight days is nothing."

"Not if the Visionary is still looking for us and shows up in force," Maddox said.

"Then let us hope she doesn't arrive within the next eight days," Ludendorff said.

-41-

The days passed quickly as Ludendorff, Andros and Galyan built a photon convertor for the starship's engine room. Ludendorff explained it to Maddox as the captain looked in on what they did.

The convertor area was beside the main engine compartments. Huge domelike machines glowed as photonic pulses struck the inner surface, causing the area to glow brighter.

"The photons are bouncing in there like billiard balls," Ludendorff said. "In reality, the domes will act like batteries in the null region." The professor thought about what he'd said. "We *hope* they act like batteries. I can't promise you they'll work."

"If they don't," Maddox asked, "how will we power the tractor beam?"

Ludendorff shook his head. "We won't."

"Then, the voyage will have been for naught."

"Yes," Ludendorff agreed.

"Let's hope your miraculous batteries work then."

"I quite agree, Captain. Now, unless there something else you need, I must get back to work."

Maddox indicated the professor should go. He watched them toil for a time. Finally, the captain took his leave.

***

Two days later, Maddox sat in his quarters. He'd decided to make his final decision on the photon suits. They were bulky

184

and unwieldy, but they might allow a person to think and act normally while in the null region. Ludendorff, Andros and he would each use a suit. The last suit was where Maddox had a hard time deciding. He could give one to Dana or Valerie.

Dana understood more and had a quick mind. Yet, she'd undergone excessive mental trauma lately. Maybe the added stress would be too much for her. Valerie had shown herself to be clever, with practical solutions to tough problems.

The hatch opened and Meta came in. "Oh," she said. "Am I disturbing you?"

"No, no," Maddox said. He turned his chair and sat back. "I'm having trouble making my last choice for the photon suit." He gave Meta his reasoning for the two choices.

"I think you're forgetting something critical," Meta said.

Maddox raised his eyebrows.

"Each has excellent qualities. But that isn't the issue. What kind of judgment will they have while drugged?"

Maddox's eyes brightened. "That's an excellent point." He turned back to his desk, staring at the names. Thus, he didn't hear Meta leave.

How would Dana or Valerie act while drugged? He needed the one who could do her job while heavily under the influence.

"I've forgotten one other person." Maddox wrote *Keith* onto the paper.

He might need the best pilot in the best possible shape in order to pull this off. Keith was the best pilot, and he used to be a drunkard. As a drunkard, Keith must have learned how to act semi-normally while deeply under the influence. He might act the most normally while under the happy pill, if experience could help a person cope while drugged.

Maddox stared at the names for a long moment before finally picking up his pen and circling Keith's name. The captain had chosen the fourth member of the null region team.

***

Given the latest insight, Maddox had Dana test each of them. She injected them with the drug and gave them problems to solve to determine what they could or could not do.

185

"I'm not sure I agree with your method," the professor told Maddox later.

They were in a testing area. It looked more like a child's playpen with mats, balls, giant building cubes and other items.

Maddox waited. His head still ached after having taken the drug.

"The point of the drug is to dull the person to the Ska," Ludendorff said. "If a person becomes too used to the drug, that might weaken his protection against the telepathic attacks."

"I have to know if a person can function while drugged," Maddox said.

"I realize that—"

"And we have to learn to act while drugged."

"Yes, yes," the professor said. "I don't need you to explain the situation. I'm simply saying there is a risk to your 'training', if we can call it that."

"Do you have a better idea?"

"Not yet," Ludendorff hedged.

Maddox said no more, and finally Ludendorff took his leave.

-42-

The selected terrestrial planet swung around the cool star. As it did so, its biggest moon orbited in a highly elliptical manner. Finally, the system bodies aligned as closely as they were going to.

Lieutenant Noonan fed the coordinates into the flight computer. Galyan over-watched the process, correcting small anomalies.

Maddox sat in his command chair. A team of technicians waited with his photon suit.

"This won't be exact," Valerie said. "But it's the best we can do, sir."

Maddox felt jittery. He did not often feel this way. They were picking up the dice of fate. He could almost feel them rattling in his cupped hands.

Keith looked back at Maddox.

The captain felt the pressure build in his chest. Did humanity's fate rest on today's actions? If they failed to drag out at least one Destroyer, did that mean the Alliance Fleet would succumb to the incredible Swarm masses?

Why else are we doing this? Maddox asked himself.

"Let's get started, Lieutenant," he told Keith.

The Scotsman stood and turned to his bulky suit. It was golden colored with a massive square pack on the back. Tubes ran everywhere. The helmet was extra bulky, making it even heavier.

187

Maddox turned to his own photon suit. Techs opened seals, leaning the suit toward him.

"Sir," Galyan said. "I have just detected cloaked vessels."

"Where?" Maddox asked.

"At the distant edge of the star system," Galyan said.

"Can you tell their—?"

"They are Spacer craft," Galyan said. "I am detecting more of them. Sir, I believe they are the Visionary's ships."

Maddox studied the main screen, finally shaking his head. "Let's hope she's too late to do anything. Are you ready, Valerie?"

"Give the word, sir," she said.

"Start whenever you're ready," he said.

Valerie sat poised at her panel. The backup pilot sat at Keith's vacated spot.

While that happened, Maddox shoved his feet into the photon suit. He put his arms in next. The techs began to seal up the suit.

Maddox watched as they sealed up Keith. "Can you hear me, Lieutenant?"

"Loud and clear, sir," Keith said.

As they suited up and tested the comm units, Valerie, the pilot and Galyan used the tractor beam, locking onto the lunar surface.

"Now," Valerie said as she watched her panel, "turn on the star drive and wait. We'll attempt to jump out of here at the same coordinates as before."

Starship *Victory* began to strain, the jump process interrupted by the tractor beam.

"We're building up jump power," Valerie shouted.

At that moment, a saucer-shaped vessel appeared. Likely, it had used its own star drive to jump from the edge of the system to this point. Five more of the saucer-shaped vessels appeared after the first, one after another.

"Keep her steady," Valerie said.

"The Spacer ships are powering up their weapons," Galyan said. "They have targeted us."

"Steady," Valerie said. "We still have—"

The first Spacer beam struck the shield. The second Spacer vessel also opened fire.

"We must cut the tractor beam," Galyan said. "We are motionless, the perfect target."

"Wait," Valerie said. "We're not ready yet."

The other Spacer ships began firing. In unison, their beams struck the main shield. It turned red and began to go brown.

"They are powering up all their weapons," Galyan said. "I am cutting the tractor beam."

"It's too soon," Valerie said, as her hands flew over her panel. "I'm overriding you, Galyan."

"You are not, Valerie. This is for the best. I cannot allow *Victory's* destruction. I have—"

At that moment, as the Spacer beams turned the shield a deep brown color, the tractor beam snapped off. With the built up energy, the ancient Adok starship jumped.

-43-

Maddox stood on the bridge of Starship *Victory*. With the movement of his chin, he began the "happy-pill" process. Hypos hissed inside the photon suit and a cool feeling swept over his mind.

Around him on the bridge, the others slumped over. The lights dimmed, but they did not go out completely. Unlike last time, the main screen still worked. The captain stared at a vast expanse of darkness.

He laughed as the drug took hold of his emotions. Despite the Spacer interference at the last moment, the ancient Adok starship had slipped into the null region.

Maddox heard laughter over his helmet speakers. It took him time to understand. Finally, he turned slowly in the bulky photon suit. Keith Maker used his photon-suited gloved hands to lean against the piloting board. The second pilot lay on the floor, unconscious, while Keith laughed like a moron.

Maddox cleared his throat. He was going to admonish the ace for…for…Maddox smiled hugely. He felt good, better than he had for a long time. If he just stayed here…

A thought intruded. He needed to do something.

A dim holoimage stood before him, waving its ropy arms.

With his chin, Maddox opened the helmet's audio receiver.

"Captain Maddox?" Galyan asked.

"Yes…?" Maddox asked in a slow voice.

"You are drugged, sir. You are not thinking clearly."

That came as somewhat of a shock to Maddox. He was the world's clearest thinker. To imply… "Oh," the captain said, vaguely understanding what Galyan was saying. They had tested—

Maddox's will began to assert itself. It strove against the pleasant feelings of his contentedness. Keith was still laughing uncontrollably.

"We are farther from the brightness than last time," Galyan said.

Maddox forced himself to focus on the main screen. Yes, he could see a pin-dot of light in the darkness.

"I am detecting a mass, Captain," Galyan said. "I do believe I have found one of the Destroyers. Would you like me to pilot the ship there?"

"Yes," Maddox managed to say.

"It has begun," Galyan said. "May I say, sir, that I feel more energized than last time. The photon batteries are working, but we are draining them at a prodigious rate."

Maddox stared at the talking hologram. It really could babble on and on.

"Would you like me to power down unnecessary systems?" the AI asked.

"Yes," Maddox said.

"They are powering down, sir," Galyan said. "That should give us two to three times as much time as otherwise."

Maddox blinked, trying to process that.

"I believe this is working, sir," Galyan said.

Maddox still blinked, listening to Keith's moronic laughter, wondering if maybe he should join in. The crazy laughter sounded like fun.

***

The Elder Ska sluggishly began to realize that he was not alone. He had divided, and that had given him youthful zest and energy for a time. What he'd forgotten, though, was a split Ska needed time later to rest and recuperate. The Elder was finding it difficult to keep his awareness up.

He struggled to understand. This was interesting. The warm life forms came in a strangely energized vessel. How were they doing that? It was a miraculous technology.

"I must feed," the Elder Ska told himself. If he could move fast enough, he might roll onto the energized ship and feed off their induced terror.

Thirst and hunger began to accelerate the process of his awakening. The Elder Ska lusted to feed. He had not fed for eons, and had now become a shriveled weak thing compared to his former glory.

The Ska propelled himself toward the energized ship. He quickly discovered a problem. The vessel moved faster than he could. No matter how much he strove, they had the advantage. That galled and maddened the Elder. After all this time, after all—what was this? More hard material ships began to pop into existence in the null region. They were saucer-shaped vessels—and they held warm entities. Not only that, but the ships possessed almost no energy and little speed.

If the Elder Ska was capable of laughter, he would have chortled now. This was an amazing piece of luck. The saucer-shaped hard material objects popped into existence like food sacs, here to energize him.

The Elder Ska did not believe in a Creator, in anything greater than himself. He knew that he was self-made, evolved throughout the ages into this perfection of being. Nothing was superior to him. This was merely one of those fortunate accidents of life that helped instead of hurt.

The Elder Ska swerved aside from the energized ship. He headed for the saucer-shaped vessels, lusting to feast on terrified entities so he could warm himself with their emotions.

***

The Visionary tottered from her throne. She'd given the order to follow the desperado Captain Maddox. He'd caused the death of her son. He tried to free the Ska. She was willing to sacrifice herself to stop him. That included doing the same trick they had caught on the recorders.

Thus, she had been the first to pop into this strange realm. Because of their modifications, more Spacers remained awake than among the crew aboard *Victory*.

The Visionary turned suddenly. She felt something. The Visionary straightened and stood frozen in that position. She saw others on the bridge do the same. At that moment, something dripping with evil invaded her mind. The dark thing played on her worst fears.

"No, no, please…" the Visionary moaned. In her imagination, she saw wicked things that twisted her stomach with revulsion and terror.

"No!" she howled. "Stop! Stay out of my mind!"

The others awake on the bridge likewise began to shriek in unholy terror. Two curled up into fetal balls.

The Visionary began to tremble as she chewed on her lips. The dark visions burning through her thoughts became even more ghastly. She threw her head back, and her throat fully unlocked. At that point, the Visionary howled like a demented soul.

***

The Elder Ska boiled through the first Spacer ship like an alligator spinning over and over again as it tore off hunks of flesh from a drowned carcass. He warmed himself by their terror. It felt so glorious to heat up, to absorb what he needed to sustain his life force. This was grand. This was unbelievable.

He chomped, as it were, in fierce gluttony. Maybe he should have savored the creatures given to him like this. Instead, he increased the power of his telepathic invasion, inducing shock and death in some of the cases. He wasn't worried at the moment. He was going to tear through each morsel and energize himself. Then, he would deal with the fast, energized, hard material object over there and devour all of them one by one as well.

-44-

A strange lassitude had gripped the four photon-suited individuals aboard Starship *Victory*. Keith no longer laughed and Captain Maddox no longer contemplated his existence. Instead, Keith sat at his piloting board, staring ahead like a man in a trance.

Maddox sat in his command chair, looking at the viewing screen and the slowly growing Destroyer.

The brightness in the distance had grown from a pin-dot size to that of an eraser on the end of an old-fashioned pencil.

The main hatch to the bridge opened, and a photon-suited individual staggered through. No one turned to greet the newcomer. Maddox and Keith remained in their statuesque poses.

"Galyan," said Andros Crank.

The holoimage no longer appeared like a real person. He had his former shape, but he'd faded considerably. In places, one could even see through his "body."

The holoimage turned. "Hello, Andros."

"Are you..." Andros stumbled against a station, sitting down. For some reason, the Chief Technician found that funny. Andros didn't burst into moronic laughter, but a fit of the giggles instead.

If Galyan could have rolled his Adok eyes, this would have been the moment. He turned back to the main screen.

"We have a visitor on the bridge, Captain," Galyan said.

Maddox used his feet to slowly turn his chair until he faced Andros. He grinned in a loopy manner inside his bulky helmet.

"It's...there," Andros said, pointing at the main screen.

Maddox continued grinning.

A red light began to blink on a board. No one seemed to notice at first, not even Galyan.

Andros's giggles changed pitch.

That caused Maddox to tilt his helmet. "What is it?" he asked, with a note of laughter in his voice.

"The blinking light," Andros giggled. "It's...funny."

Maddox's helmet turned so he could take in the blinking light. That meant something, something that wasn't funny. With an effort of will, Maddox pushed himself to his feet. He did not stagger, although he did walk slowly. Finally, he leaned his gloved hands against the board and examined the blinking light.

"What's that?" he said.

No one answered.

"Galyan," Maddox said. "What's this light mean?"

The holoimage floated to the station. "Shall I change the screen's images, sir?"

Maddox couldn't figure that one out. So, he just nodded.

The images on the main screen changed. The bright light in the distance and the inert Destroyer vanished. In their place appeared—

Maddox's head swayed back. Those looked like Spacer vessels.

Galyan announced them as Spacers a second later.

It took an effort on the captain's part. A deeper part of him believed they'd received too strong a dose of the happy-pill. He could hardly think straight.

"Spacers followed us into the null region," Maddox said.

"That is the likeliest explanation," Galyan said.

Maddox almost frowned. "That could be a problem."

Galyan seemed to fade just a little more. Did that mean his computer system was slower?

"What's happening over there?" Maddox asked.

"Unknown, sir," Galyan said.

"Why aren't their ships moving?"

"Unknown, sir," Galyan said.

"What is the most reasonable explanation?"

"There are two equally reasonable explanations," Galyan said.

"What are they?"

"They lack any motive source," the half-faded Adok holoimage said, "or the Ska is among them feeding."

A grim sensation broke through Maddox's drugged state. For just a second, he thought to hear crunching bones and mangled flesh. He thought to hear terrible screaming and terror that devoured one's sanity.

He sought to understand what that meant. He tried to "hear" these things better. The drug swept over him, over his emotions. The thought of Spacer bones snapping and flesh grinding as their terror fed the Ska made him snort in a humorous manner. It would serve the Visionary right for having failed to help Star Watch at this critical time.

The snort turned into a genuine mocking laugh. The Visionary had thought to threaten him. Of course, the goggled fool must have seen their trick of entering this place and ordered the same. Now, they were feeding the Ska through their stark terror.

Maddox nodded a few times, chuckling in appreciation of the ironic joke. That humor kept him from feeling fear or terror. Without those sensations, it appeared the Ska had no way of communicating with him. Captain Maddox shrugged a few moments later. "She wanted to follow us in order to kill me, and instead, the Visionary is caught by some cosmic ancient horror. That's her problem, not mine. I have my own worries."

Maddox no longer looked up at the screen. "Galyan."

"Yes, Captain?"

"Show me the Destroyer. I don't care about the Spacers. And get ready to attach the tractor beam to the neutroium-hulled vessel."

"Yes, Captain," Galyan said. "We are almost in position to begin."

196

-45-

The Elder Ska rampaged through the nine Spacer vessels. He used his strengthened power to wake up those who'd lacked the fortitude to remain alert. He terrorized them, warming himself, waxing more powerful and repeating the process with greater malice and thus delight.

After a time, he felt satiated, almost bloated, although that was a temporary feeling. He could feed for generations after the starvation he'd known in this place. Yet, he now had enough strength to make a few observations and calculations.

The glowing exit had appeared again. Clearly, the hard body creatures had done that. He observed the first vessel, the one full of energy. It dragged one of his ancient vessels.

That was provocative vandalism, a deadly insult to his greatness.

The Elder Ska came to another quick conclusion. The ship dragged the great Destroyer toward the glowing exit. It was conceivable the beings were trying to drag his property from this realm.

Pulses of rage coursed through the Ska.

With his renewed power, he concentrated on the lively vessel. A profound shock struck him. The ship possessed a part of himself. That was inconceivable—a vast elation struck him. Of course, that must be from his other half's attempt to break out. The attempt had succeeded in part.

The Elder Ska gathered his resources and called to the former self-part. It responded by tearing loose from the hard body where it had resided and racing to him.

The Ska realized the Spacers weren't going anywhere, so he left their clustered ships and began to propel himself toward the clot of Ska-ness heading toward him.

The enemy ship slowly dragged his property. Thus, there was time for him to figure things out.

Soon enough, the zooming clot merged into the Elder Ska. Information flowed out of the clot. A panorama of sensations jolted the Elder Ska. Scenes, tastes, sights and smells slammed upon his ego. It was confusing. It was delightful. He luxuriated in this flood of knowledge. This was almost as joyful as warming himself on the terror. He had not sensed such things for millennia. The sensations caused an almost drunken-like state.

Time passed, more time and even—wait! What was this?

The Elder Ska struggled with these sounds, sights and smells, putting them into understandable categories. That formed logic strings. He could almost understand the enemy captain's—

Captain Maddox was his enemy. Captain Maddox, a mere vessel of flesh and blood, had definite plans to leave the null zone. The captain and his cursed energized ship had come to steal his prized vessels. Not only that, the foul hard energy creature planned to keep him trapped in this place forever.

The coursing rage built with bitter intensity. How dare such a creature attempt to thwart him? How dare a puny thing match wits against a god?

Nothing could kill the Elder Ska, at least nothing in this hard matter reality. In the old reality, it had been much different. In this present realm, he and his kind indeed were unconquerable gods.

The Ska realized two things. One, the puny vessel dragging his hard matter object neared the glowing exit. Two, he was going to warm himself off Captain Maddox's terror to such a degree that the flesh and blood thing would lose all logical coherence. He would drive Maddox into a raving lunatic mewling for an end to his pitiful existence.

198

-46-

Captain Maddox sat in his command chair, twirling around and around, smiling in an indulgent manner that would have surprised Brigadier O'Hara and the Lord High Admiral. The captain did not laugh aloud like Keith, who was banging a discordant open-handed tune on the piloting board.

Keith banged away, only occasionally making an adjustment as *Victory* strained to reach the bright light. Behind the starship followed the gigantic Destroyer.

The thing was fifty kilometers long with a vast open orifice. The neutroium hull was pitted and incredibly old. The neutrons had been smashed together to form a dense hull of amazing durability. Destroyers did not need electromagnetic shields because their hull armor was impervious to almost everything. Given such an armored hull, and because of the size, the Destroyer had vast mass.

Neither Maddox nor Keith marveled that their starship could tow the Destroyer in any manner whatsoever. Likely, it was due to some facet of the null region. Galyan understood the near impossibility of what they were doing, but he could not make the others understand.

Professor Ludendorff was in his laboratory spinning around and around as he sang "Ring around the Rosy" at the top of his voice. He had already become hoarse and he'd fallen plenty of times. That had brought on bouts of laughter. Each time, Ludendorff had gotten back up to begin twirling again.

Galyan realized it was all up to him. He just hoped the Elder Ska could not target him. As a computer, he should be safe. As a deified program of the former Driving Force Galyan, he was not so sure.

"Sir," Galyan said.

Maddox stopped whirling himself around in his command chair. His head moved from side to side. He had to work to focus. That seemed funny for some reason. It made his lips hurt because he was smiling so hugely.

"Sir, can you understand me?" Galyan asked.

"I can hardly see you," Maddox declared.

The Adok holoimage had become faint indeed, a bare outline of his former self.

"I am finding it difficult to exist, sir," Galyan said. "Both *Victory* and the Destroyer have gained a bit of momentum. Unsurprisingly, this realm drains momentum. Thus, there is little power left for me."

"A shame, a terrible shame," Maddox said with a snort.

"That isn't why I am worried, sir."

"You're worried, Galyan? I'm not worried."

"That's because your mind is fogged with the drug."

Maddox shrugged.

"Sir, something is approaching us. I have never detected its like. I think it may be the Ska."

"Let him come," Maddox said, slapping his chest. "Let him come."

"The Ska is our enemy."

"Galyan, I know very well—"

Maddox abruptly stopped talking. An evil sensation radiated at him. He could feel the edges of panic tickle his mind. It wasn't funny, and that was weird.

"Are you well, sir?" Galyan asked. "I am having difficulty seeing you. I sense a fog, a cloud of evil enshrouding you. Can you hear me, Captain Maddox?"

Maddox could not hear Galyan. The Elder Ska had reached the starship and encircled the one known as Captain Maddox. The Ska strained with his regained might to penetrate the happiness armoring the weak mind.

Maddox felt pressure. He did not snort with humor at the feeling. He did not use his feet to twirl around in his command chair. He no longer had any desire to do that. He had become like a happy drunk man suddenly and inexplicably sobered to a hard reality.

Maddox blinked inside his helmet. He tried to understand what this meant. It seemed terribly important to him that he gain understanding.

"Captain Maddox," Galyan shouted.

Maddox had become frozen, not in sleep, but in a titanic struggle between the Elder Ska and him. The thing sought to reach his fear. At the same time, Maddox clung to the drugged hilarity because he sensed with growing alarm that something hideously evil waited just beyond his understanding. If he should leave the happy place, he might well howl in terror for the rest of his miserable existence.

At that thought, something penetrated his consciousness.

"*Captain Maddox,*" a powerful entity boomed at him.

"Yes?" Maddox said tentatively.

"*You are a worm.*"

"What are you?"

"*I am a god. I am the Destroyer. You must bow before me, Worm.*"

Maddox blinked several times. The way the Ska said that…a wry grin slid onto the captain's lips.

"*It's not funny,*" the Ska said.

Now, *that* was funny. Maddox snorted to himself.

"*Snort at this, Worm.*"

A bolt of purified hatred struck the captain's mind. It was more than the happy pill could take. On the command chair, Captain Maddox cringed in sudden fright.

"*That is more like it, Worm. Now, you and I are going to have a talk.*"

Maddox cringed, and a wave of self-loathing struck him. He despised cringing in fear. A coward died a thousand times. Better, then, to bravely face a horror and die than to run and have it kill you a thousand times over by repeated whimpering.

"*That is wrong, Worm. Fear me. Fear this—*"

201

Horrors descended on the captain's mind. The fear of smothering to death, the fear of heights, of having your belly slit open with a razor, of speaking in public when you knew everyone would laugh at you. The terror of the stealthy step coming upon you in the dark forest, the fear of a lion springing to rend you to death, the fear—

Hundreds and thousands of fears beat against Captain Maddox. He did not stand like a lighthouse in a howling hurricane. He did not brave it like a stalwart soldier holding his shield and spear as a horde of raving berserkers hit the line. But he did resist like a man holding onto a tree root as the tornado tried to lift him into the air. He closed his eyes and shuffled his feet toward the stage where everyone he cared about would ridicule his lousy performance.

Maddox strove with the habit of a brave man. He struggled to take one more step before giving up.

The two beings fought each other. One battered at the weaker being's sanity. The Ska huffed and puffed but could not quite blow down Maddox's last shred of courage.

On the command chair, the captain shook and trembled. Yet, he refused to despair and wail in terror. He simply would not do that. In the end, pure stubbornness refusing to give up, to quit and say no more, drove the captain to a few more seconds of resistance.

In that time, *Victory* reached the bright exit.

"*You will not take my hard material object. It is mine. It belongs with me. I do not give you leave to go yet.*"

"I want to go home," Maddox whispered. He said it with longing and desire.

In that second, a terrible reversal took place. The Elder Ska remembered all the sensations of his former self. It had used the guttered exit, and it had faced searing agony and near devouring of self. Only the tiny clot had escaped into the passing Spacer. The Elder Ska knew this thing, and he feared that such a thing might happen to him if he went with Maddox through the opening.

Logically, that should not be the case. Logically, the Elder Ska would exit the null realm through the bright exit, but only while it was bright. He did not know that, however. He knew the other thing. Such was his fear of non-existence that he quailed at the last second to do it. It was a risk, and he had not taken a real risk since journeying from the other reality to this one.

"I will hound you for eternity, Captain Maddox. I will find a way to crush your psyche and turn you into a blithering idiot."

Maddox clung to his sanity even as he strove to keep his dignity by not howling in terror. At the same time, he desperately wanted to go home.

"Captain," a robotic voice said, "stay in this star system. If you jump with a thought such as you held in your mind before, you might leave the Destroyer behind."

Those words penetrated. Despite the fear beating at his mind, Maddox thought about this star system.

Victory passed through the bright light—the Elder Ska shouted in rage as Maddox fled. That beat against Maddox's soul for the last second. His logic departed. He clung with stubbornness, and he thought, *I want to go home*.

-47-

Last voyage, the Methuselah Man Strand had beaten Maddox and company to the Sind System. There were several reasons for that. One of the keys was the strange process the Builders must have built into the bright-light exit from the null region.

Perhaps it had something to do with the placement of the null region—where it really existed. The process of thought-projection travel had many constraints that Strand, Ludendorff, Galyan, Andros Crank, or any rational being except for the Builders, could not understand.

Captain Maddox had desired home as his objective. Home to him was Earth, the heart of Star Watch. *Victory* traveled through a strange realm in a seeming instant of time. It was the same realm the starship had traversed last voyage to get from the null region to the Sind System.

That seeming instant of travel time only seemed so to an internal observer. If there could have been an outside observer, he or she would have seen that the voyage took considerably longer. In this instance, the voyage took *much* longer.

As *Victory* moved through the strange realm, the mighty Destroyer followed behind it. The tenuous grip of the tractor beam was enough, in this realm, to bring the ancient vessel along for the ride. The two spaceships remained together just long enough. Thus, after much longer than anyone could have guessed, *Victory* appeared in low Earth orbit. A half a kilometer behind it, the pitted, ancient Destroyer also appeared.

With the appearance, Star Watch command went into high emergency status, certain this had to be the dreaded second Swarm attack with a hyper-spatial tube.

***

Captain Maddox groaned on his command chair. His head pounded and his heart thudded painfully.

His eyelids fluttered as he fought for coherence. Despite the long outside time between his struggle with the Elder Ska and his journey home, it had seemingly been a matter of heartbeats for him. In reality, something much different had occurred.

Klaxons rang all around Maddox. They were dull beats against his mind. He was like a man with a terrible hangover. What he didn't want to deal with right now was loud noises or having to make decisions. Even so, a deep sense of duty stirred in him.

Maddox probed deep within himself, finding a hard core of outrage. He had to find the New Man that had raped his mother. He would kill his father for having abused his mother. He would even the score. He would—Wait. There was something else. He would aid his mother's people against all adversaries. That meant he would work with the regular humans. He would save their planet—his planet, from invasion. That meant something else…

At this point, the noise of the klaxons intruded upon his reason. He understood what the horrible racket meant.

With stiff fingers, Maddox plucked at the buckles of his photon helmet. He unsnapped them one by one and tore off the heavy helmet.

Everyone lay unconscious on the bridge. Like last time, he had been the first to stir.

With grim effort and an explosive grunt, he rose to his feet. He tottered toward the comm board. He couldn't talk yet. Thus, he couldn't summon Galyan. The AI may have been unable to respond to the summons.

Finally, Maddox reached the panel and tapped it. The main screen brightened as Maddox turned toward it, staring at a woman.

She asked a garbled question that he did not understand. He stood helplessly, opening and closing his mouth, unable to form words. The woman disappeared. In her place appeared an older woman with gray hair. She had a matronly image, and she soothed something in Maddox.

He croaked a sound.

"There is no need for haste," the woman said in a familiar voice. "I take it arriving here the way you have…"

"Brigadier," Maddox wheezed.

"Hello, Captain," she said. "You look horrible. I've never—never seen you like this."

"Reporting in, Ma'am," Maddox said in a hoarse voice.

"I see you've brought a Destroyer with you."

He managed to move his head up and down, which was exhausting.

"Are there aliens aboard the Destroyer?" she asked.

"Unknown," he panted.

"Please, sit down. You look like you're going to keel over any second."

He stood there staring at her. He knew there was something more he had to do.

"What…?" he said.

"Are your intentions hostile?" she asked.

"No," he said, managing to convey his outrage at the question.

"Do you realize it's almost two years since you left Earth?" she asked.

"What…?" he asked, hoarsely.

"We thought you were dead. The scanner, the Builder Scanner, lost track of you many, many months ago."

"I don't understand."

"Neither do we."

"Two years?" he asked.

"The Swarm has smashed the Tau Ceti System, Captain. They have made it into the Laumer Points. They're a mere three jumps from Earth."

"What?" he said.

"Does that Destroyer work?" she asked. "We have to have it operational tomorrow, if you understand my meaning."

"Two years have passed?" Maddox asked, bewildered. His mind had taken too many beatings for it to have retained its normal resiliency.

The klaxons finally stopped blaring.

Maddox rubbed his forehead. He saw a body stir on the bridge's deck.

"Is another Destroyer coming?" O'Hara asked. "We could use two."

Maddox stared at her. He couldn't believe they had been gone for two years, almost two years. What had happened to make it so long?

"Well?" she asked.

"I have just the one, Ma'am," he said.

O'Hara tried to hide her disappointment, but she failed.

"We were lucky to get this one," Maddox said, nettled.

"Oh, I'm sure you were. Welcome back, Captain. We have much to discuss before the Swarm strikes again. We're going to have to figure out what to do with that Destroyer of yours. I have a feeling the New Men are going to want to help man it. I'm afraid there's going to be trouble…"

Brigadier O'Hara shook her head. "I'm sending med teams to your ship. We're going to need *Victory* for the coming battle. We've built the biggest fleet—"

O'Hara shook her head again. "I'll give you an hour to get your bearings. Then, I don't think you're going to get a full night's sleep until we win or lose the coming Battle for Earth."

PART II
THE BATTLE FOR TAU CETI

-1-

Nearly two years *before* Captain Maddox returned to Earth with the Destroyer, Commander Thrax Ti Ix and his cleverest aides moved through the Golden Nexus of the conquered Chitin System over two thousand light-years away from the human home in the solar system.

In Swarm terms, this was Sector 34: Section 13: Mark 98 of the Great Imperium. The Reigning Supreme of the Left Swing Arm—her name was AX-29—had taken temporary command of all the Swarm warships in the star system. The Queen of the Imperium had given AX-29 direct orders: utterly annihilate the origin planet of the Human Race, Earth. After that, AX-29 was to conquer every outpost and vestige of the bipedal mammals. She was to wipe the slate clean of aliens. That was normal Imperium procedure, paving the way for future colonization.

The Queen had given AX-29 the rights to half the surviving warships in the Golden Nexus System. The rest of the warships would continue the war against the Chitin Empire.

Commander Thrax Ti Ix scuttled through the main control rooms of the Golden Nexus as he seethed with indignation. Thrax was huge in human terms, as large as a Holstein bull. Yet, he was shaped like a praying mantis. His dangling tools clinked against each other from the harness attached to his abdominal region.

As Thrax scuttled, he clacked his pincers in agitation. This was too much, simply too demeaning and awful. Thrax had escaped the Builder Dyson Sphere some time ago, traveling in a hyper-spatial tube as the sphere detonated. Thrax had taken tens of thousands of hybrid Swarm creatures like himself with him.

Following his birth and during his stay at the sphere, Thrax had been taught many wonders by the Builder. In return, Thrax had inserted an ancient Swarm virus into the Builder, which had eventually brought about the creature's demise. Thrax had yearned to join the Imperium. During his years in the sphere, he'd envisioned great honors plied upon him for the gifts he'd bring to the Imperium. Thrax had assumed, naturally, that he'd be given his choice of star commands, and that he would become the greatest Swarm conqueror in the species' long history of stellar conquest.

It all seemed reasonable to Thrax. Then, he'd achieved his dream, giving the Imperium Laumer-Point technology. That was revolutionary to the Swarm and would go a long way to speeding their conquest of the galaxy. Thrax had also brought many saucer-shaped vessels with large bulbous centers from the sphere. Each of the spaceships had star-drive jump capability just like *Victory*. Thrax had preened upon his arrival to the Imperium, boasting to the first Hive Masters that spoke to him about what he could do for the Swarm.

Everything had gone downhill after that, the dream brutally shattered.

Thrax stood motionless in the central Golden Nexus control room. Even his eyestalks were frozen. The other three hybrids quietly scuttled to the back of the chamber. They feared Thrax and his strange moods even as they agreed with his outrage. He'd long promised them glory. He had—

An odd hissing sound escaped from Thrax as he recalled the many indignities heaped upon him by the Hive Masters. They had tested him and declared Thrax an immoral monstrosity. The majority of the Hive Masters had urged the Queen to destroy Thrax and his freakish brood.

Imperium policy was clear. Workers worked. Soldiers fought. Hive Masters thought. To merge the three functions in one creature was blasphemy against nature and ancient custom. Thrax's story of the alien Builder warping hybrids such as himself stuck in the craw of the majority of the Hive Masters.

Yet, there had been one Hive Master high in the Queen's council that had urged otherwise. He suggested the Imperium use the immoral monster to stab at the outer alien fringes of the galaxy.

"Do not give him the command he seeks," the Hive Master had told the Queen. "But let him use his Builder knowledge to help us eliminate future thorny problems."

Thrax had learned all of this through his brief meeting with the Queen. She'd told him everything because she'd obviously wanted him to realize how generous she was being with him. Instead, Thrax realized that not only would he never become the great conqueror of the Imperium of his dreams, but he would become a low-rank menial instead, hated and despised by those he helped through his hard work and sacrifice.

To the Queen, it was simple. Swarm creatures obeyed. That was one of the essences of their kind. The Builder had produced something different in Thrax and *his* kind. They obeyed commands a thousand times better than humans did, but in Swarm terms, they were seething rebels at heart.

Not understanding this difference was, perhaps, the Queen's chief mistake in dealing with Thrax. She must have believed him Swarm enough to obey any command given him. Besides, the Imperium needed his intellect and understanding if they were to accelerate the galaxy's conquest.

The Imperium took Thrax's saucer-shaped ships from him, giving them to the Reigning Supreme AX-29. He'd also lost command status, gaining the new rank of technical assistant to the Reigning Supreme. Through Thrax's carefully crafted strategy, the Swarm had defeated the Chitin defenders of the Golden Nexus System.

"Technical Assistant," his third helper, Vim, said, "The Assault Master demands haste."

Thrax scuttled around to face Vim. The third helper was smaller than Thrax and had been with him on the Builder Dyson Sphere. Vim had long ago lost a chunk of his left pincer in a Kai-Kaus trap.

Thrax's hot words of rage died in his thorax.

Vim held up a large screen with his pincers. The screen was aimed at Thrax. On the screen was the Assault Master aboard the command vessel.

The Assault Master was a grotesque mass of exoskeleton with tiny, wiggly appendages on the bottom of his bulk. Beside him were feeders, inserting tubes into his clackers, pumping royal mush into him. The Assault Master made sucking sounds as mush dribbled from his clackers. A feeder used a cloth, wiping the mush from the glistening exoskeleton "chin."

Thrax seethed at this, too. He despised watching royalty eat. They seemed like little human sucklings. Worse, if he questioned the Assault Master at a time like this, it could result in his immediate destruction.

Finally, the feeders withdrew the dripping mush-tubes.

"Well?" the Assault Master demanded. "Are you ready yet?"

"We are still deciphering the coding language," Thrax said.

"I'm not interested in methodological jargon. Yes or no, Technical Assistant. Are you ready?"

"No," Thrax managed to say.

"The Reigning Supreme demands *action*," the Assault Master said. "She wishes to attack the humans *now*. She is growing impatient with your continued delays."

"I've only been in the nexus for a single day," Thrax pointed out.

"You claimed to understand the Builders that fashioned the nexus."

"I do understand them."

"Yet, you are delaying. The two concepts do not mesh."

"The Builder codes in this nexus are unlike the ones I learned."

"Are you suggesting you are useless?"

"Can *you* reconfigure the codes?" Thrax dared ask.

The Assault Master drew up in outrage as much as his tiny, wriggly appendages could force his bulk upward.

"You dare to impugn my status, you low-rank mongrel? I am the essence of strategic thought. I am not a *technical*, an appendage of superior thinking. I *am* the thinking. Never make

211

such a slur against me again, Technical Assistant. Otherwise, I will order soldiers to snip off several of your legs. After that, you will drag your carcass around with your pincers. Perhaps the degradation will finally teach you to tame your blasphemous mouth."

"I am corrected," Thrax forced himself to say. "You bring light to my imbecility."

"True, true," the Assault Master said, somewhat mollified. "To be honest, Thrax, I find talking to you to be utterly agitating. You fill me with disgust and loathing. I cannot comprehend the Builder that bred you into the mongrel hybrid you are. Perhaps the Builder hated the Imperium."

"No," Thrax said. "The Builder searched for a way to improve the Swarm."

"Vile!" the Assault Master said. "It was a *vile* deed. How can you stand to exist?"

"I live to serve the Queen."

"I suppose that proves you are Swarm, then. It is hard to believe, at times. Your freakishness—well, enough about you. It is a boring topic. I demand that you ready the hyper-spatial tube in another hour. The fleet is ready to move. It is time to attack. Do not disappoint the Reigning Supreme, Technical Assistant. She is growing increasingly impatient with you."

A second later, the Assault Master vanished as the connection ended.

Vim the Third Helper lowered the screen. Thrax and he exchanged glances.

"How has the Swarm conquered one seventeenth of the galaxy?" Vim asked. "The royalty are conceited asses."

"Mass and obedience drowns out everything else," Thrax said. "The Swarm outbreeds all others. The workers fashion more starships, and the soldiers obey every command, winning due to obliterating mass and a willingness to accept all casualties."

Vim bobbed his praying mantis-like head.

Thrax took in the other two hybrids. "Are you with me in this?" he asked them.

"We are agreed," Vim said for himself and the others.

212

The other two helpers bobbed their heads in unison. Each of the helpers had nearly the same brainpower and training as Thrax. They also seethed at their low status.

"Then let us begin Operation New Hive," Thrax said.

-2-

Thrax and his helpers worked tirelessly as only Swarm could. They tore down the chief computer system of the Golden Nexus, using advanced Builder tools brought from the destroyed Dyson Sphere. They learned many of the facts Maddox had found here several voyages ago. Thrax did not unduly care about those facts. He merely stored the data in receiver units.

The Assault Master called twenty-nine hours later. This time, he was not as accommodating as before.

"The Reigning Supreme is livid," the Assault Master told Thrax. "She is almost ready to expunge you."

"Who will make the hyper-spatial tube then?" Thrax asked.

"That is the only thing keeping her from ordering your destruction."

"Is her agitation with me logically reasoned?" Thrax asked.

"Never question me in such a way again. You are—" The Assault Master's puny pincers clacked with annoyance.

At that moment, a hatch slid up in the control room of the Golden Nexus. Five huge soldiers scuttled into the chamber. They had armored exoskeletons and razor-sharp pincers. Smaller soldiers scuttled in afterward, aiming zappers at Thrax.

"Do you understand that I am royalty and you are little better than a worker?" the Assault Master asked through the screen.

Fear surged through Thrax. He lowered himself onto the floor. "I abase myself at your glory," he forced himself to say. "I am a mere cog in the Great Machine of the Imperium."

The Assault Master panted on the screen. "Never forget that again. Otherwise, I shall enjoy watching the soldiers tear you apart. The Reigning Supreme is ready to flush you from her presence. Hurry, Thrax, or you will become mush in the food vats."

"I hear and obey with vigorous zeal."

"That's better," the Assault Master said.

Once again, the connection ended. Vim lowered the screen.

Thrax and his three helpers stared at the soldiers.

"Are you staying?" Thrax finally asked.

"Work," the smallest soldier said. "Work fast, or we will ask for new orders."

Thrax understood the threat. The soldiers would remain. They would not shoot, however, unless the Assault Master gave them the order. That order would have to come from the Reigning Supreme, AX-29.

"Before we complete the work, the four of us must discuss the correct…method," Thrax told the smallest soldier.

"Do it fast," the small one said.

Thrax moved away from the soldiers, motioning the helpers to join him. The four of them congregated as far from the soldiers as the chamber would permit.

"Does the Reigning Supreme suspect our plot?" Vim asked in fear.

"I doubt it," Thrax said. "She's impatient, that's all."

"But to kill you for such a spurious reason…"

Thrax waved that aside with a pincer. "We have a dilemma," he said quietly. "We have dealt with Captain Maddox before. He is a deadly foe. Star Watch will have advanced Builder technology because of him."

"You are not working," the small soldier said. "You are motionless. Must I ask for new orders?"

"We're thinking first as I said," Thrax told him.

"Workers *work*!" the small soldier barked.

"Call the Assault Master, then," Thrax said, nettled. "We're working in ways you cannot comprehend."

The small soldier seemed dazed by Thrax's outburst.

Thrax took that as a sign that the soldier's logic centers were confused. He thus gave his full attention to his helpers.

As he did, Thrax's bearing altered. He stood taller and spoke more crisply. He outlined a strategic plan for their rebellion. It was wrong that they, the so-called hybrids with superior abilities, should truckle to a hidebound system that demeaned them to such an intense degree.

"We are greater than any in the Imperium," Thrax reminded the others. "We are solving the present problem. However, if we allow too many warships into Human Space, we will never achieve our private goal."

"But if we don't take enough warships with us, the humans will defeat our fleet," Vim said.

"That is the dilemma," Thrax agreed. "So, how many warships do we let through?"

"And how do we ensure that the hyper-spatial tube cuts off at the correct moment?" Vim asked.

Thrax looked at the other three. He lowered his head as if being subservient. The smaller soldier was watching him carefully.

"We're going to have to take a calculated risk," Thrax said in a low voice. "I don't see any other way around it."

"What kind of risk?" Vim asked.

"We're going to have to rig an explosive," Thrax said. "We're going to have to destroy the Golden Nexus."

"What if we're in the hyper-spatial tube when that happens?" Vim asked.

"What if we're on the wrong side of the tube when that happens?" another helper asked.

"That is the nature of a calculated risk," Thrax told them. "We won't know the answer until it happens."

The other three looked nervous, but finally, they bobbed their heads in agreement. Soon thereafter, the four of them began to program the main computer of the Golden Nexus.

-3-

Half a day later, Thrax stood on the chief warship of the Conquering War-Fleet 1,021. The giant vessel was similar to the motherships that had destroyed the Adok System over six thousand years ago.

The ship would have dwarfed *Victory*. This one did not hold any assault craft, but carried immensely huge laser cannons. Ships such as these engaged in the heaviest space battles, pounding enemy vessels with hot beams. The ship did not possess an electromagnetic shield. It relied on heavy hull armor for protection, along with vast Swarm numbers.

Thrax stood near the Reigning Supreme, AX-29. She had an even grosser bulk than the Assault Master. Her exoskeleton had a glossy sheen from endless buffing. Several feeding tubes were stuck in her mouth as royal mush flowed through them. She burped from time to time, which caused mush bubbles to form and pop.

Thrax did not have human-like disgust at the sight. He did, however, find her immense immobile bulk nauseating. Yes, she could think. Her thinking was excessively hidebound, but she could comprehend complex subjects when she put her mind to it. What she could not do was move on her own. Workers would do that for her. She ate, though, and defecated, each to a great degree. As the Reigning Supreme, she also possessed a bloated ego. That meant she, too, hated Thrax because of his hybrid nature.

Thrax worked to keep from clacking his pincers in nervousness. From experience he'd found that she hated hearing him make noise. Her pincers were rather soft and thus much quieter. When Thrax clacked, his pincers sounded hard like a soldier's.

The control area seethed with activity as special sub-Hive Masters watched screens and relayed commands to the anxious fleet.

There were more than a million warships waiting to launch the great invasion of Human Space. With these numbers, they would have a hundred thousand times as many vessels as the soft-skinned mammals. It would be a crushing conquest.

Thrax did not presently have access to a screen. He was a technical assistant waiting in the background with throngs of others. He and his helpers had completed their plan. Now, would the command ship go through the hyper-spatial tube last as was the custom? That had been one of their thorniest problems.

Thrax had been sure he could get himself posted elsewhere. That had been the first failure regarding his grand scheme. If the Golden Nexus blew up with the command ship on this side of the hyper-spatial tube...Thrax waited for the perfect moment to speak up. He could not do it too soon—

A buzzing sound commenced in the ship as power surged through the Golden Nexus.

"Over there, Reigning Supreme," the Assault Master said. "That must be the hyper-spatial tube's opening."

Thrax observed a large screen that had just popped up. The swirling vortex in space was indeed the beginning of the hyper-spatial tube. According to his calculations, the tube would stretch over two thousand light-years away.

Thrax had studied the enemy star systems while in the Golden Nexus. His orders had been to project the tube into the Solar System. Thrax had done otherwise in order to implement his plan.

Over ten thousand hybrids like him were in the fleet. Most of them were posted to the star-drive-jump saucer-shaped vessels. Ten thousand was less than a drop in a bucket compared to the millions of Swarm creatures in the war fleet. But ten thousand was ten thousand times better than one.

Thrax waited for the Reigning Supreme to ask him if that indeed was the opening. She did not. Instead, she ordered the Assault Master to send through the first scouts.

Masses of Imperium warships waited nearby. The First Scouting Arm headed for the tube. Soon, ships entered the swirling mass, disappearing as they began the nearly instantaneous journey to Human Space.

The Reigning Supreme and her court watched the proceedings with interest.

Thrax swayed nervously from side to side. He yearned to give a warning to the Reigning Supreme, but he also feared to speak out of turn. He had to get her ship through before the Golden Nexus exploded and thus ended the hyper-spatial tube. Thrax thought furiously. The longer the entrance swirled, the more agitated he became.

The Assault Master glanced at him from time to time, but he said nothing.

"What are you staring at?" the Reigning Supreme demanded.

"I hesitate to say," the Assault Master said.

The Reigning Supreme's appendages wriggled in annoyance. "Does it have anything to do with Thrax? He is behind me with my functionaries, and that is where you keep staring."

"It does," the Assault Master admitted.

"I could feel his nuisance along my exoskeleton. Well, what is he doing now?"

"Swaying as if agitated," the Assault Master said.

"Stop it at once," the Reigning Supreme said without trying to scuttle around to look at Thrax.

"Forgive me, Great One," Thrax said in an outburst, "but I'm worried."

The Reigning Supreme's appendages wriggled even more. She addressed the Assault Master. "Did I or did I not give the hybrid an order?"

"You did indeed," the Assault Master said.

219

"How am I supposed to enjoy this moment if the technical assistant interrupts all the time?"

"Should I summon soldiers?" the Assault Master said.

"I worry, Great One," Thrax said, "for your safety."

Silence filled the command area. The feeders dared not move, the touchers dared not polish the Reigning Supreme's shiny exterior. The sub-Hive Masters all froze lest AX-29 notice them and send them to the crushers, to squeeze their life juices into the feeding vats.

"Why do you spout such nonsense?" the Reigning Supreme finally asked. She hadn't turned yet. It almost seemed as if she didn't want to look at Thrax.

Thrax understood that she found him repulsive. That hardened his resolve. He'd outwitted a Builder. He could surely outwit the bloated Reigning Supreme, and in that way, he would prove his superiority over her. He would, in fact, prove that he was superior to the entire Imperium.

It was at this moment that Thrax had the first inkling of his true goal. He did not dwell on the inkling, but it had burst up from his subconscious during this fearful moment.

"Great One," Thrax said.

"I am not 'the Great One,'" AX-29 said angrily. "I am the Reigning Supreme. Can you not even use Imperium titles properly?"

"Forgive me," Thrax said, "I am in error."

"That is a constant problem with you," she said. "Why must you ruin my greatest moments?"

"I am worried the swirling entrance may be unstable," Thrax said in a rush.

"Is this instability due to negligence on your part?" she asked.

"On no account, Great—Reigning Supreme We did our task perfectly."

"Then why should there be a risk?"

"It is the Builders' fault," Thrax said.

As a hybrid, Thrax was perhaps the greatest liar in the Imperium. Most Swarm had no conception of lying. Only the Hive Masters and above could conceive of the concept. Since

AX-29 viewed him lower than that, she tended to take Thrax's statements at face value.

"Do you understand what he is spouting on about?" AX-29 asked the Assault Master.

"I do not, Reigning Supreme. Should you let him elaborate?"

"I do not want to," she said, "as I loathe hearing his voice. It always sounds wrong, as it is much too harsh. Do you not agree?"

"I had not realized, Reigning Supreme," the Assault Master said. "Yes, I *do* find his voice repugnant."

"That you feel so speaks to your high breeding, Assault Master."

"You are generous in your praise."

"There you are wrong," AX-29 said. "I am *perfect* in my pronunciations."

"I am honored by your words," the Assault Master said. "You guide us with perfect intellect."

"Do you hear that, Technical Assistant?" she asked Thrax.

"Yes," he said.

"Yes, he says," she sighed. "He speaks in such a loutish way. We have refined ourselves through intense selective breeding. He is repulsive with his heavy appendages and constant movement. Does he not realize that stillness aids our intellect?"

"I do not think he does, Reigning Supreme," the Assault Master said.

"The Queen has tasked me with a hard duty," she said. "Thus, I will use the freak's knowledge because I must."

"Glory to you," the Assault Master said in a ringing voice.

"Very well," AX-29 said. "Thrax, hurt my sight by coming into my line of vision."

Thrax scuttled from the court behind her, coming into view. He was quicker, but she was many times bigger. Thrax had to restrain himself from thinking of cutting up her exoskeleton. How he would love to hear her shriek in pain.

"What is that stupid-looking expression on your face?" she asked.

"The look is due to the honor you do me."

"I do you no honor at all. This is a horror to me."

"Then I am glad you accept my—"

"Silence, Thrax. The taint of your pheromones makes me want to vomit. Now, without your breath reaching me, tell me about this danger."

"The entrance of the hyper-spatial tube may produce instabilities in the general region," Thrax said. "Those instabilities could damage the harmonics of the nexus's hyper-generators. You see, the vibrations—"

"I did not ask for a tedious explanation," AX-29 said. "Thus, spare me your boring lectures. How can you fix the problem? That's what I wish to know."

"The problem will become worse over time," Thrax said. "By that I mean, the vibrations will grow—"

"Speed it up with your warning," she said. "This is taking too long, and I am becoming hungry."

"I suggest you enter the hyper-spatial tube sooner," Thrax said. "Thus, you will spare your command vessel and your person from possible harm. Those who wait have a greater chance of—"

"I see," she said, cutting him off. "That is enough. Go back so I don't have to look at you and fear smelling your stink."

Thrax scuttled out of her view. The various feeders scuttled away from him as if he had a disease.

"Assault Master," AX-29 said. "Begin moving the command vessel toward the entrance."

"May I suggest another possibility?" the Assault Master said.

The Reigning Supreme and the court grew silent. "What?" she finally asked.

"Perhaps Thrax could turn off the hyper-spatial tube for a time and restart it later," the Assault Master said.

Thrax almost interrupted to say that would only make things worse.

"No!" AX-29 said. "We will enter the tube now and await our war fleet on the other side."

Thus, in minutes, the great command vessel and many of her defending ships headed for the hyper-spatial tube.

-4-

Against all protocol, the command vessel moved during the first ten percent of the conquering fleet's maneuvering. It was an unprecedented act.

Thrax silently preened as he stood in the back of the court. He'd known he could convince these so-called intellects. Imperium theory said that stillness aided thinking. Thrax thought otherwise. He believed that his motion, his ability to fight, run and slink aided his thinking. Motion helped to stimulate his thoughts. He did not always try to rest secure, either. He put his own being in danger in order to implement his plans. The Hive Master class seldom faced danger. They sent others to kill and die, while they claimed all the glory for having thought up the strategies.

Thrax thrilled to travel through the hyper-spatial tube, popping out much closer to the end of the Orion Arm Spiral. He knew that the nearest star system was Tau Ceti, twelve light-years from the prized Solar System.

Other motherships came through the hyper-spatial tube. Afterward, more scout vessels poured through the opening. Medium warships slipped through next—and without warning, the exit to the hyper-spatial tube vanished.

At first, only Thrax noticed. But then, he'd been watching the monitors for it to happen. Fortunately for his further plans, all the saucer-shaped jump ships he'd brought from the Builder Dyson Sphere had already made it to this side of the now vanished tube. In those ships were his only allies in the universe.

Soon, the Assault Master on his pallet began to issue orders to the screen monitors.

AX-29 must have noticed. She gulped faster, draining her feeding tubes. Only then did she spit the tubes out of her mouth. The feeders had been giving her the highest-grade royalty mush, her favorite.

"What is the problem?" she asked the Assault Master.

"I'm not sure there is one yet," he replied evasively.

"You've upset my feeding schedule," she said. "So, you might as well tell me what you're worried about."

"It is the hyper-spatial tube exit, Reigning Supreme."

"What about it?" she asked.

"It is gone," the Assault Master said.

Silence filled the spongy-floored deck.

"Technical Assistant!" shouted AX-29. "Come forth and explain this cessation."

Thrax scuttled forward as his hearts beat rapidly. This was the next critical moment. He had to survive it. If he didn't— Thrax refused to allow himself that possibility. Still, if she ordered his death, he would attack and try to scar that lovely polished exoskeleton. While he hated the Reigning Supreme, he could still appreciate beauty when he saw it.

He bowed low before her bloated bulk.

"What is the meaning of the exit's disappearance?" she asked.

"I hope the fools at the entrance did not push in too fast," Thrax said in feigned anger.

"Reigning Supreme," the Assault Master said. "Could I ask the technical assistant a question?"

"By all means, do so," AX-29 said.

"Why would ships crowding the entrance cause the exit to disappear?" the Assault Master asked.

"It is obvious," Thrax said in a scathing tone. "You mean to tell me that you don't see it?"

"Impertinence," the Assault Master declared.

"Me?" asked Thrax. "I'm not the one speaking out of turn."

224

"Reigning Supreme," the Assault Master said, looking to AX-29.

"Stop this bickering," she said. "Answer the question, Technical Assistant."

"If several ships tried to cram into the opening at once," Thrax said, "they could have upset the harmonics of the tube. If they did it violently enough, they might have caused the tube to collapse."

"How long until the tube…reappears?" asked AX-29.

"That is an imponderable," Thrax said.

"I do not like your answer," the Reigning Supreme said. "We hardly have any ships here at all, a mere 80,000 according to that monitor. Are you suggesting the hyper-spatial tube won't appear any time soon?"

Thrax assumed his plan had succeeded. That meant the Golden Nexus would never manufacture another tube, because the nexus would be drifting junk in space. He did not dare say that, however.

"That is possible," Thrax told her.

"Assault Master," the Reigning Supreme said, agitated. "What is your suggestion?"

"I do not understand," the Assault Master said.

"We are in—where are we?" she asked the Assault Master.

He barked orders. Workers moved screens before him. Soon, the Assault Master said, "We are in empty space."

"Why are we not in the Solar System?" she asked.

"I imagine Thrax has failed you in this, too," the Assault Master said.

"Thrax," she said. "Where are we?"

"Twelve light-years from Earth," Thrax said. "Earth is the human species' origin planet."

"I know very well what Earth is," she said. "Twelve light-years is too far. I will be aged before we arrive there."

"Only if you headed straight there at sub-light speeds," Thrax said.

"How else would I get there?" she asked.

"Use the Builder-made jump ships."

"There are only four hundred of those with us," the Assault Master said. "Are you suggesting we attempt to conquer Human Space with a mere four hundred warships?"

"You must use surprise against the humans," Thrax said.

"I am outraged," the Assault Master said. "Our 80,000 vessels are barely enough in this place for a defensive position. Now, the mongrel speaks of conquering with a mere four hundred jump ships? I think the trip has unhinged him."

"That isn't how I see the situation," Thrax said. "We have plenty of vessels to annihilate the inferior mammals."

"Are you seeking to give us strategic advice?" the Assault Master asked, outraged.

"If 80,000 vessels are all we have," Thrax said, "then let us conquer the humans with them. That is better than running back to the Imperium admitting gross defeat."

"Reigning Supreme, I demand—I *request* that my soldiers—"

"You demand?" Thrax asked, having noticed the slip. "Who are you, Assault Master, to order the Reigning Supreme as if she is your technical assistant?"

The Assault Master turned to AX-29 in horror. "I did not mean that—"

"Yet you said it in a commanding tone," Thrax added. "We all heard you. I wonder, Assault Master. Did you engineer the craft to block the entrance so you would leave the Reigning Supreme with only a handful of vessels? Have you lost your mind, hoping to supplant her in power?"

"Reigning Supreme," the Assault Master said. "He is a lunatic—"

"Because I see your subtle threat against the Reigning Supreme's position?" Thrax asked. "Yes, I am only a technical assistant. But as one, I see the nature of your threat with greater clarity. I cannot believe your perfidious—"

"Silence!" AX-29 shouted.

Thrax fell silent, knowing he'd taken a terrible gamble in speaking like this. The Assault Master was cunning. If the master plan was going to work, he had to weed out the other strategic thinkers until he alone was left. Thrax had reasoned this out carefully. Yes, AX-29 hated him. But the royalty did not realize other Swarm could think and plot. In truth, they could not. But he was a hybrid. Yet, because they held him in such contempt, they would not expect such devious behavior from him.

The Reigning Supreme stared at Thrax. He stood frozen in obedience. "How is it you can see a threat in the Assault Master?" AX-29 purred.

"Because he despises me," Thrax said, "he has grown careless by what he has said around me."

"I cannot believe this," she said.

Thrax dared to play his ace card. "I have a recording of it, Reigning Supreme."

"What?" both the Reigning Supreme and Assault Master said in unison.

"Look how the Assault Master talks out of order," Thrax said, "speaking at the same time as you as if his words have equal weight. That is a sure sign of his rebellious nature."

"Reigning Supreme," the Assault Master pleaded. "Let me call the soldiers so they can shred this foul beast to pieces."

"I would hear the recording first," she said. "Retrieve it, Thrax."

"I happen to have it on my person, Reigning Supreme."

"Why do you have it so handy?" the Assault Master demanded.

"Oh," Thrax said. "I see. I am to answer you first and not the Reigning Supreme?"

"Play the recording," AX-29 said.

Thrax unhooked the recorder, set it on the floor and pressed PLAY. Soon, the Assault Master spoke in a low voice out of it, describing his plan to supplant AX-29. According to the words from the recorder, the Assault Master thought the Reigning Supreme stupid and vain, declaring that he would build the Imperium better than she could ever think to do.

"Reigning Supreme," the Assault Master said in a weak voice. "These are lies. That is not my voice."

"Soldiers," the Reigning Supreme shouted. "Soldiers!"

Huge soldiers burst onto the spongy command deck. They stared at her with readiness.

"Reigning Supreme," the Assault Master cried. "I beg you, listen to me—"

"Cut him up into small pieces," AX-29 shrieked. "Destroy the Assault Master and bloody the floor with him."

"No!" the Assault Master shouted. "Kill Thrax—"

The soldiers reached him, and with their heavy pincers they began to cut apart his exoskeleton. It was brutal and fast. Soon, the Assault Master no longer squirmed or howled in agony. His blood and guts and pieces of exoskeleton littered the spongy deck.

"Foul treason," AX-29 whispered. "I cannot believe this happened. What are we going to do now?"

No one answered, not even Thrax.

"Can no one suggest anything?" AX-29 asked.

"I have a small idea," Thrax said. "I grew up in this region of space, so I probably know it better than anyone else in the war fleet."

"We are so few," the Reigning Supreme said.

"Compared to the weak mammals," Thrax said, "we still have an amazing number of vessels. I believe, with your genius, that you can conquer all of Human Space with what you have."

"That seems like vain boasting, Thrax."

He waited.

"Still…" the Reigning Supreme said. "Tell me your idea."

It was at that point that Commander Thrax Ti Ix began to outline his carefully conceived strategy.

-5-

Weeks after the Swarm's appearance three-quarters of a light-year from the Tau Ceti System, a meeting took place out in the Beyond, many hundreds of light-years away. This was a special place, one that Admiral Fletcher and his officers had tried to find but failed to do so. Fletcher and the Grand Fleet were already headed back for Earth.

The special place was the Throne World of the New Men. Strand and Ludendorff had colonized this world a long time ago with genetically selected colonists.

The system had an Earth regular G-class star. It possessed four terrestrial planets and three gas giants. The third terrestrial planet from the star was an Eden-like place with low mountains, blue seas and green pastures. Several large battle stations orbited the Throne World. These stations had heavy fusion cannons and possibly the strongest force screens among the human races. Near the battlestations were large scaffolding docks. Within the docks were new star cruisers. These had disruptor cannons instead of fusion cannons, as well as improved screens.

The Throne World System seethed with activity. The New Men lacked the Commonwealth's numbers and lacked the great industrial base. Still, they were the most highly efficient humans in space. They could retool better than others and could accept new ideas quicker. They could also take existing technical systems and improve them through superior thought.

They were the New Men, faster, stronger and smarter than regular humans. Their great fault was singular in nature. They could not sire girls, only boys. Thus, they had to keep raiding the sub-men in order to replenish their stock of women.

Since the Commonwealth Invasion, that was less of a problem than previously. Despite their having to retreat, the New Men had taken a vast haul in sub-men and women. That, incidentally, had been one of the reasons that Admiral Fletcher was so hot to find the Throne World. He desired to free the enslaved Commonwealth people.

Originally, Strand and Ludendorff had bred the New Men as defenders of the human race. After a time, the defenders realized they should be the rulers. A hard war had followed. Since retreating from the Thebes System, the New Men had been retooling and re-thinking their strategies and tactics.

The meeting was held in the palace of the Emperor of the New Men. At the meeting were the captains of the star cruisers. They were the highest-ranked among the superiors, as they conceived of themselves. They realized that a smarter and more talented group would be impossible to find in the galaxy.

The capital city shone with brilliance. Tall, mirrored buildings reflected the star's light. The palace was a white mansion with extensive gardens. In the palace was a great room and a vast round table. The table was patterned from the lore of King Arthur and his Knights of the Round Table. It had a marble top, with large chairs surrounding it. At the de facto head of the table sat the Emperor on his throne.

The Emperor was the tallest man in the chamber. He wore a golden crown and a velvet cape. He had golden-hued skin and long facial features, with deep-set eyes that shone with strength of will.

There were others who could almost match the Emperor in height and bearing. The greatest of them was Golden Ural, an equally tall and slender superior.

One man at the table did not captain a star cruiser. His name was Darius. He'd returned to the Throne World with Methuselah Man Strand in tow. He'd brought Strand from the Sind System. Darius had also told the Emperor of Ludendorff's wish for the New Men and sub-men to unite against the terrible threat of the coming Swarm assault.

Now, news of the Swarm invasion and talk with the Lord High Admiral of Star Watch had caused the Emperor to summon his star cruiser captains. It was time to decide on the correct strategy for the master race.

-6-

As Golden Ural sat at the improved Round Table, he picked at his silver uniform. He wore the Sunburst Star, a gold medal set with precious diamonds. It wasn't for courage in battle. All superiors were expected to show courage. The Sunburst Star was for excessive cleverness in battle. He'd won the star at the end of the Commonwealth Invasion because he'd taken great quantities of woman from the sub-men, and had made the theft stick without further war.

Admiral Fletcher had been hot to attack at the time. Many of the star-cruiser captains had wanted to demolish the sub-men's augmented Third Fleet. Now, even the hottest fighters in both factions were glad they had not destroyed or wounded each other in an annihilating battle.

The Emperor had just finished giving a holographic report of the Swarm Fleet. Thousands upon thousands of Swarm warships streamed for Tau Ceti. The vast number staggered the imagination. Many of the insectoid ships were vast things. As impossible as it was to believe, the enemy tonnage was even greater than their numbers.

"I do not believe the Commonwealth will survive the coming assault," the Emperor said. "The Swarm used Builder technology—a hyper-spatial tube, I am told—to cast the fleet against the Commonwealth. According to the Lord High Admiral, the jump was over two thousand light-years in extent."

A relatively short New Man stirred at the table. He was not short in actual terms, but compared to his brethren he was.

This New Man's name was Lord Drakos. Perhaps in compensation for his "shortness," Drakos had wide shoulders and was famous for his quickness and mental acuity. He had green eyes, and golden skin shades lighter than anyone else at the table. In the past, a few superiors had suggested DNA testing to see if Drakos had the genetic quality to maintain his higher status. Naturally, Drakos resented the whisper campaign directed against him. At the same time, he championed genetic purity above all else. Perhaps he reasoned that in championing the issue, others would relent about the DNA testing, believing he must have the best genetic purity if he publically argued as he did.

Drakos had fought splendidly during the Commonwealth Invasion. He'd also had a knack for picking the choicest loot. That meant he was one of the richer star cruiser captains.

Lord Drakos stirred at the table and said with a sneer, "What grandiose titles the sub-men give themselves. Lord High Admiral indeed."

"We are not here to debate titles," the Emperor said. "The point is that Admiral Cook has never lied to us. We are here to debate on the correct strategy concerning the Swarm Invasion."

"As you say, Lord," Drakos replied smoothly, although his green eyes smoldered at the rebuke.

As Golden Ural watched the exchange, he calculated swiftly.

Lord Drakos represented the hardliners, those who desired genetic annihilation of the sub-men. The hardliners had chaffed at the peace, wanting to renew the invasion of so-called Human Space.

Clearly, the Emperor knew all this. Ural wondered how his cousin would prepare the hardliners for his bombshell.

The Emperor stared at Drakos as he said, "The Lord High Admiral desires a war alliance with us against the Swarm."

Ural raised his eyebrows. His cousin had decided on directness and shock. That was interesting. Ural examined the others around the table.

As expected at such a pronouncement, surprise showed on many faces. Others seemed thoughtful. A few laughed quietly, nudging a neighbor.

Drakos spoke with controlled heat. "Can chimpanzees ally with men, Emperor?"

A murmur of assent rose from the hardliners.

"A moment," Golden Ural said lazily. He championed the realists, as they called themselves. They were greater in number than those following the hardliner philosophy.

Drakos faced him, forced to look upward due to Ural's substantially greater height.

"In the interest of clarity," Ural said lightly, "I am formally asking if *you* mate with chimpanzees."

A new murmur drifted around the table.

Drakos rose from his chair, his features frozen with anger.

The breach of protocol caused an even greater stir than the Emperor's or Ural's words.

Ural knew his target, had studied him for quite some time. Drakos did not like anyone forcing him to any particular action. With him, reverse psychology often proved successful.

"Do you wish to challenge me to a duel?" Ural asked in a mocking manner.

Perhaps Drakos understood his boorishness by standing in the Emperor's presence at the Round Table when all other captains sat.

"Such a question gives me legal cause for a duel," Drakos snapped.

"Does it indeed?" Ural asked, pressing his case. "Maybe you should first answer the question in order to discover its intent."

"This is rankest slander," Drakos declared, growing angrier.

"Nonsense," Ural said. "If you would simply answer the—"

"A moment," the Emperor said, interrupting the exchange.

Everyone fell silent, although Drakos visibly struggled to do so. He sat, though. Because the Emperor spoke, protocol demanded that he resume his seat.

"I...*request* that my captains keep personal slurs out of the debate," the Emperor said, staring at his cousin Ural. "Unless, of course, there is someone who would care to duel to the death with *me*."

No one dared take up the Emperor on his offer. He was, without a doubt, the finest duelist among them. In his day, he'd slain six champions, those hoping to dethrone the Emperor and take his place.

"No!" Drakos said, his answer like a rifle shot. "I have no chimpanzees in my zoo. Why, do you?" he asked Golden Ural.

"How many women have you impregnated?" Ural asked blandly.

"Hundreds!" Drakos boasted, as he looked around the table. "I have also sired hundreds of sons."

Ural nodded. "Thus, your actions prove that sub-men are not chimpanzees, for you do not mate with chimps. Furthermore, if you sire sons from sub-women, are they truly sub-women at all?"

"Of course they are," Drakos said. "We must medically heighten the fetuses so they become like us."

"Ah," Ural said. "Do you find sub-women ugly, perhaps?"

"Emperor," Drakos said. "Must I answer these continuous slurs?"

The Emperor took his time answering. "Let us see where Golden Ural is taking us."

Drakos glared at Ural. "I only mate with the most beautiful women," he boasted. "They are privileged to have lain with me and sired such noble sons."

"No doubt, no doubt," Ural said. "Now, I wonder, if the Commonwealth lies in ruins, the bugs have slain all the sub-species, where will your sons find women to breed?"

Drakos stared at Ural. He must have finally understood the thrust and finality of the argument. He became thoughtful. While Drakos could act hot-headedly, he could also shift direction and sometimes swiftly, showing his New Man nature in that.

"That is well-reasoned," Drakos said at last. "Why should we let the bugs destroy our harem supply by blotting out the sub-men? If the Swarm destroyed everything…"

"No more beautiful women for the superiors to bed," Ural said. "Given that truth, I suggest we help Star Watch defeat these monsters. I, for one, wish a bountiful supply of ladies for my lusty sons."

A ripple of laughter spread across the giant table.

"There is a problem, though," Drakos said. "I counted the number of Swarm ships. What can we gather to face such mass? One hundred star cruisers perhaps, maybe one hundred and ten?"

"One hundred and thirty," Ural said. "There are a few secret ships—"

Drakos waved that aside as he snorted. "I'll grant you one hundred and thirty star cruisers for the sake of argument. Among those, only a handful possess the new disruptor cannons. What can Star Watch muster?"

"Three hundred first class fighting vessels," Ural said. "By those I mean capital ships."

"I would count it a little differently," Drakos said. "But I'll grant you that as well. Let's add another four hundred lesser vessels, patrol boats, missile launchers, frigates and such. We might finish another ten star cruisers before we engage in battle. Let us grandly allow that the sub-men and we could gather 800 ships. Now, I ask you, how do 800 spaceships defeat 80,000?"

Lord Drakos scanned the throng. "Can we destroy one hundred Swarm ships for every one loss of ours? If we do, we each break even. Our one hundred and thirty star cruisers is the extent of our might. If we lose them, we have lost too much. If the sub-men lose their larger number of vessels, they can more easily replace them in the future as they have a greater industrial base."

"Our one hundred and thirty star cruisers can do a staggering amount of damage compared to the sub-men's ships," Ural said.

"Of course," Drakos said. "My point is that there are no good solutions. If we wait for the Swarm to annihilate the sub-men—"

"What is your suggestion?" the Emperor asked Drakos.

"We must gather more ships, Excellency," Drakos said. "In his report, Darius spoke of Juggernauts earlier. We could use such vessels against the Swarm."

"An excellent point," the Emperor said. "Darius, do you believe you could hijack the Juggernauts from the Sind System?"

Darius took his time answering. "I'd have to talk with Strand first," he finally said.

The Emperor scowled, shaking his head. "That is out of the question."

Many of the superiors appeared puzzled.

"Strand is the most cunning man in existence," the Emperor said. "Even in these dire times, we dare not give him leeway. He has ruled us in the past with an iron fist. Later, while on the run, he controlled some of us through wicked means. No, we will not talk to Strand."

"Sire—" Drakos said.

"No!" the Emperor said. "My mind is made up on this. The only way Strand will see the outside of his cell is if someone kills me first."

That ended the majority of the debate. Thus, after another half hour, the captains of the star cruisers decided to work with Star Watch in order to defeat the massive Swarm Fleet. They would send one hundred star cruisers to Human Space, leaving the rest in the Throne World System as a last-ditch defense.

At the Emperor's insistence, Golden Ural would lead the star cruisers. Ural's tasks, in order of descending importance, were to defeat the bugs, save as much of the fleet as possible and make sure no star cruisers "accidently" fell into the hands of the sub-men. In the meantime, Darius and his crew would use one of the newly completed and improved star cruisers to return to the Sind System and bring as many Juggernauts as possible to the Solar System.

-7-

As the Swarm Invasion Fleet accelerated for the Tau Ceti System, the elected officials of the Commonwealth debated on various actions. As word seeped out of the coming Swarm attack, panic spread. Tens of thousands of the richest people in the Tau Ceti System fled. Vast sums exchanged hands as people paid fortunes for a berth on a spaceship. Independent contractors raced to Tau Ceti to make a killing.

Even so, those that left hardly dented the overall population. Riots seethed on the Tau Ceti planets and space habitats. The riots grew until chaos threatened Star Watch's plans to turn the system into a fortress and Swarm killing zone.

Finally, Brigadier O'Hara asked to speak to the assembled electors of the Commonwealth. She worked on her speech for days, keeping the content secret. On a Thursday, she went to the Hall of Electors. Those in the vast auditorium waited impatiently for the old woman to give her talk. Many electors were indignant that the secret police chief of Star Watch would dare to address them.

O'Hara trembled as she approached the podium. There were a thousand and ten seats for the electors. Each elector also had several aides in attendance. Above them, masses had packed the galleries. The giant auditorium brimmed with people.

The microphone came on, and Mary O'Hara spoke quietly to the democratically elected officials who ran Star Watch. She spoke about Ancient Rome and one of its terrible times of trouble. That had been in 458 B.C. An implacable enemy had threatened the new republic with annihilation. In their combined worry, the Roman Senate turned to a respected warrior by the name of L. Quinctius Cincinnatus. Representatives of the Senate had found him at his plow. Once Cincinnatus reached the Senate, the senators offered to make him dictator with full authority over everyone. The senators believed Rome needed a strong hand to end their bickering so they could concentrate on the enemy. The key to such a decision was in choosing the right man. He needed wisdom and the courage to lead them to victory. What made L. Quinctius Cincinnatus so interesting was that he gave up his dictatorship earlier than the law required. He had led Rome to victory. And afterward, Cincinnatus returned to his farm and plow, content to become a normal citizen of Rome once again.

Mary O'Hara paused, searching the one thousand and ten electors. Most of them watched her on big screens sprinkled throughout the auditorium.

"We have such a respected warrior among us in our time of trouble," O'Hara said. "He is a man who loves the Commonwealth and has never attempted to acquire power for the sake of ruling over others. I refer, of course, to Lord High Admiral Cook. I suggest, my dear electors, that you beg the Lord High Admiral to take the post of dictator for as long as the Swarm Fleet exists. The bugs threaten our existence. If they win, not just the Commonwealth will die but the entire human race. This is the moment, my dear electors, for us to unite under one mind and will. But it must be a man we all trust. I ask you, is there anyone more qualified to lead us at a time like this than Admiral Cook?"

The great auditorium became deathly silent.

"We have proof of his abilities," O'Hara said. "Admiral Cook saved us from the New Men. He helped overthrow the androids. His brilliance and foresight has readied us for the Swarm. Even now, our best starship and captain search for secret weapons to aid us in this fight."

If Mary O'Hara had expected her speech to rouse them to instant action, she was proven gravely wrong.

Twenty-eight different speakers debated the issue that day after she departed the podium. It took three weeks and four days for the electors to vote on the issue. The assembly voted 611 to 481 with 8 abstentions to give the Lord High Admiral temporary dictatorship over the Commonwealth.

The wisdom of the decision was proven when Lord High Admiral Cook highhandedly demanded and got a fleet of the largest space haulers. He had the haulers begin moving the Tau Ceti population to neighboring star systems. Unfortunately, that caused vast unrest, riots and confusion in said systems. It meant those systems tottered politically. Twelve of the electors from those systems retroactively changed their votes.

What the move allowed, however, was legions of technicians and workers a free hand in changing the Tau Ceti System into a fortress.

The exodus of the general population and the work in the system continued even as the Swarm ships reached the outer Tau Ceti Oort cloud.

"All the scenarios are clear," Cook told his assembled war leaders at the main Luna Base war-room. "We're going to lose Tau Ceti. We should be clear about that. But we're going to start whittling down the Swarm advantage at Tau Ceti."

"A mere ten percent loss will hardly cripple the bugs," Lord Drakos declared.

Cook turned his white-haired head, facing the golden-skinned New Man across the conference table from him.

"A *twenty* percent loss won't cripple them," Cook said. "But we have to start somewhere. Do you have a better idea?"

Drakos stiffened at the question. The other New Men at the table watched him.

Ural knew Drakos thought of Cook as a chatty sub-man, little better than a chimpanzee hooting about this or that.

"I do have a better idea," Drakos said. "It is madness to use our ships in the system. At this juncture, we dare not risk their loss. We must fill the system with missiles as you're already doing. Only, we must move in more missiles and do it even faster now that the bugs have entered the Oort cloud."

Cook spread his big hands. "We are filling the system with hundreds of thousands of missiles. We also have vast

240

automated laser batteries. If we don't back that up with our battlefleets, the Swarm will swat our missiles and lasers aside. We have to at least threaten them with our fleets so the bugs won't concentrate everything on the missiles. That will give the majority of our missiles time to reach their targets."

"Risking our fleets at this point is senseless," Drakos said. "First you must whittle the Swarm down. Only at that point do you unleash your heaviest squadrons."

Maybe the words stung Cook. He looked tired, and he'd been working tirelessly for over a year and a half. He wasn't a young man anymore.

"Do New Men dislike risks?" Cook asked in a heavy voice.

Drakos stared flat-faced at the Lord High Admiral as his eyes narrowed.

Ural spoke before Drakos could utter a sound. "We accept calculated risks, sir. Drakos must simply be wondering how calculated this risk is."

"Very," Cook told Ural. "I plan to save every ship we have."

"That's flatly impossible," Drakos said. "If you engage our combined fleet against the bug masses, we will not only take losses but heavy ones."

"I agree that we will take losses," Cook said. "Hopefully, we won't take too many."

"Hopefully?" Drakos asked in scorn. "One must calculate, not merely hope."

"That is why I'm talking to you, sir," Cook said. "I seek your battle wisdom."

Drakos might have said more, but Ural intervened with smooth words.

It meant that Ural had to work harder later to soothe hardliner feathers. But it was much too early to let the alliance break apart due to Drakos' temper. The breakage would come later. Ural had realized months ago that his task was making sure a greater percentage of star cruisers survived than Star Watch vessels. At that point, it might be possible to win everything they had lost in the Thebes System several years ago.

-8-

The Tau Ceti System was in the Constellation Cetus. The star was spectrally similar to the Sun, although it only had 78 percent of the Sun's mass. It was also rather deficient in metals. Tau Ceti was the closest solitary G-class star to Earth. The system had five planets, two of them in the inhabitable zone.

Tau Ceti had ten times as much dust orbiting the star as the Sun possessed. Because of the greater debris disc, more stellar objects struck the planets, satellites and in-system spaceships. That meant spaceships had to move more carefully here than elsewhere. Carefully meant slower than ordinary. That hurt during the present crisis, as giant haulers brought more and more missiles to the system and took more people elsewhere.

The greater debris had its pluses, however. Those would show up later when the Swarm ships actually began to leave the Oort cloud for the Outer System. It meant the Swarm vessels would be unlikely to move through the system at high speeds. Logically, the Swarm ships would have to slow down first, which would give the defenders a little more time to get ready.

The entire Commonwealth's industrial might had churned out munitions for the coming battles, working nonstop for months upon months upon months.

As Napoleon might have walked over a possible site for battle, the Lord High Admiral and his staff moved through the Tau Ceti System.

Every larger piece of debris could conceal a certain number of missiles. The bigger pieces of debris also sheltered laser satellites. For months on end, for over a year, the Alliance members prepared Tau Ceti for the massed might of the Swarm Imperium.

It should have been a simple mathematical formula. The Swarm ships had a certain mass and speed—but it wasn't that easy. The enemy fleet had four hundred saucer-shaped vessels. According to Captain Maddox's data collected at the Builder Dyson Sphere, those ships had the ability to jump independently of Laumer Points. That meant four hundred enemy ships could conceivably attack at any time and at any point. Those four hundred ships could seriously harm the overall plan.

"The question is," the Lord High Admiral said during a strategy session on Tau Ceti Prime. "How will the Swarm use those jump-capable vessels?"

No one knew the answer. Oh, almost everyone had a *theory*. Those theories had always been worked out in exacting detail by the person or persons propounding them. But at the end of the day, no one *knew* how Imperium bugs would use those ships.

Because of that and the existence of a sly creature named Mr. Murphy, no one really knew how the first battle for survival would go. Worst of all, no one knew which Laumer Points the bugs would attempt to use after the battle. That would decide... well, just about everything.

What that meant in practical terms was more work for everyone and months of endless handwringing and worry about what was going to happen. It also meant various simulations about what would happen if the bugs used that Laumer Point instead of this one. At the terminus of each Laumer Point waited vast numbers of thermonuclear warheads.

Cook had decided to use standard war theory in regard to the Laumer Points. Star Watch would hammer Swarm ships exiting the various Laumer Points. Yet, given enemy numbers, the warheads would not stop such an advance. Cook had seen from the beginning that endless attrition to whittle down bug numbers was the only way he could eventually get to a set-piece battle that might win the war for survival.

Almost everyone else thought Cook was overly optimistic about facing the Swarm in a set-piece battle. Cook was counting on luck, and on getting his hands on some Destroyers. If Maddox could return with three Destroyers, the Alliance Fleet just might be able to pull this off.

What Cook didn't want to think about was the possibility that Maddox would fail. The captain had always come through in the end. Yet the question remained, what in the Hell had happened to *Victory*, and why couldn't the Builder Scanner find the elusive vessel?

The weeks lengthened into months. In two months' time, maybe a little more, the first Swarm warships would leave Tau Ceti's Oort cloud and enter the Outer System. Then the feces would hit the proverbial fan.

-9-

Thrax had endured his low position for almost two years now. That was galling, as he'd thought his moment had come at the Assault Master's grisly death.

Reliving the moment in his memory was one of the few ways Thrax relieved the tedium and worry of his existence. He'd plotted for almost two years for a way onto a jump ship. If he could reach there, he would implement his long-term strategy. He was so sick of his low station that anything would be better than this. Maybe the Swarm would win. It no longer mattered to Thrax as a menial, a highly glorified worker.

He'd had little contact with his fellow hybrids. He—

The hatch to his general work area slid up. Three armored soldiers scuttled in. They glared at him.

Thrax quailed inside. Was this it? Had the Reigning Supreme discovered his deception? The thought of that—

"Come," the biggest soldier said.

"Where?" asked Thrax.

"Now," the soldier said, clicking his oversized pincers. Those could cut him in half with hardly an effort. The soldiers were not only bigger and more heavily armored than he was, but they were faster. The only thing he had on them was brains.

"Bring him," the soldier said.

"Wait," Thrax pleaded.

The other two soldiers rushed in, grabbing him. Thrax tensed for a killing cut, but it didn't come. Instead, the two soldiers carried him unceremoniously, following the biggest soldier through the ship corridors.

Thrax looked around. He realized the soldiers were taking him to the hallowed area of the ship where the Reigning Supreme held her strategy sessions.

"I can walk," Thrax said.

The soldiers paid him no heed.

"Why don't you set me down?" Thrax suggested.

"You had your chance," the big soldier said.

"I've reconsidered."

The trio ignored him. They followed orders. They always followed orders. They could do no less, no more.

Ten minutes later, a big hatch slid up. The trio moved into a vast area. AX-29 faced four others smaller than her. They watched a holograph of the approaching star.

The fleet was in the Oort cloud. In this instance, that was still a long way out from the system's major planets.

The soldiers approached the Reigning Supreme, stopping short and waiting.

One of the assault leaders motioned to the soldier.

"What is it?" AX-29 asked, unable to see the soldiers and Thrax because they were respectfully behind her.

"The soldier has brought the Assistant Technician," the chief Assault Leader said.

None of the assault leaders had been elevated into Assault Master status yet. If they found that galling, none of them had ever dared complain.

"Thrax," the Reigning Supreme called.

The head soldier made clicking noises. The two carrying Thrax brought him before the Reigning Supreme and dumped him onto the spongy floor.

Thrax scrambled to his feet with what dignity he could muster.

"Why did you carry him here?" AX-29 asked.

"He would not come immediately," the big soldier said.

"Are you that incorrigible?" AX-29 asked Thrax.

"I misunderstood the soldier's meaning," Thrax said.

The soldier said nothing to that.

AX-29 studied the soldier and then Thrax. She spoke to the assault leaders. "Have I erred in summoning the technical expert?"

None of the assault leaders answered.

Thrax covertly eyed them. He understood then that each one of them hated him. They must hold him personally responsible for the Assault Master's death. In that, they were correct. If they weren't careful, Thrax would engineer their deaths as well.

"He schemes, Reigning Supreme," the chief Assault Leader said. "I can see the cunning in his eyes."

Thrax opened his mouth to retort. He happened to glance at the big soldier. He understood something in that moment. The soldier had gained the Reigning Supreme's respect because he'd acted in the accepted manner. Thrax now waited.

That seemed to surprise AX-29. "Do you plot against the fleet?" she asked suddenly.

"No," Thrax said.

"Do you wish to accuse the Assault Leader who spoke against you?"

"No," Thrax said.

"Is he wrong?"

"Yes," Thrax said.

The Reigning Supreme fixed her eyes on the Assault Leader who had spoken. "What do you make of his answers?"

"He is clever, as I said," the Assault Leader replied. "He is learning our ways."

"*Our* ways?" the Reigning Supreme asked.

"He is a hybrid. He is not truly like us."

"Perhaps that is why he fills me with disgust," AX-29 said.

"Yes," the Assault Leader said.

Thrax couldn't hold his tongue at that. It pleased him to be different while it also terrified him. He was a Swarm creature. How could the Assault Leader speak otherwise? He had brought the Imperium great gifts. Yet, the royalty had treated him like trash. That was wrong.

"Reigning Supreme," Thrax said boldly. "Perhaps it is true I am different. But maybe that is exactly what the fleet needs at a moment like this."

"Heresy," the chief Assault Leader said. "Now is the time to follow accepted Imperial procedure. That is how the fleet shall gain victory over the mammals."

"How could your villainy possibly help us?" AX-29 asked Thrax.

"I see problems and possible solutions that you, in your accepted normality, might miss."

"Vile thing," the chief Assault Leader said in horror. "I beg you, Reigning Supreme, destroy the thing before his wickedness destroys us all."

"Did I in my wickedness give the Imperium wonderful advantages?" asked Thrax.

"Assault Leader," AX-29 said, "outline the approaching problem to the hybrid."

The chief Assault Leader hesitated only a moment before saying, "I obey."

For the next hour, the Assault Leader tediously showed Thrax the Tau Ceti System, the debris cloud, the planets, the spaceships and the obviously half-hidden missiles waiting behind a thousand rocky objects. The Assault Leader used the holograph to pinpoint possible enemy spaceship concentrations.

"Should I go on, Reigning Supreme?" the Assault Leader asked at the end of the hour.

"Yes," AX-29 said.

"According to our calculations," the Assault Leader said, "we shall receive eleven percent casualties in the coming battle."

The number staggered Thrax. That was incredibly high against such a small number of enemy ships.

"Take a moment," AX-29 told Thrax. "Think about what you've seen. Do you have any technical suggestions that could lower the eleven percent rate of our coming casualties?"

"May I ask a question, Reigning Supreme?" Thrax asked.

"You may," she said.

"Although high, I believe eleven percent casualties are within the Imperial norms," Thrax said.

"Answer him," AX-29 said.

"If we had normal resupply routes," the chief Assault Leader said, "we could accept even fifty percent casualties as normative. Not that we would accept such a loss with the low enemy numbers. But we lack any resupply. Thus, to conquer the entirety of Human Space, we need to keep our ship numbers high until we build resupply centers."

"I understand," Thrax said.

"Conjugate on possibilities," AX-29 said.

Thrax stood respectfully silent for three-quarters of an hour.

"Well?" AX-29 asked. "Haven't you thought of anything yet?"

Thrax bobbed his head. "I have a suggestion. I was still mulling over its ramifications."

"Speak, Thrax," the Reigning Supreme said. "I do not really expect anything useful from you. I merely want another creature's insight. I doubt your war-planning can surpass that of my assault leaders."

"The humans are clever," Thrax said. "I found them able to change their battle plans quickly. Normally, I do not think—"

"Refrain from long-winded speeches," the Reigning Supreme said. "Just give me your insight."

"The humans have calculated like Imperial battle commanders," Thrax said. "They see our rate of advance and our tonnage. I suggest you modify your attack in order to throw their defenses into chaos."

"What can you have possibly seen that we did not?" the chief Assault Leader demanded.

"You have not used the jump ships in your calculations," Thrax said. "The vessels can leap ahead of the main fleet, striking enemy concentrations. Once they have done so, the jump ships will use the star drive to retreat out of danger and attack elsewhere on the battlefield."

"How could that change the outcome of the battle?" the Reigning Supreme asked.

Thrax waxed eloquent on the use of the star-drive jump. He'd thought for endless months about how to use those ships. It surprised him the assault leaders hadn't seen the possibilities yet. Perhaps they were too hidebound by Imperial customs or maybe because they'd never used such ships before, their uses escaped them.

After Thrax finished talking, the chamber fell silent.

"May I address his perfidy?" the chief Assault Leader asked.

The Reigning Supreme made a subtle gesture.

"The star-drive ships are our secret weapon," the Assault Leader said. "We are saving their use for a truly desperate battle. This is not it."

"Why not use your greatest advantage in the beginning?" Thrax countered. "The humans are likely throwing everything they have into this battle. Now is the time to shift as much as we can in our favor so we keep as many of our ships intact as we can."

"What?" the chief Assault Leader asked. "The enemy has sent minuscule numbers against us. They must be gathering their main strength elsewhere. Surely, you can see that?"

"The humans think differently than we do," Thrax said. "They use technology in lieu of mass. They will never have anything approaching our numbers. They have gathered their main strength. Now is the time to use the jump ships."

"You cannot possibly know that," the chief Assault Leader said.

"Haven't you read my report on the humans?" Thrax asked.

"Your report?" the Assault Leader asked, as if outraged by the question.

"Explain your statement," AX-29 said.

"I wrote a detailed study on the humans," Thrax said. "I have watched the Swarm battle against them for my entire life."

"Are you talking about your time on the Builder Dyson Sphere?" the Assault Leader asked.

"Yes," Thrax said.

"That knowledge is meaningless for two reasons," the Assault Leader said in a scoffing way. "One, you were all hybrids. You were not Imperial soldiers. Two, they were modified humans in an enclosed system. Those humans did not have spaceships. What you learned there is meaningless to these particular humans."

"I beg to differ," Thrax said. "I learned—"

"Reigning Supreme," the Assault Leader asked. "I have listened to the Technical Assistant for quite some time. He overreaches himself now. Must I endure this indignity?"

"Is it an indignity to save our fleet from excessive casualties?" Thrax countered.

"He speaks before you ruled," the Assault Leader said in horror.

"Forget about the star-drive ships," AX-29 told Thrax. "They are a secret weapon we shall save for a greater moment of need, if that need should ever arise. Do you have anything else to say?"

"I do," Thrax said.

"Then do so quickly," she said.

"I suggest you do anything other than a mass rush into the Outer System. I think the humans will expect that. Normally, Imperial fleets swamp an enemy. This time, we should use clever tactics."

No one spoke.

"I suggest two possibilities," Thrax said, emboldened by the silence. "One, maneuver around the star system. Find the Laumer Points. Head for the nearest one. In this way, we avoid their concentration of preparation. We will use speed of maneuver to surprise them elsewhere."

Still, none of them spoke.

"If that is not to your liking," Thrax said, "send a mass of missiles ahead of the main fleet. Let the humans expend their missiles on our missiles. Granted, that will use up our finite supply of missiles faster, but that will keep more of our spaceships intact. It will be easier later to manufacture more missiles than to build more spaceships."

Finally, the Reigning Supreme stirred. "I find one of Thrax's suggestions interesting. Instead of a full system-wide assault, let us use a narrow front attack. We will use attrition against attrition on a limited basis. The humans will not expect that."

"No," Thrax said, "because that throws away our advantage of greater numbers. I suggest we do anything except for that."

"Assault Leaders?" asked AX-29.

The assault leaders glanced at each other. Likely, they realized that Thrax was correct.

"Perhaps we could modify your ingenious plan," the highest-ranked Assault Leader told the Reigning Supreme. "Let us use three narrow frontal assaults. At the last moment, however, we will expand to a regular assault, enveloping the humans with our superior numbers."

The Reigning Supreme might have realized her plan was flawed, and the assault leaders had given her a way to change her mind to try a normal attack as originally planned.

"Go," AX-29 told Thrax. "Take your strange ideas with you. The Imperium does not need them. I had thought... It does not matter now. You have disappointed me, Technical Assistant. I should have known better."

"Perhaps I should go the saucer-ships and inspect—" Thrax said.

"Soldiers," AX-29 said. "Remove the Technical Assistant. He is not moving fast enough."

Thrax thought about trying to scuttle away before the soldiers came, but he realized that would only bring a worse punishment. He'd tried to get to the jump ships. Maybe another chance would come later.

His first strategy would have proven sound. Even so, the present Imperial Fleet would crush the humans in this carefully prepared star system. The question was, how many hits would the Imperial Fleet take in order to prevail?

-10-

Golden Ural sat in his command chair aboard his Star Cruiser *Boreas*.

It was amazing how quickly the past twenty-two months had passed. He'd managed to eke out a few Star Watch secrets from the Lord High Admiral. Those "secrets" had improved the star cruisers. Now, seventy-eight percent of them had a more powerful shield capability, while sixty-two percent had disrupter cannons instead of the old fusion cannons.

The Lord High Admiral had asked for nothing in return except for hard fighting when the time came. Ural understood the human's thinking. Anything and everything that could strengthen the Allied Fleet was good. Cook only thought about victory because defeat meant species death. If the Alliance should win, there were many who would accuse the Lord High Admiral of mistakes. Chief among those mistakes would be the strengthening of the New Men. But could the Alliance win without it?

During the past months, Ural had sent several of his best spies into the Commonwealth to ferret out even more secrets. Some of his commanders had questioned the wisdom of that.

"No," Ural told them. "We must take every risk to win this fight. That means learning every new technology we can."

There was another factor at play. Ural believed in keeping the lower species alive. For one thing, the Throne World needed a constant supply of women. For another, the humans were a good foil for the superiors, as it kept the Throne World honest by providing enemies to fight. If the sub-men died...

Ural found a strange sadness tightening his chest at the thought.

The cone of battle was to the far left of the approaching Swarm mass, hidden behind a gas giant. Every star cruiser in Human Space was in the cone, a large squat formation that could pour heavy firepower into a concentrated area. The cone was in direct opposition to the Swarm method.

The bugs advanced upon a broad front. Their commanders surely believed in smothering envelopment. A year ago, that would have been a reasonable tactic against the cone. Now—

Ural sat straighter in his chair. One of the greatest improvements in each star cruiser was star-drive jump ability. Superior mobility might be their greatest weapon against the incredibly more numerous Swarm ships.

Still, it was one thing to plan a battle and it was another to fight it. This one was going to last more than a few days.

"Screen," Ural said.

A moment later, the Tau Ceti System appeared on the main screen. The vast Swarm Fleet approached the Outer System, the next region after the Oort cloud. The Swarm ships had begun hard deceleration a month ago. On the last day, the bugs had begun launching incredible masses of missiles.

Those missiles did not accelerate or decelerate. Yet, because the Swarm vessels continued to decelerate, the missile mass pulled ahead of the broad-front fleet. Many of those missiles would wreck due to the system's debris cloud. Many more would continue to advance and target human missiles waiting for the Swarm Fleet to edge just a little closer.

***

As Golden Ural waited behind the farthest gas giant, Admiral Fletcher paced on his flagship. He was a big man with harsh features. He was worried but tried hard to shield that from his officers and crew. This was the first big test against the invaders.

The Allied Fleet had readied the star system for over a year. Still, their hardware did not begin to approach the mass heading for them. Now, the Swarm had launched a blizzard of missiles. They just kept coming and coming.

Fletcher had secretly been hoping the Swarm would dash through the star system, letting the heavy debris cloud obliterate most of the enemy vessels for them. Alas, such was not going to be the case. They were going to have to fight this one and do it at terrible odds.

Fletcher rubbed his fingertips together. He knew he should stop pacing, but his nerves seethed. He had to move or he'd start yelling at the top of his lungs. That wouldn't help anyone. It could positively shatter fleet morale if the news got out.

This was going to be messy. The engagement was so huge that the Swarm mass might nullify some of humanity's advantages. How did one eliminate 80,000 warships? He'd never had such a problem in the Academy. It would have been unthinkable.

Fletcher wondered about the secret report concerning the Swarm. According to Captain Maddox, the enemy had even greater numbers than this. That kept troubling Fletcher. What if this wasn't the only fleet? What if more showed up? Would another vast Swarm fleet sneak up elsewhere? Maybe this fleet, as massive as it was, was simply a diversion.

Fletcher snarled to himself. He wouldn't get anywhere by magnifying his problems. He had to face what he had today. Tomorrow would take care of itself.

"If we have a tomorrow," Fletcher whispered.

The big man stopped. He put his beefy hands behind his back. The battle wouldn't end in a day. This was going to be a marathon session. It was possible the jump drives in some of the ships would burn out before some of the crews dropped from overworking themselves.

"Are you ready?" he whispered to himself. "Can you begin yet?"

Fletcher didn't want to begin. Yet, he wanted to get this over with as soon as possible. The seething in his guts was driving him crazy. One way or another, the beginning of the annihilation of the human race would arrive in a few hours, or the beginning of its salvation.

It was just about time to get the process going.

-11-

The Battle of Tau Ceti was easily the largest battle that humanity had ever found itself in. It had the greatest number of enemy ships and the largest number of human vessels, and it was likely to produce the most casualties and breakdowns. Those breakdowns would undoubtedly prove to be a combination of nervous, physical and mechanical.

The Swarm advanced on a broad front, with a blizzard of missiles preceding the main fleet. They simply moved with an astounding number of vessels, no doubt expecting to smother any opposition. Most of the Swarm vessels in the invasion fleet had faced the Chitin, who fought in the same style and numbers. Throughout their long reign, the Swarm had found their present operational method successful more often than not.

As the 80,000-plus enemy fleet advanced, Star Watch's battleships, monitors, heavy cruisers and carriers hid behind the vast number of asteroids, comets, large pieces of debris, planets, planetary rings and heavy dust clouds. Other ships hid with them. Those included Windsor League hammerships, Wahhabi *Scimitar*-class laser-firing vessels, Syndicate missile ships and others. The New Men waited behind a gas giant, ready to employ their famous and deadly battle cone.

The hidden vessels watched the enemy horde roll toward them.

Far to the rear of the waiting capital ships was the rest of the Combined Fleet. Those were the smaller vessels, the missile boats, destroyers, frigates and others. Fletcher kept them back there for a reason. Most of those ships lacked the independent star-drive jump. They would all have to use the Laumer Points to escape the system.

In his heart, Fletcher dreaded the knowledge that he would sacrifice almost all of those smaller ships as a screen for his bigger vessels to get away. But that wouldn't happen for several days, at least.

It was always easier to build another frigate than to construct another *Conqueror*-class battleship.

"It starts," Fletcher whispered from the bridge of his flagship. It didn't start with a command on their side. The automated systems had been set into place many months ago.

The opening salvo started with missiles versus missiles. The horde of Swarm missiles approached the first thick area of debris.

Proximity detectors beeped. Signals went out, and the first human-built missiles accelerated from their launch points. They maneuvered around the pieces of debris and raced toward the oncoming horde of enemy hardware.

For the next twenty-three hours, missiles accelerated at each other and detonated. Endless thermonuclear explosions created local white spots on thousands of sensor screens. X-rays and gamma rays seethed in every direction. Heat billowed, but those heat waves were short in duration and range. The cold of space soon caused the heat to dissipate. EMP blasts washed over thousands of missiles. Sometimes the EMP was enough to short critical electronics. Sometimes, the hardening of those electronics proved tough enough.

In this type of battle, high technology was important. Mass, especially *vast* mass, proved more critical.

The Swarm command was used to such a fight. The humans had never seen its like. The Swarm horde continued its forward rush, never wavering.

On many human ships, some crews began to crack before they engaged in direct battle. The endless missile destruction ate at their morale. Most of the captains implemented stern measures to stem any mutiny. A few did not. Those ships turned tail and fled in-system. Those ships also became enemy targets.

There was another change because of those feckless crews. After several minutes of debate, the Swarm missiles began to target every piece of debris big enough to hide a capital ship.

"Damn it," Fletcher said. He sat in his command chair. "What happened to the ones whose crews cracked?"

What happened was something that was going to happen a lot more in the next week, but only to the crews on the human side. None of the Swarm crews had any thought about breaking under the strain. Such a thought would never enter a Swarm brain.

The front-most robotic laser satellites now began to maneuver into firing positions. They beamed at Swarm missiles before eventually dying under hot radiated explosions.

As the Swarm horde advanced on its broad front, the left fringe of the mighty host approached the first Tau Ceti gas giant. It had taken time for the Swarm mass to move this deeply into the Outer System.

"Now, we're going to see," Fletcher told his bridge crew. Now, the admiral of the Allied Fleet gave his first real battle orders. Those orders set into motion the second stage of the overall plan.

-12-

With flawless precision, the New Men's star cruisers accelerated out from behind the gas giant. They all headed to their right, toward the farthest edge of the approaching Swarm mass.

The star cruisers cleared the gas giant and its rings and formed into their dreaded cone of battle. This cone was squat and wide, meaning all the star cruisers were within three ranks of the front.

The instant the cone formed, the uniformed star cruisers began to target and fire. At first, the cone's combined beams reached out and swept aside any remaining Swarm missiles. Shortly thereafter, the cone targeted the first Swarm ships.

These were scout vessels in Imperial terminology. In Star Watch terms, they were as big as heavy cruisers. They also possessed extraordinarily thick hull armor.

Such hulls were little protection against the chief power of the cone. The combined star cruisers poured one hundred concentrated disrupter and fusion beams at a single vessel. Under such a hellish barrage of firepower, the enemy hull cracked like a walnut pressed by a nutcracker. The combined beams obliterated the scout in a titanic explosion.

As Golden Ural directed the other ninety-nine vessels, the combined beams switched targets and annihilated another Swarm ship in the same elapsed time.

The cone chewed into the Swarm mass, and yet the great enemy fleet continued to sweep forward. As fast as the New

Men could destroy Swarm ships, others surged forward. Their commanders also began to turn inward at the cone of battle.

The process produced massive casualties on the Swarm side. Soon, though, the Swarm scout ships would be in overlapping firing range.

Golden Ural did not give the Swarm ships such an opportunity. The cone broke apart, firing at new missiles accelerating at them. As the star cruisers did this, they rotated so their nosecones aimed inward. Seconds later, the silvery vessels began to engage their star-drive jumps, leaping in a bound to the next gas giant one and a half billion kilometers away. That put them well out of the conflict for the moment.

Unfortunately, not all the star drives worked as advertised. Three malfunctioned for various reasons and did not jump. On those, the captains fought until masses of Swarm missiles detonated the star cruisers one by one.

Two other star cruisers failed to appear in empty space. Perhaps they jumped into the gas giant. Perhaps they jumped somewhere else completely. Whatever the case, they were gone.

Despite a magnificent display of martial power, the New Men had just lost five of their precious star cruisers.

At the other edge of the Swarm mass, Star Watch deployed the bulk of their capital ships. They did not operate in a cone or any other unitary formation. Instead, the ships worked in teams of three or more, always hitting Swarm vessels with a superior number of ships and beams.

The *Conqueror*-class battleships had heavier and longer-ranged beams than Swarm lasers. They pounded the bug vessels, backed up, and pounded the enemy ships more.

The Star Watch, Windsor League and former Wahhabi ships did not perform as flawlessly as the New Men vessels. Still, there were more of them. Most were bigger than star cruisers, with heavier armor of the new kind.

For a longer duration, the human ships fought the oncoming edge of the Swarm. Unfortunately, beam coils burned out on some. On others, fueling lines erupted or cores overloaded.

Soon, those human ships that did not have jump drives accelerated away, racing for the next line of debris-hidden missiles and robotic laser satellites.

The bigger and better ships fought on to cover the retreat, pouring heavy fire at the Swarm vessels. Now, though, missiles and Swarm lasers began to hit.

A *Conqueror*-class battleship lost its drive power. Swarm missiles concentrated on it. Although it lashed out with its disrupter beam, it proved too little. The ant-like missile mass rushed in and finally blew the battleship apart.

"Pull out," Fletcher ordered on a broad-beam message. "Everyone, pull out now."

The ship captains heard the message and most obeyed. Three could not, and those ships died under the continuous Swarm advance.

As the great horde of invaders continued moving through built-up inertia, they set accelerating missiles ahead of them at the visibly retreating human ships. It was a race, and too many of the human ships lost it.

A day later, a quarter of those ships had been obliterated by the Swarm.

At that point, the next line of debris-hidden missiles and laser satellites began to thicken and engage the forward Swarm commanders. As the new missile barrage advanced against the horde, the surviving human ships raced for various Laumer Points.

Admiral Fletcher and Golden Ural held a tight-beam conference. Their ships had maneuvered and jumped near each other.

"How are your men holding up?" Fletcher asked.

The golden-skinned Ural's face never changed expression. Yet, it seemed as if his features stiffened in some manner.

"The...New Men will fight," Ural said.

Fletcher had never gotten used to working with the New Men. Even as allies, he found their arrogance maddening. He wished he could have been advancing on the Throne World. To work with these bastards—

"The Swarm are relentless," Ural said. "Incidentally, you have fought better than many of my captains expected."

If Ural thought Fletcher was going to thank him for such a backhanded compliment, the New Man had another thing coming.

"It is as I expected, however," Ural said. "Without a star drive, ships will perish in too great of numbers. I have made the calculations. With our combined forces, we have inflicted less than one hundred to one losses. That hardly dents the enemy horde. Without your masses of preset missiles, I do not believe we will continue to inflict such lopsided casualties against the Swarm."

"You're right about that," Fletcher said. "We've already expended half our missiles, a supply that took us over a year to gather. If we'd thought this battle was going to be like the English facing the Spanish Armada, we had another—"

"Excuse me," Ural said, interrupting. The lean New Man had cocked his head. "Are you referring to the ancient battle in 1588 A.D.?"

"Yes," Fletcher said.

"The Spanish Armada...how are the Swarm possibly like them?"

"The Spanish Armada sailed against England. The Spanish had to carry all their shot and gunpowder aboard their ships with them. The English fought close to their ports. So, once the English ships ran out of shot and gunpowder, they sailed back into port and got more, or supply ships brought them more. The Spanish soon had to conserve their shot because they'd run too low too quickly and couldn't resupply."

"I see, I see," Ural said. "The Swarm have conserved nothing as they battle us. They expend missiles even more prodigiously than we do."

"That's my point," Fletcher said. "The Swarm..." He shook his head.

"The battle has just begun," Ural said. "You must not lose heart."

"You'll lose it before I do," Fletcher spat angrily.

Ural's strange eyes seemed to swirl with something. He did not retort, though, but held his tongue.

I need them, Fletcher reminded himself. *Humanity needs the New Men*. It was a galling admission, but true nonetheless.

Thus, Fletcher swallowed his distaste. It was likely Ural did the same. The two of them began to discuss the next phase of battle…

***

The Battle of Tau Ceti lasted three weeks of fighting, maneuvering, repairing, sustaining, plotting, and more executing.

That wore the men down, those who survived. Too many Star Watch vessels had exploded for one reason or another. The majority of those died to enemy missiles. The next highest category of attrition was some kind of engine or core failure. The sustained firing took a toll on far too many vessels. The last category was Swarm lasers. The human ships seldom allowed themselves to get caught close enough, or for long enough, to take the deadly laser fire.

By far, the largest number of ship losses came in the lesser vessels, those without star drive jump capability. The greatest number of Swarm losses were from their scout vessels.

At the end of the three weeks, Fletcher gave the order to retreat full scale. All the carriers had survived because he hadn't thrown any fold fighters into the mix. That would be for the toe-to-toe slugging matches if it came to that.

And the admiral had a bad feeling it would come to that before humanity was ready for it.

Fletcher held a short briefing aboard his flagship with his tactical team. The team told him they had inflicted 54 to 1 losses against the enemy. That was in terms of ship losses. Star Watch had lost 241 ships and inflicted a little over 13,000 kills against the vast armada of 80,000 warships.

The New Men had done better. They had slaughtered 86 to 1 loss, having seen 33 of their star cruisers destroyed or lost during the conflict. But as good as the ratio looked, they had only annihilated 3000 enemy ships.

The smaller number was due to having almost no New Man missiles in the system. A large majority of Star Watch's kills had come from the incredible number of missiles and laser satellites stuffed into the system.

Altogether, the Allied Fleet had destroyed nearly 16,000 enemy vessels and lost 274 warships.

In the war of averages, humanity in all its forms was losing the battle for survival. At this rate, the bugs would have ships left after the New Men and Star Watch had lost everything. The Swarm could afford these staggering losses and still come out victorious.

"We fought better than we've ever done before," Fletcher told the Lord High Admiral. "But that still means we didn't fight good enough to win."

Golden Ural had a different conversation with Lord Drakos. The two of them had just retreated from the Tau Ceti System.

"Did you learn anything?" Drakos asked from a screen.

Ural nodded. "The mission was a success."

"And?" Drakos asked.

"We've captured bugs, a saucer-shaped ship of them. It will take time for our scientists to figure out Swarm command structure and ranks."

"We need something *now*, Commander," Drakos said.

"I know," Ural admitted.

Several hours ago, three cloaked star cruisers had slipped in behind the vast enemy formation. They had moved to a clot of the saucer-shaped vessels. Ural had noticed earlier that the bugs kept those ships well out of the fighting. Those ships seemed quite different compared to the other Swarm vessels. He wanted to know why. Even better, he'd seen an opportunity to learn more about the enemy.

If they were going to defeat the Swarm, they had to outwit them. The only way they could do that was by knowing more about the bugs.

Like wolves prowling a giant herd, the cloaked star cruisers had moved against a straggler. They had employed a stasis field, freezing the saucer-shaped vessel. They'd sent special commandos and filled the ship with knockout gas. Afterward, the cloaked ships used tractor beams, locked onto the Swarm vessel and jumped with it in tow.

Even now, scientists began to dissect and study the bugs and attempt to learn their alien language.

"I hope you're not going to share our hard won knowledge with the sub-men," Drakos said, his features stiff with displeasure.

"I see no reason to do so," Ural said. What he meant was that he did not see a reason *yet*. There might come a time when he would tell Admiral Fletcher, but he wasn't going to tell the hardliner Drakos that.

Drakos seemed to delight in the hidden information. Even so, he cut the connection soon thereafter.

Ural studied a manifest. It surprised him to learn the saucer-shaped vessel had star-drive jump technology. That was very interesting, very interesting indeed.

Why hadn't the bugs used that tech during the battle? Did it mean the bugs were too stupid to use star-drive tech?

Ural shook his head. He didn't know, but he planned to find out. They were going to lose the war at this rate, and that he could not stomach.

-13-

The Swarm Fleet had taken twenty percent losses while inflicting a miniscule number of kills against the human ships.

The Reigning Supreme could not understand it and she raged at her assault leaders. How could they have devised such an inefficient attack schedule? The assault leaders gave her unsatisfactory answers. In desperation, she remembered the offensive Thrax. Despite her dislike at the prospect, she summoned the hybrid to the command chamber.

***

Thrax lowered himself before the Reigning Supreme. Unlike last time he'd been here, there were no assault leaders present. He knew that meant something. What he didn't know was if that was good or bad. He assumed bad but pretended it was good.

"I hurried here as soon I received word," Thrax said.

"What else would you have done?" the Reigning Supreme demanded.

She sounded upset. Thrax remembered he was supposed to have let her speak first. If he was going to—

"Do I have your attention, Technical Assistant?"

"Most assuredly," he said.

"Your eyes glazed over like a worker thinking of its after-work treat."

Thrax almost spoke again. Just in time, he kept his clackers from moving.

"Better," AX-29 said. "Better… Thrax, I have a dilemma. Surely you have seen the ratios of destruction."

Thrax had, but he wasn't going to admit to it just in case this was a test.

"Well?" she demanded. "Have you seen the ratios or not?"

"I have not," he lied.

"But I thought…" She waved her tiny appendages under her vast bulk. Polishers buffed her more vigorously. Feeders thrust tubes at her.

"No! Not yet," she said in a miff. "I want to savor the mush, and I can't do that seeing this freak twitching before me."

Thrax was certain this was it for him. She must have convened this meeting to inform him—

"Technical Assistant, didn't you hear my question?"

"I'm sorry, no," Thrax admitted. She had just spoken and he hadn't been paying attention.

"I asked why you haven't seen the reports. I sent them to you."

"Oh, *those* ratios," Thrax said. "Yes, yes, I forgot that—"

"How are you supposed to help me when you can't even understand simple questions?"

"Help you?" asked Thrax.

The vast Reigning Supreme grew quiet as she studied Thrax. Finally, she sighed.

"I have grown weary of the timid and unimaginative advice of the assault leaders. I miss the Assault Master. Now, there was a war thinker. He would have known what to do. It was a shame the soldiers had to destroy him. Perhaps…well, never mind. It doesn't matter now. We have what we have, and that is the crux of the problem."

Thrax waited as his hope rose. Perhaps his guile was going to pay off after all.

"I am in a unique situation," the Reigning Supreme said. "I have hopped across the spiral arm, leaving my supply base two thousand light-years behind. We are effectively cut off from any reinforcements."

"That was always going to be the case," Thrax said.

267

"Don't you think I know that?" she shouted. "We have such a tiny fleet with which to conquer such a vast area. What I don't understand is why the humans only used such a small portion of their fleets against us."

Thrax cocked his head.

"What does that mean?" she asked. "Do you disagree with the analysis?"

"The humans will not have anything like the mass we do," Thrax said.

"Explain that?"

"We likely faced the massed might of the human star fleets."

"That is ridiculous," the Reigning Supreme said. "You saw the extent of their missile barrage. That was close to Imperial norms. Certainly that was how the Chitin spaceships fought us."

"Chitins are insectoid creatures," Thrax said. "Mammals simply cannot marshal mass like we or the Chitins are able to do."

"Do you truly consider yourself a Swarm creature?" AX-29 asked, changing the tone of her question.

"Yes," Thrax said. What else could he say?

"What a concept," she said. "And yet, I think I have need of your hybrid outlook. The staggering losses for the pinprick enemy kills have shaken my belief in eventual victory. I would not have summoned you otherwise."

Thrax was stunned at this reversal of fate. He could not believe it. If he hadn't destroyed the Golden Nexus this never would have happened.

"Why do you preen yourself at this news?" she asked.

"I believe there is a way to understand the humans better," Thrax said hastily.

"Why would we do that?"

"In order to exploit one of their weaknesses," he said.

"I suspect you have other reasons."

"I do," he said.

"Explain them."

"We must discover the local wormhole routes," Thrax said. "We must fully understand their military capabilities. I have studied the Chitin campaign. Great thought went into our latest victory against them."

"You are boasting," she said. "The plan was yours."

"Yes, I suppose it was," Thrax said, as if surprised.

The Reigning Supreme eyed him again, growing silent. Could she have made a mistake earlier concerning Thrax? That seemed inconceivable. And yet, she had lost twenty percent of the invasion fleet. That was a monstrous loss for such little gain.

"Perhaps normative Imperial actions are not the correct procedure in my situation," the Reigning Supreme said.

Thrax wanted to agree, but waited instead. He could not believe this stroke of luck. He must exploit this to the best of his ability.

"Yes…" she said. "I am assigning you a new task. You are to gather a landing army. You will collect Hive Master-level humans and study them. You will bring me these wormhole charts. I also want to know why the humans have thrown so few spaceships into this battle. Once I discover that…I shall proceed with the next phase of the operation."

"I would like to suggest one other possibility," Thrax said.

"I give you leave to speak," she said.

"Perhaps we could begin to set up production centers," he said. "We expended a great quantity of missiles last battle. It would behoove us to replenish what we can while we may."

"Now I see why I summoned you, *Commander*."

"What?" he asked, surprised.

"Yes," she said. "I am elevating you from Technical Assistant to your former rank of Commander. Now go. Discover these things for me."

Swelling with pride, Thrax turned and headed away.

Several minutes later, the Reigning Supreme motioned her soldiers. They carried a pallet with a bloated chief Assault Leader upon it.

"Did you listen to our talk?" the Reigning Supreme asked.

"Yes," the Assault Leader said.

"Do you think he believed me?" she asked.

"All the signs of his hybrid nature point to that."

269

"I think you are correct. I found the experience befouling in the extreme."

"He is a strange being that can dare to call himself Swarm."

"I found that insulting," AX-29 said. "Still, I do not understand how Thrax could have brought harm to our fleet."

"I know that it is almost impossible to fathom," the Assault Leader said. "But Thrax is cunning. He has the qualities of a Hive Master."

"I would have thought that preposterous seven days ago," the Reigning Supreme said. "Now, I have begun to wonder. If you are correct about this...I now elevate you to the Assault Master position."

The newly elevated Assault Master bowed low on the spongy deck.

"I have begun to believe your suspicion," the Reigning Supreme said. "I think Thrax had a hand in the collapse of the hyper-spatial tube. I can almost believe this is a Builder plot. The Queen and her Council have long believed the Builders have departed our region of space. Now...now it appears they are playing a cunning hand against us. I will be very interested to see what Thrax will find on the planets."

The Assault Leader—the new Assault Master—bobbed his head.

The feeders approached with dripping tubes. The Reigning Supreme's clackers twitched. The new Assault Master backed away. Then, the feeders shoved the tubes into her mouth and began to pump mush into her bloated form.

As the Reigning Supreme ate, she wondered which of her lies would end up being the truth. She was playing Thrax and the new Assault Master against each other. She had told each what they wanted to hear. Twenty percent losses for only a few hundred enemy kills—that was horrifying.

In order to console herself, the Reigning Supreme continued to ingest more royal mush.

***

Thrax landed on Tau Ceti Prime and began collecting humans from various sources. The cityscapes smoked from the planetary bombardments while fires raged everywhere. Many of the human survivors were dragged from underground shelters.

Thrax, Vim and the others worked tirelessly. In a matter of a week, they had gathered enough. The interrogations began shortly thereafter, producing excellent results.

Thrax found a shipping center and downloaded shipping routes, soon having a detailed Laumer Point map of the various routes. He wrote reports regarding Star Watch, the Windsor League and the former Wahhabi Empire. It was quite possible he gained faster intelligence than any normative Swarm creature could have done.

Even while all that took place, he inspected the most promising industrial sites. Two weeks after the end of the Battle of Tau Ceti, new Swarm missiles came off an assembly line.

The influx of new missiles surprised the Reigning Supreme. She summoned Thrax to report to the command ship.

Before the Reigning Supreme and before the new Assault Master and his aides, Thrax showed them the wormhole route map.

"Show me Earth," the Reigning Supreme said.

Thrax did so with a pointer.

"Three Laumer Point jumps away," the Assault Master said thoughtfully. "The first Laumer Point leads to an uninhabited system, at least according to your intelligence report. The second Laumer Point will take us to this Alpha Centauri System and the third and last to the Solar System."

"I suggest we make an immediate attack," Thrax said.

The Assault Master moved his appendages in sudden agitation.

"You do not agree?" the Reigning Supreme asked him.

"This could be a clever trap," the Assault Master said. "I have learned one thing from these humans. They are cunning."

"They are desperate," Thrax retorted. "They built up Tau Ceti for over a year, and we swept that aside with ease. This is the moment, Reigning Supreme. I have given you the path to victory."

"I do not agree," the Assault Master said, nettled. "Consider the possibilities. Surely, the humans expect a direct

271

attack as we showed them here, our normative way. We lost twenty percent of our fleet this time. I suggest that is not *sweeping them aside* as Thrax so callously said."

The Reigning Supreme silently agreed.

The Assault Master seemed to recognize that. He spoke more confidently. "If we lose another twenty percent in the empty system and another in the Alpha Centauri System and a final twenty percent in the Solar System—"

"Then we have achieved complete victory," Thrax said, interrupting. "We will have won."

"What is your hidden agenda in saying that?" the Assault Master asked. "I have studied your stellar map of the Commonwealth. They have vastly more star systems than these paltry four."

"I realize that," Thrax said. "What you seem unable to understand is that the humans are almost defenseless now. They hoped to stop us at Tau Ceti, building up as we traveled here. In some manner, they knew we were coming and this was their great and studied attempt. Need I remind you that their attempt failed? Now, we must simply do as ordered, destroying Earth, and we win the war. The mammals *must* defend Earth. As they do so, we will smash their last concentrations of ships. The rest will be mopping up operations. I have uncovered their weakness. I have given you victory, Reigning Supreme."

"How can the mammals have known about our secret assault for so long?" the Reigning Supreme asked. "That is not logical."

"I don't understand that either," Thrax said. "Yet, I suspect Captain Maddox had a hand in that."

"Who is this creature?" the Reigning Supreme asked.

"A human I fought at the Builder Dyson Sphere," Thrax said.

The Reigning Supreme recoiled at the mention of a Builder. She eyed the hybrid anew, remembering that Thrax had grown up on a Dyson Sphere, trained by the Builder. Perhaps the Assault Master was correct. This could all be an elaborate Builder trap. How could she know the truth one way or another?

Maybe the Assault Master took her silence the wrong way. "I beg you, Reigning Supreme," he said. "Give me twenty-one extra days to continue repairing our ships. Many have taken extensive damage. Twenty-one more days will see us substantially stronger."

"Waiting that long is a mistake," Thrax said. "We must hit the humans while they are reeling from the Tau Ceti fight."

"What can the humans do in twenty-one extra days?" the Reigning Supreme asked.

"In truth," Thrax said, "I don't know. Every instinct tells me—"

"I have heard enough," the Reigning Supreme said, interrupting him. "We will attack, as that is the Imperial norm. I will no longer deviate from standard strategy and tactics. We are the Swarm. We will survive by acting like Imperial servants. But, we will first wait twenty-one more days and finish the repairs to the most heavily damaged ships. In that time, we will also continue to replenish our missile stocks."

She eyed them both.

"I have taken a little advice from each of you," she explained, "and mixed it with the normative tactics. After the end of the twenty-one days, we will achieve glorious victory over the mammalian cowards who fled from the battlefield."

-14-

As the Swarm engaged in further repairs, as the humans, new and old, engaged in bitter debates and arguments about what to do next, Starship *Victory* appeared in Earth orbit along with the alien Destroyer.

Those weren't the only reinforcements to arrive. The New Man Darius brought five Vendel Juggernauts to the Solar System. They were filled with Vendels ready to assist Captain Maddox because of everything he'd done for them.

Meanwhile, the final Destroyer was no longer in the null space. Neither was the long-suffering Ska. They had yet to leave the strange realm through which they journeyed. Where they would appear...that was anyone's guess.

PART III
THE EXTENDED BATTLE FOR EARTH

-1-

As the Kai-Kaus chief technicians and their many subordinates moved through the neutroium-hulled Destroyer, cataloging and realigning alien systems so Captain Maddox and company could use the craft in the coming battle, Sergeant Riker had a bad dream.

Riker was in his quarters aboard *Victory*. He slept fitfully, tossing and turning. He had been on an alien Destroyer before, and he'd hated the experience. The place had felt too alien, too evil and bizarre. Riker loved growing green things; flowers, carrots, bushes and trees. He loved something essential about them. Some said he had a green thumb.

But the Destroyer...whoever had fashioned it long ago— the Ska, he knew. Yes, the Ska as a species had a brown thumb. Everything they touched turned to shit.

Riker moaned in his sleep. He hated the Ska. He was a lover of life. They represented death. Having the taint of death on his person—

Riker's eyes shot open. He stared upward, not seeing anything in particular. Instead, he heard a call. It was distant thing. It was not a siren call that lured him. It was like an ogre roaring a challenge. However, since the creature making the roar was far, far away—

"It's coming," Riker said in a gruff voice, with his eyes still not seeing anything in particular.

The distant call sounded again, and it seemed closer than before. It seemed to be hurtling toward—

Riker sat upright in his bed. He shook his head several times. He blinked repeatedly.

"Oh," he said, waking up, finding himself staring at nothing as he sat up in bed.

Riker rubbed his forehead. What had that been about? It couldn't mean anything. If dreams were supposed to mean stuff, he would have done a thousand crazy and immoral things in his time.

Riker swung around so he could put his feet on the floor. He lurched upright, heading for the hatch.

***

Riker moved through the corridors, his naked feet slapping against the cold deck. He hadn't passed anyone yet. Most of the crew was still on leave, on Earth.

Victory was closer to Mars, though. That's where the Destroyer was too, three hundred kilometers away in space.

Riker moved robotically as if hardly aware of what he was doing. He rounded a corner—

"What in blazes are you doing, man?"

Riker kept walking.

"Sergeant," Ludendorff called. "What's wrong with you?"

The voice finally penetrated Riker's senses. He stopped, turned around and regarded the open-mouthed professor.

"I think it's coming," Riker said.

"Never mind about that," Ludendorff said. "Why are you wandering around the ship in your underwear?"

Riker frowned and moved his head as if rusted. He looked down at himself and found that Ludendorff was right. He wore tighty-whiteys and nothing else.

"My dear, boy," Ludendorff said, "don't you know that those went out of style hundreds of years ago? They hug your junk much too tightly. It shows a repressed nature to wear such ridiculously binding clothing around your privates. You certainly don't want one of the fairer crewmembers seeing you like that. She'll tell others and none of them will want to test your mettle under the covers. You're sabotaging yourself, my boy. If you're going to be outrageous, better to wander around in the buff. That will get tongues wagging, but in the right direction. Some of the women will believe—"

"Shut up!" Riker shouted, grabbing his head as if the professor's words hurt him. "Shut up and let me think. I can't think."

"I see," Ludendorff said, who seemed not to have taken the slightest offense at the outburst. Instead, the Methuselah Man studied the sergeant as if seeing him for the first time.

"What did you say before?" Ludendorff asked.

"I can't remember now."

"Wasn't it: 'It's coming?'"

Riker nodded as understanding swirled in his eyes. "What do you think that means?"

Ludendorff snorted. "I would think that obvious even to an outmoded individual like yourself. You must be referring to the Ska. What else could have caused this...?" Ludendorff waved a hand.

Riker kept blinking as if his mind had gone into auto mode.

"Galyan," Ludendorff called.

The AI holoimage appeared a moment later.

"Galyan," Ludendorff said. "Why don't—"

"Professor," Galyan said, interrupting. "Why is Sergeant Riker only wearing underwear? Isn't that odd?"

"Do you see what I mean?" Ludendorff asked Riker. "Even Galyan finds the tighty-whiteys obscene. It's time for a change of style, my boy."

Riker seemed to find it harder to think the longer he stood there.

"This is decidedly odd behavior for the sergeant," Galyan said. "According to my analysis, it indicates a deeply troubled mind."

"Ah, yes," Ludendorff said. "Galyan, I want you to play back the sergeant's passage through the corridors as far back as you can."

"Will that help to solve his strange behavior?" Galyan asked.

"That's the hope," Ludendorff said.

Two seconds later, Galyan produced a holoimage of Riker moving down the corridors. Ludendorff moved closer to the holo-recording, studying it.

"Can you play any audio?" the professor asked Galyan.

The AI did so. At certain times, the others could hear Riker's slapping feet.

"Notice his eyes," Ludendorff said. "They're glazed over." He turned to Riker. "Do you know what caused this?"

Riker shook his head.

"Where were you headed?"

"I...I was—I'm looking for Maddox. I have to warn him that it's coming. I could feel..."

"Yes, yes," Ludendorff said. "What could you feel?"

"A brown thumb," Riker said.

"As opposed to a green thumb, perhaps?" asked Ludendorff.

"Yes," Riker said, as he snapped his fingers. "I dreamed of death, approaching death, a killer, a—"

"A Destroyer," Ludendorff said in a hardening voice. "You knew the captain was in danger before against the Visionary on the Fisher world. This must have something to do with the Ska, and possibly with the Visionary or Spacers, as well. Yes. Go find Maddox."

Ludendorff turned around.

"Where are you going?" Riker asked.

"This is Dana's area of expertise," the professor said. "I want her to hear and see this. I have a feeling your dream is vitally important."

-2-

Captain Maddox stood beside Ludendorff in an observation room. On the other side of a two-way mirror, Riker lay on a couch in dim quarters. The sergeant wore his uniform, although he did not presently wear any boots or socks.

Dana sat beside the sergeant on a chair. She had an open notebook and a pen on her lap. She spoke quietly to Riker, having already administered a special drug to him.

"You're not saying much," Ludendorff said quietly.

Maddox didn't reply or look at the professor. He'd been speaking with Mary O'Hara earlier. She'd shown him the last images from Tau Ceti as found by the Builder Scanner.

The majority of the Swarm Fleet had moved near the Laumer Point to Epsilon 5, an empty system that led, among other paths, to the Alpha Centauri System. That was the fastest route to Earth. The implication from the Swarm Fleet's location was they knew what they were doing concerning wormhole routes.

O'Hara had shown him other things, as well. He'd seen Tau Ceti Prime and some of the renewed industrial output there. The Swarm worked astonishingly quickly. Of course, that made sense with millions of Swarm workers working overtime on the surface. He'd also seen repair ships fixing heavily damaged Swarm vessels.

There had been one other interesting holo-vid, a recording. It had shown three cloaked star cruisers. O'Hara had shown Maddox the stasis field in operation. The New Men had captured a bug ship, jumping to a different place with it. If Golden Ural knew about the operation, the New Man had not shared it with Star Watch yet.

Those and other worries had Maddox preoccupied. This incident with Riker—

"I say, my boy," Ludendorff said. He shook Maddox's right forearm. "Are you listening to me?"

Maddox turned abruptly, snatching his forearm out of the professor's grasp. He did not like people touching him, except for Meta.

"I'm not diseased," Ludendorff said.

Maddox gave him a curt nod.

"Yes, yes, I know. You have strange phobias. I suppose that goes with your..."

Maddox's eyes had begun to smolder.

"With your many responsibilities," Ludendorff said, undoubtedly changing what he'd been about to say concerning Maddox's hybrid nature.

The two of them fell silent as Dana began questioning Riker. The sergeant twisted about on the couch and kept repeating, "It's coming."

Dana tried to dig deeper. It didn't help. Finally, Riker's eyes snapped open as he glared at the doctor.

"It's coming!" the sergeant shouted, with spittle flying from his lips. "Don't you get it? It's coming! It's going to kill us all! There's nothing we can do! It's—"

Dana moved in, trying to press a hypo against his side. Riker lashed out, hitting her wrist with his bionic arm. Dana's arm swung back as something cracked. She whitened, swaying, seeming ready to faint.

Ludendorff headed to the hatch.

Maddox beat him to it. He flung open the hatch. "Sergeant," he said sternly.

Riker turned haunted eyes on him. "It's coming," the sergeant said in a pleading tone. "Why won't anyone listen to me?"

"Come with me," Maddox said.

Riker seemed as if he was about to flare up again. Finally, he nodded. "Something is seriously wrong with me, isn't it, sir?"

"Maybe," Maddox said.

"Please," Riker said. "Don't lie to me."

"Yes. Something is wrong with you."

"Is there a cure for this...taint?" Riker asked.

"I don't know," Maddox admitted. "If there is, I'm going to find it."

Riker nodded again, but it seemed a hopeless gesture.

By that time, medics had arrived, taking a shaken Dana with them. She cradled her broken wrist and seemed afraid to look at Riker as she departed.

"I want my old life back," Riker said.

"I think the entire Commonwealth wants its old life back," Maddox said.

"Why is this happening?" Riker asked.

"Because we're alive," Maddox said. "As long as we're alive, we're going to have problems. That is the nature of life, a constant struggle for survival."

"Begging your pardon, sir," Riker said, "but that sounds like a New Man philosophy."

"Perhaps it is."

Riker stared at him, finally nodding once more. "I wish I could tell you more."

"Don't worry about it, Sergeant. We've always won through in the end."

"We've never faced these kinds of problems before, though."

Maddox shrugged. "Either we win or we lose. The critical thing is that we fight. We will never stop fighting until we're dead, and that includes against the taint the Ska put on you."

Riker blinked several times. A tired smile crept onto his face. "That's good advice, sir. I'll keep fighting,"

Maddox moved closer, and he clapped Riker on his fleshly shoulder. Then the captain turned around. He needed to speak to Ludendorff. The Methuselah Man had likely departed with Dana. So Maddox headed for the med center.

-3-

Maddox pulled Ludendorff out of the medical chamber where medics worked on Dana. He pulled Ludendorff along, heading into the corridor.

"That's quite enough," Ludendorff said, trying to shrug his arm out of the captain's grasp.

Maddox merely tightened his hold, forcing the Methuselah Man to keep stumbling in order to keep up.

"I say, old boy, this has gone on long enough. If you don't release me—"

Maddox stared at Ludendorff as if daring him to do something.

"Don't say I didn't warn you," the professor said.

Maddox's grip tightened even more. Then his hand flew off as a terrific shock jolted him. Maddox staggered backward, his hand feeling as if it burned with fire. He shook his hand and finally regarded Ludendorff with some surprise.

The professor wore a smug look. "I tried to warn you, but no…you couldn't bother giving a man the same courtesy you demand for yourself."

Maddox flexed his hand, covertly examining it. The flesh did not seem burned although it still felt raw.

"Neuro-lash," Ludendorff said. "Works every time."

Maddox's hand froze, as he looked up, staring at Ludendorff a second time. "A lash," the captain said.

"What's gotten into you, my boy? I'm the one who should be upset. Look at what your man did to Dana. That was an outrage."

"What do you know about the Ska?"

"We've been over this before to a tedious degree," Ludendorff complained. "I've already told you what I know."

"Professor, you often say such things. Just as often, you keep the juiciest tidbits to yourself in order to wring some perceived advantage for yourself later."

"My *modus operandi* has served me well thus far," Ludendorff said with some pride.

"Perhaps," Maddox said. "Perhaps you should understand, though, why I probe further. Now, what do you know about the Ska?"

"Hmmm...well," Ludendorff said, running a thumb underneath the small gold chain around his neck. "It appears to be coming here, if that's what Riker is warning us about."

"That is my own conclusion," Maddox said. "I suspect it's using the thought-travel route as we did—or whatever the process is. If the Ska isn't using the route directly, the person he controls is doing so."

"If that's the case," Ludendorff said, "we're wrong about the null space being a permanent trap for it."

"I've already accepted that as a given."

"Yes, yes," Ludendorff said. "I knew that, too, but it's good to lay out the parameters in order to arrive at the correct conclusion. So... If Riker is correct, the Ska is coming here, maybe coming after you or the Destroyer. Likely, the Ska is coming with the other Destroyer. Presumably, the Ska will appear in the company of at least one Spacer. I would tend to think more."

Maddox nodded.

Ludendorff cocked his head. "The question is: when will it appear?"

"Soon," Maddox said.

"Is soon a week, two weeks, what?"

"Is it an hour or a day?" asked Maddox.

"This is maddening." Ludendorff looked up suddenly. "I think it's going to be longer than a day."

"Why?"

"The nature of the warning shows that," Ludendorff said. "I suspect Riker's subconscious recognizes the nearing Ska. The first tendril of that coming monster likely spawned your sergeant's nightmare."

"I suppose that sounds logical."

Ludendorff turned away, his thumb trying to rub the small chain smooth. After a time, he faced Maddox again.

"This is a disaster," the professor announced.

"If you haven't noticed," Maddox said dryly, "the Swarm Fleet is also a disaster."

"Two disasters at once," Ludendorff muttered. "Even if we could figure out how to prevent the one, the other will finish us off."

"We have our Destroyer, the Juggernauts—"

"I hope you don't seriously think those additions are going to turn the tide of battle," Ludendorff said. "Even if we could capture the second Destroyer, I doubt that would be enough against the Swarm."

"Maybe we don't have to have enough to defeat the Swarm, just enough to drive them away."

Ludendorff smiled. "Galyan would tell you that the Swarm never retreats. You either destroy it or it destroys you."

"Is Galyan correct in thinking that? Thrax retreated from us at the Dyson Sphere."

"Is Thrax truly Swarm, though?"

"He looked Swarm enough to me," Maddox said. "The Kai-Kaus certainly thought of his kind as Swarm creatures. Even the Builder believed so."

"Fine," Ludendorff said. "So now that we've established that…now what?"

Maddox looked off into the distance before regarding the professor. "Isn't there some way to directly hurt the Ska?"

"My boy, we've been over this—"

"Then let's go over it again," Maddox said testily. "We were both on the Fisher world. We both saw the mural. The Fishers drove the dark cloud with rays of light. They seemed to push the Ska away with the light rays. I'd call that direct harm."

"I suppose you might have a point," Ludendorff conceded.

"Well...?" Maddox asked. "What does the ray of light in the mural represent?"

"I frankly don't know."

"Does Strand?"

"If I don't know," Ludendorff said with a scowl, "then Strand isn't likely to have any idea—"

"You told me Strand is smarter than you."

Ludendorff stiffened. "I said no such thing. I told you he knew more about the Ska than I did."

"Then he's smarter than you concerning the Ska."

"Are you deliberately trying to goad me?" Ludendorff asked suspiciously.

"Without a doubt, I'm trying," Maddox said. "Am I succeeding?"

"Only in pissing me off, my boy," Ludendorff said. "I resent your—"

"Professor Ludendorff," Maddox said. "We're almost out of time. The Ska is coming. The Swarm Fleet will soon launch its next assault. Earth hangs in the balance. You have Strand's notebook. You have your memories of the Fisher world. I suggest you do whatever it is you do at times like these. Make that mind of yours function overtime."

"Are you suggesting I ingest mind-altering drugs?"

"If it gives you even a chance of figuring this out, then yes."

Ludendorff grunted in a peeved manner.

"Give me something to work with," Maddox said.

Ludendorff's head jerked up. "You? This is all about you saving the day yet again. Is that right?"

"*Us* saving the day," Maddox said. "This is all about us saving the day, if we can, if you can decipher ancient archeological finds quickly enough."

"Hmm..." Ludendorff said. "I am the greatest archeologist since the Builders. If anyone could do this, I'm the likeliest candidate." The professor nodded. "My boy, that was a brilliant observation just now. Yes, this is all up to me, isn't it? This may be the reason the Builder modified me in the first place. Oh, I'm not saying the Builder had prophetic powers. But it must have seen that humanity would need a Methuselah Man around in order to survive a few of the more outlandish dangers in the galaxy. Yes. You're quite right. It's time I holed up in my laboratory and truly began to think."

Ludendorff eyed Maddox. "Good day, Captain, I have much work to do."

Maddox watched the professor march away. The Methuselah Man was possibly the most conceited person in the galaxy. Ludendorff was probably several orders of magnitude more conceited than the New Men. Yet, humanity's survival likely rested on his ability to figure out a way to push the Ska away from them.

That still left the Swarm fleet. Could the Destroyer and the Juggernauts turn the tide against more than 60,000 Swarm warships? The Combined Fleet had roughly three-quarters of its ships left, but only a fraction of the missiles it had deployed at Tau Ceti. How could humanity use that to halt the Swarm Invasion?

-4-

The days passed with furious activity.

The Kai-Kaus chief technicians led their squads through the fifty-kilometer-long Destroyer. The neutroium hull-armor meant the neutrons were packed side by side. It meant the Destroyer had more mass than the rest of the Combined Fleet put together. The five-kilometer-wide firing aperture meant the eventual beam would be like nothing the New Men, the *Homo sapiens* or even the Spacers could think of having. It would pour amazing destructive power upon the enemy.

Some of the Wahhabi ships had videos of the former Destroyer annihilating life on Al Salam. They had video of the Destroyer obliterating the main Wahhabi Home Fleet. Star Watch officers and selected New Men watched those videos in order to plan better.

The Kai-Kaus soon reported that they had restored the Destroyer's power sources. Now, they were working on relinking the main cannon, if that was even the right word for it.

Meanwhile, according to the Builder Scanner, the bulk of the Swarm Fleet was moving in the Tau Ceti System. The 60,000-plus warships headed for the Laumer Point that linked Tau Ceti to Epsilon 5, the empty star system.

The Lord High Admiral called a meeting of the highest-ranking officers. There were Star Watch admirals and rear admirals and two New Men representatives, Golden Ural and Lord Drakos. There were Syndicate and other high commanders. A few Spacers had shown up. They were heretics to the prevailing Spacer cult. The Vendel commander of the Juggernauts sat at the conference table. Three chief strategists were there, Ludendorff, Galyan and Captain Maddox, as well as Brigadier O'Hara.

Surprisingly, no androids had shown up to help.

"They've run far away if I know the androids," Ludendorff whispered to Maddox. The two of them sat together at the large table. Galyan stood at Maddox's other side. The holoimage had leaned near to hear the professor's aside.

The Lord High Admiral now opened the meeting with an acknowledgement of the Builder Scanner. It had been an open secret until now. Cook did this partly because he showed the assembled officers the moving Swarm Fleet on a holo-recording.

"We're going to know in several weeks, maybe two months at the most, whether or not Earth stands," Admiral Cook said in a grave voice. "I have instructed the admiral of Epsilon 5 to begin preparations for a main force Swarm advance. Hopefully, Admiral Quinn can inflict staggering losses against them. She knows her duty, and I doubt any of her squadron will flee."

Cook turned to the New Men. "Do you have anything to add so far?"

Drakos scowled as if Admiral Cook had blown bad breath into his face.

Golden Ural made a lazy gesture. "Are you thinking about anything specifically?"

"If the Swarm breaks through to Epsilon 5 with minimal casualties," Cook said, "that will diminish our chances of victory."

"An interesting observation," Ural said.

Drakos stared at Ural.

"They know," Ural told Drakos.

"Know what?" Drakos growled.

"About the alien jump ship," Ural said.

Drakos shook his head.

"It doesn't matter if I tell them," Ural said.

"No!" Drakos said. "My spies..." He let his voice fade away.

"Please," O'Hara said from farther down the table. "Tell us what your spies have uncovered from us."

Drakos gave her a burning stare.

O'Hara turned to the Lord High Admiral. "I believe Lord Drakos was about to tell us that his spies have uncovered knowledge of Captain Maddox's journey to the Builder Dyson Sphere. It was there that Thrax's saucer-shaped vessels escaped. Drakos knows that we know those ships likely have star-drive jump tech."

"Ah…" Ural said, as he turned to the Lord High Admiral. "That's why you've gone into such depth about the Builder Scanner."

"What are you talking about?" Drakos hissed at Ural.

"It's clear they used the scanner to watch our operation earlier," Ural told Drakos. "They know we have captured a saucer-shaped vessel."

There were no murmurs at the table, no shocked looks in any direction.

"Yes," Ural told Cook. "I would like to give you the specifics of the saucer-shaped ship. I would also like to warn you about the danger of those ships appearing near the Laumer Point at Epsilon 5. That would be an excellent use of the four hundred jump-capable enemy vessels."

The Lord High Admiral nodded sagely.

"Better late than never," Ural added.

Admiral Fletcher slapped a big hand against the table. "This is too much—"

"Fletcher," the Lord High Admiral said abruptly. "That's enough of that."

"But, sir—"

"I said it's enough," Cook replied in a stern voice. "These men are our allies. Like any human," he said, staring at the New Men, "they have flaws. I can forgive a man a flaw if he fights in my defense."

"Are you saying we're just like you?" Drakos asked in a dangerous voice.

"No," Maddox said.

All heads turned toward the captain.

"You're not like us," Maddox told Drakos. "You lack the same honor."

Drakos rose from his chair, with his balled fists resting on the table. "That is a slur directed against a superior."

Maddox stared at Drakos and slowly stood as well.

The Lord High Admiral traded glances with Brigadier O'Hara. She shook her head. The Lord High Admiral did not intervene this time. He watched and waited like everyone else.

"Do you know what it signifies to stand as I stand?" Drakos asked.

"Of course," Maddox said. "It means a duel."

Drakos' eyebrows shot up. "Do you believe yourself my equal because a New Man sired you?"

"No," Maddox said.

Some of the tension eased from Drakos' wide shoulders.

"I consider myself your superior," Maddox said.

For a moment, shock twisted Drakos' face. Then, a cruel smile slid into place. "That is the worst slur of all. I demand satisfaction."

"Since you have challenged me," Maddox said. "I have the choice of weapons."

"I see you are knowledgeable concerning Throne World customs."

Maddox dipped his head slightly.

"What is your weapon choice?" Drakos asked.

"No!" the Lord High Admiral said, intervening at last. "This is an improper use of a high-level strategy meeting."

Drakos seemed reluctant, but he tore away from looking at Maddox to face Cook. "This is a personal matter. I demand that you do not interfere in our affairs."

"It is not a personal matter when I need both of you," Cook said. "You will wait until the emergency is over before indulging yourselves in duels. Is that clear, Captain?" Cook asked.

Maddox inclined his head, although he never took his eyes off Drakos.

"Then I bid you sit down, sir," the Lord High Admiral asked Drakos. "And I order you to sit down, Captain."

Maddox sat without another word or gesture.

"What's gotten into you?" Ludendorff whispered.

"His face…" Maddox said, and after that, he could say no more.

Ludendorff covertly studied Drakos' features as the New Man sat. Ludendorff leaned near Maddox, whispering again, "So the New Man looks a little like you. Do you think that's significant?"

Maddox did not answer, but the emotional heat radiating from him said enough.

In the meantime, the Lord High Admiral showed another holo-vid. Perhaps he did so to get everyone's mind off the Maddox-Drakos incident. As the holo-vid progressed, the number of people glancing slyly at the two dropped off until the tiff seemed to have been forgotten.

There were more discussions, arguments and some dismay at the disparate strength levels. The vast missile attack in the Tau Ceti System was supposed to have destroyed more Swarm ships. Star Watch had hoped for greater than 100 to 1 ratios. Instead, they'd only had 54 to 1. Could the Destroyer and Juggernauts make up the difference this time?

"It's going to depend on how hard we can hit the Swarm ships coming through the Laumer Points," the Lord High Admiral said at the end. "We have some traps in case any Swarm jump-ships show up. If those traps don't work…"

"Whatever happens," Golden Ural said into the silence, "the time for planning is almost over. That will leave us facing the time for hard fighting."

-5-

Commander Thrax Ti Ix outperformed himself on Tau Ceti Prime.

The industries poured out missiles, with heavy lifters roaring into space almost every seven minutes, each with a new cargo-load for the fleet. Thrax broke his captured humans and downloaded reams of information on Star Watch, the Commonwealth, the Windsor League, Spacers, New Men, the Patrol, the Destroyers—

The Reigning Supreme summoned Thrax to the command ship.

Soon enough, Thrax stood before her. AX-29 seemed agitated. There were no feeders in evidence, and the buffers sulked in the corner. It seemed as if soldiers had struck several, an almost unprecedented occurrence.

AX-29 began speaking immediately. "What did you discover about these Destroyers?" she demanded.

"One invaded the Solar System several years ago," Thrax said. "The Destroyer—"

"How many?"

"One, as I said," Thrax told her.

"You are certain of this?"

"Oh yes," Thrax said. He wanted to ask if that was important. By now, he knew better than to do that.

"What happened to the Destroyer?"

"The reports are garbled," Thrax said. "I would say Captain Maddox forced the Destroyer to maneuver into the Solar System's star."

"And that act demolished the Destroyer?"

"Of course," Thrax said.

"No, no, no," the Reigning Supreme said. "You do not understand the significance of the Destroyer. How could you? Only highly ranked Hive Master-class Swarm receive the Higher Knowledge."

Thrax waited, yearning to obtain this knowledge. He thought back to what she could mean—

"Oh," Thrax said. "You must be referring to the Destroyers used against the Swarm ages ago."

The Reigning Supreme shrank away from Thrax to the best of her limited ability. "What do you know about that?" she whispered.

"The Builder told me," Thrax said. "Ages ago, the Builders used captured Destroyers to battle the Swarm—"

"Enough," she said. "That you know this Higher Knowledge—only the highest ranked Hive Master-class are aware of this ancient war. Not even the Assault Master knows. You must never speak of this to anyone lesser ranked than a Reigning Supreme."

She stared at him as her fear slowly dissipated.

Thrax could feel the difference in her. She was thinking about eliminating him. Likely, the normative codes said she must. If he did not give her a reason why she should keep him alive—

"I possess many such pieces of ancient data," Thrax said. "Of course, the Queen knew this," he lied.

"She did?" the Reigning Supreme asked in amazement.

"Of course," Thrax said. "She instructed me to tell you if there was any mention of Destroyers—"

"Hold Commander Thrax Ti Ix," AX-29 said. "This seems fraudulent. Yet, how could you lie? You are only—"

The Reigning Supreme made a moaning sound as her bulk shook with something approaching fear. "This cannot be," she whispered.

Thrax waited.

293

"You are a hybrid creature. You look like a soldier. The Queen gave you Technical Assistant rank. Yet, you truly have the thought-patterns of a highly ranked Hive Master. That means you are able to spout mistruths. I have taken everything you've said before this at face value. Now, I will have to check your words for possible lies. I cannot fathom that I've missed this."

"Reigning Supreme," Thrax said. "You are in a truly unique position. You are cut-off from the Imperium. You have a mere portion of your war fleet. You have faced cunning enemies and dastardly tactics. I believe the humans will practice bitter deceit against us. Even more, I believe they have secret weapons left."

"Destroyers?" she asked in fear.

"Perhaps," Thrax said. "Who can know at this point?"

"What is your point?" she asked.

"As a Reigning Supreme, duty summons you to use every Swarm facet to produce victory. I am a hybrid. This has been made abundantly clear to me. Yet, perhaps this is the moment the Imperium needs a hybrid such as me with advanced Builder knowledge. Use this fact instead of fighting against it. Instead of fearing me, discover new sources of insight to help your fleet obliterate the humans."

"Your words are difficult," AX-29 admitted. "Your sight causes loathing—"

"Yes, I know," Thrax said, interrupting. "But you were chosen because of your wisdom. This is the time to implement your wisdom to its fullest."

"How dare you attempt to instruct me."

Thrax decided to go for broke. "I dare because I am a hybrid. Yet, now more than ever you need hybrid thinking to deliver you victory. Will you use it, Reigning Supreme? Or will you throw away your best chance at ultimate victory?"

AX-29 pondered that. She squirmed. She made vomiting noises as half-digested mush dribbled from her clackers.

"What is your suggestion?" she finally asked.

Thrax bobbed his head. "This time, you must use the jump ships," he said. "As you enter the Laumer Point with the first scouts, you must send in the jump ships to attack any humans attempting to obliterate our vessels. That will be standard Star Watch tactics."

"That is a clever move. Yes."

"Let me lead the assault," Thrax said.

She studied him anew. Instead of loathing, a sense of shrewdness prevailed. "No," she said. "The Assault Master will do that. You will stay here with me, hybrid. You will give me more unusual ideas. If the humans have a Destroyer...I am going to need even more cleverness than this."

-6-

The last of the Swarm warships headed for the Epsilon 5 Laumer Point. As they did, the Assault Master joined the jump ships.

According to Thrax's suggestion, the Reigning Supreme would first send through several scout ships.

"We must assume the humans have a Builder-like ability to see our actions," Thrax told AX-29. "That is the most logical explanation for the massed missiles in the Tau Ceti System. According to my interrogations, the humans readied for us even before we reached the Oort cloud."

"That is daunting news," the Reigning Supreme agreed.

"We still defeated them, though."

"With terrible losses," she said.

"The humans will not have had such preparation time for this attack," Thrax said. "That was why I suggested before that we attack at once."

"You did not know those things before."

"That is true…" Thrax said. "I retract my last statement."

"You can maneuver mentally," the Reigning Supreme said in wonder. "How did I fail to see this earlier?"

Thrax did not tell her that her bigotry had blinded her to the truth. He was still amazed at this fantastic turn of fortune. It told him that one must always strive. Only quitters truly lost. As long as one fought, one had a chance to turn things around. He would remember that and implement it later, if needed.

Sixty thousand plus warships took time to maneuver delicately. The lower-ranked assault leaders had worked out a careful schedule in order to push through as many warships in as short an amount of time as possible.

"Now," Thrax told the Reigning Supreme, "we must sprint to the Solar System in an avalanche of attacks."

The Reigning Supreme gave the order, and the first scout ships entered the Laumer Point.

***

On the other end of the wormhole in the Epsilon 5 System, Admiral Quinn's patrol boats reported enemy ships appearing.

"In what number?" Quinn asked from her heavy cruiser flagship.

"They're still coming, Admiral. No. It looks like they've stopped. I count twenty vessels. They came through in force."

"No nukes to clear their way?" Quinn asked.

"Nothing, Admiral."

"Excellent," she said. "Maneuver the first mine and detonate it when in position."

Near the Epsilon 5-Tau Ceti Laumer Point, a heavy mine maneuvered toward twenty drifting enemy heavy-cruiser-sized warships. The bugs aboard those vessels and possibly the electronics in the vessels were experiencing severe Jump Lag. Thus, there was no counter-fire against the approaching mine. It appeared as if this was going to be a textbook Jump Lag attack.

The heavy mine maneuvered inward…and detonated. The terrific thermonuclear explosion slammed against the Swarm ships. Several of the nearest tore apart. Others took hard blasts. Those enemy hulls proved tougher than expected, though.

A second mine moved in as some electronics began to wake up on the least damaged enemy ships.

The second thermonuclear detonation savaged more enemy vessels. Likely, it blinded all the awakening enemy sensors.

"Can this be for real, Admiral?" the chief patrol boat commander asked in glee.

"Don't worry about that," the admiral said. "Send in another mine. Let's finish them off. Then start maneuvering more of your mines closer to the Laumer Point. I think the bugs are as dumb as stumps when it comes to wormhole travel."

"Yes, sir," the patrol boat commander said.

***

On the Tau Ceti side of the wormhole, more Swarm ships waited to enter the Laumer Point.

"Why hasn't one of the scout ships returned to tell us about the conditions over there?" the Reigning Supreme asked in her command chamber.

"We should give them a little more time," Thrax said.

"No. We must send through a stronger force to help them."

"I would not advise that, Reigning Supreme."

"Do not overstep your bounds, Commander. I can still send you to the crushers. I will drink your juices in delight in that case."

Thrax stopped talking, deciding there was only so much he could do in this short of a time.

***

"Look at that, Admiral," the patrol boat commander said over the comm line. "This time, forty enemy heavy cruisers have come through. The new ships are drifting in the debris of the old ones."

"Get your mines into position," the admiral said. "We're going to assume the bugs aren't going to learn any time soon, but will just push through massive amounts of reinforcements. This could be our golden opportunity."

"Yes, Admiral," the patrol boat commander said.

Shortly, twin thermonuclear explosions, one on each end of the drifting Swarm ships, struck the enemy vessels. The results were predictable: more enemy hulls shattered. Those farther away from the blasts took less damage.

A few short minutes rectified the oversight as another mine detonated, and the formerly intact enemy warships joined the growing debris in space.

"Sir," the patrol boat commander said. "I just had a brainstorm. Would you like to hear it?"

"I would," Admiral Quinn said.

"We should reverse the process on the bugs. Usually, the enemy sends a few nukes through to clear the path. They must be on the other side en masse. Let's send a few nukes onto their side and blow them to bits."

"That is an excellent suggestion, Commander. Make it so."

"You bet, sir," the patrol boat commander said.

***

The Reigning Supreme was in her command quarters, watching screens that showed the Laumer Point.

"I am getting frustrated," she told Thrax. "Why haven't—"

The great bulk leaned forward as the Reigning Supreme stared at a screen. "What just came out of the Laumer Point? That does not look like a Swarm scout. It has a most odd shape—"

A vast white explosion occurred as a heavy cobalt bomb shredded the nearby Swarm vessels waiting to enter the Laumer Point.

"What is happening?" the Reigning Supreme shouted.

"The humans are clever indeed," Thrax said bitterly. "They are sending nuclear bombs through the Laumer Point at us."

"You should have thought of that."

"Have any of your assault leaders recognized the problem as quickly as I have?" Thrax asked defensively.

"No," the Reigning Supreme admitted. "What should I do?"

"Unleash the Assault Master and his jump ships now," Thrax said. "We have waited too long. Draw the main fleet back from the Laumer Point. More enemy bombs will surely come through."

"Those are excellent suggestions," AX-29 said.

"Oh," Thrax added. "Make sure the Assault Master does not jump too near the Epsilon 5 Laumer Point. He will have to shrug off the sleeping sickness before his ships can fight. He does not want to give the enemy easy kills."

"Contact him," the Reigning Supreme said. "Give him those instructions."

Thrax scuttled to a comm unit and began to do just that.

***

299

Admiral Quinn jumped up from her command chair in shock. "Give me a close up of that," she told her sensors officer.

A moment later, she viewed drifting saucer-shaped vessels. They were two million kilometers from the Laumer Point.

"How many are there?" she snapped.

"One hundred and eighty-seven," the sensors officer said.

Quinn absorbed that. She had nine heavy cruisers, lots of mines and a willingness to fight to the death if she had too. This was a volunteer assignment. Everyone knew the score about the war.

"Use the black-ice-coated mines," she said at last. "Accelerate them for now while the enemy is caught in Jump Lag. Let the mines drift as their sensors come online. We want to catch those bastards by surprise."

"Admiral," communications said. "More Swarm heavy cruisers are coming through the Laumer Point."

"Let's keep giving them hell while we can," she said. "The odds are going to turn against us soon enough."

***

It took several days to move the entire Swarm Fleet through the cleared Laumer Point. Sixty thousand plus vessels was a lot of ships to move through such a narrow aperture.

The Assault Master's jump ships took 69 losses altogether. The scout vessels on both sides of the wormhole took 567 losses from various explosions. In return, they had destroyed nine scout-sized enemy ships and eleven escape-pod-sized vessels.

"The first were heavy cruisers," Thrax told the assembled war council. "The last vessels were called patrol boats."

The Reigning Supreme, the Assault Master and various assault leaders were in attendance.

"We lost 639 ships and destroyed 9 major enemy vessels and 11 minor vessels for a total kill of 20 ships," the Assault Master said. "Given the nature of Laumer Points and the possibilities, we achieved a grand success, a mere 32 to 1 loss ratio."

300

"Yes," the Reigning Supreme said. "I am pleased. After the struggle in the Tau Ceti System, I expected much more from the humans."

She eyed Thrax speculatively. "Maybe the humans are not as dangerous as I feared."

"The correct usage of the independent jump ships saved you grievous casualties," Thrax pointed out. "My suggestion that you send the jump ships a distance away from the Laumer Point likely saved you that fleet. However, I would like to point out that losing 69 jump ships out of 200 was a much graver loss than the 567 scout ships. The jump ships are unique for us and intensely valuable, out of proportion to their minuscule numbers."

"I take strenuous objection to your slurs against my command decisions," the massive and nearly immobile Assault Master said.

"You should not have lost *any* jump ships," Thrax told him. "I certainly would not have lost any if I had commanded them."

"That is a preposterous boast," the Assault Master said. "Reigning Supreme, I implore you."

AX-29 eyed Thrax. "I see what you are attempting to do, Commander. You wish to gain glory through leading the jump ships and will thus say anything to gain command status. Is advisory status so repugnant to you?"

"Not at all," Thrax lied. "It has been a fantastic honor to serve you in whatever capacity you deem wise."

"Then let me hear no more about you leading any ships," she said. "You are going to remain on the command ship, Thrax. I have decided that you are very clever, too clever by far to let you out of my sight."

"Reigning Supreme?" asked Thrax.

"We attained a marvel," she said. "We broke through into the empty star system with ease. The humans could have saturated the system with missiles. They did not, and thus, we took negligible losses."

"Because they lack such quantity of missiles," Thrax said. "As I keep trying to tell you, they used the bulk of their missiles in the Tau Ceti System."

"That still seems too impossible to believe," the Reigning Supreme said. "The humans could have filled Epsilon 5 with these black-ice-coated mines. They practically let us into this system. Consider, foul surprises have plagued our mission at every step. I expect more to come. Each time we believe something, the opposite happens. No. We will approach the next Laumer Point with great caution. The humans are devious beyond any race we've ever faced."

"Reigning Supreme—"

"Silence, Thrax," she said. "I am forming the next phase strategy. I have watched you. I have watched our new Assault Master. Now, I am taking matters into my own pincers. This…last surprise… this poorly defended Laumer Point…means something awful likely waits for us in the Alpha Centauri System. The humans want us to believe we can waltz right in. We will devise a few clever ruses of our own this time."

Thrax, the Assault Master and the other Hive Master-class insects bobbed their heads in agreement.

"For the moment, the fleet will move cautiously toward the next Laumer Point," the Reigning Supreme said. "Then, I will decide what to do next."

-7-

Captain Maddox marched through Star Watch HQ on Pluto. He was headed to the office of the Lord High Admiral.

It was a smart idea for Cook to stay near the Builder Scanner. It meant he could order the scanner to look anywhere, instantly. With a Builder communicator, Cook could speak to specially selected representatives. They could pass on his orders, and thereby give humanity a great advantage in knowing what the enemy was doing as he did it in real time.

This was greater than the advantage of Ultra in World War II on Earth long ago. Back in that day, the Allied side could intercept German messages, but the Germans had still surprised the Allies. They did so by keeping important orders off the encrypted machines and only giving such orders by face-to-face messengers. Thus, the Germans had totally surprised the Allies with the Battle of the Bulge attack.

Maddox had been wondering lately how refined the Builder Scanner could focus. Could the scanner see through walls as it were? The only thing better than seeing what the enemy was doing…was listening in to his planning sessions.

Maddox entered the Lord High Admiral's outer officer as the secretary looked up from her desk.

"Captain," Cook shouted from his inner office. The door was open. "Do come in, young man."

Maddox nodded to the secretary, a pretty warrant officer, and entered the spacious inner office, closing the door behind him. This had to be the biggest office on Pluto. Here, space was at a premium. You couldn't tell it by Cook's vast ceiling and wide "elbow room." Three different screens were on, showing various Earth scenes: the ocean, a pine forest and what had to be a Himalayan mountain.

"Sit, sit," Cook said, as he scribbled on a computer screen with a stylus.

Maddox settled into a comfortable chair.

Several seconds later, the Lord High Admiral looked up. He was a big, craggy man with thick white hair. He wore his signature white admiral's uniform. He had thicker fingers than Admiral Fletcher. His facial skin looked more leathery than Maddox recalled from previous visits. The bags under his eyes looked baggier.

Maddox didn't envy the Lord High Admiral his position, nor the great weight of responsibility on those shoulders.

Cook set down his stylus, flattened his big hands on the desktop and squared his shoulders. "Ah," he said, perhaps seeing something on Maddox's face. Cook leaned so far back in his chair it creaked in complaint.

"What can I do for you, Captain?"

"Give me Lord Drakos," Maddox said flatly.

A half smile had grown on the Lord High Admiral's face. Now, the smile vanished.

"Surely, you haven't come here to waste my time on something so frivolous," Cook said in a grave voice.

"There is nothing frivolous about the request, sir. I have a feeling—more than a feeling—that we could lose this war."

"I don't like any of my officers saying that, least of all you, young man."

"Yet, that is a stark truth," Maddox said. "The possibility of defeat exists. After watching the bugs swat our defenders from the latest Laumer Point—"

"I've heard enough about that," Cook said. "You have no idea how little people regard my station. I have taken heavy blame for the lack of more defenders at the Epsilon 5-Tau Ceti Laumer Point. The next time—"

"Sir, I watched the Builder Scanner holo-recording several times already. It's obvious the bugs did not know about the tactic of hurling nukes through a Laumer Point in order to clear the way. They know it now, though, because we did it to them."

Cook nodded abruptly. "Is there anything else?"

"As I said, sir, I would like the head of Lord Drakos. I want to kill him as soon as I can."

"What's the rush, if I may ask?"

"If the bugs wipe us out, sir, I'll never have had the opportunity to fulfil one of my chief promises."

"It won't matter then," Cook said. "You and Drakos will both be dead. We all will."

"It will matter to my mother, sir."

"Your mother?" asked Cook, looking astonished. "What does she have to do with this?"

It seemed Maddox wouldn't speak, as if his face walled up. He picked at his trousers, seemed to reconsider his attitude and said in a low voice, "I believe Drakos forced himself upon her, sir. I believe…" Maddox took a breath. "I believe he is my sire."

Cook stared at Maddox in obvious shock. Finally, the big man shook his head. "What do you base this on?"

"Our resemblance, sir."

"Your resemblance? Captain Maddox, this is sheer frivolity. I wonder if the strain of command has finally gotten to you."

Maddox waited.

"For one thing, we need the New Men and that cone of battle of theirs. We cannot afford to poison our rather tenuous relationship with them. Your killing Drakos would certainly do that. But there's another issue here. You must make certain of this…lineage. Besides, despite his crimes against your mother—if he indeed is your father—you cannot kill him."

"Believe me, I can, sir."

Cook shook his head. "That's not what I mean. Of course, if you put a gun to his head and pull the trigger, you are capable of killing him. It won't do you any good, though, to slay your own father. That will create repercussions in you that you do not want to deal with."

"Respectfully, sir, I'm not worried about that."

Cook banged a fist on the desk. "Well, son, you'd better damn well give it some thought. I know that parents often do bad things to their kids. But hating them the rest of your life warps you. Bitterness is an awful thing. Bitterness will hollow out your soul. I've seen it happen many times. I urge you to give up this vendetta."

Maddox stared at Cook, stared longer, and abruptly nodded. "I have an idea that might take my mind off killing Lord Drakos."

"Yes?" Cook asked.

"I ask permission to take the Destroyer out and attack the Swarm Fleet, sir."

Cook blinked several times. He leaned forward and clasped his hands together, resting them on the desk. The big man's eyes had narrowed.

"What are you talking about?" Cook finally asked.

"I know about the strategy debates, sir. I know others have already pressed you with this idea."

"Then you must know about my objections to the plan."

"I do, and I believe you should reconsider. We can't win this fight, sir, at the present exchange ratios, anyway. You know that. I know that. Likely, the bugs know that, too."

"That's tommy rot," Cook said. "We already took out twenty percent of their fleet at Tau Ceti. I'd say with the Destroyer and the Juggernauts in the Alpha Centauri System—"

"I'm sorry, sir," Maddox said, interrupting. "Forgive me, but please listen. That won't be enough. That's the point. We have to risk the Destroyer out there in order to make the Alpha Centauri stand work. I suspect you already know that. I suspect the thought of losing the Destroyer out there makes you sick at night. We're not going to win the battle of Alpha Centauri without the Destroyer. But if we don't seriously whittle down their fleet beforehand…"

"Okay," Cook said. "I'm listening."

"The trick is the Destroyer's unique jump drive. It first creates an ion storm—"

"I know all about that," Cook said heatedly. "Please do get to the point, Captain."

"The point is simple, sir. I command a crew aboard the Destroyer, jump to the Epsilon 5 System, fire up the giant beam and blast a great section of the enemy fleet. As soon as I'm done, the Destroyer jumps away. Once the crew is ready again, once the Builder Scanner has pinpointed the enemy again, I repeat the process. I continue repeating the process until the Destroyer drives the bugs mad with fury. But you already know all that. The strategists have suggested the same thing. This is an impossible situation. Believe me, I know all about those. This isn't the time to play it safe. We have to take calculated wild risks."

"That is an oxymoron."

"Yes and no," Maddox said. "You calculate and see where you have to take the wild risk in order to make the rest work."

Cook frowned. "The way you say that, Captain, makes it sound as if you're talking about something else."

Maddox allowed himself to think about the Ska and Ludendorff. When there weren't any answers…

"We have to whittle down the enemy fleet," Maddox said. "It's so huge, we can't do it all at once. The Destroyer is the perfect weapon system to use against them in Epsilon 5. We have to take the risk in order to save the Earth, maybe save humanity."

Cook looked away. "We might attempt a trial run… Let me ask you this. What if something goes wrong during one of the Epsilon 5 attacks?"

"We'll make sure it doesn't, sir."

Cook laughed bleakly as he regarded Maddox. "I've read the accounts of every one of your missions, Captain. Many things went wrong in each one."

"True. We'll fix the problems along the way. It's what we always do."

Agonized indecision was stamped on Cook's face.

"We have to attack now, sir. If we wait too long, it will be too late."

"What gives you your confidence, Captain?"

Maddox shrugged. "I study the situation and weigh the odds. Once I see that playing it safe will result in defeat, I look for outrageous answers. Once I find the best outrageous

307

answer, I tackle it with gusto because nothing else makes sense."

"I understand your reasoning…" Cook bit his lower lip. He looked up suddenly. "Earlier—did you really expect I'd give you Lord Drakos?"

"No."

"Was that to get me to think about this?"

Maddox stared at the Lord High Admiral and slowly shook his head.

"I suppose you should know, sir. Every time I think about Drakos with my mother…an animal grows in me. At those times, all I can think about is destroying him. It finally occurred to me, if we're going to lose anyway, I might as well tackle the problem I can still fix. That gave me the…energy to speak to you about the Destroyer."

"I see," Cook said. "If I agree to the Epsilon 5 Attack, will the situation with Drakos continue to be a problem?"

Maddox blinked several times as the animal desire welled up in him. Talking about Drakos fed the beast, as it were. That was unlike him, he knew. Usually, he could keep his composure better than anyone. For just a moment, he wondered if this "animal" had anything to do with the approaching Ska.

"I'm waiting," Cook said in a heavy voice.

Maddox hated the idea of another entity controlling or influencing like this. If this was the Ska interfering with his emotions—he would squash the feeling.

"Drakos won't be a problem, Admiral."

Cook didn't appear to like the late assurance, although finally he nodded, effectively ending the meeting.

-8-

Captain Maddox's skin crawled with revulsion as Keith piloted the shuttle toward the main Destroyer hangar bay.

The ancient Destroyer was teardrop-shaped, a colossal vessel fifty kilometers long with an outer shell of neutroium armor. As the shuttle drifted toward the hangar opening, Maddox felt an ancient pulse of evil in his chest. The hull was not of one smooth piece. It was pitted from thousands of lifetimes of operational usage.

The Nameless Ones had served the Ska, destroying one species after another in a long war against other life. Long ago, the Builders had defended this area of the Orion Arm from them. Some of these ancient relics still survived in the new world of lesser races battling for survival against each other. Could humanity have survived among such technological giants in the past ages?

There was something Maddox didn't like to admit even to himself. *Is the ancient vessel haunted from its long existence as a killer of things, a genocidal machine?* The Kai-Kaus had reported more mentally fatigued workers than on any other project. It seemed they felt the lingering evil, too.

Maddox took a deep breath to calm his nerves. The Lord High Admiral had given him permission to attack the Swarm mass in the Epsilon 5 System. It was time to whittle down the incredible enemy numbers. If and when the Ska showed up, and if it showed up with another Destroyer—

"Are you well, sir?" Keith asked, glancing at him.

309

The words brought Maddox back to reality. He glanced at Keith, finding it impossible to say more than, "Yes."

"If you don't mind me saying so, sir, you seem a bit faint."

Maddox said nothing, although a frown touched his lips.

Maybe that was enough of an answer. Keith concentrated on the controls, easing the shuttle past the hangar bay opening and into the belly of the ancient beast.

***

The sense of evil was worse as Maddox strode through the ancient corridors. The deeper he moved into the huge vessel, the greater the sensation grew. Finally, it seemed like an ancient heart pumped the vileness at him. Maddox struggled not to break into a sprint.

This was preposterous.

A hatch slid open and Maddox practically stumbled onto the bridge. As the hatch shut, he felt a small sense of relief.

He looked around.

The Kai-Kaus had added new bulkheads and installed regular Star Watch panels. It gave a feeling of normalcy. Yes. The bridge was like an island amid an evil ship of annihilation, one with moaning ghosts kept at bay by these thin walls.

Shaking his head to rid himself of the ghostly imagery, Maddox sat in the command chair. Unfortunately, Galyan wouldn't be with him this time. He was on his own here. The Adok AI was running *Victory* with a skeleton crew. Ludendorff and Dana were aboard *Victory*, as the two tried to solve the puzzle of the Ska.

"We're ready when you are, sir," Valerie said.

Maddox accepted the lieutenant at her word, and began to run through a variety of tests…

***

Later, Maddox looked around with something approaching satisfaction. The ship was ready enough to fight. He realized they could spend months refining the giant vessel. What it could do now, though, was jump through the ion-storm-created portal and deploy its massive beam afterward. The two actions were all that really mattered.

"We will attack in two hours," Maddox said. "Thus, I want each of you to take a cat-nap. Then, we're going to surprise the Swarm and hammer them if we're able."

***

The two hours passed fitfully for Maddox as he stared at the ceiling of his quarters. He began to wonder if he could fall asleep on this vessel. Every time he closed his eyes, he felt the vile vibrations in his soul. He didn't know how else to explain it.

Wouldn't that be…absurd, he supposed, if they had this grim vessel of war, but could only use it for short runs? He would inquire later if the Kai-Kaus had slept while working on the Destroyer. If none had, that would be telling.

Finally, Maddox arose and strode purposefully to the bridge. He saw the others had already gathered there. This didn't seem like the time to question if any of them had gotten any sleep. If the Destroyer was haunted by its past actions, this was a bad time to bring it up.

"Mr. Maker," Maddox said. "Are you ready?"

"That I am," Keith said.

Something about the way the ace said that more than implied he wanted to get this over with. A new thought intruded. Was it the mass killings that had tainted the vessel, or was it the Ska's presence these many millennia?

Maddox balled up these ideas and shoved them into a drawer in his mind, deciding he no longer had the mental energy to worry about such things. It was time to do his duty.

"I'd like to see the latest intelligence from the Builder Scanner," Maddox said.

With a few manipulations, Valerie brought it up on the main screen.

Maddox stood, studying the massed Swarm Fleet in the Epsilon 5 System. "Does their formation look different to anyone else?" he asked.

"It does," Valerie said shortly. "They seem more spread out. They didn't travel like that before."

"When was the scan taken?" Maddox asked.

Valerie checked her panel. "A day ago, sir."

"The Swarm have changed their dispositions since then."

"It would seem so, sir," Valerie said.

Maddox shook his head. This was an inauspicious beginning. Hopefully, the difference would not hurt the effectiveness of the coming attack.

"Here," he said, using a pointer. "I want you to bring the Destroyer here, Mr. Maker."

"Yes, sir," Keith said, with less enthusiasm than normal.

"If you have an objection or a better idea," Maddox said. "I'd like to hear it."

Keith turned around in wonder. "Uh, no, sir. I'm fine with your placement."

Maddox nodded, realizing he'd miscalculated. More than ever, the crew did not want a wishy-washy captain. They wanted a decisive man of action. If the Destroyer was haunted, they needed someone to lean on in order to bolster their morale.

"How long until you're ready to jump?" asked Maddox.

"Fifteen minutes," Keith said.

"Make it ten," Maddox said. "Fifteen minutes in the middle of battle later will be too long. We're going to get it right from the start."

"Yes, sir," Keith said.

The pilot worked with haste.

Two minutes later, a vast ion field appeared around the Destroyer. Purple ionized bolts flashed everywhere. The ion storm grew in size and power until the huge vessel began to shake.

Maddox refrained from asking if there were any problems. He let the pilot and the anxious Kai-Kaus on the bridge do their jobs. None of them turned to him to report problems. Thus, he would not pry it out of them.

"Jump in two minutes," Keith said, with only a hint of a tremor in his voice.

Maddox checked a chronometer. "You've already taken three minutes more than I asked, Mr. Maker. I expect more speed next time."

"Yes, sir," Keith said.

"Lieutenant," Maddox said. "Are you prepared?"

"Yes, sir," Valerie said.

The next two minutes ticked slowly as the ion storm raged around the Destroyer.

"We're jumping," Keith said. This time the tremor in his voice was more evident.

Outside the ship, a giant opening appeared in the middle of the ion storm. The Destroyer slid into the opening, heading toward battle against the massed enemy.

-9-

An ion storm had appeared at the beginning jump point and now one did on the other end, as well. The new storm happened, as plotted, in the Epsilon 5 Star System. Seconds later, the massive Destroyer popped into the new ion storm.

It took time for the storm to dissipate and time for the people inside the Destroyer to gather intelligence about the Swarm.

"There," Valerie said. "I finally have a visual, sir."

Maddox sat forward on his command chair. The vast Swarm Fleet spread out before him.

Sixty thousand warships was an incredible number. Humanity had yet to produce a fleet of one thousand ships, never mind something sixty times as great. Yet, as mind numbing as 60,000 might be, it was dwarfed by the immensity of space. It made a difference that most of the Swarm warships accelerated. The acceleration created thrust, which made the ships a hundred times easier to see than otherwise.

One thing Maddox soon noticed. Whoever controlled the Swarm Fleet had spread out the warships in widely spaced clusters. The ships were everywhere in the system instead of bunched closely together like before.

"It's almost as if the bugs know we have a Destroyer," Valerie said.

Maddox nodded curtly. He wasn't going to worry about that right now. "Chief Technician?" he asked Andros Crank. "Is the beam ready?"

"I'll need ten minutes or more," Andros said from his station.

"As long as that?" Maddox asked with a frown.

"There are still some technical problems that are giving us trouble."

"I didn't ask for excuses," Maddox said. "I asked if it had to be that long."

"Yes, sir," Andros said, without a change of expression. "It is regrettably going to take that long."

Maddox accepted that in silence. "Lieutenant," he told Valerie. "I want you to target that cluster over there." He used a pointer to circle a spread-out group of ships."

"Targeting, sir," Valerie said, as she began punching in the coordinates.

As the lieutenant targeted and as the Chief Technician shepherded his techs to ready the beam, five thousand or more enemy missiles launched from various ships and headed toward the ancient Destroyer.

Valerie pointed that out to Maddox.

"Thank you," he said. "Can you estimate their time of arrival?"

"The nearest will take a little over an hour at their present acceleration."

"Good," Maddox said. "We have time then."

The time ticked away as the Kai-Kaus toiled to ready the ancient generators and the rather tricky firing apparatus.

Fifteen minutes later, Maddox spoke up, "Andros Crank—"

"Ten more minutes, sir," Andros said, with sweat beading his forehead.

The new minutes ticked past slowly. All that time, the nearest Swarm ship-clusters had been spreading apart, making themselves less attractive bulk targets.

"I don't like this," Maddox muttered. "It's taking too long."

No one responded.

Twenty-five minutes after appearing in the Epsilon 5 System, Andros signaled the captain that the beam was ready for firing.

315

"Mr. Maker," Maddox said, "engage the engine. We're going to give chase. I want to fire into a thicker clot of warships."

"Any—" Keith said.

"Those warships there," Maddox said, using his pointer to circle a group farther away.

"Uh…" Valerie said. "If we do that, sir, the missiles in Vector 3 are going to reach us."

"That's why we have neutroium armor," Maddox said.

Valerie stared at him. "I don't know that it's a good idea to take direct nuclear hits, sir, not even with this ship."

Maddox swiveled around to gaze at Valerie. "Perhaps you're right," he muttered ten second later. He studied the main screen. "Very well, target the original group."

"Firing," Valerie said, as she punched that in.

Outside on the teardrop-shaped monster, the five-kilometer orifice swirled with terrible energies. All at once, a vast beam speared out of the orifice, traveling one hundred and fifty thousand kilometers. The terrible beam smashed Swarm ships as if they were constructed of tinfoil. The vessels simply shriveled up and dissipated. The hard radiation spewing outward from the beam crippled many other vessels. It was an awesome display of ancient technology.

However, the Swarm had already taken evasive action, and that saved many ships that might have otherwise perished. Still, many nearby Swarm crews died from radiation poisoning. And that was despite the fact that the Swarm creatures could take harder doses of radiation than humans could.

"Rotate the ship, Mr. Maker," Maddox said. "We're going to fire into another cluster."

"Sir," Andros said, speaking up. "I regret to inform you that it's going to take at least another twenty minutes before we're ready to fire again."

"That long?" Maddox asked again

Andros did not reply.

The captain studied the approaching missiles. It was no longer five thousand of them converging on the Destroyer, but three thousand five hundred. The other fifteen hundred no longer existed or drifted aimlessly due to the giant beam. Still, those thirty-five hundred missiles were getting much too close.

"We're going to have jump again," Maddox said. He pinched his lower lip. "How long will that take to implement?"

"Ten minutes, sir," Keith said.

"Fine," Maddox said. "Let's see…where we should go."

He and Valerie studied the spread out enemy fleet, finally choosing a thicker cluster much nearer the Epsilon 5-Alpha Centauri Laumer Point.

Fourteen minutes later, the ancient Destroyer deployed the ion storm. The ball of energy grew, and that shorted the electronics of the nearest enemy missiles heading for the ship.

Finally, the Destroyer slid through the new opening and appeared at the other end of the star system.

There, much like before, it took longer to fire the giant weapon than Maddox would have liked. It allowed those bug ships time to disperse.

Still, the beam fired. Swarm ships died, and the missiles fired at the Destroyer failed to reach the giant teardrop-shaped killer.

Four times, the Destroyer jumped. Four times, it took too long to fire the beam. At the end of the fourth jump, masses of Swarm missiles crisscrossed the star system. Valerie pointed out that it was going to be harder to find a relatively empty place to appear where they could still hit the enemy ships one hundred and fifty kilometers away.

"The ion storm can act as a shield against any missiles," Maddox said.

Valerie shook her head as if that was a poor idea.

Andros spoke up, saying he would not vouch for all the missiles shorting out due to the ion storm. Some would get through, reaching the hull.

Thus, after a grueling four jumps, the Destroyer jumped a fifth time. It went to the Alpha Centauri System to join the main fleet getting ready to face the approaching Swarm mass.

-10-

The Destroyer sent awful tremors through the Swarm Fleet. The lazy way it went about picking off heavy warships terrified the Reigning Supreme. The fact that it had waited so long, letting missiles almost get into detonation range bespoke human pride.

AX-29 summoned her advisors. Soldiers dragged pallets holding the Assault Master and his aides. Of the Hive Master-class, only Thrax scuttled in on his own power.

The Reigning Supreme spoke. "The humans have a Destroyer. I know you have each studied the numbing assault. The vessel moved at will, jumping, annihilating, jumping elsewhere and annihilating again. That it moved precisely each time tells me that Thrax's theory about a Builder helping the humans seems more plausible as time goes by. This is a terrible day. I have doubts about the coming assault."

"Reigning Supreme," the Assault Master said, scenting the air with powerful pheromones. "We are an Imperial assault force. We shall prevail against these humans. They have shown faintness of heart, running away each time. With remorseless power, we have advanced one step at a time upon the Solar System. Only the Alpha Centauri System stands in our way now. Can you doubt the humans will run from it as well?"

"Our losses," the Reigning Supreme said. "They keep inflicting losses on us. This time, the humans annihilated 1,074 heavy ships of the line. We were unable to even scar the Destroyer."

"One thousand ships are as nothing," the Assault Master said.

"I must concur," Thrax said. "Given the nature of the enemy vessel, I found their assault highly ineffective. The missile barrages kept the ancient ship at bay each time."

"You are gloating again," the Reigning Supreme told Thrax. "The missile barrage was your idea."

"And it worked," Thrax said. "I am not boasting. I am declaring that I know how to defeat the enemy. I tell you that I would have gladly taken ten times those losses and still I would feel confident about our coming victory. The humans will have to stand and fight soon. When they do, we shall annihilate them utterly."

"I feel uneasy," the Reigning Supreme said. "There is a taint I cannot shake."

"The Destroyer ran from us," Thrax said. "The Assault Master is correct in his analysis."

"I do not need your concurrence," the Assault Master told Thrax.

"You are jealous because I thought up the missile barrage defense," Thrax said.

"No!" the Assault Master cried. "I shall finally tell you—"

"Enough!" the Reigning Supreme said. "Swarm councils are not the place for bickering. This is a strategy session. Here, calm reason shall prevail."

"Of course," Thrax said. "I beg your pardon."

"Yes, Reigning Supreme," the Assault Master added.

"We must work out an assault schedule," she said. "What if the Destroyer shows up again as we use the Laumer Point? What if the enemy launches more nuclear bombs through the wormhole? They have the advantage of advance knowledge. We…"

"We have superior numbers," Thrax said. "We have Swarm courage. I have long studied the humans. They have weak wills, easily swayed by blood and death. A steady attack panics them. Have we not seen this time and again?"

"We have," the Reigning Supreme admitted.

"The humans have pricked us," Thrax said. "However, even against a Destroyer, our losses are miniscule. We are winning, Reigning Supreme. We are winning in part because we know we will prevail. Soon—"

"Yes, yes," the Reigning Supreme said. "I have heard enough about our greatness. Now, it is time to decide how to invade the Alpha Centauri System without sustaining debilitating casualties."

"Reigning Supreme," the Assault Master said. "I have developed an advance-to-attack movement schedule that allows for the Destroyer hitting us at the same time. It accounts for enemy nuclear bombs appearing at will through the Laumer Point. However, I must point out that we will undoubtedly have to accept a high number of casualties. Their superior intelligence system and superior movement capabilities means we can only trump them through our main strengths of numbers and will power."

"Unfortunately, I believe you're right," AX-29 said. "Yes. Show us your schedule."

The Assault Master gave swift orders. A holoimage soon appeared, and he ran through the detailed attack plan.

Thrax was appalled at the losses the Assault Master envisioned. Wasn't there another way? Maybe with a more aggressive use of the jump ships… No! He needed to save the jump ships and his fellow hybrids for the day he could gain command of them. They were his bolt hole in case the attack failed. Above all else, he must survive.

"Thrax," the Reigning Supreme said. "Do you have anything to add to the attack schedule?"

"A few minor adjustments," Thrax said.

"Tell us," she said.

Thrax's adjustments amounted to a more careful use of the jump ships. "We must treat the jump ships like the Queen's eggs, a precious commodity."

"Your speech is almost blasphemous," the Reigning Supreme said. "To speak of the Queen's eggs in such a light—"

"I am ashamed," Thrax said, lowering his bulk to the floor. "I meant no disrespect to the Queen or the Imperium. I will—"

"Yes, yes," the Reigning Supreme said. "It is enough that you are contrite."

AX-29 questioned the Assault Master and then questioned Thrax concerning the coming attack. Afterward, she seemed calmer than before.

"I have done well by elevating Thrax and by elevating you, Assault Master. We have arrived at a good plan. We will begin to implement it at once. While I dislike losing Imperial vessels and crews, I am eager to engage the enemy in head-to-head battle that will lead to our ultimate victory. This time, in this place, we will crush the humans."

-11-

Star Watch and the New Men readied their fleets against the approaching Swarm mass. This time, they would contest the Laumer Point with the full fury at their disposal.

However, they would do so in a layered defense.

The first stage of defense was going to be the Destroyer. It made the most sense, as it hit with staggering force and exposed the least number of personnel to any nuclear devices that could and likely would precede the first enemy ships.

One hundred and fifty thousand kilometers away from the Epsilon 5-Alpha Centauri Laumer Point the Destroyer waited patiently.

Maddox and the crew had discovered that they could sleep only fitfully aboard the vessel. They universally had bad dreams and woke often. It meant the crew and the captain were bleary-eyed and cranky on the day of battle.

Captain Maddox paced behind his command chair. He had a slightly wild look in his eyes. He strove to master his unease, but it was proving difficult. That was so unlike him that others noticed.

"Sir," Valerie said, "if you would sit down, please. You're making the rest of us nervous by your pacing."

Maddox wanted to shout at her. He barely stopped himself in time. Reluctantly, he sat. Nervous energy still ate at him. The feeling tightened his gut and loosed butterflies within.

I am Captain Maddox, he told himself. Even so, he struggled to maintain his decorum. He hated this ship. He loathed the vile feelings it left in his mind. He was tired. He felt edgy as his mind boiled with ideas.

Maddox had sent Meta to *Victory* two days ago. Was the Ska approaching? Was that why he felt like this? Riker was aboard *Victory*. Should he call the sergeant and tell him to—?

"Sir," Valerie said. "Look."

Maddox's head snapped up. On the main screen, he saw a large device tumble out of the Laumer Point.

"Well?" he snapped.

"It appears to be a thermonuclear device," Valerie said as she studied her board.

As if to confirm her words, the bomb detonated with terrible energy. It had been a massive bomb almost on par with the cobalt weapon Star Watch had used several days ago.

Nine minutes later, another Swarm bomb tumbled through the Laumer Point.

"They're making certain," Valerie said.

Maddox nodded.

The blasts from the nuclear bombs sent gamma and X-ray radiation outward in a wide radius. The neutroium hull stopped any from reaching into the Destroyer. The Swarm would have to do worse than that by a long shot to hurt them. It was one of the chief reasons why the Destroyer held the forward post.

Seventeen minutes after the third nuclear bomb went off, the first Swarm ships shot through the Laumer Point. These came through with some speed. They kept coming, too, one right after another. Jump Lag struck the ships, but the velocity was such that it made room for over 328 vessels before the first batch stopped coming.

"Chief Technician?" asked Maddox.

"Two more minutes," Andros said.

At the end of two minutes, the mighty Destroyer's beam flashed one hundred and fifty thousand kilometers. The five-kilometer-wide beam devoured the 328 Swarm vessels, leaving cinders in a few places, but little else besides.

Time passed.

"Captain," Valerie said. "I've just received a message. The New Men have spotted several Swarm jump ships. Some are five million kilometers away, while others are ten and twenty million kilometers from the Laumer Point. They are clearly acting as scouts. To confirm this, two of the enemy jump ships have jumped to places unknown."

"Likely they're reporting back to the hive," Maddox said.

"Maybe not," Keith said. "Is that another nuclear device coming through?"

On the screen in the debris floating before the Laumer Point, another bomb tumbled into existence. It detonated, rearranging the debris and sending heat, EMP and radiation outward.

Soon thereafter, another group of Swarm vessels came through, this time to the tune of 237 ships.

Four minutes later, the Destroyer struck once more, beaming the Jump Lagged enemy ships and annihilating them with the most amazing beam in the Orion Arm.

The process continued for the next eight hours. The Swarm debris began thickening before the Laumer Point. The enemy ships no longer came through at speed. Several had wrecked in the debris.

More enemy scouts had jumped back to the Epsilon 5 System, no doubt reporting on what happened.

Eight hours took its toll on the personnel aboard the Destroyer. It took its toll on the ancient equipment that supported the terrible beam. It tasked the operators working on the equipment.

Perhaps it taxed the Swarm, too, but no one on the human side was asking.

After eight hours of one-sided destruction, over ten thousand Swarm vessels had become junk or drifting particles floating in the Alpha Centauri System.

"Why won't they pull back?" Valerie shouted. Her hair was disheveled and her eyes wild. "Sir, this is too much."

"Steady now, Lieutenant," Maddox said. He was tired, but his guts no longer seethed. He didn't feel the ancient evil the way he had hours ago. Maybe the fatigue had numbed that part of him. It allowed him to act more like his old self with cool confidence.

"Here come some more," Keith said.

Three hundred and nineteen Swarm ships tumbled through the Laumer Point.

"Fire when ready," Maddox said in a hoarse voice.

The second ticked away and nothing happened. Finally, Maddox swiveled around.

"Well, Andros?"

The Kai-Kaus Chief Technician threw his hands into the air. "Something has gone wrong. The beam isn't going to fire. I'm surprised we've been able to keep this up for so long."

Maddox stared at the man. "No quick fixes, Chief?"

Andros Crank wearily shook his head.

"Very well," Maddox said in a smooth voice. "Valerie, instruct the Lord High Admiral that the Destroyer will have to pull back."

"He's not going to like it," Valerie said, adding a belated, "sir."

"Maybe not," Maddox said. "But do not think he hasn't planned for the eventuality. We've done our share for the moment. Now, it's time to let others shine. Mr. Maker, if you would turn this ship around and get started, I would appreciate it."

Keith nodded as his hands trembled. "Yes, sir, Captain."

The ancient Destroyer thus turned away from the Laumer Point. It did not engage the ion storm and special portal. Instead, under regular power, the fifty-kilometer-long killing machine began accelerating away.

Meanwhile, the Swarm ships suffering Jump Lag began waking up.

-12-

Now began a bitter and highly uneven struggle. The next to attack the Laumer Point area were the Juggernauts.

The five heavy spaceships—the largest vessels after the Destroyer—moved in from an area five hundred and fifty thousand kilometers away. They moved fast, and they warmed up their weapons enroute.

Soon, the Juggernauts began launching missiles and firing their beams. They killed the Swarm vessels trying to shrug off Jump Lag.

As before, more Swarm jump ships entered the Alpha Centauri System and some exited the system as well. By now, several clots of Swarm jump ships twenty vessels strong had staked out areas far away from the battle zone. They were obviously the eyes of the Swarm, reporting to Swarm High Command in the Epsilon 5 System.

The bugs now sent through powerful nuclear devices. They detonated, and because the Juggernauts had to come in closer to fire their weapons, the hard radiation struck their vessels.

Even so, the Juggernaut shields held.

The bugs sent more nuclear devices through, forcing the Juggernauts to back off.

Eleven minutes later, the bugs switched again. Now, they sent heavy squadrons through. Four hundred and fifty-three Swarm heavies came through the Laumer Point.

However, the tactic had been rather obvious. The Lord High Admiral had ordered Star Watch nuclear devices into the region. Those detonated, destroying the enemy ships.

Afterward, the bugs went back to the cat and mouse game. Sometimes they sent through nuclear devices. Sometimes they sent war vessels.

That began a shift in the battle as some Swarm vessels finally survived long enough to begin operating.

The first time that happened, the Juggernauts attacked harder, boring in closer and closer, using their powerful missiles and beams. The awakened Swarm ships came out to fight, trying to buy time for their side. The fight seesawed until the Swarm stopped sending reinforcements through the wormhole and sent through more nuclear devices. That caught one of the Juggernauts too near the Laumer Point. The Juggernaut's shield collapsed and the hull cracked from the nuclear blasts.

This time, the Swarm High Command timed it right. They poured ships through the Laumer Point into the debris-laden zone. The debris had thickened considerably and now acted like shielding particles. Because of that, the Juggernauts couldn't kill fast enough. More of the Swarm heavies woke up. They battled savagely, recklessly and fearlessly.

Finally, after more than twelve and a half hours of constant battle, the Swarm achieved their first kill, destroying the Juggernaut with the cracked hull.

By this time, the Swarm had taken 9,623 ship losses. It was a staggering ratio, the greatest of the battle so far by many magnitudes.

Perhaps if humanity had fought a different kind of alien, the losses would have been too much for the enemy. But these were Swarm soldiers and crews. They'd been bred to die for the Imperium. Instead of showing fear and hesitation, the Swarm chugged more warships into the Alpha Centauri System.

The invading fleet still had approximately 50,000 vessels to complete their mission. Even so, not even the Swarm could continue to take 9,623 to 1 ship losses and hope to win.

This phase ended as the four remaining and battered Juggernauts pulled out of the battle zone and headed away.

***

Star Watch moved in with *Conqueror*-class battleships. The New Men brought their cone of battle, using almost every surviving star cruiser.

It was a war of attrition fought in a unique and brutal manner. The Swarm kept pouring ships through the Laumer Point. The New Men and humans closed in upon the Jump Lagged vessels, battering them with disrupter beams. It was a cauldron of destruction as the New Men and humans came within 40,000 kilometers of the Laumer Point.

The combined beams of the cone of battle and the teams of beams used by the *Conqueror*-class battleships shredded a monstrous number of Swarm vessels. In the annals of human history, no enemy had ever tried to force such a small pass in the face of such determined defense.

"They're wearing us down by heating our beams too long," Lord Drakos declared.

If that was the Swarm strategy, it finally started working. The New Men and the old could only destroy so many vessels in a certain amount of time. As some of the star cruisers overheated, as some of the battleships retreated due to malfunctions of various sorts, more and more Swarm vessels remained intact long enough to fire back.

Two hours after engaging the third line, the Swarm finally had enough vessels to push the cone of battle and the battleships back. That allowed the arriving Swarm ships to survive en masse.

Within another half hour, the Swarm had three thousand sluggish warships moving against the cone of battle and 82 percent of the Alliance battleships that had started the Alpha Centauri fight.

"Retreat," the Lord High Admiral ordered. "Retreat across Alpha Centauri. We did what we could. We slaughtered the Swarm. I count over 15,000 enemy wrecks. Now, we have to move back and prepare for the next phase."

It was an admission of amazing generalship and planning, and—ultimately—defeat. The humans, new and old, had simply not destroyed enough Swarm vessels yet. Despite the lopsided victory at the Laumer Point, humanity was going to lose the Battle for Earth if this kept up.

-13-

Sergeant Riker was in his quarters aboard *Victory*. The starship was near Proxima Centauri, the red dwarf of the triple-star system.

Riker had watched the ongoing battle for quite some time. Everybody on the ship had been watching, including Galyan. In fact, the Adok AI had watched with absorbing interest. The little holoimage had not said a word since then.

In any case, Riker had returned to his quarters. He'd felt uneasy, had been feeling uneasy ever since the start of his bad dreams.

Riker sat at his desk, debating whether he should write to his nieces. They'd fled Tau Ceti along with millions of other displaced persons. The war with the Swarm had seen great misery so far. In actual numbers, it was almost as bad as the New Men invasion. Tau Ceti had been a heavily settled star system. Those who had remained in the system were now dead, hundreds of millions of people. Fewer people had been able to flee elsewhere. If one also added in the annihilation to Tau Ceti property and industry…

Riker shook his head. He pushed the notepaper away. He did not feel like writing a letter. He *could* not write a letter. He felt wrung out, faded, even.

The sergeant nodded. Yes, that was the correct word. He felt faded, as if he was passing away like a bad hologram. It almost seemed as if he'd been stretched thinner and thinner. If this kept up, soon, he would simply fade away.

Riker pushed his chair back, stood, and remained frozen for three seconds. He slumped back onto the chair and grunted as if someone had punched him in the gut. The air went out of him. His eyelids fluttered. All at once, he began to shiver and shake. It continued to worsen until it became uncontrollable. He vaulted backward out of and over the chair, foaming at the mouth as he twisted on the floor.

The feeling worsened as he broke out in a cold sweat. Agony twisted his stomach until it felt as if his guts were on fire.

Riker contorted. Fear bubbled through him, but a knot of stubbornness survived the first wave. That stubbornness forced him to roll onto his belly. The mulish part of his nature got him up onto his hands and knees. He crawled for the hatch and realized that he would never make it. Switching direction, he headed for the nightstand.

The second wave of nausea struck. He did not shake this time. He did not foam at the mouth. Terror nearly swamped him, but he hung on. He realized what he had to do or everything that he'd worked his entire professional life to protect would burn up along with everything else.

"No," Riker grunted. "Not going to happen."

From on the floor, he reached the nightstand and began to shake it. Finally, his communicator fell off. With trembling fingers, he pressed the correct buttons. Nothing happened. He pressed again, and again, and—

"Sergeant Riker," Galyan said. The little Adok holoimage stood in his room. "What is wrong with you?"

Riker tried several times to form the words. It was so hard to do.

"Sergeant?" asked Galyan.

"It's here," Riker whispered.

"If you are referring to the Swarm Fleet—"

"No," Riker said hoarsely. "*It's* here."

"Could you mean the Ska?"

"Yes. Tell...tell Ludendorff it's time."

Galyan disappeared.

Riker could not hold on any longer. He crumpled fully onto the floor and thankfully passed out.

-14-

"Sir," Valerie said from her station on the Destroyer's bridge. "I have a high priority message from Galyan."

"Put it on the screen," Maddox said.

"I would, sir, but Galyan said this is for your ears only."

Maddox stared at Valerie for several seconds as if he didn't want to take the call. He had a bad feeling that this had something to do with the twisting in his guts that had started approximately ten minutes ago. He could not shake the feeling—

"Captain?" asked Valerie. "Are you well?"

Maddox snapped out of it, standing. "Yes, his message—"

"I can patch it through to a pair of headphones, sir."

"Good," Maddox said, sitting. He took a pair of headphones, slipping them onto his head. "Galyan," he said.

"Captain," Galyan said. "You must come immediately. I cannot open the professor's door. I cannot materialize in his chamber, either."

"We happen to be in the middle of a losing battle, Galyan. I'm getting ready to run interference for the fleet. If the Destroyer can't slow down the Swarm advance, too many Star Watch ships won't have time to get through the wormhole to the Solar System. So if you don't mind—"

"Riker believes the Ska has arrived, sir. As per your instructions—"

"What? You're sure?"

"Positively, sir," Galyan said.

Maddox sat frozen in thought. The Ska had arrived at the worst possible instant. It must have come in the other Destroyer. If the Ska leagued with the Swarm—black disaster threatened, an end to any hope to save the Solar System.

Maddox glared at the floor, thinking furiously. When hope flickered like a candle in a hurricane, one had to grasp at the impossible. He'd had premonition about Ludendorff and the Builders. Could he stake everything on that premonition?

What choice do I have? We're out of options.

Maddox sat up as he raised his head. Bitter determination burned in his eyes. His mouth was dry and the words came hard. His chest actually ached.

"I'm on my way, Galyan. We'll be there shortly."

"Yes—" Galyan said.

Maddox didn't hear anymore as he tore off the headphones. "Mr. Maker," he said crisply, "plot an immediate jump to *Victory*."

"Sir?" Keith asked. "I thought we were heading for the Swarm."

"There's been a change in plans," Maddox said. "You will plot a star-drive jump to *Victory*. It is in the vicinity of Proxima Centauri."

"I know where it is, sir," Keith said in a dubious tone. He waited, but Maddox said no more. Thus, the ace began to plot the jump.

"Sir," Valerie said. "The Lord High Admiral is on the line."

Maddox studied her. Had she just called Cook? It seemed more than possible.

"Put him on the main screen," Maddox said.

A second later, the Lord High Admiral appeared on the screen.

"Captain Maddox," Cook said, without any greeting. "A foreign Destroyer has just appeared near Alpha Centauri A. We're attempting to hail it, but so far, the vessel has refused to respond. I thought you might know if this—"

"It's the Ska, sir. It's here, with the second Destroyer from the null space. It must have followed us."

"I was afraid of that," Cook said. The admiral seemed to diminish, to find it difficult to speak the next words. "Will the Ska attack us, do you think?"

"Without a doubt," Maddox said in his crisp manner.

Admiral Cook looked away. When he looked back, he seemed to have become suddenly decrepit, the life drained from his face.

"It's over," the Lord High Admiral said listlessly. "Star Watch is in full retreat with the Swarm coming after us. If that Destroyer attacks, it's going to finish whatever chance we have—"

"I have an idea, sir," Maddox said, interrupting.

The aged Cook peered at Maddox. "I don't see what you can possibly do," Cook grumbled.

Maddox leaned forward as the intensity glowed from him. "I want you to listen to me, sir. This is critical. We have a chance. It's as slender a thread as you can imagine, but it's still a chance. You must get every ship you can out of Alpha Centauri and into the Solar System."

"What are you talking about?"

"Some of our ships have the star drive," Maddox said. "They must use it and flee. The rest have to race to the Laumer Point and hope they have time."

"Captain..." Cook said.

"We've lost Alpha Centauri," Maddox said. "The enemy Destroyer means you have to forget everything we planned. My Destroyer is good for several beams, maybe. That wouldn't be enough to take on the new Destroyer. The enemy Destroyer will undoubtedly help the Swarm. That means we cannot possibly—"

"I understand that," Cook practically cried out. "We're doomed."

"No, sir. Not yet," Maddox said. "I have a plan—"

"What plan?"

"I can't tell you now," Maddox said as he stared intently at the Lord High Admiral. "We're facing a being unlike anything you've ever conceived. It has...supernatural powers, for want of a better word. It can eavesdrop on minds, I believe."

Cook blinked several times as if trying to comprehend what Maddox hinted at.

"You have to give me something, Captain."

"This is like one of my missions, sir. Spur of the moment you must order whatever ships can to escape this star system. If you don't, it's likely Star Watch will lose every warship here."

The despair of the situation beat strongly on the Lord High Admiral's face. Yet, like a drunken bum sleeping on the street, he would move because the cop had a nightstick and he knew this cop would use it.

"I'll give the order," Cook said. "I hope you know what you're doing."

Maddox nodded, and the connection cut out a moment later.

A terrible sense of grimness welled up in Maddox. He'd made some hopefully shrewd guesses about Ludendorff and the Fisher planet. Still, these were guesses. It was more than possible he'd guessed wrong. But there was a possibility he'd guessed right, and if so, then heaven help him for what he was about to do.

***

Maddox sat in his command chair as his gut seethed, his face a frozen mask. The others kept watching him out of the corners of their eyes. At this point, Maddox did not dare to think concretely about his plan. As he'd told Cook, the Ska had what appeared to be supernatural powers. The alien creature might still be in shock due to the journey, but once the Ska fully woke from its—

"Why is this taking so long?" Maddox asked curtly.

"We've strained this ancient machine beyond its limits," Andros said. "One can't just snap his fingers and make a wish. The battle taxed every system in the ship. We're repairing what we can, but…"

Maddox stood as something animal-like rose to the surface. The beast looked out of his eyes as he said in a quietly intense voice, "Get us to *Victory* now, Andros."

The Kai-Kaus Chief Technician grew pale. So did several others on the bridge. Whatever arguments they might have marshaled died inside them. Maddox took his seat again. In another seven minutes, an ion storm began to rage around the Destroyer.

Maddox sat forward, gripping the chair rests with his fingers. This could be the countdown for the human race. Pieces of a puzzle began to tumble in his mind, things he'd known but hadn't allowed himself to put together.

I've been acting on intuition, he realized. When he'd stood before the mural on the Fisher world—that was when the process had begun. Some of the things Ludendorff had told him back then had seemed off. How could the star boil away a planet's oceans and the planet yet retain an atmosphere? Why would the Ska destroy the Fishers who had supposedly worshiped it? The white beams they'd used hadn't been a representation but a real thing. The idea that Strand and he had been there at a dig two hundred years ago didn't match up with Ludendorff's history.

Maddox rubbed his head. He had a feeling there were gaps in his memory. Things had happened on the Fisher world. Things had happened to him, but had also most certainly happened to Ludendorff. The professor had never properly accounted for having run off ahead of him.

Now, Maddox believed he knew why that had happened. He also realized why he'd given Ludendorff the strange orders several days ago.

As the ion storm raged around them, as Keith readied the controls, Maddox began shaking his head. If this worked how he thought it might, he was going to be the most hated man in the Commonwealth. He couldn't worry about that, though. He had to save the human race. He had to destroy the Ska while it was possible.

The nonsense about picking up Strand's old notes—no, Maddox realized that had been a dodge, which he should have recognized then. The captain laughed bleakly. This time he had a feeling that not even Ludendorff understood the entire picture.

Why am I seeing this?

Maddox pondered that as Keith piloted the Destroyer toward the new opening. Maybe the Builders or Builder who had manufactured the safeguard—if he was right about that—had used hidden methods on the Fisher world.

The stone mural—it was as if Maddox saw for the first time the full range of pictures on the mural. Something had kept his mind from seeing everything back then.

A terrible sense of awe caused goosebumps to pimple his arms. The Ska was, possibly, the most terrible life form in the galaxy. The Builders had known that. According to the stone mural, the Builders had constructed a weapon that no one should ever wield except under the direst circumstances.

This was one of those moments.

Maddox balled his fingers into fists, squeezing, hating the Builders, but hating the Ska even more. He did not like the idea of anyone using him. Maybe no one had exactly. Maybe this was an ancient Builder failsafe against the horror of the Ska. That failsafe must have been programmed into Ludendorff's mind a long time ago. The programming was why Ludendorff had insisted they go to the Fisher world first.

The question, the real question, was would he have enough time to implement the ancient weapon before the Ska began rampaging among the sheep of humanity?

-15-

Maddox sprinted down the corridors of Starship *Victory*. A terrible sense of lateness added urgency to his haste.

Galyan floated beside him.

Outside the starship, the vast Destroyer waited inertly, its crew as baffled as those aboard the ancient Adok vessel.

"The Lord High Admiral wants to speak to you," Galyan said.

"Is the fleet leaving Alpha Centauri?"

"No, Captain," Galyan said. "That is what the Lord High Admiral would like to—"

"If they don't leave at once, they're all dead. I already told him that. Why's he bothering me about it now?"

"How can you say such a thing?" Galyan asked.

"History tells me I'm right."

"Earth history? Adok history?"

"No," Maddox panted. "Fisher history, the real story, not the cock and bull tale Ludendorff tried to sell us before."

"Captain, I am not following your logic. Normally— Captain, are you listening to me?"

Maddox could barely hear Galyan speak. It was like a tinny noise down a long tube. The sense of evil he'd been feeling before had grown exponentially. The sense had become smothering, demanding more and more of his attention.

"*Mite,*" a dark voice called in his mind. "*Mite, can you hear me?*"

338

Maddox blocked the voice by concentrating on mathematical formulas. He did his multiplication tables, running through them starting with 1 x 1 = 1.

The darkness in his mind increased, making it harder to think. Yet, he had to think, he had to block the Ska for just a little longer.

A sob of effort escaped Maddox's throat. That caused the holoimage to stare at him in consternation. The alien AI lips opened, and presumably, the being spoke. Maddox did not hear any words now.

"*I am coming for you, mite,*" the dark voice said. "*I am going to devour your soul and make you mine. I am going to feast forever and ever on your species.*"

"Which one?" Maddox managed to ask.

"*What? I do not understand.*"

Greater awareness grew in Maddox as the Ska slackened its concentration against him as it pondered the strange question.

Maddox squeezed his eyes shut and focused his thoughts as he'd never done. He opened his eyes and sprinted until he reached the professor's closed laboratory hatch.

"Open up, Ludendorff!" the captain shouted. "It's me, Maddox."

Nothing happened.

"It is as I told you," Galyan said.

Maddox hammered against the hatch. "You old goat!" he shouted. "Don't you realize it's time? I'm here. I want it now."

Still, nothing happened.

At the edge of his consciousness, Maddox could feel the Ska gathering itself. He believed it might still be on the other Destroyer. The bizarrely alien creature was waking up after the slumber of its journey from the null space. If Maddox didn't get to the weapon in time...

"This is why you were made, Ludendorff!" Maddox shouted. "You always thought it was to help mankind on its long journey upward in civilization. Maybe that was part of it, I don't know. But I'm beginning to believe that the real reason was to act as one of the fail-safes against the Ska. How do you fight a spiritual entity, or whatever the Ska really is? We don't have the weapons to face it. But I think the Builders stumbled onto a weapon. I think they used the weapon in the Fisher System. The weapon destroyed everything, though. That's the real story. That's what happened. The Ska wasn't going to destroy its slaves because the creature never made a deal with the Fishers. The aliens used the weapon and forced the bizarre entity into the star, and that did something to the Ska, something nothing else can do. But the Fishers paid for the weapon with their lives, with their entire civilization. I know that's what going to happen here. If the Ska had taken longer to show up, that's what would have happened to Earth. But now we have a chance, Ludendorff. If you can just open the damn hatch and quit sulking about this—"

The hatch clicked. It began to open.

Maddox grabbed the edge and flung it open. Ludendorff stood before him in rumpled clothes. The Methuselah Man stank. He probably hadn't showered for days on end. He had bags under his red-rimmed eyes.

Maddox forced Ludendorff stumbling backward into the laboratory. It was a mess, with objects and devices strewn everywhere. Dana sat on a chair with her head resting on folded arms on a counter. She snored softly.

How long had she been working overtime helping the mad Professor Ludendorff?

"The voice," Ludendorff said, as he clutched his head. "It won't stop rattling off theorems, vectors and licker codes. It won't stop. I hate it. I'm the professor. What did the Builder do to me?"

Maddox looked around the nearly trashed chamber. He spotted a gleaming metal object with two prongs curving up. It had handgrips for two hands. The thing looked heavy. It appeared a man used the handgrips to hold it up so the flattened ends of the prongs would rest against his forehead.

"Is that it?" Maddox asked.

Ludendorff moved slowly as his eyes blinked owlishly. "I do not understand. No one can know about this."

Maddox strode toward the silvery gleaming device on the counter.

"No!" Ludendorff shouted, rushing to block the captain's way.

Maddox shoved Ludendorff aside so the Methuselah Man stumbled, crashing against a table and falling to the floor. There, Ludendorff began to weep softly.

As Maddox approached the strange machine, he saw "Strand's" open notebook. Curious, Maddox paused by the book. In the pages were silvery symbols scribbled in a way that made his chest ache. He realized that he recognized those as Builder symbols. It occurred to Maddox that Strand had never written the book. A Builder had. That's what Ludendorff had gone to get at the Fisher world. Maybe Ludendorff really believed in his heart that Strand had written the book. Maddox knew now the Builder who had made the first device for the Fishers had left instructions for making the terrible tool a second time.

"Captain," Galyan said. "I do not understand what is going on."

Maddox faced Galyan. The captain wondered if he could live with himself once this was done. Well, if he couldn't, that didn't mean the rest of the crew felt the same way.

"Listen to me closely, Galyan," the captain said. "You have to be ready to use the star drive and take us to the Solar System. Tell Keith he has to move the Destroyer there now, going to…Pluto. Tell him to go to Pluto. Send a message to the Lord High Admiral. If he hasn't already, he is to order every ship that can to jump to Earth, to the Solar System. If he doesn't to that now, those ships are going to disintegrate in the next hour."

"That is a fantastic message, Captain. How can it be true?"

"If you don't do it, Galyan—"

Maddox stopped talking as the Ska resumed its spiritual attack against him, blocking everything else from the captain's senses.

-16-

The next few seconds were among the most grueling in Maddox's existence. A power struck him that seemed to hurtle him backward in time and space. He tumbled like paper in a sandstorm, the particles rasping against him.

Maddox saw the world around him in his memories. He saw a large arm holding him. He felt the beat of his mother's heart close to his. They were on a space hauler. Maddox had no idea how he knew that. His mother was in third class together with a group of ruffians. The ruffians kept eyeing her. Maddox could read their intentions on their faces. He struggled against his mother's arm, and realized with shock that he was just a baby. He could not talk. He could only coo or cry. Right now, Maddox began to cry in rage because he couldn't hurt those who threatened his mother.

Finally, the thinnest ruffian with the wickedest grin stood up and approached her.

"Set down the mewling brat," the ruffian said. "I'm horny," he said, rubbing his groin and swaying his hips suggestively.

Maddox's mother set him down. She did it so very gently. Then she approached the ruffian with a sultry smile, pushing herself against him.

"That's what I'm talking about, bitch," the ruffian said. He grabbed the back of her head roughly—his eyes widened. He looked down at her and shoved her away so she stumbled.

"What did you do to me?" he shouted. The ruffian rubbed his side. "What did you do?"

Maddox's mother held up a small needle. A drip of something green glistened on the tip.

The ruffian stared at her as drool began running from his moist mouth. "What the—?" he said, stumbling backward until he struck a bulkhead. The ruffian slid down, beginning to make gagging noises.

"What did you do to him?" a bigger ruffian demanded.

"The same thing I'll do to you if you mess with me," she said.

The bigger ruffian glanced at his friend. That one had started convulsing. The bigger ruffian scowled, advancing a step at Maddox's mother.

"You can die just like him," she said. "Or you can keep away from me and live. It's your choice. I don't really care, because I've already been to hell and back. One more killing won't make any difference to me."

The bigger ruffian muttered darkly. Then he turned to the hatch, banging on it, demanding a medic.

In Maddox's memory, his mother scooped him up, rocking him gently back and forth, cooing to him, telling him that she loved her little man.

The word "love" acted like a tonic on Captain Maddox in the here and now. The memory faded and he realized he stood frozen in Ludendorff's laboratory aboard Starship *Victory*. The Ska attacked him. It strove to feed off him by creating terror—

Maddox rubbed his eyes until he saw splotches before his vision. During that moment, he saw the Builder machine on the counter. He staggered for it—

"*No, Captain*," the Ska said, "*you shall never reach the object.*"

Maddox rubbed his eyes as hard as before. He saw the thing and stubbornly took another step. He lunged at the machine, touching the cool metallic surface.

"*What is that?*" the Ska asked.

Maddox gripped the handles, grunted as he picked it up, and shoved his forehead against the two flattened pieces of the curved prongs.

As he did, the Builder machine began to purr with power.

"You slug," the Ska said. *"You won't get away as easily as that."*

The machine's purring increased its intensity. The machine built up Maddox's mind and it altered his reality. He sensed a monstrous evil behind him.

The captain turned and saw a roiling dark cloud that had to be the Ska. It wasn't fluffy, but oily and sticky and full of malice and dark desires. It hated physical life for reasons that Maddox could not understand.

"Maybe you can see me," the Ska said. *"But I can also clearly see you. This is much better, you filthy little beast. I am going to toy with you for an eon."*

As the black cloud spoke, an oily tendril grew from it. The tendril had glistening suckers on the end. Those suckers did not drain blood; they drained the soul from a person in a process that should not work. It would create soul agony in the prey.

Rage built in Maddox. He aimed the Builder machine at the thing, and a beam of purest light emitted from it. The beam struck the oily tendril—and the cloud writhed with agony.

"How did you do that?" the Ska asked.

Maddox didn't know, although he felt great weariness. In that moment, he realized that he powered the machine with something critical from himself. If he gave too much of his self to the machine, it would twist and torment him as much as if the Ska gained ascension over him.

In spite of that knowledge, maybe because he was still angry at what the ruffian had tried to do to his mother, Maddox aimed the Builder machine at the black cloud.

"It's time for you to suffer," Maddox said. He beamed a thick pure light at the cloud. He beamed it long and hard. His heart raced. His soul-energy diminished at a fantastic rate, but that allowed him to sear the dark cloud, to hammer it—

The Ska fled from the Builder machine that shot rays of soul light. It fled as it howled in agony. There was only one way it knew to heal itself, and that was inside a hot star.

-17-

The unbelievably ancient Ska veered away from Proxima Centauri, as the red dwarf was much too cool for what it needed. Instead, the Ska fled toward the closest hot star, Alpha Centauri A. This particular star had 1.1 times the mass of the Sun and it shined 1.519 times as brightly.

The strange creature from another dimension moved with uncanny speed as it traveled, just a little slower than the speed of thought. It sped past the star's atmosphere, which was composed of four parts: the heliosphere, corona, transition region and the chromosphere. Surprisingly, the chromosphere, transition region and corona were much hotter than the surface of the star.

After exiting the star's atmosphere, the Ska sped through the photosphere, the convective zone, the tachocline, the radiative zone and finally entered the incredible and soothing core of Alpha Centauri A.

Here, through nuclear fusion, the star produced its energy through a series of steps called the proton-proton chain. The process converted hydrogen to helium and slowly but remorselessly devoured the star's massive amount of hydrogen fuel.

As the Ska swam through the heated core, it soaked up the tiny amount of a mysterious substance produced under these intense conditions. In many ways, these unknown particles had neutrino-like properties. They also had a governing effect upon the star, and that was critical to what was about to happen.

For the Ska did not simply soak itself in these mysterious particles, the bizarre creature absorbed the substances. It was as if these particles ceased to exist. That began a strange and harrowing reaction within the heart of the star. Unlike the normal energy created by the proton-proton chain that took such an incredibly long time to go from the center to the outer edge of the star, this Ska-induced process abruptly affected the natural fusion reactor.

Without the neutrino-like particles, and for reasons unknown to human, Swarm and other scientists—although certain Builders could have explained it to a sufficiently intelligent species—the star of Alpha Centauri A expanded. The star did this in a moment instead of slowly as a red giant would have done in its evolutionary changes over time.

With the star's rapid expansion came a vast outpouring of stellar radiation and blazing heat and plasma. The radiation along with the heat scorched everything within one hundred AUs or a little over three times Neptune's orbit from the Sun.

That meant that almost everything in the inner and outer system burned up into cinders or into nonexistence. In that moment, the several billion human inhabitants of the Alpha Centauri System ceased to exist. The planets heated and killed their people. The space habitats disappeared, turned red hot or received such massive doses of radiation that everyone died. Perhaps a few deep miners survived for the moment. Almost every one of them would die a lingering radiation-poisoned death.

The expanding star did not spare the remaining spaceships of Star Watch that had failed to fleet, the Wahhabi survivors or the Windsor League vessels that made up the Alliance Fleet. Those ships in the star system vaporized under the hellish conditions of the expanding star. Although the New Men had paid heed to Maddox's warning—all the star cruisers had already jumped to the Solar System—none of the civilian vessels in the system survived.

The Spacers that had arrived with the Ska from the null region in the second Destroyer, including the Visionary, all gained their mental freedom as the wounded Ska journeyed to the star. However, the intense heat from the expanding star boiled away the neutroium armor. It took a little longer than other vessels, although the heat cooked and killed the crew long before the ancient vessel altogether ceased to exist.

The large majority of the Swarm Fleet did not escape damage, either, even though most of the vessels were farther away from Alpha Centauri A than the human ships.

Perhaps two-thirds of the remaining Swarm ships broke apart under the intense heat and lashing radiation. Half of the rest received terrible doses of radiation. Fortunately for the Swarm creatures, they could take much more radiation than a human and live. Unfortunately for those creatures, that meant a terrible lingering death full of agonizing pain.

However, a group of Swarm ships escaped the dreadful destruction. Those ships, including the command vessel and most of the jump ships, were behind a huge gas giant at the moment of the expansion.

Thus, as the heat and radiation annihilated everything around them, these vessels escaped the mass death as the gas giant sheltered them from the expanding star. The gout of heat and radiation from the abrupt expansion that slaughtered so many did not last long.

In the end, 6,318 Swarm vessels survived the cauldron of death. Among that number were 174 jump ships.

After everyone except for the stranded Swarm creatures had passed away, the Ska inside the expanded star began to grow queasy. It slowly dawned on the other-dimensional creature that the mysterious particles had flowed too heavily into its being.

With terrible clarity, it realized the particles had healed the damage inflicted by Captain Maddox, but at a frightful cost. Those neutrino-like particles had accelerated its aging process to a monstrous degree. In a word, it was dying from advanced age.

Maddox! the Ska thought. *I must avenge myself on Captain Maddox.* As it had these desires, the Ska lost more and more of its mental coherence. So, even though it left the star and began the journey to Earth, it had started to seriously fade. Whether it would reach Earth in time to hurt Maddox was going to be a running question.

-18-

The magnitude of the death and destruction awed even the Reigning Supreme and her Hive Master-class advisors. The sudden disappearance of most of the fleet paralyzed the command structure.

AX-29 was supposed to have invaded Human Space with several hundred thousand warships. Instead, she had arrived with a little over 80,000 vessels. Now, she was down to 6,318 ships. Perhaps as bad, she was stuck for the moment behind the boiling gas giant. Did the Laumer Point between Alpha Centauri and the Solar System still exist? If it didn't, she was looking at years of travel to reach the target.

AX-29 grieved her situation. Her advisors stared blankly at nothing. Thrax...

The Reigning Supreme looked around. Where was Thrax? What had happened to the little hybrid Swarm monster?

**

Thrax scuttled as fast as he could go through the corridors of the command vessel. His mind was numb with shock; he worked off instinct alone.

What could have possibly caused the system's largest star to expand like that? It was unprecedented. It had destroyed on a massive scale. He thought he'd seen mass destruction in the Golden Nexus System. The monstrous war between the Chitins and the Swarm had beggared his imagination. But this...

Thrax clacked his pincers. The star had expanded. It had devoured. The Swarm Fleet—

Thrax clacked his pincers harder as he continued to scuttle at maximum speed.

It was only through sheerest luck that this part of the fleet had survived. The expanding star must have changed the Laumer Points. The gravitational eruptions, the particles spewed into space—Alpha Centauri had become a death zone. For the moment, at least, the fleet was trapped behind the gas giant. How long would he survive in such a situation?

Thrax did not give himself good odds. The Reigning Supreme would surely revert to her old ways. She would come to loathe him. Likely, she would come to blame him for the awful disaster, even though it wasn't his fault.

Thrax clacked his pincers more as he scuttled madly for the hangar bay. If he hadn't destroyed the Golden Nexus, how many more Swarm vessels would have perished today to the expanding star?

The hybrid Swarm creature created by the Builder on the Dyson Sphere laughed in an odd manner. Few other Swarm creatures could laugh or even understood the concept of humor.

Thrax halted. His head swayed back and forth. By slow degrees, he gained control over himself and thought furiously. He was dead if he stayed. Yet if he tried to leave—

"Act," Thrax told himself. "This is not a time to think. This is a time to do."

Commander Thrax Ti Ix did exactly that. He'd used his head on the Dyson Sphere. That had been a terrible disaster, too. He'd survived that. He would survive this horror, as well. He would show—well, maybe he would just show himself. But he would prove that the hybrids were the superior Swarm creatures. And he would do that by acting decisively before the others could gain their bearings. But he could only do that by staying on the run until he was free.

Thrax raised his pincers high and clacked three times in rapid succession. That's what he desired. He wanted to be free again instead of part of a system that ultimately despised him. He'd given the Imperium much, and it had repaid him with scorn.

Thrax charged to the hangar bay, determined to reach the jump ships and get the heck out of here. Where would he take the jump ships—given that he could gain control of them?

"I don't know," he whispered. "Far away from humans and far away from the Imperium. I'm sick of both."

* * *

Hours later, AX-29 finally began to regain control of herself and her advisors. What solidified the full return of her sanity was a message from a soldier.

"Turn on the screen," AX-29 said.

Soldiers did her biding. A moment later, a bloated Hive Master-class commander appeared on the screen.

"Reigning Supreme," the commander said. "I am calling because these orders seem out of protocol. I realize this is a trying moment—"

"Get to the point," AX-29 said.

"The jump ships are not responding to my calls. They have begun to edge toward the gas giant. They are to move aside—"

"Who is commanding the jump ships?" AX-29 said.

"I have been unable to confirm that."

"Why?"

"No one is answering me."

"That should change nothing."

"The command jump ship was destroyed in the star blast."

"I will take charge of the situation as of now."

"Thank you, Reigning Supreme. The situation on my own ship—"

"Take charge there," AX-29 said. She motioned soldiers. They rearranged her pallet. Moments later, she began hailing the jump ships.

The jump vessels showed on the main screen, slowly maneuvering from the rest of the fleet.

"I demand that you answer my call," AX-29 said. "If you fail to answer, I will target—"

The screen wavered. A moment later, Thrax appeared on the screen.

350

"What is the meaning of this?" AX-29 said. "I am attempting to contact the jump ships. Why are you on the comm?"

Thrax clacked his pincers. "I am attempting to correct the problem, Reigning Supreme."

"What does that mean?"

"I am on a jump ship," Thrax said.

"I did not give you permission to leave the command vessel."

Thrax clacked his pincers again.

"Stop that," AX-29 said. "I find the noise irritating."

Thrax did not stop, but clacked his pincers more loudly than before.

"Did you hear my command?"

"I did," Thrax said. "I have simply chosen to ignore it."

AX-29 stared at him. "Are you rebelling, Thrax?"

"I am the superior Swarm creature," Thrax told her. "How do I know? Because I will survive this disaster, a disaster of your making."

"How dare you speak to me like that?"

"You are as good as dead," Thrax said. "You led us to destruction. I despise you, and I despise your bloated bulk. Good-bye, AX-29, and good riddance."

"Fire!" the Reigning Supreme raged. "Fire on his jump ships."

"We need them," the Assault Leader told her.

"Thrax!" the Reigning Supreme shouted.

Thrax likely did not hear, as the first of the jump ships used its special drive to leave the Alpha Centauri System.

-19-

Captain Maddox collapsed shortly after appearing in the Solar System. He had tried to explain to Galyan what had happened in his battle against the Ska. As Maddox spoke the first words, he'd fainted, falling onto the floor with a heavy thud.

The first medic reaching him declared that the captain had gone into a coma. The woman didn't know it, but the captain had used up too much of himself in powering the strange Builder-conceived weapon.

Soon enough, Maddox lay in *Victory's* medical center. Three times the first night, he almost quit breathing. Meta held his hand each time, stroking it and whispering quietly that he'd better not leave her.

"Keep doing that," the doctor said. "It's helping. It seems to stabilize his cardiopulmonary rhythms."

Meta held Maddox's hands for hours. She sat in a chair, speaking quietly to him the entire time. Fifteen hours later, she was still doing that, although her voice had grown ragged.

"Let me sit with him," Riker said. "You need to get some sleep."

With bleary eyes, Meta peered up at the sergeant. She'd been weeping quietly many times. "If something happens to him…you come and get me immediately."

"I promise," Riker said.

Valerie helped Meta stand and guided her out through the hatch.

Riker sat down beside Maddox. The sergeant did not take the captain's hand. The old sergeant looked at the young whippersnapper for some time. He looked at the smooth face.

If anyone had any real inkling of what had happened to Maddox when he faced the Ska, it was Riker. The bad feeling had left the sergeant. He did not sense the Ska anymore.

Riker didn't know it, but the Ska had faded away as it tried to reach the Solar System. It had aged too swiftly to make the journey. A lingering malice tainted the farthest region of the Solar System's Oort cloud, but that was all that was left of the incredibly ancient creature.

What Sergeant Riker did know was that the captain had stood in the gap when no one else could have done so. Maddox had faced an evil creature all by his lonesome. The young fool had used up something essential of himself to do it, too.

Riker knew because he'd been linked, however tenuously in the end, to the monstrous thing from another dimension. These thoughts did not come as certain knowledge, but as feelings, intuitions.

On the second night, Maddox began to buck and wheeze horribly. Riker had been napping, with his chin resting on his chest. The older man's head snapped up. He stood, hollered for medical help and grabbed Maddox's nearest arm.

Riker quailed inside at the thought of Maddox's passing away. Tears sprang to Riker's eyes. He did not wipe them away. He gripped the young man's arm with fierce strength as he leaned in and began whispering into Maddox's ear.

The tears made tracks on Riker's face as they dripped onto the captain's hospital gown. The older man kept talking.

The medics rushed in and went to work. At the doctor's orders, they left Riker alone. Finally, Maddox quit bucking and began to breathe evenly again.

By that time, Meta had arrived. She pried Riker's hands off Maddox's arm, patting the sergeant's arm. Then she lay on Maddox's chest, crying softly, telling him to fight, to live. She needed him. She wanted him to come back and live the rest of his life with her.

For the next five days, Meta, Riker, Valerie, Mary O'Hara, Galyan and Keith kept the captain company at all times.

353

"Keep talking to him," the doctor instructed. "Your words are doing more than anything I can do to keep him alive."

On the sixth day, Dana appeared. She spoke quiet words into Maddox's ear.

On the eighth day, Ludendorff showed up. The Methuselah Man looked like a wreck. He seemed to have aged an incredible number of years. He moved slowly like an old man. His hands trembled when he lifted them.

"I want to talk to him alone," Ludendorff said.

Everyone left but Meta.

"You too, my lovely," Ludendorff said.

"No," Meta said. "There's something about you I don't like."

"Come now," Ludendorff wheezed.

"No," Meta said. "You mean to harm the captain. I can feel it."

Ludendorff seemed indecisive, finally nodding. "Have it your way, then," he said. "Stay and see how wrong you are."

The professor put his hands on the cot's bar, but he did not touch the captain.

"How did you guess, old boy?" Ludendorff asked in a plaintiff voice. "What did the Builder to do me? There are so many things I'm not sure about anymore. You did this to me…"

Ludendorff stopped talking as Meta stood and walked around onto the other side of the cot. Her features were set as she studied Ludendorff.

"Is something wrong?" Ludendorff asked petulantly.

"Why are you blaming him?" Meta asked.

Ludendorff made a vague gesture. "He's always striving. He's always poking around."

"You made the machine that gave us victory," Meta said. "But you're still up and around. Maddox paid the cost of using the machine. You have no reason to blame him for anything."

Ludendorff grumbled quietly to himself.

"Blame the Builder if you have to blame someone," Meta told him.

"Blast it," Ludendorff said, with some of his old fire. "Don't you understand? The Builder is dead. I can't touch him. Look what they did to me."

"Do you mean giving you incredibly long life?" she asked.

"Bah," he said. "You can't understand."

"If you weren't so completely self-absorbed you might be able to think of someone other than yourself for once."

"Don't lecture me. I saved humanity."

"You built the weapon," Meta said. "He," she touched Maddox, "saved humanity. He stood in the gap against the evil that would have devoured us. That's why you're upset. Building the weapon cost you, but he's gotten all the credit."

"For murdering billions of people in Alpha Centauri," Ludendorff spat.

Meta shook her head. "Everyone in Alpha Centauri died so the rest of us could live. Are you so self-absorbed with only your own ego that you can't see the truth?"

Ludendorff's eyes burned with hatred and his lips trembled. "Tell him, if he ever wakes up, to never look for me again. If he does, I'll kill him."

"I'll tell him."

It seemed as if Ludendorff would say more. Abruptly, the Methuselah Man turned around and hobbled out the door.

After Ludendorff was gone, Meta stroked Maddox's arm. "Wake up, darling. Come back to me. Please, come back..."

-20-

The last vessels of the Swarm Fleet made it to the Alpha Centauri-Solar System Laumer Point and used it to reach the Outer System.

The bugs had taken too long, however. Andros Crank and his Kai-Kaus technicians had fixed the Destroyer enough for it to beam seven times.

The four Juggernauts, the New Man cone of battle and the rest of Star Watch with its remaining *Conqueror*-class battleships, carriers, fold-fighters with anti-matter torpedoes, the monitors and heavy cruisers together with Windsor League hammerships and Wahhabi *Scimitar*-class vessels crushed the Jump Lagged Imperial vessels.

Humanity took losses—numbering 18 ships—but they wiped out the Swarm menace. Later, scientists determined that all the bugs had been dying from radiation poisoning. That and the Jump Lag accounted for the wretched operational fighting on their part.

The New Men readied to depart. Before they did, Golden Ural visited *Victory*. The tall New Man asked for permission to see Captain Maddox.

Meta and Riker flanked the New Man. Ural stood over Maddox, fingering his chin as he looked down upon the hybrid.

Whatever Ural thought, he kept to himself. Finally, the New Man turned to go.

"Is that it?" Meta asked him.

Ural examined her frankly. It made Meta flush.

"You are the captain's woman?" Ural asked.

"I'm his wife," Meta declared.

"Ah," Ural said. "Yes, I approve." The New Man then took his leave.

Meta looked at Riker. "What was that all about?"

The sergeant shrugged. He had no idea.

They both turned to study Maddox. He still lay in a coma, fifteen days now since facing the Ska.

"Do you think he'll make it?" Meta asked the sergeant in a small voice.

"Now, now," Riker said. "Don't give up hope. Our Captain Maddox is a fighter. If anyone can survive what happened, it's him."

"I'm afraid, Riker. I don't want him to die."

"Neither do I," the sergeant said softly.

***

As Captain Maddox lay inert on the medical cot, his mind wandered in a dazed fog. He had not dreamed during this time. He had hung between life and death for fifteen long days.

It almost seemed as if he were lost. Did he search for a way back to life? What did it mean to use a Builder weapon that used soul energy as its power? The cost to his essence had been terrible indeed.

Yet, on the fifteenth day of his mind's wandering, the self of Captain Maddox broke through the dazed fog. He perceived an old memory in a dim manner.

He lay cradled against a bosom and saw a great and lovely face smiling sadly down at him. He was a baby again as his mother held him.

Maddox looked up at the face with absorbing interest. He had never known his mother. Actually, the more precise term would be that he could never remember her.

As the baby Maddox, he stared up at her, trying to pierce his earliest memories. Her lips curved so sadly and the blue eyes were clouds of loveliness.

Maddox waved his chubby little fists. He opened his mouth and made cooing sounds.

His mother laughed quietly. "You are my little man," she said.

Maddox cocked his head. What a lovely angelic voice.

The looming face came down nearer. He could smell her breath. It was so good. It was his mother.

"Listen to me, my sweet, sweet child. You are all I have now. You are to grow up to be a strong man. You must be brave and good, and help those in need. I don't think I'm going to get to watch you grow up. I don't think you can ever buy me lunch and talk about our good times together."

She hugged him, kissing him so tenderly.

"You must stop the New Men, darling. You are going to be a hero, I just know it. Oh, my darling baby, I will miss you so much. Be a good boy, Maddox. Be a good man. Live a straight life and never allow them to corrupt you."

Maddox listened intently. He wanted her to kiss him again, and hug him again and—

Maddox abruptly stopped. His mother was gone. She no longer held him. He was alone on a dry beach, a young man in a Star Watch uniform.

Maddox turned slowly in a circle. It was just this beach of sand. There was no ocean, no cliffs, no wind—

"The Fishers," Maddox said. "I'm back on their world."

In the distance, then, he saw the same creature he'd seen before. It beckoned him to follow.

"Why are you so far away?" Maddox shouted.

The shimmering creature raised a tentacle, beckoning.

"I'm tired," Maddox said. "I've done my part."

The Fisher would not stop beckoning.

Finally, Maddox began to trudge after the Fisher. It kept ahead of him on the sand. After a time, the Fisher entered a fog.

"Nope," Maddox said. "You don't get to escape me this time."

He began to run, soon entering the fog after it. He ran and ran, and he shouted for the Fisher to dare to show itself again.

It did not.

As he ran, Maddox thought he sensed light in the distance. The light meant pain. The light meant sorrow and great regrets.

The light also meant Meta and Riker, Galyan, Valerie, Keith, O'Hara and the others.

Was that enough to keep running for life? Maddox wasn't sure. If his mother were waiting for him in the other direction…

Something fierce grew on Maddox's face. He still hadn't settled with his father. He still hadn't paid the man back for harming his mother, for using his mother.

"I'm not finished," Maddox said. "Do you hear me? I'm not finished."

He continued to run in the fog toward the light, and as he did, Captain Maddox of Star Watch came back to himself in the hospital quarters of Starship *Victory*. He opened his eyes to see Meta's teary smile as she laughed with joy at his return.

"You're alive," Meta declared.

"Yes," Maddox said in such a weak voice.

Meta rushed near and held his face, showering him with kisses.

"Say it," he whispered.

Meta laughed and cried all at once. "I love you. I love you. I love you."

"And I love you, babe," Maddox whispered. "Now, help me up. I have a lot of work to do."

THE END

SF Books by Vaughn Heppner

LOST STARSHIP SERIES:
The Lost Starship
The Lost Command
The Lost Destroyer
The Lost Colony
The Lost Patrol
The Lost Planet
The Lost Earth

DOOM STAR SERIES:
Star Soldier
Bio Weapon
Battle Pod
Cyborg Assault
Planet Wrecker
Star Fortress
Task Force 7 (Novella)

EXTINCTION WARS SERIES:
Assault Troopers
Planet Strike
Star Viking
Fortress Earth

Visit VaughnHeppner.com for more information

Made in the USA
Columbia, SC
03 August 2017